A NOTE ON THE AUTHOR

JAMES RUNCIE is Head of Literature at the Southbank Centre, an award-winning film-maker and the author of six novels. *Sidney Chambers and The Perils of the Night*, the second of 'The Grantchester Mysteries' series was published in 2013. James Runcie lives in London and Edinburgh.

www.jamesruncie.com
www.grantchestermysteries.com
@james_runcie

The GRANTCHESTER MYSTERIES

SIDNEY CHAMBERS
AND
The Shadow of
Death

JAMES RUNCIE

BLOOMSBURY
LONDON · NEW DELHI · NEW YORK · SYDNEY

First published in Great Britain 2012
This paperback edition published 2014

Copyright © 2012 by James Runcie

The moral right of the author has been asserted

Bloomsbury Publishing, London, New Delhi, New York and Sydney

Bloomsbury Publishing Plc, 50 Bedford Square, London WC1B 3DP

Bloomsbury is a trademark of Bloomsbury Publishing Plc

A CIP catalogue record for this book is available from the British Library

ISBN 978 1 4088 5770 0

Typeset by Hewer Text UK Ltd, Edinburgh
Printed and bound in Great Britain by CPI Group (UK) Ltd, Croydon CR0 4YY

MIX
Paper from
responsible sources
FSC® C020471

www.bloomsbury.com/jamesruncie

For Marilyn

Contents

The Shadow of Death

CANON SIDNEY CHAMBERS had never intended to become a detective. Indeed, it came about quite by chance, after a funeral, when a handsome woman of indeterminate age voiced her suspicion that the recent death of a Cambridge solicitor was not suicide, as had been widely reported, but murder.

It was a weekday morning in October 1953 and the pale rays of a low autumn sun were falling over the village of Grantchester. The mourners, who had attended the funeral of Stephen Staunton, shielded their eyes against the light as they made their way to the wake in The Red Lion. They were friends, colleagues and relatives from his childhood home in Northern Ireland, walking in silence. The first autumn leaves flickered as they fell from the elms. The day was too beautiful for a funeral.

Sidney had changed into his suit and dog collar and was about to join his congregation when he noticed an elegant lady waiting in the shadows of the church porch. Her high heels made her unusually tall, and she wore a calf-length black dress, a fox fur stole and a toque with a spotted veil. Sidney had noticed her during the service for the simple reason that she had been the most stylish person present.

'I don't think we've met?' he asked.

The lady held out a gloved hand. 'I'm Pamela Morton. Stephen Staunton worked with my husband.'

'It's been a sad time,' Sidney responded.

The lady was keen to get the formalities out of the way. 'Is there somewhere we can talk?'

Sidney had recently been to see the film *Young Man with a Horn* and noticed that Mrs Morton's voice had all the sultriness of Lauren Bacall's. 'Won't you be expected at the reception?' he asked. 'What about your husband?'

'I told him I wanted a cigarette.'

Sidney hesitated. 'I have to look in myself, of course . . .'

'It won't take long.'

'Then we can go to the vicarage. I don't think people will miss me quite yet.'

Sidney was a tall, slender man in his early thirties. A lover of warm beer and hot jazz, a keen cricketer and an avid reader, he was known for his understated clerical elegance. His high forehead, aquiline nose and longish chin were softened by nut-brown eyes and a gentle smile, one that suggested he was always prepared to think the best of people. He had had the priestly good fortune to be born on a Sabbath day and was ordained soon after the war. After a brief curacy in Coventry, and a short spell as domestic chaplain to the Bishop of Ely, he had been appointed vicar to the church of St Andrew and St Mary in 1952.

'I suppose everyone asks you . . .' Pamela Morton began, as she cast an appraising eye over the shabby doorway.

'If I'd prefer to live in the Old Vicarage: the subject of Rupert Brooke's poem? Yes, I'm afraid they do. But I'm quite content here. In fact the place is rather too large for a bachelor.'

'You are not married?'

'People have remarked that I am married to my job.'

'I'm not sure what a canon is.'

'It's an honorary position, given to me by a cathedral in Africa. But it's easier to think of me as a common or garden priest.' Sidney stamped his shoes on the mat and opened the unlocked door. 'The word "canon" just sounds a bit better. Please, do come in.'

He showed his guest into the small drawing room with its chintz sofas and antique engravings. Pamela Morton's dark eyes swept the room. 'I am sorry to detain you.'

'That's quite all right. I have noticed that no one knows what to say to a clergyman after a funeral.'

'They can't relax until you've gone,' Pamela Morton replied. 'They think they have to behave as if they are still in church.'

'Perhaps I remind them too much of death?' Sidney enquired.

'No, I don't think it's that, Canon Chambers. Rather, I think you remind them of their manifold sins and wickedness.'

Pamela Morton gave a half-smile and tilted her head to one side so that a strand of raven hair fell across her left eye. Sidney recognised that he was in the presence of a dangerous woman in her mid-forties and that this gesture alone could have a devastating effect upon a man. He couldn't imagine his interlocutor having many female friends.

Mrs Morton took off her gloves, her stole and her hat, laying them on the back of the sofa. When Sidney offered her a cup of tea she gave a slight shudder. 'I am so sorry if this seems forward but might you have something stronger?'

'I have sherry, although I am not that keen on it myself.'

'Whisky?'

This was Sidney's favourite tipple; a drink, he tried to convince himself, that he only kept for medicinal purposes.

'How do you take it?' he asked.

'As Stephen had it. A little water. No ice. He drank Irish, of course, but I imagine yours is Scotch.'

'It is indeed. I am rather partial to a good single malt but I am afraid that I cannot really afford it.'

'That is quite understandable in a vicar.'

'You knew Mr Staunton well, I take it?'

'Do you mind if I sit down?' Pamela asked, walking towards the armchair by the fire. 'I think this is going to be a little awkward.'

Sidney poured out the Johnnie Walker and allowed himself a small tumbler to keep his guest company. 'It is clearly a delicate matter.'

'We are not in church, Canon Chambers, but can I presume that the secrets of the confessional still apply?'

'You can rely on my discretion.'

Pamela Morton considered whether to continue. 'It's not something I ever imagined telling a priest. Even now I am not sure that I want to do so.'

'You can take your time.'

'I may need to.'

Sidney handed his guest her whisky and sat down. The sun was in his eyes but once he had established his position he thought it rude to move. 'I am used to listening,' he said.

'Stephen and I had always been friends,' Pamela Morton began. 'I knew that his marriage wasn't as happy as it had once been. His wife is German; not that it explains anything . . .'

'No . . .'

'Although people have commented. It seemed an odd choice for such a handsome man. He could have chosen almost anyone he wanted. To marry a German so soon after the war was a brave thing to do, I suppose.' Pamela Morton stopped. 'This is harder than I thought . . .'

'Do go on.'

'A few months ago, I went to the office to pick up my husband. When I arrived I discovered that he had been called away. There was some fuss about a will. Stephen was alone. He said he was going to be working late but then he suggested that we go out for a drink instead. It seemed perfectly innocent. He was my husband's business partner, and I had known him for several years. I had always been fond of him and I could see that something was troubling him. I didn't know whether it was his health, his money or his marriage. I think that's what most men worry about . . .'

'Indeed.'

'We took a drive out to Trumpington, where I suppose Stephen thought that we were less likely to meet people we knew and we wouldn't have to explain to anyone why we were having a drink together. So, thinking about it now, I suppose it all began with something complicit.'

Sidney was beginning to feel uncomfortable. As a priest he was used to informal confession, but he could never quite reconcile himself to the fact that it often contained quite a lot of detail. There were times when he wished people wouldn't tell him so much.

Pamela Morton continued. 'We sat in the far corner of the pub, away from everyone else. I had heard that Stephen liked a drink or two but the speed surprised me. He was on edge. It was the usual chatter to begin with but then he changed. He told me how tired he was of his life. It was a strange thing to say; the intensity of his feeling came on so suddenly. He said how he had never felt that he belonged in Cambridge. He and his wife were both exiles. He said that he should have gone straight back to Ireland after the war but that the job was here. He didn't want to sound ungrateful to my husband for giving it to him, and besides, if he hadn't, then he would never have met me. When he said that, I started to worry. I wondered what I would have to tell my husband, and yet there was something compelling about the way he spoke. There was an urgency, a desperation and a charm to it all. He had a way with words. I've always admired that. I used to act, you know. In a small way. Before I married.'

'I see,' said Sidney, wondering where the conversation was going.

'Despite the blarney, I knew he was telling me that his life was a shambles. Anyone who heard him speak might have thought that he was beginning to be suicidal but they would have been so wrong.'

Pamela Morton stopped.

'You don't have to tell me everything,' Sidney answered.

'I do. It's important. Stephen spoke about how he longed to get away and start again somewhere else. Then, when we were still in the pub, he looked me in the eye for a long time before speaking and . . . oh . . . do you mind if I have a drop more? Dutch courage, you know.'

'Of course.'

'You must find this all rather seedy. You know what I am going to say, don't you?'

Sidney poured out the drinks. 'No, I don't think I do,' he said quietly. 'Please go on.' He had learned never to stop a narrative in full flow.

'Stephen told me that he couldn't stop thinking about me; that every part of his life without me was a misery; and that he loved me. I couldn't believe it. He said what a miracle it was that we had the chance to be alone so that he could tell me. He only lived for the times when we saw each other and that if only we could be together then his life would have purpose and meaning and he would drink less and be happy.'

Pamela Morton looked up, expecting Sidney to ask what she had done. 'Go on . . .' he said.

'As he was speaking,' Pamela continued, 'I felt this strange heat inside me. I don't know where it came from. I thought I was going to faint. My life seemed to fall away from me. I hadn't ever thought about it before but he was saying all the things I thought myself. I could see that my life did not have to be a dead end in a small provincial town. I could begin again. We could run away, escape our own past and live without history, pretending that there had been no war, we had lost no friends and that we had no family. We could just be two people with the future before them. We could go away, anywhere, Stephen said. He had some money saved and all I had to do was think about it. He didn't want to rush me. All he wanted was for me to say yes . . .'

'And did you?'

'I thought it was mad and impossible. I was frightened and thrilled at the same time. He talked about getting back in the car and driving away there and then, down to the coast, and taking a boat across the Channel. I didn't know what to say. He told me to imagine how we'd laugh, thinking of the havoc we'd wrought. We could drive all the way through France, staying at hopelessly romantic hotels while everyone else continued with their humdrum lives back in Cambridge. We would be free. We would go to Nice and the French Riviera and we would dress up and dance on warm summer nights under the stars. It was crazy and it was wonderful and although we knew we couldn't leave there and then it was surely only a matter of time. Anything was possible. Everything could change.'

'When was this?' Sidney asked.

'It was just after the Coronation. The pub still had its bunting up. Four months ago.'

'I see.'

'I can understand what you're thinking.'

'I am not judging you in any way,' Sidney replied, knowing that he was not sure what to think. 'I am listening.'

'But you must wonder. If we were that impetuous why has it taken us so long? My children have left home but, even so, I thought of them. Then, as soon as we got back home, I became frightened of what it all meant. I began to lose heart. I couldn't quite believe what had happened. Perhaps it had been a dream and Stephen had never said those things, but then we started to meet each other in secret and I knew that it was the only thing I wanted to do. I was obsessed. I could not believe that no one had noticed any change in me. "Surely they can tell?" I thought to myself. I hardly dared to believe that I was getting away with it. The more it went on the more I couldn't wait to leave. I was no longer myself. In fact, I didn't know who I was, but I told Stephen that we had to be sure that we had everything settled before we could do something so rash and that we should go in the New Year.'

'And he agreed?'

'As long as he saw me, he said, he believed that anything was possible. And we were happy.'

'And no one else knew of your plans?'

'I have a friend in London. She . . . it's difficult to explain, Canon Chambers. She let me pretend that I was staying with her . . .'

'When, in reality?'

'I was in a hotel with Stephen? I'm afraid so. You must think me very cheap.'

Sidney was taken aback by her frankness. 'It is not for me to pass judgement, Mrs Morton.'

'Pamela. Please, call me Pamela . . .'

It was too soon for such familiarity. Sidney decided to try not to offer his guest another drink.

'So you see why I have come, Canon Chambers?'

Sidney couldn't see anything at all. Why was this woman telling him all this? He wondered if she had got married in church, if she had ever considered her marital vows and how well she got on with her children. 'What would you like me to do?' he asked.

'I can't go to the police and tell them this.'

'No, of course not.'

'I can't trust them to keep it a secret. My husband is bound to find out and I don't want to stir things up.'

'But surely this is a private matter? It is no concern for the police.'

'It has to be, Canon Chambers.'

'But why?'

'Can you not guess? I can't believe Stephen killed himself. It is totally out of character. We were going to run away together.'

9

'So what are you suggesting?'

Pamela Morton sat up and straightened her back. 'Murder, Canon Chambers. I mean murder.' She fought to find a handkerchief from her handbag.

'But who would want to do such a thing?'

'I don't know.'

Sidney was out of his depth. It was all very well for someone to come to him and confess their sins but an accusation of murder was a different business altogether. 'This is quite a dangerous thing to suggest, Mrs Morton. Are you sure that you really think this?'

'I am certain.'

'And you have told no one else?'

'You are the first. When I heard you speak in the service about death and loss I felt sure that I could trust you. You have a reassuring voice. I am sorry I don't attend church more often. After my brother was killed in the war I found it hard to have faith.'

'It is difficult, I know.'

Pamela Morton spoke as if she had said all that she had to say. 'What I have said is the truth, Canon Chambers.'

Sidney imagined his guest sitting through the funeral service, restraining her grief. He wondered if she had looked around the congregation for suspects. But why would anyone have wanted to kill Stephen Staunton?

Pamela Morton recognised that Sidney needed to be convinced. 'The idea that he took his own life is absurd. We had so much to look forward to. It was as if we were going to be young once more and we could be whoever we wanted to be. We would start again. We were going to live as we have never lived. Those were the last words he spoke to me. "We will live as we have never lived." Those are not the words of a man who is going to shoot himself, are they?'

'No, they are not.'

'And now it's gone. All that hope. All that wasted love.' Pamela Morton took up her handkerchief. 'I can't bear it. I'm sorry. I didn't mean to cry.'

Sidney walked over to the window. What on earth was he supposed to do about this? It was none of his business; but then he remembered that, as a priest, *everything* was his business. There was no part of the human heart that was not his responsibility. Furthermore, if Pamela Morton was correct, and Stephen Staunton had not committed what many people still believed to be the sin of suicide, then an innocent man had been unjustly killed and his murderer was still at large.

'What would you like me to do?' he asked.

'Talk to people,' Pamela Morton answered. 'Informally if you can. I don't want anyone to know about my involvement in all this.'

'But who shall I speak to?'

'The people who knew him.'

'I'm not sure what I can ask them.'

'You are a priest. People tell you things, don't they?'

'They do.'

'And you can ask almost any question, no matter how private?'

'One has to be careful.'

'But you know what I mean . . .'

'I do,' Sidney replied, as cautiously as he could.

'Then you could keep what I have said in mind and, if the moment comes, perhaps you might ask a question that you might not otherwise have asked?'

'I am not sure that I can make any promises. I am not a detective.'

'But you know people, Canon Chambers. You understand them.'

'Not all the time.'

'Well, I hope you understand me.'

'Yes,' Sidney replied. 'You have been very clear. I imagine this must have been terrible. To bear it alone . . .'

Pamela Morton put her handkerchief away. 'It is. But I have said what I came to say. Are you sure I can rely on your discretion?' she asked, looking up at him, vulnerable once more. 'You won't mention my name?'

'Of course not.' Sidney answered, already worrying how long he could keep this secret.

'I'm so sorry about all of this,' Mrs Morton continued. 'I'm ashamed, really. I couldn't think how to tell you or the words that I was going to use. I don't know anything at the moment and I've had to keep so quiet. I've had no one to talk to. Thank you for listening to me.'

'It is what I am called to do,' said Sidney and immediately wondered whether this was true. It was his first case of adultery, never mind murder.

Pamela Morton stood up. Sidney noticed that, despite the tears, her mascara had not run. She pushed back that strand of hair again and held out her hand.

'Goodbye, Canon Chambers. You do believe me, don't you?'

'It was brave to tell me so much.'

'Courage is a quality Stephen said I lacked. If you find out what happened to him then I hope you will inform me first.' She smiled, sadly, once more. 'I know where you are.'

'I am always here. Goodbye, Mrs Morton.'

'*Pamela* . . .'

'Goodbye, Pamela.'

Sidney closed his front door and looked at the watch his
father had given him on his ordination. Perhaps there would
be time to look in at the wake after all. He returned to his
small drawing room with the tired furniture his parents had
bought for him at a local auction. The place really did need
cheering up, he thought. He gathered the glasses and took
them through to the kitchen sink and turned on the hot
tap. He liked washing up; the simple act of cleanliness had
immediately visible results. He stopped for a moment at the
window and watched a robin hopping on the washing line.
Soon he would have to get round to his Christmas cards.

He noticed the lipstick marks on the rim of Pamela Morton's
whisky glass and remembered a poem by Edna St Vincent
Millay he had read in the *Sunday Times*:

> 'What lips my lips have kissed, and where, and why,
> I have forgotten, and what arms have lain
> Under my head till morning; but the rain
> Is full of ghosts tonight . . .'

'What a mess people make of their lives,' he thought.

Sidney's friend Inspector Keating was not amused. 'It could
hardly be more straightforward,' he sighed. 'A man stays on
in the office after everyone has gone home. He sets about a
decanter of whisky and then blows his brains out. The cleaner
finds him in the morning, calls the police, we go in, and that's
it: clear as my wife's crystal.'

The two men were sitting at their favourite table in the RAF bar of The Eagle, a pub that was conveniently situated not far from the police station in St Andrews Street. They had become friends after Sidney had taken the funeral of the inspector's predecessor, and they now met informally after work every Thursday to enjoy a couple of pints of bitter, play a game of backgammon and share confidences. It was one of the few off-duty moments in the week when Sidney could take off his dog collar, put on a pullover and pretend that he was not a priest.

'Sometimes,' he observed, 'things can be rather too clear.'

'I agree,' said the inspector, throwing a five and a three, 'but the facts of this case are as plain as a pikestaff.' He spoke with a slight Northumbrian accent, the only remaining evidence of a county he had left at the age of six. 'So much so, that I cannot believe you are suggesting that we set out on a wild goose chase.'

'I am not suggesting that.' Sidney was alarmed by his friend's assumption that he was making a formal request. 'I am merely raising an eyebrow.'

Inspector Keating pressed his case. 'Stephen Staunton's wife told us that her husband had been depressed. He also drank too much. That's what the Irish do, of course. His secretary informed us that our man had also started to go to London on a weekly basis and was not in the office as much as he should have been. She even had to cover for him and do some of his more straight-forward work; conveyancing and what have you. Then there is the small matter of his recent bank withdrawals; vast sums of money, in cash, which his wife has never seen and no one knows where it has gone. This suggests . . .'

Sidney threw a double five and moved four of his pieces. 'I imagine you would think the solicitor was a gambling man . . .'

'I certainly would. And I would also imagine that he might have been using some of his firm's money to pay for it. If he wasn't dead I'd probably have to start investigating him for fraud.' The inspector threw a four and a two and hit one of Sidney's blots. 'So I imagine that, when the debts mounted up, and he was on the verge of being discovered, he blew his brains out. It's common enough, man. Re-double?'

'Of course.' Sidney threw again. 'Ah . . . I think I can re-enter the game.' He placed his checker on the twenty-three point. 'Did he leave a note?'

Inspector Keating was irritated by this question. 'No, Sidney, he did not leave a note.'

'So there's margin for error?'

The inspector leaned forward and shook again. He had thought he had the game in the bag but now he could see that Sidney would soon start to bear off. 'There is no room for doubt in this case. Not every suicide leaves a note . . .'

'Most do.'

'My brother-in-law works in the force near Beachy Head. They don't leave a lot of notes down there, I'm telling you. They take a running jump.'

'I imagine they do.'

'Our man killed himself, Sidney. If you don't believe me then go and pay the widow one of your pastoral visits. I'm sure she'd appreciate it. Just don't start having any ideas.'

'I wouldn't dream of it,' his companion lied, anticipating an unlikely victory on the board.

The living at Grantchester was tied to Sidney's old college of Corpus Christi, where he had studied theology and now took tutorials and enjoyed dining rights. He enjoyed the fact that his work combined the academic and the clerical, but there were times when he worried that his college activities meant that he did not have enough time to concentrate on his pastoral duties. He could run his parish, teach students, visit the sick, take confirmation classes and prepare couples for marriage, but he frequently felt guilty that he was not doing enough for people. In truth, Sidney sometimes wished that he were a better priest.

He knew that his responsibility to the bereaved, for example, extended far beyond the simple act of taking a funeral. In fact, those who had lost someone they loved often needed more comfort after the initial shock of death had gone, when their friends had resumed their daily lives and the public period of mourning had passed. It was the task of a priest to offer constant consolation, to love and serve his parishioners at whatever cost to himself. Consequently, Sidney had no hesitation in stopping off on his way into Cambridge the next morning to call on Stephen Staunton's widow.

The house was a mid-terrace, late-Victorian building on Eltisley Avenue, a road that lay on the edge of the Meadows. It was the kind of home young families moved to when they were expecting their second child. Everything about the area was decent enough but Sidney could not help but think that it lacked charm. These were functional buildings that had escaped wartime bombing but still had no perceivable sense of either history or local identity. In short, as Sidney walked down the street, he felt that he could be anywhere in England.

Hildegard Staunton was paler than he remembered from her husband's funeral. Her short hair was blonde and curly; her eyes were large and green. Her eyebrows were pencil-thin and she wore no lipstick; as a result, her face looked as if her feelings had been washed away. She was wearing a dark olive housecoat, with a shawl collar and cuffed sleeves that Sidney only noticed when she touched her hair; worrying, perhaps, that she needed a shampoo and set but could not face a trip to the hairdresser.

Hildegard had been poised yet watchful at the service, but now she could not keep still, standing up as soon as she had sat down, unable to concentrate. Anyone outside, watching her through the window, would probably think she had lost something, which, of course, she had. Sidney wondered if her doctor had prescribed any medicine to help her with her grief.

'I came to see how you were getting on,' he began.

'I am pretending he is still here,' Hildegard answered. 'It is the only way I can survive.'

'I am sure it must feel very strange.' Sidney was already uncomfortable with the knowledge of her husband's adultery, let alone potential murder.

'Being in this country has always seemed strange to me. Sometimes I think I am living someone else's life.'

'How did you meet your husband?' Sidney asked.

'It was in Berlin after the war.'

'He was a soldier?'

'With the Ulster Rifles. The British Foreign Office sent people over to "aerate" us, whatever that meant, and we all went to lectures on *Abendländische Kultur*. But none of us listened very much. We wanted to go dancing instead.'

Sidney tried to imagine Hildegard Staunton in a bombed-out German ballroom, dancing among the ruins. She shifted position on the sofa and adjusted the fall of her housecoat. Perhaps she did not want to tell her story, Sidney wondered, but the fact that she would not look him in the eye made it clear that she intended to continue. Her speech, despite its softness, demanded attention.

'Sometimes we went out into the countryside and spent the nights drinking white wine under the apple trees. We taught them to sing "Einmal am Rhein" and the Ulstermen gave us "The Star of County Down." I liked the way Stephen sang that song. And when he talked about his home in Northern Ireland, he described it so well that I thought that this could be my refuge from all that had happened in the war. We would live by the sea, he said, in Carrickfergus, perhaps. We were going to walk by the shores of Lough Neagh, and listen to the cry of the curlews as they flew over the water. His voice had so much charm. I believed everything he told me. But we never did go to Ireland. The opportunity was here. And so our marriage began with something I had not been expecting. I never imagined that we would live in an English village. Being German is not so easy, of course.'

'You speak very good English.'

'I try hard. But German people are looked on with suspicion, as I am sure you know. I can see what they are thinking still, so soon after the war. How can I blame them? I cannot tell everyone that I meet that my father was never a Nazi, that he was shot at a Communist protest when I was six years old. I do not think I have done anything wrong. But it is difficult for us to live after such a war.'

'It is hard for everyone.'

Hildegard stopped and remembered what she had forgotten. 'Would you like some tea, Canon Chambers?'

'That would be kind.'

'I am not very good at making it. Stephen used to find it amusing. More often he drank whiskey.'

'I am rather partial to Scotch myself.'

'His was Irish, of course.'

'Ah yes,' Sidney remembered. 'With a different taste and a different spelling.'

Hildegard Staunton continued. 'It was Bushmills. Stephen called it the oldest whiskey in the world. It reminded him of home: a Protestant whiskey, he always said, from County Antrim. His brother sends over two cases a year, one on Stephen's birthday and the other at Christmas. That is, two bottles a month. It was not enough. Perhaps that is why he went up to London before he died. It wasn't for business. It was to collect more whiskey. We couldn't find Bushmills in Cambridge and he wouldn't drink anything else.'

'Never?'

'He said he would prefer to drink water. Or gin. And when he did that he drank it like water in any case.' Hildegard gave a sad smile. 'Perhaps you would like sherry instead of tea. Priests often have sherry, I think?'

Sidney did not want to have to explain his dislike. 'That would be kind . . .'

Mrs Staunton moved to the glass cabinet on the sideboard. There were not many books, Sidney thought, but he noticed an upright Bechstein piano and some tasteful reproductions of landscape paintings. There was also a collection of German porcelain, including a fiddler wooing a dancing lady, and a Harlequin twisting a pug dog's tail. Most of the figurines were of children: a boy in a pink jacket playing the flute, a girl in the same coloured top with a basket of flowers, a little ballerina, brothers and sisters sharing a picnic table.

Sidney remembered his reason for coming. 'I'm sorry if I am intruding. But I like to think that you are one of my parishioners . . .'

'I am Lutheran, as you know. We are not regular churchgoers.'

'You would always be welcome.'

'*Kinder, Küche, Kirche.*' Hildegard smiled. 'The German tradition. I am afraid I am not very good at any of them.'

'I thought if there was anything I could do . . .'

'You took my husband's funeral. That was enough, especially under the circumstances.'

'They were difficult.'

'And after so much death in the war. To choose to die in such a deliberate way after you have survived. It's hard to understand. I am sure you disapprove.'

'We do believe that life is sacred, given by God.'

'And therefore God should take it away.'

'I am afraid so.'

'And if there is no God?'

'I cannot think that.'

'No. As a priest that would be a bad idea.' Hildegard smiled for the first time.

'Very bad indeed.'

Hildegard Staunton handed Sidney his sherry. He wondered why he had got himself into all this. 'Will you go back to Germany?' he asked.

'Some people say there is no Germany any more. But my mother is in Leipzig. I also have a sister in Berlin. I do not think I can remain here.'

'You don't like Cambridge?'

'It can be dispiriting. Is that the right word? The weather and the wind.'

Sidney wondered if the Staunton's marriage had ever been happy. 'I was thinking,' he began tentatively. 'Did your husband share your feelings?'

'I think we both felt that we were strangers here.'

'He was depressed?'

'He is from Ulster. What do you think?'

'I don't think all Ulstermen are depressed, Mrs Staunton.'

'Of course not. But sometimes with the alcohol . . .' Hildegard let the sentence fall into the silence between them.

'I know . . . it does not help.'

'Why did you ask that question?' Hildegard continued.

'I apologise. It was intrusive, I know. I was only wondering if you had any fears that this might happen?'

'No, I did not.'

'So it came as a shock?'

'It did. But then nothing surprises me, Canon Chambers. When you have lost most of your family in war, when there is nothing left of your life, and when the only hope you have turns to dust, then why should anything shock you? You fought in the war?'

'I did.'

'Then I think, perhaps, you understand.'

If Sidney had been a better Christian, he thought, he would try to talk to Hildegard about the consolation of his faith, but he knew that it was not the right time.

The conversation was unsettling because there were so many subjects moving through his mind: the nature of death, the idea of marriage and the problem of betrayal. To concentrate on any one of these issues was likely to upset Hildegard and so he tried to keep the conversation as neutral as he could.

'And you are from Leipzig?' Sidney continued.

'I am.'

'The home of Bach.'

'I play his music every day. I studied at the Hochschule in Berlin with Edwin Fischer. He was like a father to me. Perhaps you have heard of him?'

'I think my mother might have one of his recordings.'

'It is probably *The Well-Tempered Clavier*. His playing was filled with air and joy. He was a wonderful man. But, in 1942, he went to Lucerne, and I lost my confidence.'

'The war, I suppose.'

'It was many things.'

'And do you teach?'

'In Germany I had many pupils. You know that work is our weapon against world-weariness.'

'*Weltschmerz.*'

'You are familiar with the word?' Hildegard smiled once more. 'I am impressed, Canon Chambers. But here, work is not so easy. When I return to Germany, then, perhaps, I will teach every day. I need to work. I do not know what my husband did with money.'

'He left no will?'

'I do not think so.'

'Perhaps your husband's business partner was waiting until after the funeral to tell you about it?'

'I do not know him well. My husband was private about his work. He told me that it was unfulfilling. All I do know is that Clive Morton felt the same. I think he was more interested in golf than law.'

'Perhaps I could enquire on your behalf, if it might be helpful?'

'I would not like to trouble you.'

'It is no trouble,' said Sidney.

'There is nothing that is urgent . . .' Hildegard Staunton continued. 'I have my own bank account and enough money for now. It is only that I am so tired. I think it must be the sadness. It is like looking down a lift shaft. The gap is dark. It goes down and you can see no ending.'

Sidney sat down beside her. 'I'm sorry, Mrs Staunton. Perhaps I should not have come.'

Hildegard met his eye. 'No, I am glad. I am not myself. I hope you will excuse me.'

'You have had a terrible loss.'

'I was not expecting it to be so violent. I knew that Stephen kept his revolver from the war. He told me that sometimes he thought about what he had done with it. The people he had killed. He had such a conscience. I think it was too much for him, the memory of that conflict. Perhaps marrying me was an attempt to make up for what had happened, but I think it made it worse. He kept thinking that he might have killed people I had known; teachers, friends, relations. It was hard to know what to say to him. It was not good.'

Sidney remembered his own war, fighting in the last year with the Scots Guards, the long periods of waiting, the sleepless nights before moments of violent activity, risk and death. He didn't remember the killing so much as the guilt and the loss: men such as Jamie Wilkinson, 'Wilko', whom he had sent out to have a look at the enemy lines and who had never come back. He recalled the fear in men's faces; the sudden bursts of action and then, afterwards, the swift, brutal burial of friends. No one spoke about it and yet Sidney knew that they had all kept thinking of the things that had happened, hoping their thoughts and fears would recede. The rest of their lives would be lived in the shadow of death, and they would spend time involved in activities that were unlikely to have as much impact as anything they had done in those years of war.

'Are you listening?'

Sidney remembered where he was. 'I'm very sorry.'

Hildegard was almost amused by his lack of attention. Sidney saw the beginnings of a smile. He liked her mouth.

'You were perhaps dreaming, Canon Chambers. Such a thing is normal for me, even more so than what is real.'

Sidney remembered why he had come. It was not going to be easy to continue but he had to do his best to discover the truth. 'I meant to ask you a question. I hope you do not mind.'

'I hope I can answer it.'

'I know this may sound strange,' Sidney began tentatively. 'But do you think anyone would have wanted to harm your husband?'

'What a question!'

'I am sorry to have asked.'

'Why should anyone want to hurt him? He was good enough at harming himself.'

'Yes, I can see that.'

'Everyone loved my husband, Canon Chambers. He was a charming man.'

Sidney finished his sherry. 'I wish I had known him.'

He was about to make his excuses and leave when Hildegard Staunton continued. 'Of course, you should also speak with his secretary.'

'Why "of course"?'

'You have met Miss Morrison?'

'I don't think I have.'

'She was at the funeral. She organised his life and knew everyone who saw my husband. She would be able to answer your question if you go to ask about the will. They spent all their time together at work. I sat in this house.' Hildegard looked away as she said this.

On the mantelpiece Sidney could see another porcelain figurine, of a little girl feeding chickens. *Mädchen füttert Hühner* was inscribed in Old German at the base. He wondered who had given it to them, or if it had belonged to Hildegard's family, bought when she was a child. There were so many questions he could not ask.

'We could not have children,' she said, as if in answer.

'I'm sorry. I didn't mean to upset you or intrude,' he said.

'I do not know why I said that. I sometimes think people who live in England prefer their pets to their children. But I do not worry about that any more. I will try to come to your church. It was kind of you to take the funeral; you have a gentle face.'

'Thank you,' said Sidney, 'if that is true.'

'Come again,' Hildegard offered, 'after you have visited Miss Morrison. If you see her then perhaps she will tell you more.'

Hildegard Staunton held out her hand and Sidney took it. Her grasp was firm and she looked at her guest with a gaze that did not falter. 'Thank you for coming. Please visit me again.'

'It would be my privilege.'

Sidney walked back to church and felt unutterably sad. Something was very wrong. He thought of a field in a foreign country, a summer's evening, white wine and apple trees, an

Irish boy and his German sweetheart at the beginning of their adventure together and a man singing:

> 'From Bantry Bay up to Derry Quay
> And from Galway to Dublin town
> No maid I've seen like the sweet colleen
> That I met in the County Down.'

They had once had all of their lives before them.

The offices of Morton Staunton Solicitors were located on the ground floor of a single-storey building that abutted the yellow brick loggia of Cambridge Railway Station. To the left lay a waiting room and Miss Morrison's office. To the right lay the rooms of the two partners, Clive Morton and Stephen Staunton.

On arrival, Sidney was somewhat surprised by the appearance of the victim's secretary. He could not remember seeing her at the funeral and was now guilty of a presumption. He had been expecting a cliché: a woman in a green tweed skirt with her hair pinned into a neat bun; someone who had been educated at Girton and now lived with her mother and a couple of cats. What he discovered instead was an elegant and petite woman in her late thirties with swift eyes and finely angled features. She was dressed entirely in black and white and wore silver jewellery that matched her elegantly styled grey hair.

'Miss Morrison . . . I don't think we've met.'

'I scurried away after the service, I am afraid. It was all too upsetting as I am sure you must appreciate.'

'I can imagine,' Sidney began, already regretting the fact that he had come.

What was he doing getting involved in all this? he thought to himself. As an ordinand he had imagined the tranquil lifestyle of a quiet country parson, but now here he was, poking his nose into other people's business, involving himself in matters in which he was plainly out of his depth. He had to concentrate on the official reason for his visit: the acquisition of Stephen Staunton's will.

'I hope I am not calling at an inconvenient time?' he asked.

'There is still so much tidying up to be done. But my job is half of what it used to be and I am not sure whether we will be getting another partner . . .'

Sidney looked down at Miss Morrison's desk, with its papers scattered beside a well-used typewriter. A bag of lemon drops rested on top of what appeared to be a thick Russian novel.

'What can I do for you?' she asked

'I have come on behalf of Mrs Staunton,' Sidney began. So far this was, approximately, true. 'As you can imagine, she is not feeling particularly strong at the moment. I offered to enquire as to whether her husband had left a will.'

'I have thought about this, Canon Chambers, and it is an odd thing. He did not. Like many solicitors they may be good at drawing up instructions for other people but they are absent-minded when looking after themselves.'

'And Mr Staunton needed a bit of looking after?'

'My employer was not the most methodical of people.'

'But you kept his diary, managed his appointments, that kind of thing?'

'Of course.'

'You organised his life?'

'Not entirely.'

27

'I don't understand.'

'He liked to be mysterious at times.'

'I suppose most people like to have an area of their life that is private. I know I do myself.'

Miss Morrison began to explain. 'Mr Staunton kept his own pocket diary and so if people spoke directly with him then he would write it down there and it often led to confusion. If he made arrangements in the evenings, for example, and then didn't tell me the next morning, we would have a number of double bookings; but, in general, we rubbed along very well.'

'So he didn't always tell you everything?'

'He liked his privacy. And he did not want to be pinned down by too many appointments.'

Sidney found the matter-of-fact tone unconvincing. 'I am sorry to have to ask this, Miss Morrison, but was your employer a difficult man?'

'He wasn't easy but when you've been with someone for so long you get used to their ways.'

Sidney was about to ask a leading question about the state of Stephen Staunton's mind at the time of his death but a train steamed past so loudly that it shook the windows. 'Good Heavens,' he said.

'It's only the express that makes that much noise. They're every two hours so it isn't too bad. You get used to it.'

Sidney had planned to return to what he hoped was a subtle interrogation when Clive Morton looked in. He was a tall man with greying blond hair that was swept back, lotioned and in need of a cut. Dressed in a blue blazer with grey flannel trousers, a white Oxford shirt and a Savage Club tie, he clearly saw himself as the public face of his firm.

'Canon Chambers,' he began. 'I don't think I've seen you since the funeral? I trust my secretary has been catering for your every need.'

Miss Morrison interrupted. 'He was asking about a will.'

The solicitor appeared surprised. 'I didn't know that was your department?'

'On behalf of Mrs Staunton . . .'

Clive Morton already appeared to suspect Sidney's motives for coming. 'I see.'

This was the man that Pamela Morton had wanted to leave. Sidney felt uncomfortable with the knowledge. 'I was just passing when . . .'

'He was not that fond of paperwork, our Stephen. He could be rather slapdash. Don't think he bothered about a will. He didn't even have the courtesy to leave a note explaining why he had done such a dreadful thing. Poor Mrs Hughes . . .'

'I beg your pardon?'

'Our cleaner. She found him.'

'So there was definitely no explanation for what he did?'

'There's not much need to explain something that dramatic. He downed enough whisky to give him the courage and off he went.'

'Had you been partners for long?'

'Just coming up to five years. We read law at Trinity and got back in touch after the war.'

'So you were friends?'

'Most of the time. We did have the odd contretemps but nothing too serious. Although it has to be said that Stephen could be bloody moody. The charming Ulsterman who drinks too much and then tells you it's all hopeless; you know the type . . .'

29

Clive Morton's presence dominated the room. Miss Morrison gave a little nod and left. She seemed upset. 'If you'll excuse me . . .'

Sidney pressed on. 'Did he have a temper?'

'Oh, he had a temper all right. I remember I once remarked that it was rather amusing that a man with a German wife should have to initial all his paperwork "SS". He went berserk!'

'I can imagine that he would.'

'Never one to take a joke, our Stephen.' Clive Morton moved towards the drinks table and began to open a bottle of sherry. 'Would you like a drink, Canon Chambers? It's nearly lunchtime and it's been sticky round here recently, as you can imagine.'

'I shouldn't . . .'

'Go on . . .'

'A small whisky perhaps.'

'Oh,' Clive Morton paused. 'I had you down as a sherry man.'

'Most people do . . . but I'd prefer whisky if that's possible.'

'How do you have it?

'Neat, please, from the decanter.'

'Stephen was very partial to the whiskey; the one spelled with an "e". I'm more of a gin and tonic man. I'm sure Miss Morrison will bring in some ice. She knows I need a bit of fortification before lunch.'

Sidney took a sip of the whisky that had been poured from the decanter. It tasted exactly as it did at home. 'Is this from Stephen Staunton's supply?'

'I wouldn't know. Miss Morrison stocks the cupboard. We normally offer a gin or a sherry. If a client is particularly upset we do have some medicinal brandy. Stephen, however, stuck to his whiskey.'

Sidney was no aficionado but he had spent enough time with his friends in the Ulster Rifles to recognise that he was not experiencing Stephen Staunton's favourite blended whiskey. There was no smoky aroma, no fruity sweetness redolent of vanilla and bitter toffee. In short, it was not Bushmills.

'Of course, Stephen used to drink far too much,' Clive Morton continued. 'And it always gets to you in the end. I've seen it in so many friends, especially those who couldn't settle down after the war. They come home and can't explain what they've been through. So they drink to cheer up, the alcohol depresses them, and then they drink even more to get through the depression. Did you fight yourself, Canon Chambers, or were you a padre?'

'I fought, Mr Morton. With the Scots Guards . . .' The reply was more insistent than he had intended but Sidney did not intend to be patronised.

'Good for you!' his host continued.

Sidney remembered bayonet practice on the Meadows, running into sandbags and being told how important it was to hate his enemy. He had never been much good at that but he guessed that he had seen more of death than Clive Morton.

'Is this all that's left?' he asked. 'In this decanter?'

'Why? Do you want another?' His host laughed.

Sidney remembered Hildegard Staunton's words. 'You cannot get Bushmills in Cambridge and he wouldn't drink anything else.' 'Oh no,' he said. 'This is quite enough.'

There was a pause. Sidney knew that he should leave but thought that if he let the silence hold a little longer then Clive Morton might say more.

'Do you think Mr Staunton's affairs will be complicated to settle?' Sidney asked, and then felt compromised and guilty about using the word 'affair' in the presence of Pamela Morton's husband. He wondered if his wife's adultery had been a form of secret revenge.

'Lawyers are a bit like doctors, Canon Chambers. We neglect our own lives, perhaps because we think we are immortal. An occupational hazard.'

'But in Stephen Staunton's case . . .'

'Well, I suppose it was inevitable . . .' Clive Morton continued.

'You think so?'

'Don't get me wrong,' Clive Morton continued. 'I liked the man. We used to be close but, as I've implied, he had become much more distant of late: remote and moody to boot. And you can't work with a partner who is half-cut after lunch.'

'I wonder if Miss Morrison may have had to cover up for him?'

'Well spotted, Canon Chambers. It was getting ridiculous. I told Stephen I was prepared to turn a blind eye in the evenings but you can't employ a man who can get drunk twice in a day.'

'It was as bad as that?'

'Sometimes. I'm not saying he was an alcoholic. It's that his mind wasn't on the case in hand. I had to warn him, of course.'

'That he might lose his job?'

'Yes. Even though we were partners something had to be done.'

'And he knew this?'

'Of course he knew it. I was the one that told him.'

'And do you think the idea of losing everything might have made him despair?'

'I am not going to feel responsible for Stephen's death if that is what you are getting at, Canon Chambers. He had plenty of opportunities to sort his life out. I won't pretend it was easy but I always dealt with him fairly – no matter how many times he went to London or disappeared without telling anyone. At least Miss Morrison kept tabs on him. She could always be relied upon to finish off the paperwork and let us know where he was in the event of an emergency. He didn't seem to have any problems with her. It was the rest of the business that suffered from his rather cavalier approach. But, if you'll excuse me, it's my golfing afternoon.'

'Golf?'

'Every Wednesday. It helps to break up the week. I sometimes combine it with business. So much easier when you are out of the office . . .'

'And were you playing golf the afternoon that your colleague died?'

'Afternoon? He died after work, didn't he? We always shut up shop early on a Wednesday. That's how Stephen made sure he couldn't be stopped. It's a terrible business. When a man decides to do something so drastic there's nothing you can do to stop him, don't you think?'

'I suppose not,' Sidney replied. 'And there were no big arguments with clients, that sort of thing? No one who might have a grievance against him?'

'None, as far as I am aware. Solicitors can sometimes get on to the wrong end of things but I was always confident that Stephen could charm his way out of a tricky situation. What are you getting at?'

Sidney paused. 'It's nothing, I'm sure,' he replied. 'I am sorry to have taken up so much of your time.'

'That's quite all right. I don't mean to rush you but I don't think we were expecting you. We don't have much call for clergymen in the office . . .'

'And I admit that, in the church, we don't have much call for lawyers . . .' Sidney replied, more testily than he had intended.

He had never taken such dislike to a man before and immediately felt guilty about it. He remembered his old tutor at theological college telling him, 'There is something in each of us that cannot be naturally loved. We need to remember this about ourselves when we think of others.'

On the way out of the office, Sidney felt ashamed of his rudeness. He worried about the kind of man he was becoming. He needed to return to his official duties.

He bicycled over to Corpus and arrived just in time to take his first seminar of the term. It was on the synoptic gospels, a study of how much the life of Christ found in the accounts of Matthew, Mark and Luke was dependent on a common, earlier source known as 'Q'.

Sidney was determined to make his teaching relevant. He explained how, although 'Q' was lost, and the earliest surviving gospel accounts could only have been written some sixty-five years after the death of Christ, this was not necessarily such a long passage of time. It would be the equivalent of his students writing an account of their great-grandfather just before the turn of the century. By gathering the evidence, and questioning those who had known him, it would be perfectly possible to acquire a realistic account of the life of a man they had never met. All it needed was a close examination of the facts.

Sidney spoke in familiar terms because he had discovered that when students were first at Cambridge they required encouragement as much as academic tuition. On arrival, those who had been brilliant at school soon found themselves in the unusual position of being surrounded by fellow students who were equally, if not more, intelligent than they were themselves. This, matched by the superiority of Fellows who didn't actually like teaching, meant that undergraduates in their first year were often prone to a vertiginous drop in confidence. The gap between a student's expectation of academic life and his subsequent experience could prove dispiriting. At the same time, the University itself displayed little sympathy for their disorientation, believing that those in their charge should understand that it was a privilege to be at Cambridge and they should either shape up fast or go crying back home to Mummy. Sidney therefore saw it as one of his duties to look upon the more vulnerable undergraduates with more sympathy than that shown by his colleagues, especially towards those theological students who found the rigorous investigation of some of the more unreliable biblical sources a challenge to their faith. Sidney, as in so many other areas of his life, had to ensure that those in his charge took a long view of life and held their nerve. The race was not always to the swift, nor the battle to the strong, he told himself. Time and chance happened to them all, and it was vital, above all, to hold a steady course.

It was a lesson he still needed to learn himself.

Although Sidney knew that he would see Inspector George Keating for their regular game of backgammon the following day, he decided that he really did need to telephone his friend, even if it might incur wrath. This it did, as the inspector had made it clear in the past that he never liked to have open and shut cases questioned and he was still smarting from England's loss at football to the Hungarians the previous evening.

'6-3! And to think we invented the game, Sidney. Wembley Stadium is the home of football and a team no one's ever heard of put six goals past us. Unbelievable!'

'I don't know why you are so fond of football,' his friend replied. 'It always leads to disappointment. Cricket is the game . . .'

'Not in the winter . . .'

'Then Rugby Union. Perhaps even hockey . . .'

'Hockey!' Inspector Keating exclaimed. 'You think I should start taking an interest in hockey? Next thing it will be bloody badminton. Why are you on the telephone, man?'

'There is something I wish to discuss with you.'

'Can't it wait until tomorrow?'

'It could but I don't want it to ruin our game of backgammon . . .'

The inspector let out a long slow sigh. 'You had better pay a visit to my office, then. If you can fit me in between services . . .'

'I think you are rather busier than me.'

'Come to St Andrews Street, then.'

Sidney had never been invited into the inner sanctum of the police station and had been expecting something alto-gether more organised, modern and scientific than the sight that greeted him on arrival. Inspector George Keating's private space was not the methodical hub of an organised crime-fight-ing force but a mass of manila files and papers, notes, diagrams, paper bags and old cups of tea that covered every conceivable space: desks, chairs and bookcases. The windows were lightly steamed from the heat of a two-bar electric fire, the ashtray was full and the desk-light had blown. The whole interior could easily have been mistaken for the rooms of a university don, an effect the inspector would not have intended.

Sidney often wondered whether he should say something about his friend's demeanour. He was a man who was two inches shorter than he wanted to be, which was not his fault, and his suit needed pressing, which was. His tie was askew, his shoes were scuffed and his thinning sandy-coloured hair was not as familiar with a comb as it should have been. The demands of the job, three children at home and a wife who kept a tight control on the family finances were perhaps beginning to take their toll. There were times when Sidney was glad that he was still a bachelor.

He knew that his visit was something of an imposition and felt increasingly guilty, but his suspicions were on his conscience and he needed to share them. He reported what he had discovered and conveyed his concerns about the whisky.

'Stephen Staunton's wife specifically told me that he only drank Bushmills, which, as you may know, has a distinctive smoky, vanilla and bitter-toffee taste. However, the whisky in the office was of the more common or garden variety. Johnnie Walker, I suspect . . .'

'Which leads you to conclude?'

'That the whisky was placed on Stephen Staunton's desk to give the illusion of Dutch courage but that he never drank any of it . . .'

'Nor, I suppose you are about to tell me, did he put his revolver in his mouth and shoot himself?'

'I seem to remember that there were no fingerprints on the revolver, Inspector?'

Sidney was not going to call his friend by his Christian name in the office.

'None. We did check.'

'And do you not think that is suspicious too?'

'You're suggesting the gun was wiped clean?'

'It's a possibility. Did you examine the decanter?'

Geordie Keating was now, if such a thing were possible, even more irritated. 'Not especially closely. We didn't really see the need. You'll have to provide more evidence than this, Sidney. What you have told me just won't do. Who would have killed Stephen Staunton, anyway? What was the motive? He didn't have any enemies as far as we can make out. He was simply a hard-drinking and depressed solicitor from Northern Ireland. That is the beginning and the end of it.'

'Yes, Inspector, only I don't think that it is.'

'Well, you'll have to find more information from somewhere if you want me to do anything about it . . .'

'But if I do so then you will investigate?'

'If further evidence comes to light of course we will investigate; but in the meantime I've got a runaway teenager, a couple of burglaries and a nasty case of blackmail to contend with.'

'Then I am sorry to have troubled you.'

'Don't be ridiculous, Sidney. If something comes up then of course we will investigate. You must know that we need more to go on than this. Jesus didn't settle for one or two miracles, did he? He went on until people believed there was proof.'

'I think we are quite a long way from Jesus, Inspector.'

Sidney left the police station, mounted his Raleigh Roadster and bicycled along Downing Street and past St Bene't's church. As he did so, he dreaded to think how Isaiah Shaw, the current vicar, would regard his current activities. Sidney could sense the man's disapproval not only whenever they met but every time he passed his church. For Isaiah had let it be known that he disapproved of his colleague's early rise through the ranks of the Church of England.

Sidney was forced to acknowledge that Isaiah had a point. He had, indeed, been fortunate. Following the untimely demise of his predecessor, the new Bishop of Ely, a Corpus man, had wanted to install his own domestic chaplain in Sidney's place, and had therefore moved him swiftly onwards and upwards to the fortuitously vacant parish of Grantchester. This promotion to such a plum position at the relatively young age of thirty, followed by his acquisition of a canonry only two years later, was regarded with considerable jealousy by colleagues of a similar age who found Sidney's effortless friendship with the senior clergy nothing less than an affront to their piety and hard work. There was more to being a priest, they argued, than their rival's easy charm.

Consequently, Sidney felt that he had to prove himself not only to his parishioners, but also to his rivals. He had to earn his position as Vicar of Grantchester *after the fact*. This was not always easy, and so he took it upon himself to throw himself into as many situations as possible, doing whatever he could to bring a Christian perspective to everyday events.

He turned into Trumpington Street. There, even though he knew that it might ruin his appetite for lunch, he decided to stop off at Fitzbillies for a consoling Chelsea bun. He wondered what Mrs Maguire, his daily help, might have left for him back at the vicarage. On a Wednesday it was normally sausages. For some reason he didn't fancy sausages, but then halfway through his bun he found that he didn't feel like something sweet either. He was out of sorts.

He returned to his bicycle and set off down Mill Lane towards Grantchester Meadows. He hoped that the wind against his face might freshen him up a bit but nothing seemed to make any difference. A group of students in duffel coats and long college scarves were talking loudly on their way to lectures, walking off the pavement and into the road, paying no heed to passing cyclists. A sign writer was repainting the façade of the butcher's shop and a window cleaner was at work above the new bank. Both of their ladders spanned the entire pavement, so that those of a superstitious nature, who did not want to walk under ladders, swayed on to the road and into the traffic. How removed all this was from the desperate world of suicide, or, more likely, murder, Sidney thought.

He passed Hildegard Staunton's house and headed off across the fields to Grantchester. When he arrived home all was as he had expected. Mrs Maguire had done some of her famous tidying, moving papers that Sidney had carefully left in separate and organised stacks on the floor, and piling them all together on his desk so she could vacuum. There were sausages in a Pyrex dish in the kitchen and potatoes she had peeled and left in cold water. There was also a note:

'More Vim please. And Harpic. Fish tomorrow. Not Friday.'

Sidney found it hard to address these concerns. He turned on the wireless and listened to the news. The Queen had just arrived in Canada on her Commonwealth tour. The Piltdown Man had been exposed as a hoax; and the Salvation Army were about to open a café in Korea. Sidney listened, ate his sausages and wondered what impact any of this information would have on the people of Cambridge.

As he cleared away his lunch and contemplated the possibility both of a cup of coffee and the second half of his Chelsea bun – there might even be a few quiet minutes in which he could listen to a bit of his beloved jazz music – there was a knock on the door.

Sidney opened it to find Miss Morrison standing on the step. 'I hope I am not disturbing you,' she apologised. She was wearing an elegant dark mackintosh and her hair was wet and windswept. 'I saw the bus to Grantchester and just stepped on to it.'

Sidney had not noticed that it had been raining. 'This is a surprise,' he replied.

'I hope a not unpleasant one.'

'Of course not. Do come in . . .'

'I won't stay if you don't mind, Canon Chambers. It's only that I have something that I think you should see . . .'

'What is it?'

Miss Morrison produced a piece of paper from her hand-bag but appeared reluctant to hand it over. 'I'm very sorry. It's evidence. I should have told you about it earlier. In fact I should have given it to the police but it's private. I hope I won't get into trouble.'

'What is it?'

'A letter; or rather a note . . .'

'To you?'

'Yes. It's addressed to me. From Mr Staunton.'

'May I see it?'

'Yes. But if you could just read it and give it back I would be very grateful. It's rather upsetting.'

'I see . . .' Sidney took the note. 'Where did you find it?'

'Mr Staunton left it on my desk. It's very short. But it leaves you in no doubt as to what must have happened.'

'Are you sure you won't come in?'

'I'd rather not if you don't mind.'

Sidney stood in the doorway and began to read:

A,

I can't tell you how sorry I am that it has come to this. I know you will find it upsetting and I wish there was something I could do to make things right. I can't go on any more. I'm sorry – so sorry. You know how hard it has been and how impossible it is to continue.

Forgive me

S

It had begun to rain again, and it was absurd that they were both still standing in the doorway of the vicarage, but Stephen Staunton's secretary remained in righteous defiance.

'I can see how upsetting this must be, Miss Morrison, but it would have been helpful if you had shown this to the police. I notice that he refers to you by your initial: A. Was that his usual practice?'

'We both used to initial everything to show that we had read things. He'd sign a single "S" for me and a double "S" for Mr Morton's papers – that is, until Mr Morton made a joke of it. They did not get on as well as they once had . . .'

'And "A"?'

'My name is Annabel, Canon Chambers.'

She waited for Sidney to return the note. This he did not do.

'Miss Morrison, there are some unusual features about your employer's death in which the police have become interested.'

Sidney knew that he was exaggerating Inspector Keating's level of concern but decided that it was the only way in which Miss Morrison would grant the request he was about to make.

'Are there?' Miss Morrison looked shocked. 'I don't understand.'

'I don't think it is anything to worry about but I very much hope that you will allow me to keep this note so that I can show it, in confidence, to my friend Inspector Keating in order to set his mind at rest. As soon as I have done so, then I will return it. May I have your permission to do this? I can assure you that the information would remain confidential.'

'I won't get into trouble, will I?

'I think that is unlikely. The police are convinced Mr Staunton died by his own hand and this note appears to prove it.'

'Appears? It states it quite clearly.'

'Indeed it does,' Sidney admitted. 'And so I am sure that it will be returned to you shortly. The only strange thing is why it has come to light now.'

'I explained. It is private. I was upset. And it is mine. Meant only for me.'

Sidney realised that he would have to give Inspector Keating the note and accept the reality of what had happened. All that he had been doing was to complicate a straightforward case and arouse doubt. He should never have listened to Pamela Morton's suspicions or been railroaded by her charm. Clearly the pressure of the infidelity had been too much for Stephen Staunton and he had taken the only escape route that he could find.

And yet, for reasons he could not quite fathom, Sidney's suspicions would not abate. Why, for example, would Stephen

Staunton leave a note for his secretary but not for his wife? What made Miss Morrison so hesitant to provide the police with information? And who had replaced the whiskey in the office?

Annabel Morrison looked him in the eye. 'Please return the note as soon as you can.'

'Of course.'

'I hope you can understand how distressing this has been, Canon Chambers . . .'

'I can, Miss Morrison. It has been distressing for everyone.'

'I am glad you understand that. Good day, Canon Chambers.'

Sidney closed his front door and made his way back into the hall. He was still holding the note. He looked down but could not focus on the words. And then, unbidden, he imagined Stephen Staunton's widow, Hildegard, sitting alone with her porcelain figures, due to receive Christmas cards from people who did not yet know that her husband was dead.

The following Sunday, having attended the last, and the shortest, Communion service before lunch, Pamela Morton knocked on the vicarage door. She was dressed in a dark navy coat with a wide-brimmed saucer hat that looked extraordinarily formal, even for church. She informed Sidney that she would take a very small whisky but could not stay long. She was expected for lunch at Peterhouse. A driver was waiting.

Once she had sat down her impatience was revealed. 'I am rather disappointed in you, Canon Chambers,' she began, her voice altogether more strident than Sidney had remembered. 'I was hoping that you might have something for me by now. Have you found anything at all?'

'A little,' Sidney answered. Despite the imperious charms of his guest, his attitude to her plight had cooled since his meeting with Hildegard Staunton. If any one person involved in this sorry business required his time and sympathy it was surely the widow rather than the mistress.

'Then what have you discovered?' Pamela asked.

'I am afraid that, despite my endeavours, your suspicions of foul play are going to be difficult to prove. Stephen Staunton left a note.'

'Do you have it?'

'I do.'

'Can I see it?'

Sidney crossed over to his desk and handed the piece of paper to the dead man's mistress. He knew that this was a breach of Miss Morrison's privacy and that he should have taken the evidence straight to the police as he had promised but he wanted to see what Pamela Morton had to say.

She was less interested than he had hoped. In fact she was unimpressed. 'No date, I see.'

Sidney was almost irritated by her dismissal of the only fact he had uncovered. 'It is Stephen Staunton's handwriting, is it not?'

'It is . . .'

'You hesitate to accept it as genuine.'

Pamela Morton was thinking. 'His secretary could just as well have written it. She certainly knew how to forge his signature.'

'How do you know that?'

'Stephen told me. It was a tacit agreement between them. He let her go home early on Wednesday afternoons – I think she saw her mother – and then, on other days, if he had to leave

45

before she had finished his letters, he would trust her to read them through and dash off his signature. It gave him more time to see me, he said, and then he could get home sooner without arousing the suspicions of his frumpy wife.'

'Do you think she is frumpy?'

'I wouldn't call her stylish. And no one would say she was thin.'

Sidney suddenly felt very sad. There was no need for Pamela Morton to talk like this. He had been moved and haunted by his visit to Stephen Staunton's widow and he had kept remembering it: her poised profile as she looked out of a window; the way that she would stop in the middle of a sentence as if she had suddenly remembered something else; the fact that she turned to Bach for consolation. He was upset that Pamela Morton could be so dismissive.

'You don't seem to care for the other women in Mr Staunton's life?' he asked.

'Why should I care for them? They did not make him happy. In fact, they contributed to his misery . . .'

'I am not sure Miss Morrison could be considered guilty of that . . .'

'She is an irrelevance, Canon Chambers.'

'Although she seems to know rather a lot about her employer. She knew where he went and she certainly made excuses for him when he was in places where, perhaps, he should not have been. Are you sure that your relationship with him was a secret?'

'I don't think little Miss Moribund knew a thing. There was only my friend Helen in London. The odd "seen-it-all-before" barman might have guessed but no one else.'

46

'And you are convinced that your husband did not have his suspicions?'

'I'm not stupid, Canon Chambers. I know how to keep secrets. Have you heard of Tupperware?'

Sidney was distracted by this sudden change of tack. Something Mrs Maguire had once said when she replenished the larder came back to him. 'Don't they have those American-style parties for housewives?'

'It's not the parties I'm interested in. They're plastic boxes that keep food fresh and separate. No cross-contamination. Nothing gets in; nothing comes out.'

'And so you "Tupperware" your life?'

'That's right, Canon Chambers. I keep things separate. It's like making meringues . . .'

Sidney understood the allusion but was not sure that dividing the white of an egg from its yolk was on a par with adultery.

'You have to keep things fresh, Sidney,' Pamela continued with her egg-bound metaphor, 'and discrete. Both discrete and discreet if you know what I mean. Sometimes people are not aware of the difference between the words so I think it's safer to do both. That way no one is hurt.'

Sidney could not remember allowing Pamela Morton to call him by his Christian name but was too surprised by her way of looking at human behaviour to comment. He decided to challenge her. 'There is a flaw . . . of course.'

'Which is?'

'Well, if there are two of you then you both have to be equally diligent about your Tupperware, or, indeed, your egg whites. The slightest bit of yolk . . .'

47

'That's true. But Stephen was very careful. Do you know about the private diary?'

'His secretary mentioned it.'

'Well, he certainly made sure *she* never saw it. He kept it in his jacket pocket. That was the one that could tell you what was really going on.'

'But his secretary kept an office diary . . .'

'That was for show. What he really thought and what he really got up to was in the private notebook. Miss Morrison did not know him as well as she thought she did.'

'I am not so sure about that. But I am surprised that you do not appear to accept this note as being genuine.'

Pamela Morton hesitated. 'Have you shown it to the police?'

'Not yet.'

'But you will.'

'Of course.'

'Then I hope you will be appropriately sceptical.'

'I haven't decided what I think,' Sidney replied, but knew that he would have to see Stephen Staunton's widow once more.

It was always a difficult matter for a vicar to decide when to call in on his parishioners. The traditional hours were between three and five, before Evensong and the preparation either of high tea or dinner; but clearly those hours were unsuitable for people in employment and Sidney knew that Hildegard Staunton sometimes taught piano to private pupils after school. He therefore decided to risk a visit at six-thirty, making the assumption that she would be at home and unlikely to be either dining or entertaining. This proved correct.

Josef Locke's 'I'll take you home again, Kathleen' was playing on the wireless when he arrived. Hildegard switched it off and offered him tea.

His hostess was wearing the same green housecoat and appeared nervous; embarrassed even. 'I am sorry I was in a dream when you last came. It was unfortunate. I could speak to people after the funeral because it was soon and I knew that I had to. Then afterwards . . . it was the shock, I think.'

'I did not think that you were in a dream.'

'I am sure I was rude. And sometimes, when I am sad, my English disappears. Do you speak any German?'

'*Nur ein wenig . . . Können Sie mir den Weg zur nächsten Stadt zeigen?*' Hildegard laughed.

'From the war, you understand. *Sie sind eine sehr anziehende junge Dame. Spielen Sie Fußball?*'

'No, Canon Chambers I do not play football. *Würden Sie gerne tanzen?*'

'*Ach, ich bin kein Tänzer.* I am afraid I am not a dancer.'

'*Was für eine Schande.* Did you find out about the will?' she asked.

'I am afraid that there doesn't seem to be one. But as his wife, you will no doubt be the beneficiary. This house, his savings . . .'

'I am afraid there are more likely to be debts. No doubt Miss Morrison will tell me.'

'I take it that you are not too fond of Miss Morrison.'

'I didn't see her enough to have an opinion. I think she thought that she was more responsible for my husband's well-being than I was myself. I did not mind too much. I have never found jealousy helpful . . .'

'Although she might have been jealous of you, of course?' Sidney began.

'I do not think it likely that she was in love with my husband if that is what you mean. But she did like to know everything that was going on.'

'I can imagine,' Sidney replied. 'But I gather he had a separate diary. So she can't have known everything . . .'

'How do you know about that?'

'She told me.'

'There is nothing much in it. The police returned it to me with what they said were his "effects". I didn't understand what they meant.'

'Have you put them somewhere safe?'

'They are here,' Hildegard replied. 'Would you like me to show you?'

'You don't have to.'

Hildegard took up a box from the sideboard. 'It seems very strange now. It is like something in a museum, the few possessions of a life: a wallet, a diary, cigarettes and a pencil with a rubber on the top. Sometimes I think my husband could still come back and the house would be as he had left it. I pretend that he has not died. One morning I poured two cups of tea before I realised that I only needed one.'

'I'm sorry . . .' said Sidney.

Hildegard stood up and opened the box. 'The police also asked if I wanted to keep the gun. What would I want with a gun?' She handed Sidney her husband's diary.

'What is this life,' she asked, 'but days that have passed? My husband wrote down the things he had to remember in pencil and then when each day was over he rubbed out what had happened.'

'An unusual habit . . .'

'When I saw him doing this for the first time he smiled and told me that another day was gone. He sounded relieved. He was rubbing out his life. Sometimes he would leave the house late at night and go for a walk. He could be away for hours. I never knew where he went. He could disappear, morning or night, and when I asked he told me that he just wanted to keep the black dog away. I think he preferred the night, when there was no one to trouble him. That's why he slept in the day – another hour could be lost.'

'He slept in the day?'

'After lunch; a sleep for one hour exactly, even in office hours. He stayed on into the evenings to make up for it and was always last to leave and lock up. Often he was late for dinner, or distracted, and sometimes I didn't know what I could do or say to help him. I asked him if perhaps it made life worse, to wake up twice in a day . . .'

Sidney opened the diary. It was small and leather-bound; the leaves were of lightweight paper and it came with a rubber-topped pencil in its spine. The pages were so fragile that some had been torn through excessive rubbing out. Inside the front cover, written in an italic hand was the owner's name, S. Staunton. On one page he read the word 'Anniversary' and on the first of August 'H's birthday'. The only other markings were the traces of a pencilled division between morning and after-noon – A.M. and P.M. Perhaps, Sidney thought, they were the remnants of appointments either side of his afternoon nap.

'And he would sleep anywhere?' Sidney asked.

'It was a routine. At two o'clock every day. His last appoint-ment ended every morning at 12.30. Lunch. Sleep. And then his next appointment would be at 3.15. He was like a machine. He could sleep through anything. A bomb could go off and he would not notice. I sometimes worried that if he was ever driving the car at two o'clock he would fall asleep, crash the car and kill himself. In the end he did not need a car to do that for him . . .'

Sidney leafed through the diary. There didn't seem to be anything of note but perhaps, he wondered, he could examine it more closely at home, when he had more time. Then he might be able to work out what had been erased. 'Do you mind if I borrow this?' he asked.

'There is nothing to see.'

'I would like to think about it a little more. It might be the basis of a sermon, perhaps; the disappearance of the days . . .'

'For they are as grass.'

Sidney had a sudden memory. '*Denn alles Fleisch, es ist wie Gras*. Brahms's *German Requiem*.'

'You know it?'

'I heard it in Heidelberg, just after the war. I found it very moving: the singing in unison at the start of the second movement, the journey from pain to comfort.'

'It was popular all over Germany. It was like a death march.'

Sidney was still holding the diary. 'I know this must have a sentimental value.'

'We were not sentimental people.'

'I'm not sure that I agree with you. Your husband remembered your birthday and, it seems, your wedding anniversary.'

'He was good about those things. It was easy for him to remember. Then he could feel confident. He was a kind man who wanted to please people. I could not help him as much as I wanted to. I should have been a better wife.'

'You must not blame yourself.'

'How can I not? My husband took his own life.'

'But he must have had friends?'

'You came to the funeral. They were there. But we did not socialise. My husband did not enjoy the politeness of dinner parties. He did not like being forced to behave well. He preferred to see people on their own . . .'

'And out of office hours?'

'I did not mind who my husband saw. I did not ask questions. He was kind to me. We had this house. We had food. I was warm. And I could play the piano as much as I liked without being disturbed. It was not complicated. All I wanted in my life was someone to be kind to me and I found him. We were not happy all the time but I do not think we were ever sad. Now, of course, this has gone . . .'

Sidney wondered if Hildegard was about to cry and then realised that it was he who was on the verge of tears. He felt immense pity and yet he could not think how to express it or give her comfort. 'You have your memories,' he said quietly.

'Yes, of course.' Hildegard Staunton tried to accept Sidney's cliché. 'I have my memories. Not that all of them are good. And now I have to start again.'

'If there's anything I can do?'

Sidney knew that his offer was weak but he was surprised by the alacrity of Hildegard Staunton's response. 'You can pray for me, Canon Chambers. That would be helpful. And you can pray for my husband too. I would like to know that you are doing that; that someone will care for us. You know that some believe that people who take their own life will never go to heaven?'

53

'I am not one of those people,' said Sidney. 'And it is not for me to judge. We live as we can. If we cannot meet our hopes and expectations, then we fall short. It is, if you will forgive me, part of being a Christian. We are not as we might be . . .'

Hildegard gave Sidney the faintest of smiles. 'Is that not a very long way of saying that nobody is perfect?'

'It is,' said Sidney. 'Perhaps you should be a priest yourself . . .'

'Oh, I don't think that would be allowed.'

'You could be a deaconess . . .'

'Now you are teasing me . . .'

'I like to see you smile,' said Sidney, boldly.

'And I like it that you make me smile,' Hildegard replied.

One of the advantages of being a clergyman, Sidney decided, was that you could disappear. Between services no one quite knew where you were, who you might be visiting, or what you might be doing: and so, on most Mondays, his designated day off, he would bicycle a few miles out of town, ride out through the village lanes of Trumpington and Shelford, and then take the Roman Road for Wandlebury Ring and the Iron-Age forts of the Gog Magog Hills. In such a flat Cambridgeshire landscape Sidney liked the gently sloping elevation of the hills, the prehistoric route ways around him, the sense that he was part of a longer, more distant history, of barrows, vortexes and ley lines. This was a pre-Christian landscape that connected with an ancient folk tradition, with its reports of haunting apparitions, ghostly packs of dogs and giant chalk figures carved into the ground.

Here Sidney sat, with the ham sandwich and flask of tea that Mrs Maguire had prepared, and let thoughts come to him. It was a form of prayer, he decided. It was not asking or talking but waiting and listening.

The view was not as spectacular as that of the hills of Antrim that Stephen Staunton must have known as a child, but Sidney was content that it had a smaller English beauty; a contained, unfolding series of vistas that were never still as the sun moved through the clouds. He took sustenance and consolation from what he had come to refer to as 'healing views'. There was no one to disturb him; no telephone calls, no unwelcome letters, no knock at the door.

Autumn was his favourite time of year, not simply for its changing colours but for the crispness in the air and the sharpness of the light. As the leaves fell the landscape revealed itself, like a painting being cleaned or a building being renewed. He could see the underlying shape of things. This was what he wanted, he decided: moments of clarity and silence.

The grass and the fields were damp after the morning rain and Sidney could not sit down. Instead, he leaned on a five-bar gate, ate his sandwich and drank his tea, letting his thoughts roam. When he had finished, he decided to climb on to the gate itself, perching on its top rung, as if he were still a boy with a whole day stretching before him and nothing to do but waste it. He looked out over the surrounding countryside and wondered how many other people had been confronted with this same view over time, and thought that this was home; this was England.

He began to consider the case in which he had become involved. He was sure that Pamela Morton was right to be suspicious about Stephen Staunton's death, and all was not as it appeared, but how could he give her misgivings weight and substance? Why would a man whom so many people had been at pains to point out was clearly a potential suicide not have taken his own life? And if he had been murdered then who could have done it? Clive Morton could have had a financial motive and Hildegard Staunton certainly had cause for resentment.

Sidney was unsettled by his feelings. On approaching the Staunton residence he had felt depressed and ill at ease, but as soon as he had sat down with Hildegard he had not wanted to leave. Had her tragedy made him pity her, or were his feelings more than sympathy for her fate? Had he even, he wondered, become so fond of her that he could not believe that she could ever make a man so miserable that he would want to kill himself?

Sidney watched the low sharp light of the day start to disappear behind the trees and remembered that he had no lights on his bicycle.

He would have to get back.

He returned home, poured himself the smallest of Johnnie Walker's against the chill of the night, and looked at Stephen Staunton's suicide note once more. Then, as the whisky took care of his anxieties, the beginnings of an idea started to emerge.

He picked up the pocket diary and looked at the seemingly random arrangements of mornings and afternoons that had been added in pencil.

How could he have been so slow? It annoyed him beyond measure. To have taken the information at face value; to believe what people wanted him to believe! How had he allowed himself to be taken in?

He realised that he needed to see Pamela Morton once more, and urgently, but when he telephoned it was her husband who answered. Struck by a sudden moment of nerves, Sidney put down the receiver.

The next day, he sent her a note but it was late the following afternoon before she called on him in person. After he had poured them both cups of tea, Sidney leaned forward in his chair and said: 'I think, after all this time, that I might be making progress.'

Pamela Morton was still, surprisingly, ungrateful. 'Well, that would make a pleasant change.'

'It has not been easy, Mrs Morton, and I do think it might have been simpler if you had gone straight to the police rather than a clergyman who is ill-equipped to deal with these matters . . .'

'There is no need to be defensive, Canon Chambers. I know you would not have summoned me to your home if you did not have something to tell me. Is there the faintest chance that you might actually believe me?'

'I have always believed you, Mrs Morton . . .'

'I have told you before. *Pamela* . . .'

Sidney ignored her request. 'Although I do need to ask you to account for your movements . . .'

'On the day of the murder? You don't think I'm a suspect? That would be rich.'

'No, I am not saying that.'

'But you might be *suggesting it.*'

'Well, it would be a good way of throwing an investigator off the scent; to suggest a murder that no one has considered to be murder; to open a case that was never going to be opened. Perhaps one would only do that if one wanted to frame someone else?'

'And do you think that is what I might have been doing?'

'I don't wish to insult you, Mrs Morton. . . .'

'You're doing a pretty good job so far . . .'

'I have to think about every possibility: your husband, for example.'

'Yes, I can see why he might be a suspect but I can assure you he knows nothing. He's too busy playing golf. He's obsessed. The hobby is worse than gambling.'

'That's as may be. But I need you to be both specific and honest.'

'That's how I've always been.'

'Then I must ask you to remember where you were on the evenings of September the first, second, eighth, fifteenth and twenty-second, and the two nights of October the fifth and sixth.'

'You expect me to remember all that?'

'It's very important . . . Pamela . . .'

'And you want to know now?'

'There is only one thing about these dates that interests me . . .'

'October the sixth is the night before Stephen died. I certainly saw him then. I will always remember it. I told him that we just had to get through the winter. If we could just get through Christmas then everything would be all right.'

'And the other dates?'

'I don't have to account for all of my movements, do I?'

'You just have to tell me if these were the days on which you saw Stephen Staunton. September the first, second, eighth, fifteenth and twenty-second, and the two nights of October the fifth and sixth.'

Pamela Morton thought for a moment. 'I can't be exact without my own diary but I can tell you that we did see each other two days running because my husband was away and it probably was on the nights that you mention. If the other days were Tuesdays, then yes. I always get the 10.04 to London on Tuesdays. Stephen would follow me later. We went on separate trains. We were very careful, Canon Chambers. I want you to understand that. Why do you want to know?'

'It would make everything clear, Mrs Morton. Everything . . .'

During many a moment in the course of his investigation Canon Sidney Chambers considered once again how much he had neglected his calling. Prayer, scripture, sacrament and fellowship were supposed to be the sacred centre of the priest's life and yet he could be found wanting in all of these activities. Instead, he had been distracted. He had attended meetings of the Mothers' Union, the Women's Institute and the PCC. He had organised the flower rota, and typed up a timetable for the church wardens, the sidesmen, and the volunteers to clean and polish the brasses. He had edited the monthly issue of the parish magazine, continued with the weekly Bible study group, and run a series of confirmation classes. He had even taken a group of Scouts and Cubs on a hike, supervised the building of the Christmas crib, organised the carol singers and set up a search for a lost cat. At the same time he had continued his teaching at Corpus. Any visiting archdeacon, sent to check up on him, would have no cause for complaint, but Sidney knew that he was not at his best. He had not visited the sick as regularly as he had hoped, he was three weeks behind on his correspondence and he had not even begun to write the big Advent sermon which he was due to preach in King's College Chapel.

There were also his parents to consider. His father, a doctor in North London, was still complaining about the demands of the National Health Service. His mother had recently telephoned to say how worried she was about Sidney's brother and sister. Jennifer was, apparently, seeing a man who was 'too common by half' and Matthew had joined a skiffle band that included 'all kinds of riff raff'. Perhaps their elder brother could go and knock some sense into them, she wondered? Sidney thought that this was not really his business but the plain fact was that even before he had involved himself in this criminal investigation he had had too many things on his plate. His standards were slipping and the daily renewal of his faith had been put on the back burner. He thought of the General Confession: 'We have left undone those things which we ought to have done; and we have done those things which we ought not to have done . . .'

He started to make a list, and at the top of the list, as he had been advised at theological college, was the thing that he least wanted to do. 'Always start with what you dread the most,' he had been told. 'Then the rest will seem less daunting.' 'Easier said than done,' thought Sidney as he looked at the first item on the list of his duties.

'Tell Inspector Keating everything.'

It was a Wednesday morning, and he knew that a visit to the St Andrews Street Police Station would not be popular, but Sidney was so convinced by the accuracy of his deductions that he decided the truth was more important than Geordie Keating's impatience.

'I hope this is not going to become a habit,' his friend warned, as he pushed an old cup of tea on to a stack of stained papers and began a new one.

'Not at all, Inspector. I do have more information that I think is important.'

'My life is a river of "more information", Sidney. Sometimes I wish someone would put a dam in it. I presume that you are referring to the solicitor's suicide.'

'I am.'

'Then you had better sit down.'

Sidney wondered whether he should have rehearsed what he was going to say, written it down even, but there had been no time for such preparation. Consequently, his thoughts came out in a rush. 'I have been thinking about the circumstances of the crime, the people involved and the nature of love.'

'Oh God, man . . .'

'And I just cannot believe that Stephen Staunton meant to kill himself. I know that everything suggests that he did so but I do not believe this to be the case. Nor do I believe that he drank any of the whisky that was on his desk . . .'

'Then what was it doing there?'

'A red herring, Inspector. It was even, perhaps, a way of pointing the finger at Clive Morton, a man who does not know as much about whisky as he possibly should . . .'

'That does not make him a murderer . . .'

'I do not think that he is . . .'

'Well, that's a relief . . . it only leaves every other inhabitant of Cambridge as a suspect. I don't suppose the victim could still be responsible for his own death? That the case could in fact be suicide?'

'You remember at the very beginning of our conversation on this subject when I suggested that things could be too clear?'

'I certainly do. It was a bit cheeky of you if you don't mind my saying so.'

'I don't. But this was the murderer's mistake. Knowing that I was on the case she began to panic. In fact she panicked so much that she was forced into producing her trump card: a suicide note.'

'She?'

'Yes . . . "She" . . .'

'You're suggesting our man got his secretary to write his own suicide note? You're crackers.'

'I am not, Inspector.'

'Then what are you suggesting?'

'I am proposing that the letter is not a suicide note . . .'

'Oh, Sidney . . .'

'Look again, Geordie.'

As Inspector Keating examined the piece of paper Sidney recited the text he had memorised.

A,

I can't tell you how sorry I am that it has come to this. I know you will find it upsetting and I wish there was something I could do to make things right. I can't go on any more. I'm sorry – so sorry. You know how hard it has been and how impossible it is to continue.

Forgive me

S

'Seems pretty clear to me,' Inspector Keating replied.

'Too clear; and then again, not clear enough. For this is not a note written by a man who is about to kill himself. It is the note of a man ending a relationship.'

'Yes, I can see that it could be . . .'

'And you remember the private diary, the one with the entries in pencil that Mr Staunton rubbed out each day?'

'The one with the days marking the mornings and the afternoons? The one that might suggest a few appointments that he wanted to keep quiet? I can see what you might be saying.'

'But they are more than that. Look again.' Sidney produced the diary.

'A.M and P.M. What is wrong with that?'

'They are never on the same day. And you will note that the initials A.M. occur less frequently as the initials P.M. increase.'

'Which means?'

'Annabel Morrison and Pamela Morton. Their initials. These are the records of assignations.'

'So you are suggesting that our solicitor friend had not one but two lovers?'

'I am afraid I am.'

'How did he have the energy?'

'That is not our concern, Geordie . . .'

'But two on the go at the same time! And a wife as well. God knows, it's hard enough when you've been married for a bit. What do you think Stephen Staunton's secret was?'

'Charm.'

'Is that all?'

'That and the fact that he listened. He paid attention. According to Pamela Morton, when he spoke he made people feel that they were the only people in the world that mattered.'

'Is that what women want?'

'Apparently so. Although, being a married man, you would know more about it than I do.'

'I am not so sure about that.'

'But to our purpose . . .'

Inspector Keating was hesitant. 'I am still trying to understand it all. The man was involved with three women – if we include his wife. No wonder it all got too much. You are suggesting, I take it, that when his relationship with Mrs Morton became more intense he decided to end things with Miss Morrison?'

'Exactly.'

'And you think that she . . .'

'I am afraid so.'

'That's madness.'

Sidney continued. 'You will recall that Mr Staunton took a rest after lunch each day. You will also remember that every Wednesday afternoon Mr Morton plays golf, which leaves only two people in the office on the day of the murder . . .'

'Annabel Morrison and Stephen Staunton.'

'Miss Morrison has received the note from Mr Staunton ending their affair. What is more, she suspects that a new relationship has begun. She cannot be sure, but such is her fury, and such is her rejection, that she determines no one else will enjoy the attentions of the man she loves. We know that Mr Staunton is a strong sleeper. His wife told me he could sleep through anything; perhaps even the sound of the 2.35 train to Norwich. For it is at that moment that Miss Morrison places the gun in his open mouth and pulls the trigger of the revolver she has removed from the desk. The sound is masked by the noise of the train. She then places a half-empty decanter of whisky on the desk, little caring that it is a whisky her employer would never drink because the appearance of suicide is so strong. Only when we begin to doubt does she produce the note which, she realises, can be converted from a "Dear John" letter into an explanation for suicide. It is very clever.'

Inspector Keating did not give his friend the appreciation that he thought such reasoning deserved. 'That's all very well, Sidney, but the evidence is very circumstantial. How on earth are we going to prove all this?'

'You don't think this is enough?'

'It would be hard to secure a conviction on this alone.'

'Then I think I will pay Miss Morrison a little visit.'

'On what pretext?'

'The return of the note.'

'And then, I suppose, don't tell me, that you will try and prove your theory by engineering a confession?'

'I am not sure what I will do,' Sidney replied. 'But the truth will out.'

'Are you sure you want to do all this?'

'I have no choice.'

'And there's nothing I can do to stop you?'

'Nothing at all, Inspector.'

Sidney was relieved to discover that Annabel Morrison was alone when he called at the office of Morton Staunton Solicitors, and she was grateful to receive the return of the note.

'I hope the police are satisfied?' she asked.

'They are indeed, Miss Morrison. You have been most helpful. I am sorry it has all been such a terrible business. You must be very upset.'

'I am, Canon Chambers, I don't mind admitting it.'

'You were clearly very fond of Mr Staunton.'

'I was.'

'You must have spent a great deal of time together, more time perhaps than he even spent with his wife?'

'We did. I don't want to speak out of turn, Canon Chambers, but I am not sure that he was happy with his wife. She's German as you probably know.' Annabel Morrison gave Sidney a conspiratorial look, one that assumed the atmosphere was now safe for prejudice. 'I think he needed a bit more looking after than she was able to do.'

'It must have been a full-time job, and out of the office as well on some occasions.'

'It was. But I am not sure what you are suggesting?'

'I am not suggesting anything at all, Miss Morrison. I am merely remarking that you must have accompanied Mr Staunton on many occasions, on business, of course. I am not implying that there was anything improper.'

'We did sometimes travel together, but those times were quite rare.'

'But then Mr Staunton also travelled with other women.'

'What do you mean?'

Sidney looked at Annabel Morrison and decided to take an extraordinary gamble. 'With Mrs Morton, for example.'

'Did he?'

'I believe Mrs Morton travels down to London on Tuesday mornings.' Sidney decided to add a lie to his risk. 'I believe that sometimes they went together?'

Annabel Morrison was clearly discomfited by the question. 'This was never in the diary that I kept.'

'Perhaps Mr Staunton didn't like to tell you?'

'But if he was travelling with Mrs Morton I would have known.'

'I gather they were rather fond of each other.'

'What on earth are you suggesting?'

'I am sure there was nothing compromising or untoward,' Sidney replied, in as unconvincing a manner as he could.

He had told a second lie.

He was astonished to discover how easy it was.

The railway station at Cambridge had been built in the 1840s, in a symmetrical style in warm local stone, and was the heart of a regular service between London and Kings Lynn. When it was at its busiest the platforms were crowded with people, and this Tuesday morning was no different. A stooping elderly don kept dropping a selection of books which he had tied up with string; three girls were preparing to put their bicycles into the guard's van; and Pamela Morton was waiting for the 10.04 express train to London. She was wearing a dark burgundy coat and a matching beret, and she carried a small portmanteau. A thickset man in a double-breasted navy pinstriped suit stood to her right. He looked, to all intents and purposes, to be a man about to do business in the City but he held neither briefcase, papers nor an umbrella.

As the express train approached, a petite but determined woman with silver hair pinned in a bun, and dressed entirely in black, made her way through the crowds. She wore dark glasses, although it was November, and leather gloves. She appeared to know exactly where she needed to be on the platform and stood directly behind Pamela Morton.

The train whistled. The woman in black stepped and stretched both arms, palms facing forward. As she leaned back to gain the necessary momentum to push Pamela Morton off the edge of the platform on to the rails and under the train, one man blocked her path, a second pulled her back from behind, while the businessman next to Pamela Morton threw his arm around her waist.

'What are you doing?' she shouted, struggling to break free. 'Let go of me!'

The train braked, slowed and stopped. The businessman let go, and just as Pamela Morton was about to complain to the stationmaster she saw that the two men behind her were holding Annabel Morrison. Her face was filled with fury. 'You tart. Isn't one man enough for you?'

'What do you mean? What are you doing?'

'It's all your fault.'

'My fault?'

'He was happy with me. You never knew that, did you? He never told you.'

Pamela Morton looked at her lover's secretary. 'My God,' she said. 'You.'

'You don't know anything.' Annabel Morrison continued. 'You never knew him at all; what he felt, what he went through, how he suffered. He told me everything.'

'You tried to kill me.'

'I could kill you all.'

The doors to the train opened, and the people of Cambridge alighted and boarded. Inspector Keating came forward to make his arrest. 'Are you all right, Mrs Morton?'

'I don't understand. What is this woman doing?'

Keating gestured to his men. 'Take Miss Morrison away.'

'You'll never have him now,' she spat. 'No one will.'

Keating turned to Pamela Morton. 'I'm sorry. Sometimes desperate crimes require desperate measures . . .'

Pamela Morton looked hard at the Inspector. 'You risked my life.'

'We had two men following Miss Morrison and one man guarding you since you entered the station. I'm surprised you hadn't noticed.'

'And how did you know someone would try to kill me?'

'We didn't. It was Canon Chambers who suggested that an attempted murder might take place and that we should be ready for this. I believe you know the man.'

'I certainly do.'

'Then you can have a word with him yourself. He has been summoned.'

'I will need more than a word.'

'Go easy on him, Mrs Morton.'

'I most certainly won't,' Pamela replied, before looking at the receding figure of Miss Morrison. 'That jealous, murdering bitch.'

When Sidney finally arrived to greet Pamela Morton he could tell that he was in for a roasting. 'What on earth do you think you were doing having me followed?' she shouted.

Sidney held out his hand in greeting but it was not shaken. He let his arm fall. 'It was, I am afraid, a necessary evil.'

'Was this the only way of doing things? And how did you know it would happen here?'

'You take this train every Tuesday, I think?'

'Most Tuesdays . . .'

'Miss Morrison has always been very particular about train times. I also noticed that she liked to read Russian novels . . .'

'Fascinating. But I fail to see what this has to do with me,' Pamela Morton replied, icily.

'The first time I spoke to her I realised that she was reading *Anna Karenina*. You will be familiar with the work?'

'I have seen the film. I was not as impressed with Greta Garbo as everyone else seemed to be . . .'

'A story of adultery that begins and ends on a railway platform. I informed Inspector Keating of my suspicions and although he didn't quite believe me, he trusted me sufficiently to provide men for your protection . . .'

'And how did that woman know about me?'

'That I cannot reveal . . .'

'You told her, didn't you?'

'I told her nothing. I let her make an assumption.'

'That is as good as telling her. You promised that you would keep my secret. I could have been killed. Why didn't you warn me?'

'Sometimes it is not always what you know that matters. It is what you withhold. If you had known of the possible danger then your behaviour might have become unpredictable. It was vital that you knew nothing.'

'A bit dicey if you ask me.'

'A calculated risk. Taken by someone you could trust.'

'That's all very well for you to say . . .'

'But we finally discovered the truth, did we not? And your suspicions were proved correct.'

Pamela Morton jumped to the necessary conclusion. 'So that jumped-up little nobody did everything?'

'It appears so.'

'Then I was right.'

'You did not point the finger . . .'

'That is true. But I certainly raised the alarm. I suppose there'll be a trial?'

'Of course.'

Pamela Morton looked uneasy. 'It will be a scandal, I imagine. How public will the information become? What shall I tell my husband? How can I explain why his secretary tried to kill me?'

Sidney hesitated. 'You can tell him that Miss Morrison is a fantasist and create your own story, I would have thought. Perhaps you could say that despite it all, Miss Morrison was really in love with your husband and wanted you out of the way. Most men are flattered when they discover that they have a secret admirer. Convince him of that and it should blind him to everything else.'

'I hope you're right. Interesting that you of all people should advocate the telling of untruths.'

Sidney offered her his arm and began to escort his unwilling accomplice from the station. 'The white lie has its purposes.'

'I suppose it's easier to tell than the black.'

'I prefer white,' Sidney added before adding a barbed question of his own. 'But in your case isn't it simply a matter of preserving the status quo?'

'I am not sure either of us knows what that is.'

'I'm sure he'll believe whatever you say, Mrs Morton.'

'It's just as well I was once an actress. Do you think he's going to go along with even more lies?'

'Trust me . . .'

Pamela Morton shielded her eyes from the low November sun and gave Sidney a stern look. 'Do you know, Canon Chambers, I'm not sure that I will. I think I've trusted you enough for one day.'

That evening Sidney stopped outside Hildegard Staunton's front door. He was about to ring the bell when he heard the sound of the piano inside. The music was stark, angular, dramatic and mysterious. It seemed to hover on the edge of atonality, using all twelve notes of the chromatic scale as it built to a conclusion that was as natural as it was inevitable. It was Bach's Fugue in B Minor; the final piece in the first book of *The Well-Tempered Clavier*.

Hildegard held the final chord for a long time and let the music die away. When Sidney was certain that she was not going to continue, he rang the doorbell.

Inspector Keating had suggested that the news of Annabel Morrison's arrest would be better coming from a clergyman than a policeman, but Sidney had not decided how much to tell her about all that had happened, or how many details of the case he would leave out.

The light in the porch came on, the door opened, and Hildegard Staunton smiled. 'Come in,' she said as he stepped up and stood by her side. 'I had forgotten how tall you are.'

'I am often too tall for a room,' said Sidney. 'I try to sit down as soon as it is polite to do so.'

'I hope you don't develop a stoop,' Hildegard replied. 'I always think a man should be proud to be tall.'

'I try not to be proud,' said Sidney, sounding more pompous than he had intended.

'You have come to tell me things?'

'I have come to return your husband's diary and, yes, I have come with news.'

'I can tell already that you are nervous, Canon Chambers.'

'Sidney . . .'

'Very well, *Sidney*.'

'It is not easy.'

'I am not frightened of difficult things . . .'

'It is to do with Miss Morrison . . .'

'Ah . . . She loved my husband . . . I think . . .'

'You knew?'

'Women often know more than men think that they do.'

'Unfortunately . . .'

'Oh,' Hildegard Staunton interrupted. 'Now I see. But it can't be?'

'Yes . . .' Sidney hesitated. He wondered how much she understood.

'My husband loved me but wanted another. What did she do?'

'Your husband did not commit suicide, Mrs Staunton. He was murdered by his secretary. I am sorry to have to tell you this.'

'Why would she do such a thing?' Hildegard spoke slowly as she tried to take in what Sidney was saying.

'I think because he stopped seeing her.'

'He wanted to come back to me? He once told me that he could never leave me.'

Sidney considered his answer. There was no need to tell Hildegard about Pamela Morton. What purpose would it serve other than to hurt her? It was true that the facts could well emerge at Annabel Morrison's trial but it was likely that Hildegard would have returned to Germany by then. Besides, this was not the time for further revelation. The sin of omission was surely kinder than the telling of truths.

'No,' Sidney said quietly. 'And he never did.'

73

Hildegard stood up and started to walk round the room. She stopped by the window and looked out. It was almost dark. Sidney could hear the wind gathering outside. It began to rain.

'You are kind to tell me.'

'The police were going to come; but I thought it better . . .'

'If you came yourself? I am grateful. It is horrible but you make it less so.'

'If you would like me to leave you alone, you just have to say.'

'No,' Hildegard replied. 'Don't go. We do not have to speak. I have to think of death in a different way now. I wish I didn't have to consider it so often.'

'I will stay for as long as you need, Mrs Staunton.'

'Hildegard.'

'I am sorry. *Hildegard.*'

'Please could you sit here beside me? I will try not to cry.'

Sidney moved next to her. He took her hand and held it. Hildegard tightened her grip as she spoke. 'I do not know what I am saying, perhaps, so you may not believe me, but, to know this, to know even part of this, is relief. That he was not so sad that he killed himself. That I did not drive him to do such a thing.'

She looked at Sidney and the tears came. 'Is that so very selfish?'

Sidney felt in his pocket for a handkerchief but he was too slow. Her tears fell on to the hand that held hers. 'I don't think anyone thought that.'

'It does not matter what anyone else thought. I thought it.' She stood up and moved away.

Sidney heard the pain in her voice. 'I wish you hadn't.'

'We cannot help what we think . . .'

'But perhaps sometimes we should not dwell too much . . .'

'No,' said Hildegard as she tried to pull herself together. 'You are right. It is why I play the piano. It stops me thinking.' She sat back down beside him. 'Do you play?'

'I am afraid not.'

'Perhaps I should teach you?'

Sidney smiled. His lessons at school had not been a success. He never could get the hang of his two hands doing different things at the same time. 'I think Germany is rather a long way to go for lessons.'

'Yes,' Hildegard smiled sadly. 'I suppose it is. Will she hang, this woman, for what she did?'

'It seems most likely.'

'I am not in favour of another death.'

'Neither am I; but it is the law of our land.'

'You should change it. *Rache trägt keine Frucht* . . .'

'It is not in my power; but one day, I hope, in my lifetime.'

They were still sitting beside each other and neither of them wanted to move. Hildegard Staunton gave him a playful pat on the knee. 'And what about you, *Sidney*?' she asked. She seemed amused by the very English nature of his name. 'What about your lifetime?'

'It is very simple. I have my job. I have my calling . . .'

Hildegard smiled. 'You do not have a wife, I think?'

'I cannot imagine it . . .' he began.

'Well, there is time . . .' Hildegard said gently and then smiled. 'Why are you called *Sidney*?'

'I was named after my grandfather.'

'Is it an unusual name? I have never heard it before.'

'There was a Victorian clergyman called Sidney Smith. He was quite a character. He once said that his idea of heaven was eating *pâté de foie gras* to the sound of trumpets.'

'I am not so sure about that. In any case I think I prefer the Sidney of this world to any man of the past.'

'I think we would both have enjoyed meeting him, had we lived in those times.'

Hildegard stood up. 'I think you do not like sherry but it is all I have. The whiskey has not yet arrived. Stephen's brother told me a last case was on its way; not that I need it. Would you like some?'

'Why not?' Sidney replied.

Hildegard laid out a tray. 'What do you think I should do?' she asked. 'Perhaps I should not go back to Germany after all?'

'It would be good if you stayed here, of course. From my point of view . . .'

Hildegard handed Sidney his drink. 'It is a strange feeling to have no responsibility for someone else any more.'

'You must try not to let this darken the rest of your life.'

'It is hard to think of that now.' Hildegard looked up and smiled sadly. 'I cannot imagine the future.'

'It may be impossible. You will not forget what has happened. But I hope, if I may say so, that you might think a little bit more about yourself. There is only so much self-sacrifice we can offer . . . .'

Hildegard was amused. 'I never thought I would hear a priest telling me to be selfish. You think I have made a sacrifice of my life?

'No. All I hope is that you will find happiness again.'

'But you know that happiness is an illusion, Canon Chambers?'

76

'*Sidney . . .*'

'Nothing can last in this world. *Zeit gibt und nimmt alles.*'

'Time gives and takes all?

'Your German is better than you admit. If you come and see me you may even feel at home.'

'Oh, I don't know about that.' Sidney replied. 'Are you going back?' he asked.

'In ten days' time. I will be home for a German Christmas with my mother and sister.'

'What are they called?'

'My sister is Trudi. My mother is Sibilla. They are very German names.'

'Like Hildegard.'

'I was named after Hildegard of Bingen. The visionary. Fortunately I don't have any visions. But she wrote music and without music I do not know how I could live.'

'I am sorry that you won't be at our carol service.'

'I will be with my sister in Berlin. I will hear *Stille Nacht* in German once more. When they sing, I shall remember your kindness to me.'

'I am also sorry that not everyone has been good to you.'

'But *you* have been good, Canon Chambers, and it is your kindness which I shall remember . . . .'

Hildegard stood up and took a porcelain figure off the mantelpiece. It was of the little girl feeding chickens. 'Take this,' she said. 'On account of your kindness.'

Sidney was caught off guard. 'Oh, I don't think I could.'

'Stephen bought it for me when he thought we were going to have a child. He always wanted a girl. Perhaps you will be luckier in your life than we have been. I'd like to give it to you.'

'Your life is not over.'

'Please,' said Hildegard. 'Take it to remember me by.'

Sidney could hardly bear the days that followed. He could not concentrate on his work, not least the Advent sermon that he was due to preach at King's, and even the idea of another evening in The Eagle with Inspector Keating had lost its appeal. Their meetings had become a matter of work rather than pleasure. It was his own fault, Sidney thought, but then how could he have behaved otherwise? An injustice had been uncovered and his conscience had given him no choice.

Now he had to resume the priestly life. He remembered his Principal telling him at theological college: 'the clergyman's identity is defined not by what he does but what he is'. He was required to live an exemplary live. It would not do to sniff out murderers and sit on a widow's sofa drinking sherry.

This, however, was easier said than done. Sidney had to admit that he was distracted. Hildegard had sent him a letter to remind him of the date of her leaving, but he had been so uncertain as to what he would say, and how he might ask for her forwarding address, that he almost missed her departure completely.

A removal van was parked outside the house and Hildegard was waiting for a taxi to take her to the station. She was dressed in a dark blue coat and she held her gloves loosely over a matching handbag.

'I'm glad I arrived in time,' said Sidney.

'I would have asked the taxi to stop at your church. It is not so far.'

'I might not have been there.'

'But you are here now.' She smiled. 'And I am glad. I hope you will come and see me in Germany . . .'

'Yes, I . . .'

Hildegard saw his embarrassment. 'I do not believe in farewells . . .'

'No. Well . . . it's only that it might be difficult to arrange . . .'

'Nonsense. I will help you.'

Sidney could not understand why his words would not come. 'I've never been to Berlin. Or Leipzig . . .' he said.

The taxi pulled up and Hildegard paused, as if she was wondering whether to get in it after all. 'I will write to you. I will send you my address.'

'Yes, of course,' said Sidney.

She held out her hand. 'Thank you. You are a good man.'

'I don't know about that.'

As he took her hand, Hildegard leaned forward and kissed him lightly on the cheek. 'I will not forget you . . .' she said.

'Nor I you . . . .'

Sidney watched the taxi recede into the distance. He touched his own cheek. Then he bicycled back to the vicarage. Outside the front door was a large brown case. Hildegard had instructed the removal men to leave the case of Bushmills that she had been sent from County Antrim for Christmas. A card was attached.

'For my friend Sidney, who I know will appreciate what lies within. With love and gratitude. Your Hildegard.'

Sidney walked into his study and sat in silence.

He tried to write his sermon. It would be about hope, he decided, and grace. He remembered the flimsy pages of Stephen Staunton's diary. We cannot erase the past, he thought, no matter what we do; instead we have to let it carry us into the future.

As he wrote, he stopped to think about each stage of Hildegard's journey home. He imagined her boarding a train and leaning out of the window to wave him goodbye. He could picture her, even now, blonde and pale, dressed in her dark blue coat, standing on the stern of a ferry with seagulls cawing in its wake as the light fell. He saw her walking through wintry German streets and passing through Christmas markets where people drank *Glühwein* amidst the swaying lanterns. He wondered what Hildegard would say to her family when she first saw them, her sister Trudi and her mother Sibilla, and if she would speak about all that had happened; or if it would be like the war, which had rendered so many people so silent. Would she mention him at all, he asked himself; and how, come to think of it, would he ever talk about her?

The next evening he made his way to King's College Chapel. As the candlelight flickered over the carved wooden choir stalls, Sidney thought once more about the hope and the fragility of Christmas, the uncertain morning and evening of our lives caught amidst the unfurling of time and season, day and year.

The service made his sadness at Hildegard's parting all the more resonant. It was the end of another day, a further chance to contemplate mortality and glimpse eternity as the precentor continued the responses:

'O God make speed to save us.'

The choirboys replied:

'O Lord make haste to help us.'

'Singing is the sound of the soul,' he thought to himself. For centuries people had been singing these words. Such continuity gave Sidney hope. He was part of something greater than himself – not only history but beauty, continuity and, he hoped, truth.

He prayed for the soul of Stephen Staunton. *We will live as we have never lived.* Those had been his last words to Pamela Morton and yet, perhaps, they also spoke of a world beyond our own.

He looked up at the darkened stained glass. He had learned more about love in the past few weeks than he had known in years. He had seen some of its characteristics: how it could be passionate, jealous, tolerant, forgiving and long-lasting. He had seen it disappear, and he had seen it turn into hatred. It was the most unpredictable and chameleon of emotions, sometimes sudden and unstable, able to flare up and die down; at other times loyal and constant, the pilot flame of a life.

Sidney touched his hands together in prayer. Then he gave himself up into silence. 'How we love determines how we live,' he thought.

A Question of Trust

It was the afternoon of Thursday 31 December 1953, and a light snow that refused to settle drifted across the towns and fields of Hertfordshire. Sidney was tired, but contented, after the exertions of Christmas and was on the train to London. He had seen the festival season through with a careful balance of geniality and theology and he was looking forward to a few days off with his family and friends.

As the train sped towards the capital, Sidney looked out of the window on to the backs of small, suburban houses and new garden cities; a post-war landscape full of industry, promise and concrete. It was a world away from the village in which he lived. He was almost the countryman now, a provincial outsider who had become a stranger in the city of his birth.

He started to think about the question of belonging and identity: how much a person was defined by geography, and how much by upbringing, education, profession, faith and choice of friends.

'How much can a person change in a life?' he wondered.

It was an idea at the heart of Christianity, and yet many people retained their essential nature throughout their lives. He certainly didn't expect too radical a departure in the behaviour of the friends he was due to meet that evening.

As the train pulled in to Kings Cross, Sidney was determined to remain cheerful in the year ahead. He believed that the secret of happiness was to concentrate on things outside oneself. Introspection and self-awareness were the enemies of contentment, and if he could preach a sermon about the benefits of selflessness, and believe in it without sounding too pious, then he would endeavour to do so that very Sunday.

He put on his trilby, gathered his third umbrella of the year – he had left the previous two on earlier journeys – and alighted in search of a bus that would take him to the party in St John's Wood.

His New Year's Eve dinner was to be hosted by his old friend Nigel Thompson. Educated at Eton and Magdalene College, Cambridge, Nigel had been tipped as a future Prime Minister while still at university and had become Chairman of the Young Conservatives straight after the war. Having been elected as the Member of Parliament for St Marylebone in the 1951 General Election, he began his rise to power as PPS to Sir Anthony Eden (a man his father had known from the King's Rifle Corps), and now worked as Joint Parliamentary Under-Secretary of State for Foreign Affairs. Sidney was therefore looking forward to a few meaty conversations about Britain's role on the international stage with one of the most promising MPs in the country.

His wife, Juliette, had been the Zuleika Dobson of their generation, possessing a porcelain complexion, Titianesque hair and a willowy beauty that her dream-like manner could only enhance. Sidney had worried at their wedding whether she had the stamina necessary to be the wife of an MP but cast such masculine thoughts aside as the first intimations of jealousy.

83

Their home was a nineteenth-century terraced house to the north of Regent's Park. It had previously been the type of establishment in which rich Victorian men had kept their decorative mistresses. Sidney considered this rather appropriate as Juliette Thompson certainly had a whiff of the Pre-Raphaelite about her. Her beauty was both doomed and untouchable: unless, of course, you were Nigel Thompson MP.

Sidney got off the bus at the stop for Lord's Cricket Ground and made his way towards Cavendish Avenue. He was not an admirer of London in winter, with its wet streets, fetid air and gathering smog, but he recognised that this was where his family and friends earned their living and that if he wanted to enjoy the congeniality of their homes and the warmth of their fireplaces then he had to put up with any inconvenience in getting to them.

At least, Sidney remembered, his sister Jennifer would be at the dinner. His younger sibling had a naturally good-natured manner, with a rounder face than the rest of the family, eager brown eyes and a bob cut that framed her face and gave the impression, Sidney thought, of a circle of friendliness. She was always glad to see her brother; and he felt his heart lift every time she came into the room.

Traditionally, Jennifer was considered the most responsible member of the family but on this particular evening she was to bring a rather shady new boyfriend to the dinner: Johnny Johnson.

She had briefed her brother about him during the family telephone call on Christmas Day, and she had high hopes that Sidney would approve of him: not least because he and his father ran a jazz club. He was 'a breath of fresh air', and he did, apparently, 'a million and one amazing things'. Sidney only hoped that his sister was not going to become besotted too soon. The family trait of thinking the best of people had resulted in the past in her having rather too fanciful expectations about the ability of men to make lasting commitments, and this had, inevitably, led to disappointment.

They were to be joined by Jennifer's best friend and flatmate, Amanda Kendall, who had just begun her career as a junior curator at London's National Gallery.

When Sidney had first met Amanda, soon after her twenty-first birthday, he had been rather smitten. She was the tall and vivacious daughter of a wealthy diplomat who had once been a colleague of his grandfather. Unlike Juliette Thompson, she was not what a fashion magazine would refer to as an 'English rose', being dark and commanding and full of opinion. But she had presence, and even though her own mother had described her nose as 'disappointingly Roman', dinner parties throughout London were grateful for her conversational sparkle. It was universally considered that, although she might cause trouble with her outspoken views, Amanda could liven up any party and would be a good catch for any man who was prepared to take her on. Sidney had nurtured a faint hope that one day he might be that man, but as soon as he had decided to become a clergyman, that aspiration had bitten the dust. It would have been ludicrous for a well-connected debutante, in pursuit of the most eligible bachelor in town, to marry a vicar.

Now, after several years of careful research, Amanda appeared to have got her man. On one of her recent trips to assess the potential death duty on a series of paintings in a Wiltshire stately home, she had met the allegedly charming, undoubtedly wealthy, extraordinarily good-looking and unfortunately ill-educated Guy Hopkins. This was the man to whom she was to be engaged, perhaps even, it had been suggested, that very night.

Sidney's official companion at dinner was the renowned socialite Daphne Young, a terrifyingly thin woman who was famed both for her sharp intelligence and for the number of marriage proposals she had turned down. Consequently, he rather dreaded the disappointment that even someone so well mannered would be unable to conceal on discovering that her dining companion that evening was going to be a clergyman.

At least the other two guests at the dinner were relatively jovial: Mark Dowland, a publisher who was delightfully indiscreet about his authors, and his small and spiky wife Mary, a zoologist with piercing blue eyes and the sharpest of tongues. The softest thing about her, her husband had once remarked, was her teeth.

Sidney had never been that keen on New Year's Eve. It was, perhaps, the thought of yet another year passing, a reminder of all the time that he had frittered away in the previous twelve months and the secular conviviality so soon after Christmas. He sometimes wondered what it might be like to take to his bed until it was over, and remembered a fellow priest who, when he felt the horrors approaching, would hole up in the grimmest boarding house in the most depressing town he could find, in order to plumb the slough of despond. The idea was, that after hitting rock bottom, he would emerge into a world in which anything would seem better than his most recent experience. The town his friend had chosen to confront every demon known to man, Sidney remembered, was Ipswich. It seemed an odd choice.

Cocktails were served in the drawing room on the first floor where Mark Dowland began to recite from the work of John Betjeman, a promising new poet:

> 'Phone for the fish-knives Norman
> As Cook is a little unnerved . . .'

The other guests began to laugh at the performance but Sidney could not join in. He was already disconcerted by the fearful realisation that the party might end in charades; an activity which he always dreaded since his failure, the last time he had been at the Thompsons, to mime the five syllables of the Dickens novel *Martin Chuzzlewit*.

He accepted a gin and tonic to stiffen his sinews before facing the prospect of Amanda's potential engagement and the introduction to his sister's new inamorato.

Johnny Johnson proved to be a dark, good-looking man, and he was dressed in an extremely well-cut, thin black suit that Sidney rather admired. He began with a question. 'All right?'

'I think I am,' Sidney replied.

'Jennifer's told me a lot about you.'

'Nothing too damaging, I hope.'

'Not at all, Sidney. Although I did find it quite a turn up for the book when she told me her brother was a vicar. I thought you'd be a teacher or a doctor.'

'I think that was what was expected of me.'

'I don't go to church very much, Sidney, if I'm honest. It makes me feel like I've done something wrong.'

'That may be the intention.'

'You need to liven those services up a bit,' Johnny continued. 'Literally. You could have Sunday evenings as jazz nights. After you've done all the serious stuff.'

Sidney brightened. He had always wanted to attract more people to his church services and stem the departure of teenagers from protracted ceremonies that still felt Victorian. Sometimes he thought that the church had hardly advanced since the days of Trollope. 'That's not a bad idea,' he replied.

'I could help if you like; put you in touch with some people to get you started?'

'That would be splendid.'

Mary Dowland moved over to join them. 'You're not seriously thinking of having jazz in church, are you?'

'Why not?' Sidney replied.

'Well, you can never tell if the notes are being played in the right order.'

'That's the wonder of jazz, Mary,' Johnny explained. 'There's no right way and there's no order.'

'Don't people get very lost?'

'You can't get lost if you've got rhythm, Mary.'

Sidney was amused by Johnny Johnson's copious use of other people's Christian names. He admired his directness.

Edna, the Thompsons' maid, arrived with a further tray of drinks, offering refills, which Johnny refused.

'You're not having a cocktail?' Sidney asked.

'I don't drink alcohol, Sidney.'

'How restrained,' Mrs Dowland noted.

'I like to keep my wits about me, Mary.'

'Shall we go through?' Juliette Thompson asked, as she stood up and smoothed her hair. She was dressed in a sleeveless gown that flared out from her thin waist and Sidney noticed Guy Hopkins giving her the once over. He wished Amanda's prospective partner could have been less obvious.

The dining room was decorated in the Georgian style, with walls painted in smoking-room red, an ornate plastered ceiling and an egg and dart cornice. A narrow sideboard held two Chinese vases and a canteen of silver cutlery.

'I presume there are placements?' Daphne Young asked, turning to her host. Her halter-necked and backless dress only drew attention to her almost skeletal frame. 'I do expect to be seated to your right.'

'Then your expectations have been fulfilled,' Nigel Thompson replied.

Sidney dreaded the humiliation of this moment. At many a dinner party he was placed next to the 'difficult relation': the cousin with a slight lack, the daughter recovering from a broken engagement, the son who had lost everything in a casino and who had come home to sort himself out. He knew, for a start, that he was unlikely to be seated anywhere near Amanda Kendall but was surprised and delighted to find himself next to his hostess. He looked at the placements.

Nigel Thompson MP

Miss Daphne Young	*The Hon. Amanda Kendall*
Mr Guy Hopkins	*Mr Mark Dowland*
Mrs Mary Dowland	*Miss Jennifer Chambers*
Canon Sidney Chambers	*Mr Jonathan Johnson*

Mrs Juliette Thompson

'This all looks very congenial,' he said to his host.

Nigel Thompson was anxious that everyone should appreciate his reasoning. 'Guy,' he called out, ignoring Sidney's gratitude. 'I haven't put you next to Amanda because I am sure you have been seeing quite enough of each other recently. And besides, I rather want her to myself.'

'You can have her on loan,' Guy called out. 'Like one of her paintings. I shall need her back at midnight.'

'I am no Cinderella,' Amanda replied.

'And I am no Ugly Sister,' Mary Dowland chipped in. 'Canon Chambers, I believe I am seated next to you?'

Sidney passed her the plan.

'I see Jennifer and Johnny have been seated next to each other,' Mary observed. 'Shouldn't we swap?'

'But that would mean putting a brother and a sister side by side,' Juliette explained.

'Of course,' Mary Dowland stood behind her chair. 'Not that I have anything against sitting beside you, Canon Chambers . . .'

Jennifer cut in. 'Don't go on about it, otherwise he will think that you do. He's very sensitive about these matters, my brother. He's always complaining about how disappointed people look when they discover that they are sitting next to a clergyman.'

'But this is not just any old clergyman,' Juliette Thompson explained. 'Sidney is one of the most charming men I know. That's why he's sitting next to me.'

'Now, now,' Nigel announced. 'You'll embarrass the man. I presume we can rely on you to say grace, Sidney.'

'Blimey, Jenny,' said Johnny Johnson under his breath. 'It's a long time since I've said that.'

'You only have to say "Amen", darling.'

Sidney began: '*Benedic, Domine, nobis et donis tuis, quae de tua largitate sumus sumpturi, et concede ut illis salubriter nutriti, tibi debitum obsequium praestare valeamus, per Christum Dominum nostrum. Amen.*'

'Amen,' the group affirmed.

Johnny pulled in his chair. 'And I wasn't expecting Latin, Sidney.'

The meal consisted of French onion soup and then the braces of pheasant that Guy Hopkins had brought as a gift from his Boxing Day shoot. This was accompanied by roast parsnips, carrots, cabbage and game chips; followed by a lemon meringue pie. Nigel Thompson had provided several amicable bottles of Beaujolais. He also promised champagne for the chimes at midnight.

The conversation drifted aimlessly as the guests discussed the best kind of house party, the merits of a London home over a place in the country, and the right kind of carpet for a dining-room floor. The Thompsons were, apparently, 'between carpets' and so the dining-room floor, for the moment, consisted only of the wooden floorboards.

Sidney was a little disappointed. He had been expecting an advanced level of political and cultural debate. The increasing international escalation over atomic weapons had created the possibility that, for the first time, mankind held the means of its own extermination. Tensions between Eisenhower and Khrushchev were on the rise; and questions remained concerning German rearmament, the rescue of the Atlantic alliance and the building of a new framework for the collective defence of Western Europe. Yet here they all were talking about carpets.

Sidney was surprised that people took the conversation so seriously but was happy not to have to respond to gambits which

91

presumed that Christmas must be his 'busiest time of year'. Instead, Mary Dowland was keen to tell him about the prospective arrival of a panda at London Zoo, while Daphne Young informed Sidney that her current paying guest was a clergyman in search of a new challenge who needed a little advice.

'I'm not sure anything I say could be of much benefit.'

'Nonsense,' Daphne replied. 'Nigel tells me that you are one of the brightest clergymen in the Church of England.'

'I think that is only because he is a friend of mine.'

'He's a good friend to have. And I imagine Grantchester's a fine living. Perhaps you need a curate?'

'I have considered it.'

'Then come and meet Leonard. He's frighteningly intelligent. He's learning Russian at the moment. God knows why. I fear he thinks me rather flippant.'

'I very much doubt that.'

'It's true, I'm afraid.'

Guy Hopkins put his arm around the back of her chair. 'I'm surprised you haven't brought someone along, Daphne. Don't you have a man in tow?'

Mary Dowland giggled. 'You normally have several, don't you? I'm sure you must be in the address book of every eligible bachelor in London.'

Her husband filled his glass with more red wine. 'I wonder what happens when they get married. Do you suppose their wives cross you off?'

'It has been known,' Daphne Young acknowledged, aware that she was being teased. 'I suppose that these days I am considered rather dangerous. It can sometimes take a man rather a long time to recover.'

'A lifetime, I should imagine,' said Sidney, generously.

'You are too kind, Canon Chambers.'

Just before midnight, after the maid and the cook had been allowed to leave for the New Year celebrations at Piccadilly Circus, and as the port began to circle round the table, Guy said that he had a surprise. He stood up and placed a jewellery box in front of Amanda. 'I think you may be able to guess what this is.'

'How stupendous,' Nigel announced. 'I think this probably calls for something more than port.'

'Hold on,' his wife counselled. 'We do not know what it is yet.'

Mary Dowland would not wait for the champagne and filled up her own glass with wine. 'I think we can guess.'

'I don't know what to say . . .' Amanda began.

Guy put a protective hand on her shoulder. 'Open it.'

Inside the case was a gold ring with a large ruby surrounded by miniature diamonds.

'It's beautiful,' said Amanda.

'Try it on.'

The room was stilled, the candles guttered. Sidney hoped that it was what Amanda wanted. She smiled, nervously, almost embarrassed, at this public demonstration of love and money. 'I've never seen anything quite like it.'

'Can I see it?' Daphne asked.

'Of course. It's lovely, isn't it?'

The ring was passed round for all to admire. Nigel returned with champagne. 'There's more in the fridge. I was saving this for midnight but all it means is that we will have to drink a bit more. If I can just squeeze past . . .'

Johnny Johnson lifted his chair and was about to tuck it in behind him when Nigel Thompson tripped over the leg and stumbled.

'Bloody hell!'

The champagne bottle fell from his hand and smashed on the floor.

'Oh . . .' his wife cried. 'It's everywhere.'

'So bloody careless of me . . .' said Nigel, looking down at the floor.

'Don't swear!' his wife cut in, mopping the champagne from her dress. 'You know how it upsets me.'

'I'm quite happy with the port,' said Mark Dowland. 'Goes down a treat.'

Daphne stood up. 'Let me get a cloth from the kitchen.'

Mary joined her. 'And a dustpan and brush.'

'It's splashed up all over me,' Juliette complained. 'I will have to change.'

'Then go and do so,' her husband snapped.

'I don't want to leave everyone. I don't know what to do.'

'I'll go with you,' Amanda offered. 'There's no need to make a fuss. We can go upstairs. It's all right, darling.'

'It's all such a mess . . . .'

'Soon be midnight,' Johnny said quietly to Jennifer. 'We don't want to miss the bells. Shall we stand outside then?'

'I think we have to stay here. I'm sorry.'

'I was hoping we could be alone.'

'That comes later.'

They smiled and then looked up to see that Sidney had heard them. Guy stood back in the doorway as Daphne and Mary cleared away the champagne and the broken glass. Nigel went in search of another bottle.

Mark Dowland drank some more port. 'This is all going terribly well . . .' he said, expecting those around him to appreciate his irony. They did not.

Sidney worried how he was going to get back to his parents' house in Highgate. There were taxis, of course, but they were expensive. He had assumed that he was going to get a lift with Jennifer and Johnny but they seemed to be going on somewhere else and he couldn't imagine Amanda and Guy wanting his company on the evening of their engagement. It was curious, however, that Amanda had not technically accepted the proposal of marriage. She had merely admired the ring. If he had been in Guy's position he would have been looking for a more affirmative answer.

At last, the guests sat down once more, helping themselves to the stilton and awaiting Juliette and Amanda's return. Nigel suggested retiring to the drawing room, where they could all see in the New Year in greater comfort and settle down to some charades but he was interrupted by the return of his wife, in a black silk peignoir, and Amanda, who smilingly challenged them: 'I hope you've all been behaving. I've been looking forward to some champagne. Who's got my ring?'

There was a silence.

'I don't have it,' said Mary Dowland. 'I handed it to Sidney . . .'

'And I gave it to Juliette . . .'

'I can't remember what happened,' said Juliette. 'I can't remember anything. I think it was in front of me.'

'Well, I haven't got it,' said Jennifer.

'Nor I,' said Daphne.

'Then where the hell is it?' Nigel asked.

His wife looked frightened. 'Don't swear . . .'

'Perhaps it fell on the floor?' Sidney suggested.

'I didn't see it there,' said Mary. 'And we cleared up quite carefully, didn't we, Daphne?'

'You couldn't have swept it into the bin?' Mark Dowland asked his wife. He had not moved from his chair for the whole evening.

'No, of course not. Do you think this is funny?'

'Or could it have fallen between the floorboards?' Sidney asked.

'Not a stone that big,' Guy said quickly.

Nigel Thompson got down on to his hands and knees. 'It can't just have disappeared.'

Sidney tried to be reassuring. 'Well, we should all look. It must be here somewhere.'

The guests stood up and paced around the room, looking into the table decoration, under plates and mats, on the sideboard, across the floor and down the backs of chairs. The ring was nowhere to be found.

Guy Hopkins began to lose his temper. 'This is ridiculous.'

Amanda tried to calm him down. 'It must be here somewhere, darling.'

'But where?'

The doorbell rang. 'That will be my taxi,' said Daphne Young.

Her host was surprised. 'You're going?'

'It must be early . . . .'

'Have we missed the bells?' Mark Dowland asked.

'I asked it to come for a quarter past midnight,' Daphne explained. 'I am expected elsewhere on the half-hour.'

Mary Dowland was unable to resist the opportunity for sarcasm. 'Then it was good of you to stay with us so long.'

Guy pressed closer. 'And you're sure you don't have my fiancée's ring?' he asked.

'Of course I don't,' Daphne replied. 'What do you take me for? You can look in my bag if you like.'

'That won't be necessary,' said Nigel.

'It will,' Guy replied. 'We have to find the ruddy thing.'

Daphne opened her bag and emptied its contents on to the dining-room table without a word. Inside had been a compact, perfume, a handkerchief, a set of keys, a little diary, an address book and a small purse which she opened in front of all the other guests. Sixpences, threepenny bits and a ten-shilling note scattered across the table.

'You can look all you like,' she said. 'You won't find it there.'

'Amazing,' said Johnny Johnson. 'I've never seen inside a woman's handbag before, Daphne.'

As Guy scattered the objects of the handbag across the table, examined them and then put them back, piece by piece, Daphne returned to her place, picked up her stole, and finished her glass of port.

'Happy?' she asked.

'It's not here,' Guy complained.

'It is very bad form to look into a lady's handbag.'

'I'm sorry for the intrusion. I was upset.'

'It's positively boorish,' Daphne continued. 'Now if you don't mind, I will say goodbye to my host and hostess.'

Johnny Johnson held up his glass of water. 'Happy New Year, Daphne.'

'I am sure the ring will turn up in the morning,' said Sidney.

'The morning?' Guy exploded. 'I'm going to search this room and everyone in it.'

'If you'll excuse me.' Daphne edged past. 'Would you like a lift, Canon Chambers? I believe I may be going in your direction.'

'Perhaps I should stay, Jennifer . . .'

'It's all right, Sidney,' his sister reassured him. 'I'm sure the Thompsons won't mind.'

'I would not want to take you out of your way, Miss Young. You've been delayed already this evening, I'm sure.'

Daphne Young accepted his refusal with alacrity. 'Indeed, Canon Chambers. A Happy New Year to you.'

Nigel and Juliette Thompson accompanied Daphne into the hall, where they said their goodbyes. A further, fruit-less, search around the room ensued, and after everyone had ostentatiously opened their pockets and satisfied Guy Hopkins that they were not thieves, Jennifer and Johnny left too. They asked if Sidney wanted to come along to a jazz club with them and although her brother was tempted, he thought it better if everyone calmed down and went home.

'I suppose I'll be doing the driving,' Mary Dowland said to her drunk husband.

'Despite my celebratory consumption, I am perfectly capa-ble of driving a car,' her husband explained. 'There is nothing to it. And, on a night such as this, what more can possibly go wrong?'

Sidney spent what, on a clergy stipend, was a small fortune on a cab and stayed the night with his parents. It was strange to be back in his childhood home. No matter how often he tried to explain the nature of his vocation and the daily routine of his job, Alec and Iris Chambers regarded their son with an air of amused perplexity. They couldn't seem to understand how they could have produced a child who had become a priest.

They found it easier to talk to him as if he was still a diligent seventeen-year-old over whom they still had a measure of control. Whenever Sidney came to stay he was expected to fit in with their daily lives as if he had neither left nor grown up, assisting his father with *The Times* crossword and his mother with the preparation of the vegetables. Iris Chambers had hinted more than once that it was about time that she was a grandmother, but since neither Sidney, nor Jennifer, nor their brother Matthew, had made any progress in this area of life the three siblings were treated as children every time they came home.

Matthew was considered to be something of a night owl, and always excused himself from the family gatherings at lunchtime, but Jennifer was expected and she arrived late and in something of a state. She threw down her bags in the hall and exchanged half-hearted New Year greetings with her mother.

Alec came out of his study to greet her. He had put on his new Christmas jumper and still had his pipe in his right hand. 'What on earth is the matter?' he asked.

'Has Sidney not told you about last night?'

'Told us what?'

'As far as I can see,' Sidney replied, 'there is nothing, so far, to report. A misplaced ring is bound to turn up.'

'Well it hasn't,' Jennifer answered forcefully, before throwing herself down on the sofa. 'The whole thing is a disaster . . . .'

Her mother sat down in a neighbouring armchair. 'You will have to explain, dear.'

'Sidney can do it. I am too upset.'

There was a small pause in which her mother stood up again and began to head towards the kitchen. 'Perhaps then, Sidney, you would like to finish laying the table and tell me what happened?'

Alec Chambers was having none of it. 'But then I don't get to hear the story!'

Jennifer interrupted. 'It's very simple. Amanda was given an engagement ring last night.'

'By whom?' her father asked.

'Guy Hopkins.'

'And who might he be?'

'So Amanda is engaged?' her mother cut in.

'I don't know.'

'You don't know?'

'That is not the point.'

'I would have thought that is very much the point.'

'You never let me finish,' Jennifer complained.

Alec Chambers was trying to understand his daughter's story. 'Is this the ring that is missing?'

'What was it like?' Iris asked.

'It doesn't really matter what it's like. The fact is that it's gone. Amanda passed it round the table for everyone to admire. She never got it back. The whole evening was a fiasco. Champagne everywhere.'

'Was it very expensive?' her mother asked.

Her father would not let Jennifer answer. 'You mean to say that the ring was lost in a welter of champagne?'

Sidney tried to reassure everyone. 'I am sure there is a perfectly innocent explanation. It must have either fallen through the floorboards or someone has been absent-minded and misplaced it when the champagne bottle was smashed.'

'What a profligate waste,' Iris tutted.

'An accident, I hope?' Alec asked.

Jennifer ploughed on. 'Johnny thinks someone's stolen it.'

'Does he, indeed?'

'But you were amongst friends,' her mother cut in. 'Surely that's impossible?'

Alec continued. 'I presume you searched everywhere, including the bathroom? Perhaps Amanda took it off in an absent-minded moment?'

Jennifer explained. 'She hardly had it on in the first place. We looked everywhere. Although some of those present weren't at their sharpest.'

'Ah! I assume drink had been taken?'

'It was New Year's Eve, Daddy.'

'It sounds ghastly,' said Iris. 'But I am sure it will sort itself out. Besides, it's time to carve the joint, Alec. After we have eaten I thought that you both might like to help me with the Christmas thank-you letters. Some of your father's patients have been exceedingly generous of spirit.'

Jennifer made her way to the table. 'Well, I wish some of that generosity of spirit had been in evidence last night.'

Her mother served out the roast beef while her husband poured from a bottle of claret. 'By the way, Sidney, I found the last clue in the crossword – "Boar's head and all man? Yes." It's Hogmanay.'

'Very good; hog, man, aye.'

'Are you going to say grace?'

'I will,' Sidney replied. It was important to keep the family up to his standards even though his father had been positively agnostic of late.

'*Mensae caelestis participes faciat nos Rex gloriae aeternae.*'

After the 'Amen' his father turned to Jennifer. 'When are we going to meet this chap of yours?'

'I'm not sure he'll want to see me again after last night. It was so embarrassing.'

'Is Nigel Thompson's wife all right these days?' Iris asked her daughter.

'Juliette? I'm not at all sure. We all think she was the last to be seen with the ring in her hand but it can't have been her. She was the hostess, for goodness sake.'

'She has always had a nervy disposition.'

'Now be careful, Iris,' Alec cautioned. 'We must not jump to conclusions.'

'I'm sorry, darling, but poor dear Juliette is often her own worst enemy in life. I seem to remember . . . .'

Alec Chambers doled out the claret. 'I hope no one cast any aspersions . . . .'

'Have the Thompsons called the police?' Sidney asked.

Jennifer rested her knife and fork on her plate and gave her brother one of her steady sisterly stares. 'They don't want this to become public knowledge. Nigel's not been an MP for long and he doesn't want anything to damage his prospects. You know how ambitious he is.'

'Our future Prime Minister,' Alec smiled.' I expect Churchill's got something to say about that.'

'He can't go on for ever, Daddy.'

'You know that Gladstone formed his last administration at the age of eighty-three?'

'But that was not a success.'

Sidney felt they were straying from the point. 'So they plan to sort out this ring business amongst themselves?'

'That's the idea.'

'And how are they going to do that, Jenny?'

'I told them that you would come back and help.'

'Me?'

'Yes, my dearest brother, you.'

'I am not sure how I can be of any assistance.'

Jennifer looked at her brother as if he was slow to under-stand. She had, since she was ten, spoken to him about serious matters in emphatic italics, never quite believing that he was giving her his full attention. She employed this tactic now. 'You can help *look for the ring* and then, if it *is* still missing, you can *find out what went wrong*, without causing *a scene*.'

'A scene has already been made, I recall.'

'Nigel was going to telephone you . . .'

'You suggested it?'

'I told him that I would *talk to you in person first*. Juliette's taken to her bed, and Amanda is apparently alternating between rage and tears. Nigel is one of your *oldest friends*. I promised I'd pop you round this afternoon. You were *there at the time* and you are *the only one everyone trusts*.'

'But I have to get back to Grantchester . . .'

'There are no services tonight or tomorrow, are there?'

'No, Jennifer, but that is not the only thing I do. I lead quite a full life and need to be back tomorrow evening. I am never really off duty.'

'And that's precisely why you can be on duty now.'

'It's not even my parish. It's St John's Wood, for goodness sake. Haven't they got a vicar of their own?'

'Of course they have.'

'Then why can't they ask him?'

'Because he wasn't present at the time and their vicar is not a detective.'

'Neither am I.'

'You are going to have to become one. I have brought my car.'

Sidney looked to his father for support but found none. 'You don't appear to have much of a choice, old boy.'

It was hard for Sidney to retain his cheerfulness. Here he was, surrounded by the possibility of deceit, theft and betrayal, and now bullied into taking an unwilling part in an investigation into events at a party he had never been that enthusiastic in attending. He felt ethically compromised. He always liked to give people the benefit of the doubt and yet now, here he was, on the verge of questioning the lives and morals of his friends and acquaintances.

He saw already that if a crime had been committed he would have to look dispassionately at every member present, even his own sister, who could, he supposed, if he thought objectively, have stolen the ring out of some misguided jealousy. And yet it made him sick to be so suspicious.

Nigel answered the doorbell. He was wearing a tweed jacket and a crumpled open-necked Viyella shirt that looked as if it had been pulled straight back out of the laundry basket.

'Thank goodness you've come,' he said. 'Everyone is in pieces.'

Sidney took a step back. 'I'm not sure I can be of much assistance.'

'Your calming presence will be a good start.'

Juliette came down the stairs in the same peignoir that she had worn the previous evening. She did not appear to have slept. 'It's Edna's day off,' she began. 'But can I get you a cup of tea?' It was a question, Sidney thought, which was more commonly asked of vicars than any other profession.

'Say yes,' her husband whispered. 'We have to keep her mind on other things.'

'That would be most kind.'

The two men walked to what Sidney supposed he must refer to as the scene of the crime. 'How would you like to begin?' Nigel Thompson asked. 'We went through the room as thoroughly as we could and then put it back to normal. Juliette found it too upsetting to leave it in a mess. There were still bits of broken glass everywhere. I don't know how we missed them.'

The dining table was without its tablecloth and was set with two silver candlesticks and a lazy Susan at the centre but was, Sidney noticed, smaller than the previous night. 'There are only six places,' he observed. 'And yet the dinner party was for ten.'

'It extends,' Juliette explained as she came into the room with a pot of tea. 'You can pull it out at either end. We can even seat twelve at a push . . .'

'Late Georgian walnut,' her husband continued, 'with a rather unpredictable mechanism underneath. It's a bit of a palaver to go under the table and do it and then put it back together in the morning but it's a family heirloom. However, you're not here to discuss the furniture.'

'Indeed.'

Amanda entered the room. She was wearing a black jersey-knit twin-set and looked on edge. Sidney wondered what the outcome of the evening had been and whether she was engaged to Guy Hopkins or not. He would have to find the right moment to ask.

Juliette turned to her husband and began to cry. 'I know that everyone thinks I did it.'

'No they don't, my darling.'

'I was the last person that people can remember seeing with the ring but I know I never took it. It would never occur to me to betray one of my closest friends.'

Amanda put an arm around her while looking firmly at her husband. 'Believe me, Juliette, none of us would ever suspect you of such a thing.'

'Would other people?' Sidney asked.

'I am afraid so,' said Nigel. 'Juliette, perhaps you would like a little lie down, my darling? You know how these conversations upset you.'

'But I don't want to lie down.'

'I will take you upstairs,' Amanda offered. 'Let's leave the men to talk for a bit.'

Juliette looked frightened. 'You will come and see me in a little while, Nigel? You know how I hate to be on my own.'

'Of course, my darling. I think Sidney and I need a word in private. Amanda will be with you.'

The two men watched as the women left the room. Then Nigel Thompson closed the door. 'Can I get you something stronger now we've had the tea?'

'No, thank you. I'm sorry Juliette is so upset.'

'The theft is a disaster. It's clear everyone thinks she stole the ring because she has had her moments in the past.'

'I remember you telling me. It was a sad time.'

'I'm not sure that I confessed in full, Sidney. After we lost our first child I'm afraid there were incidents. Shoplifting. Mainly baby clothes. When she was caught I managed to appeal to the police and they turned a bit of a blind eye, thank God. I can hardly ask them to do the same thing again. I promised I would keep her in check. Now, of course, she's too scared to leave home without me. I knew she was delicate when I married her. Daphne had even warned me. She told me Juliette would need a lot of looking after, but I didn't expect this.'

'Are you sure she can't have taken the ring without knowing what she was doing?'

'We have searched the house. I've questioned Juliette quite carefully and I've never seen her frightened in this way. I wonder if she might even have seen something or if some-one has threatened her because I genuinely don't think she has done it. In the past she was never upset. She could not accept she had done anything wrong. Now she is all too aware of what has happened and she can't think of anything else; and just when her nerves seemed to be getting better. I can't understand it and it makes me furious. All these people are our friends, for goodness sake.'

'And you have no suspicions?'

'Well, I'm afraid I do, but it wouldn't be fair to jeopardise your own line of inquiry.'

'You mean Johnny Johnson?'

'I can hardly suspect anyone else, can I?'

'Even though he's a friend of my sister?'

'He was going on to a jazz bar afterwards. He could have passed off the ring there . . .'

'I won't believe it,' Sidney answered. 'You can't just arrive as a guest at a house for the first time and do something like that. And Jennifer speaks very highly of him.'

Nigel thought for a moment. 'It's difficult though, isn't it? You can hardly suspect Guy of stealing a ring that he has only just given to his future fiancée, or Amanda of taking it. I hope you don't suspect me, and I've already told you about Juliette. Apart from Johnny Johnson and your sister that only leaves the Dowlands, who don't appear to be too concerned about such things.'

'Tell me a little bit more about Daphne Young.'

'She was at school with Juliette. They were the prettiest girls in their year. Her mother died when she was fifteen and then her father went to the bad, I'm afraid. She doesn't like to talk about it but it was gambling. As a result she works in the Health Service. Does very modern work: research papers into the psychological influences that contribute to addiction, although that doesn't stop her enjoying the odd flutter herself. Research, she calls it. As you know, she's one of the most popular girls in London.'

'No money worries?'

'I can't imagine so. I think her suitors pay for whatever she wants. And she takes in paying guests. I think she has some kind of chaplain at the moment. Didn't she mention him to you?'

'She did.'

'Of course she can't have taken the ring. She emptied her handbag in front of us all before she left. And then, after we had searched everywhere and you had left, Guy went mad. He accused Amanda of being too scatty for words, careless, irresponsible, unreliable, clueless, embarrassing and stupid.'

'She is certainly not stupid.'

'The Dowlands made an attempt to stop him but Guy called them meddling know-nothings. That didn't go down too well, either. He said that if they really wanted to involve themselves then they should have done so earlier by spotting the thief. He then poured an enormous glass of port and announced that if the ring wasn't found he would go to the police and blame us all. I tried to calm him down as it's the last thing I want but then Juliette started having hysterics and I had to get her to bed and the Dowlands went home. That meant leaving Guy and Amanda to scream at each other.'

'Did Amanda put up a fight?'

'I'll say. She gave as good as she got. We didn't hear the entire conversation as we were halfway up the stairs to the bedroom but it was one hell of a barney. We did hear Guy shouting out, "three hundred and twenty-five guineas" and Amanda screaming back that she wasn't a horse to be bought at market and that if all he could think about was money then he could forget any engagement and go back to Wiltshire and marry a stable girl.'

'You heard as much as that?'

'It was impossible not to. Juliette asked me to go and make them stop but she was in no state to be left, and then all we heard were slamming doors, Guy storming out with a bottle of my finest port in his hand and Amanda collapsed in a heap. I tell you, Sidney, it's not easy to find yourself in a house with your wife shivering with fear in the bedroom and one of your guests crying on the sofa downstairs. Poor Amanda: what a night it must have been. And Juliette can't sleep at all. She keeps coming down and searching the room, trying to remember where she put the ring.'

The door opened. It was Amanda. Sidney noticed that she had changed her hairstyle, pinning her dark hair back. 'You are not telling him about my row with Guy, I hope? It is confidential.'

'If we are to avoid going to the police then nothing is confidential.'

'I can talk to him about the police. I am sure he will have calmed down, even if I have not.'

Sidney held Amanda's look. 'You will not forgive him?'

'I am not one who subscribes to the theory of *in vino veritas* but I cannot marry someone who insults me in the house of my friends.'

'Has he apologised?'

'He telephoned and tried his best but then kept repeating "three hundred and twenty-five guineas, Amanda", the very phrase that had set me off in the first place. He seems to think that the monetary value of the ring excused his behaviour.'

At this moment the telephone rang. 'I'm sorry,' Nigel apologised. 'I think I had better answer.'

Amanda looked at Sidney. 'Would you like me to stay?' she asked.

'If there is any light that you can shed on last night I would be grateful.'

She sat down next to him and, almost absent-mindedly, looked down at her ringless left hand. He had expected her to choose a seat opposite and at a distance and found her proximity and her intimacy unsettling. She had a brittle, challenging presence, and he could smell her perfume. It was the same fragrance as that worn by a girl he had met in Paris at the end of the war: *Voile d'Arpège*.

She put her hand by her side. 'I'd like to think the ring may just be lost. I try to think the best of people and I don't want to blame anyone, apart from Guy, of course.'

'I don't think he can have done it.'

'When I really hate him I think he might have done it as some kind of insurance swindle but I don't think he's capable of that. He's too stupid.'

'I wouldn't say he was stupid. He chose you.'

'Anyone can do that,' Amanda replied. 'He was probably after my money.'

'Are you very well off?' Sidney asked.

'Very, as a matter of fact; but I try not to let people know too much. It gets in the way and you start suspecting their motives. That is why it is easier to mix with rich people. It's not something that I feel proud about. Although, truth to tell, I could have bought the bloody ring myself . . .'

The grandfather clock in the hall struck the hour. It was four o'clock.

Sidney tried to imagine what it must have been like to have a proposal made and withdrawn in the same evening, with the ring stolen and a public argument following. Many women, given that course of events, would have taken to their beds or fled back to their parents. 'You seem more angry than upset,' he said gently.

'I'm furious with myself for not realising what Guy was like. My head was turned by his good looks and his courtship but the man turns out to be appalling. And to accuse me of deliberately losing the thing! I wish I had now. That would serve him right.'

'So who do you think took it?' Sidney asked.

'Are you going to talk to Johnny Johnson?'

'I am hoping to talk to everyone.'

'The Dowlands have gone down to Cornwall for a few days so you won't have much luck there. I suppose most people think it's Johnny since no one, myself included, can bear to think it's Juliette. And that's where the ring was last seen. But it's horrible to think like this. Loyalty should be at the heart of friendship, don't you think?'

'I don't think it counts for much without it. It's a question of trust.'

Amanda met his eyes and did not look away. 'So, Sidney, what are you going to do now?'

'I think Jennifer is taking me to meet up with Johnny at a jazz club tonight. It's a good excuse to talk to him, as I'm rather fond of jazz and I'd like to hear some music before I go back to Grantchester.'

'When do you return there?

'I have to prepare for Sunday, Amanda.'

'But you've only just had Christmas. Can't you have a holiday? You must be exhausted.'

'I am. I find all this rather depressing, I am afraid.'

Amanda continued to study his face as she spoke. 'Betrayal, anger and mistrust. It's not a good start to the year.'

Nigel returned to the room. 'Daphne has been on the telephone. She was asking if there had been any sign of the ring and if there was anything she could do to help. It might be worth your going to see her, Sidney.'

'I can't imagine I'd be welcome.'

'She tells me that you offered to see her lodger, although I think she refers to him as a "paying guest". Doesn't he want a job as a curate or something?'

'I didn't plan on going so soon.'

'Well, they are both ready for you now. I could give you a lift.'

'No time like the present,' said Amanda.

Nigel was putting on his coat. 'It's a twenty-minute drive across to Hereford Square. I hope you don't mind.'

It was quite extraordinary, Sidney thought, to have the control over his life taken away with such entitled ease.

It was after five o'clock when Sidney rang the doorbell of Daphne Young's flat in South Kensington. As he did so, he continued to wonder when his life was going to return to normal. He should have been in his study preparing for Epiphany, but now the only revelations in his life were all too human. The reason he felt so unsettled, he decided, was because these investigations forced him to think about life in a manner that was contrary both to his character and his faith. As a priest he was expected to be charitable and think the best of people, tolerating their behaviour and forgiving their sins; but as an amateur sleuth he found that the requirements were the exact opposite. Now his task was to be suspicious, to think less of everybody, suspect his or her motives and trust no one. It was not the Christian way.

Daphne Young was wearing a pale pink afternoon dress with bands of bright red dotted Swiss cotton alternating with ivory lace. 'Let me take your cloak,' she began. 'I always think they make priests look like vampires.'

'That is not the intended effect, I can assure you.'

'Mr Graham has left in search of shortbread. You remember that he is a clergyman who is keen to meet you? Would you like some tea?'

'I wouldn't want to detain you.'

'I was hoping to get down to Brighton this evening to see my father. He's on his own. Then I will have Sunday lunch in the country. Do you know the Longstaffs?'

'You asked me that last night.'

'Friends of the Quickmains. Lord Teversham's often there. Lovely people.'

'Your father, you say?'

'A daughter's duty,' Daphne Young replied. 'But I like to be social. It's not often I'm in town at the weekend. Now, of course, the idea of a London dinner party is even less attractive.'

'Last night was very difficult.'

'It was, Canon Chambers. Although why the Thompsons can't go to the police is beyond me. I suppose it's all to do with Nigel worrying about his reputation. He doesn't want to be in *The Times* for the wrong reasons.'

'I think it is a matter of discretion.'

'Even if the crime is obvious?'

'You think Johnny Johnson stole the ring?'

'I can't imagine anyone else doing such a thing.'

'But why would he want to do that? He'd only just met everyone.'

'Why do people steal, Canon Chambers? I suppose that is something for someone of your profession to consider. Is it the need for money or could it not also be the thrill of the crime? Could it even be seen as a kind of revenge, a political act against the wealthy, an attempt to restore some kind of social balance?'

'I see you have thought of this in the past.'

'I am a trained psychologist, Canon Chambers, as I think you know. But this case seems pretty straightforward. Mr Johnson's background certainly provides pause for thought.'

'What do you mean?'

'Don't you know?'

Sidney gave a brief shake of the head.

'His father is Phil "the Cat" Johnson: a well-known jewel thief.'

'How do you know?'

'My father is a retired jeweller, Canon Chambers. Johnson was notorious. Of course if the Thompsons had involved the police then they would have looked through their files, put two and two together, and the whole sordid business would be over and done with.'

'I had no idea,' said Sidney.

'Did Jennifer not tell you?'

'It's possible she did not know. His son is very charming, as you have seen.'

'Like father, like son,' Daphne Young smiled to herself. 'Everyone trusted Johnson. Then he robbed them blind. This is quite a simple matter when you think about it. Go to the police, Canon Chambers. I know it puts your sister in an awkward position but she'll thank you for it in the long run.'

'I think I must do this in my own way.'

'If word gets out we will be social pariahs. Invitations will cease immediately. If I had known that the Thompsons weren't intending to involve the police I would never have got in that taxi. We should have stayed and searched the room and taken all of our clothes off if necessary. Then we would have discovered where Johnny Johnson had put it. A ring can't simply disappear.'

'But it appears to have done exactly that.'

Leonard Graham entered the room and was full of apology. He was a small, well-groomed man with precise and definite manners and he was wearing a clerical cassock. This was unusual for an off-duty priest, almost as unusual as his pencil-thin moustache. A mistake, thought Sidney. A clergyman, as far as he was concerned, should either be fully bearded or clean-shaven; a moustache was neither one thing nor the other.

'I knew that I might miss you,' Leonard began 'but I went in search of shortbread as we didn't want to welcome you with tea alone. Unfortunately, the shops are closed.'

'As you know, Sidney has very kindly agreed to talk to you about your future prospects,' Daphne announced.

'And I am very grateful.'

'Would you like me to leave the room?' she asked.

'That won't be necessary,' Sidney replied. 'I think it might be more convenient altogether if I took Mr Graham to a nearby pub. It is half past five and I believe that one of them, at least, will be open.'

Leonard Graham looked alarmed. 'Isn't it a bit early?' he enquired.

'It may appear so,' Sidney replied. 'But I believe I have earned a pint. You are, of course, welcome to join us, Miss Young.'

'That is polite to the point of being amusing. You ask knowing that I must refuse. I have a train to catch. My father awaits in Brighton.'

'Then I will not keep you.' Sidney stood up.

'That would be kind,' Daphne Young answered. 'Although I hope you will not lead my lodger astray, Canon Chambers.'

'I will keep him on the straight and narrow, Miss Young, don't you worry,' Sidney replied. 'And I will bear your observations in mind.'

'You would do better to act on them, Canon Chambers.'

'I may well do, but, in the meantime, I will keep my own counsel. *Non liquet.* The case is not proven.'

'Then, Canon Chambers, you will need to keep an even mind amidst your difficulties. *Mens aequa rebus in arduis.*'

The Hereford Arms was a delightful pub on the southerly end of Gloucester Road. The two men settled down by the fire and enjoyed the reassuring nature of each other's company. Leonard had only recently completed his theological training. He had been ordained into a parish where he had spent most of his time at a private school for girls, and he now considered himself ready for a proper parochial curacy. What he had not anticipated, however, was the circuitous route that would lead him to Sidney, or the rather loose interpretation of 'pastoral duties' that his new companion seemed to follow.

Leonard had been taught that a clergyman should draw his community to God through leadership, example and self-sacrifice. It was a serious and sacred role that required a full commitment to the church and the community around it. He had never seen a priest extend his sense of social responsibility so far as to play an active role in the investigation of crime in an area that was miles away from his own parish.

Leonard therefore found himself in a curious situation. He had hoped to seize this opportunity of meeting a well-connected country parson to talk both about the latest developments in theology and his own future prospects, while Sidney was keen only to discuss the complexities of his latest case.

After a brief 'Cheers' and a polite 'Happy New Year', and with their pints of beer on the table, the inquiry resumed.

Sidney was on the offensive. 'How long have you been Miss Young's paying guest?' he asked.

'Four or five months.'

'And do you know her well?'

'As well as opportunity allows. She is out every night and every weekend.'

'Does she have any particular friend?'

'She is unattached as far as I can ascertain. There are a few regulars. One of them sends her a sonnet every day.'

'Good heavens.'

'There have been so many that she's stopped reading them. There are at least thirty on the mantelpiece in a pile.'

'Are they any good?'

'No. They are dreadful. Although the name Daphne is difficult to rhyme, I suppose.'

Sidney thought for a moment. 'Didn't Swift write a poem to a Daphne?' he asked. 'I seem to remember he referred to her as "An Agreeable Young Lady, but Extremely Lean".'

Leonard Graham smiled somewhat mischievously and his moustache followed the curvature of his upper lip. He really should shave that off, thought Sidney.

'That would be appropriate,' Leonard answered. 'Daphne Young reminds me of a whippet. She hardly eats a thing.'

Sidney remembered the poem:

> 'What Pride a Female Heart enflames!
> How endless are Ambition's Aims!
> Cease haughty Nymph; the Fates decree
> Death must not be a Spouse for thee . . .'

He drank his beer. 'Someone should write a book about the dedicatees of the great poets.'

Leonard Graham smiled. 'Or their demise.'

Sidney considered the matter. 'Death of the poets. A valediction.'

'I've always found it strange that so many of them meet their Maker in unusual circumstances. Matthew Arnold, for example, died while leaping over a hedge . . .'

'I suppose he did,' Sidney replied. 'And didn't the Chinese poet Li Po drown while trying to kiss the reflection of the moon in water?'

'Pushkin and Lermontov were both killed in duels . . .'

Sidney began to recall his classical education, 'Aeschylus was felled by a falling tortoise.'

'Euripides was mauled by a pack of wild dogs . . .'

'Neither of them strictly poets, of course . . .' Sidney cautioned.

'Although if the criteria was broadened to writers in general then we could have a field day,' Leonard Graham continued. 'Edgar Allan Poe was found in another person's clothes.'

'And Sherwood Anderson swallowed a toothpick. But we are getting distracted, my good friend. Tell me about your landlady's father. I gather she is on her way to see him.'

'He lives in Brighton, as she has informed you. Miss Young is very solicitous in her visits. I think she organises his finances and gives him pocket money; a reversal of roles at the end of a life.'

'It is interesting that he was once a jeweller.'

'You are surely not suspecting my landlady of theft? She is quite a well-known psychologist.'

'I find it uncomfortable when people are keen to pin the blame on others. But I agree that it is unlikely. Furthermore Daphne Young was seated at the wrong end of the dinner table. She has told you what happened last night?'

'Not in detail.'

'Then I will, if I may, go through it all with you.'

'It seems strange for a priest to be so involved.'

'Indeed it is, but I would find it helpful to talk it over with someone who might have an objective view.'

'I am no detective, Canon Chambers.'

'Neither am I, Leonard, but, under the circs, I have to make the best of things. Let me begin . . .'

After he had described the events of the previous evening Sidney returned to the subject of Daphne Young's keenness to implicate Johnny Johnson. 'There was quite a commotion after the champagne bottle had been dropped. I think almost any of the guests could have snaffled the ring at the time as very few people were sober, apart, of course, from Johnny Johnson . . .'

'Why, of course?'

'He does not drink. Which, curiously, puts him at a disadvantage. He was sitting next to Juliette Thompson and she had the ring. Her husband dropped the champagne bottle next to them. It would be quite simple for Johnson to act coldly and clearly amidst the confusion.'

'Unless, of course, the bottle was dropped deliberately?'

'It's a possibility.'

'The wife could have taken the ring?'

'She could indeed . . .'

'Knowing Johnny Johnson would be our chief suspect?'

'That would be too calculated, I feel. I think this was an opportunistic crime.'

'You are convinced it took place amidst the confusion of the champagne bottle?'

Sidney tried to clear his head but ending up thinking aloud. 'Unless of course Nigel Thompson dropped the bottle to warn his wife? It was a distraction to stop her taking the ring; an attempt to wake her up, as it were; and then unbeknownst to them both, Johnny Johnson took advantage of the situation. It's a difficult business. Someone took the ring and hid it. But where? I am at a loss, I must admit.'

'Is there anything I can do, Canon Chambers?'

Sidney finished his pint of beer and an idea came at last. 'There is perhaps, one thing . . .' he began.

South Kensington was abnormally quiet. The gas lamps of London were aflame, the smog had descended, and the last of the dog-walkers were returning home from the parks. Sidney made his way to the Underground and took the Piccadilly Line to Leicester Square. From there he planned to go into Soho and fulfil his assignation with Johnny Johnson. He would then take the late train back to Cambridge.

He looked at his fellow passengers on the Tube. There was an elderly lady in a fur coat with a Pekinese dog on her lap; two young men, despite the vacant seats, standing and smoking roll-up cigarettes; a man in a battered trilby reading a copy of *The Times*: 'Russian Date for Berlin Conference Accepted' was the headline. None of them looked as though they had to worry about theft or betrayal, but doubtless they had their own demons. Sidney looked at the elderly lady's hands. They were covered in rings.

Emerging from the lift at Leicester Square, and crossing Chinatown, Sidney noticed the streets were filling up. This was where everyone had gone: skifflers, jazzers and rock'n' rollers: political dissidents, free spirits, philosophers, ranters and rebels. All was noise, bustle, shout and song: street salesmen, market vendors, milk bars and music booths.

Sidney believed that time flowed more easily in Soho. Life here was no longer broken up into a series of worldly meetings, appointments and assignations that had to take place between certain hours. Instead one event merged into another. People took their own time. It didn't matter if they were early or late. They came and went as if the events they were going to had no beginning and no end. It was, perhaps, a secular incarnation of what the Church Fathers had referred to as a 'glimpse of the infinite'.

He remembered that his brother Matt was performing with his new band 'The Bottlemen' that night. He had half-promised to put in an appearance but Jennifer told him that Johnny would be at The Flamingo if he wanted a chat and Sidney thought it best to get the whole sorry business of the stolen ring out of the way as soon as he could.

He found Johnny at the far end of the bar smoking a cigarette and drinking a Coca-Cola. He was dressed in the black suit with thin lapels that Sidney had appreciated on New Year's Eve, and he wore a narrow tie. 'What are you drinking?' he asked.

'I think I had better have something soft. I have had two pints of beer already this evening,' Sidney apologised. 'A bitter lemon?'

'Have some gin in it.'

'I don't think that would be wise.'

Johnny gestured to the barman for the drinks. 'What are you doing getting involved in all this, Sidney? Couldn't you just leave them be?'

'I think it's to stop the police becoming a part of it.'

'Well, that's one good thing. I assume someone's told you about my Dad?'

'I'm afraid so.'

'No need to apologise. It was bound to come up. This is Dad's place, in fact, but I lead a different life. I work in property. Flats mainly. I buy them up then rent them out. We charge too much but it's more legal than what my father used to do. Although even he's seen the error of his ways these days.'

'You are a realist, I think, Mr Johnson, about business and about crime.'

'No point lying to you, Sidney. If the ring is still missing then I am sure they all think I did it.'

'It would have taken some nerve.'

'Believe me, I'm not so daft as to go out with your sister and steal from her best friend the first time I meet her.'

'I never imagined you did it. Unfortunately, I appear to be the only one who thinks this.'

'As well as Jennifer.'

'Yes, Jenny does too. So the only way in which I can keep the police away and deflect the blame from you is to find out exactly what happened. I am asking what you think as you were almost certainly the most sober person in the room and the theft probably took place under your very eyes.'

'Well, unfortunately I did not see anything. It obviously wasn't planned in any way as no one could have known for sure that the ring was going to be produced in the first place.'

'How do you think it was stolen?'

Johnny smiled enigmatically. 'You'd have to ask my Dad that.'

'You must have ideas of your own?'

Johnny took a sip of his Coca-Cola. 'It would have to be taken quickly. And then hidden – perhaps in a place that could be explained if it was discovered later. A place of safe-keeping.'

'And who are you suggesting?'

'No one, Sidney. I don't make accusations. Let's just say it might be someone who knew the room well.'

'But it would have to have been done by sleight of hand.'

'The port glass and the handkerchief, I suppose. You drop the ring in your glass of port. Drain the glass, dab your lips with a handkerchief, spit the ring into it, and put the two back together in your pocket.'

'And why do you think someone took it?'

'There's the need for money, of course. But if you ask me about last night I'd say it might also be about getting one over on people. Amanda Kendall has everything, doesn't she? Good looks, a career, plenty of boyfriends, I imagine – although the one she is with now is a disgrace – and so I'd say, since you're asking, that the person who stole her ring wanted to take her down a peg or two. It wasn't so much about stealing, it was about the satisfaction of the taking.'

'Intriguing.'

'I might be completely wrong. But I'd also say it was a woman. Guy's the fiancé, the MP's the host, you are a priest, and the publisher was drunk. Would you like another drink?'

'No thank you. I should leave. But go on.'

'Stay if you like. We've got a great quartet later and Johnny Dankworth's looking in. Your sister will be here in a minute.'

'To tell you the truth I'm rather anxious to get back to my job, the one I was called to do.'

'I can tell that they've bullied you into this, Sidney. I suppose it's because they think you can get more out of people. People will sometimes say more to a priest whereas if any of that lot asked me anything I'd keep my mouth shut. I only hope they're not using you.'

'Can I buy you a drink before I go?' Sidney offered.

'You don't need to worry about that.'

Sidney waited and met Johnny's eye. 'I would just like to say that I really don't think you had anything to do with this. I do want you to know that.'

'I appreciate it, Sidney.' Johnny smiled as he stubbed out his cigarette. 'I was just thinking that it would be quite funny if you found out that you were better at being a detective than you were at being a priest.'

'I like to think I have a sense of humour but I can tell you that I wouldn't find that amusing at all.'

'Jen and I might.'

Sidney was swept by a wave of insecurity. 'To tell you the truth, Johnny, at this precise moment, I can honestly say that I don't think I am very good at anything at all.'

'Nonsense. You are very good at being a decent human being.' He held out his hand. 'It's a pleasure to meet you. Any time you want to come to the club, or need a flat, or require a bit of female company, I can arrange it.'

'Thank you, but I rather feel that it's time for me to take charge of my own life. It's been getting out of hand recently. God bless you, Johnny.'

'And God bless *you*, Sidney.'

As he spoke Sidney realised that Johnny was the first person, since his ordination, ever to have given him that reply.

It was after midnight by the time he returned to Grantchester. Although he had sketched out his sermon before he had left for London, Sidney knew that he would have to rise at six in the morning in order to finish it. It was ironic that the need to preach on the subject of Epiphany, the revelation of Christ to the Wise Men, should leave him so short of wisdom on the subject himself.

He knelt down by the side of his bed and said his prayers, ending with a plea that he knew that neither he, nor his Maker, would ever be able to fulfil.

'Grant Lord, that I may not, for one moment, admit willingly into my soul any thought contrary to thy love.'

He was hopelessly restless and, after a night broken by insomnia and uneasy dreams, most of which involved a crime of some kind, Sidney made himself a pot of tea and began to think on what he might say later that morning. He would talk about Christmas presents, he decided, comparing the gifts brought by the Wise Men and the tokens exchanged by friends and family. He would improvise a few thoughts on the spirit of giving, and he would use the carol 'In the Bleak Mid-Winter' with the line: 'What can I give him, poor as I am?' He would speak about the importance of giving with your heart, something he remembered, involuntarily, and with a sinking feeling, that Guy Hopkins had singularly failed to do.

He lost himself for a moment in the memory of New Year's Eve, and then felt annoyed by his inability to concentrate. He wished he could stop mulling over the crime and meditate on the meaning of Christ's incarnation. It was so much more important than the theft of a ring at a dinner party.

It was an appropriately bleak morning and Sidney was further dispirited by the fact that his congregation was half the size that it had been on Christmas Day. This, however, was no excuse for putting in a performance that was below par, particularly as, to Sidney's surprise, Inspector Keating had brought his family.

'We never got to church on Christmas Day because our youngest had chickenpox,' he explained afterwards. 'And we felt like a change. Our own vicar can go on too long and we wanted to see if you lived up to expectations.'

'I was not at my best.'

'You made us think and you made us feel guilty. Isn't that what you are supposed to do?'

'We come to the table in good charity and in penitence . . .'

'You do, however, appear to be tired, Sidney. Is it the exhaustion of Christmas?'

'It is a little more than that, I am afraid.'

'Ominous . . .'

'I fear so. What are you doing this evening? We had to suspend our routine over the festive season and I feel in need of it now . . .'

'It can't wait until Thursday?'

'I fear not.'

'Then what about a quick pint in The Eagle at eight? Would you like to give me something to chew on over lunch?'

'I can see your wife and children are waiting. It involves a group of friends, a stolen engagement ring and my own sister.'

'Not as victim or thief?'

'No, but bad enough. I can't sleep, Geordie.'

'Well, we can't have that. I don't think I've ever seen you so low.'

'I think it is the New Year. I always find it a dark time. Another year gone.'

'A good pint of beer will sort you out.'

That evening, a thick mist descended over Cambridge and the lights of cars and bicycles glowed dimly through the gloom of the wet streets. The rain had passed but the air was damp and it still felt like the end of an old year rather than the beginning of something new. Sidney wondered where he really belonged these days, working as he did, halfway between a parish and a college, making trips to London and involving himself with the police. He was constantly between places and never at rest; but perhaps it was a priest's duty, he thought, to be a pilgrim, out in the world, a man of good courage, travelling wherever the Lord decided to take him.

Despite the consolation of faith, the religious life still contained its doubts and its loneliness; and on this dank winter evening Sidney needed the companionship of a friend.

Inspector Keating had already bought the drinks by the time he arrived and it was clear they were going to need a second round as it took nearly all of the first for Sidney to go through the salient facts of the case. He finished by asking if people sometimes collaborated to point the finger of suspicion at one man.

'That is more in the nature of fiction than reality,' Inspector Keating replied. 'Although it does happen.'

'There seem to be a number of possibilities but, apart from my sister, they all appear to think Johnny Johnson did it.'

'Then either they are correct, or they are all in it together, or they are hiding something.'

'I don't find that very helpful.'

'Then you have to start again, examine all the evidence as if you are doing so for the first time and without prejudice. In other words, you need a detective.'

'They don't want the police involved. The host is an ambitious MP who wants to keep this out of the newspapers.'

'Well, that is evidence in itself, Sidney. If they were all so certain that Johnny Johnson is guilty then they would call us in. The fact that they haven't done so might mean that they know the evidence against him will not stand up; or that they suspect someone else and are not telling you. Can you trust them? They sound a slippery lot.'

'I think I can trust my sister.'

'What does she think?'

'The wife has stolen before.'

'Then that too needs to be taken into account.'

'I don't think she did it, Geordie. We searched the room and then her husband went through all her possessions so that they could specifically eliminate her from their enquiries.'

'But none of you could be objective. Some of you had drunk too much, others were tired and, once the crime had been revealed everyone probably wanted to get out of there as quickly as possible. That's not an ideal scenario for a search.'

'Which means?'

'You need to conduct a further investigation.'

'Surely it's too late for that?'

'The ring might still be there. Even if it isn't, a search will give you ideas. I presume you looked thoroughly under the table and between the floorboards?'

'We didn't take the floor up . . .'

'You need to picture the scene all over again.'

'And then?'

'You need to call everyone back into the very same room. You need to do a re-enactment and watch everyone very closely.'

'I am not sure they will agree to that. And how will I know that some of them will not alter their behaviour?'

'Sidney, you know that this is really a matter for the police?'

'I think they are all expecting my sister to have a word with Johnny Johnson, that he will then return the ring, and the whole thing can be over and done with. The only problem is . . .'

'That he had nothing to do with it.'

'In my opinion. And that of my sister.'

'Well, you need to be careful, Sidney. You know how desperate the rich can be.'

'Do I?'

Inspector Keating finished his pint. 'Well, if you don't know now then you will soon enough.'

On Thursday 7 January, the day after the Feast of the Epiphany, Sidney found himself boarding another train to London, clambering on to yet another bus to Lord's (it was so depressing to stop there in winter, when there was no cricket), and walking up to Cavendish Avenue. He was going to search the Thompsons' dining room. By committing himself ruthlessly and concentrating hard at the scene of the crime he hoped an idea would eventually come to him.

When he arrived in the early afternoon Sidney was not altogether surprised to see that Juliette Thompson was dressed in a white nightgown but he became alarmed when she appeared to have forgotten who he was, an incident so worrying that Sidney wondered what type of medication her doctor was giving her.

Nigel himself was clearly irritated by the visit. Sidney had not been invited to lunch and his host was briskly polite. 'We did search the room quite thoroughly at the time,' he said. 'We looked all over the floor and down the backs of the chairs, as you will recall.'

'Can you extend the table to its full range, and bring in everything that was used on the night in question?'

'I will ask Edna to help you.'

'Do you have a torch and a stepladder?'

'I can't see the stepladder being of any use, Sidney. Nobody could have hidden the ring in the cornice.'

'I think I need to look at the room from every angle, if you don't mind,' Sidney replied. 'Is Juliette all right?'

'I fear we may need professional help. I do not think we can solve this particular problem on our own. It only makes me hate the thief even more, not for the actual incident or for the hurt caused to Amanda – she seems to have recovered forcefully – but for sending Juliette into such a sharp decline. I sometimes think that the person who did it knew that she would react like this.'

'Which would rule out Johnny Johnson. He had never met her before.'

'Indeed. And so it must be one of our greatest friends, but I just can't believe such a thing, Sidney. It would be such a betrayal of our trust. Perhaps it would have been a good idea to involve the police but I just can't risk it. When Churchill retires and Eden takes over, I'll be in line for a junior Cabinet post. I can't allow anything to endanger that, especially something so trivial as another person's engagement ring. The whole affair is taking up far too much time and trouble as it is.'

'I will do all that I can to help you.'

'I know that, Sidney, and I appreciate it, but do you really think this search of yours is going to do any good? The ring will be long gone by now.'

'That is probably so. But I want to spend enough time in this room to think through all the permutations. One has to have a bit of faith.'

Sidney imagined the room to be a series of cubes on a three-dimensional grid. He would move from north-west to south-east, working in a series of horizontal lines from left to right and then right to left, using both a torch and a magnifying glass. He would look at the wood, the table, the walls and the floorboard. He would open the sideboard and empty the canteen of cutlery, and he would sit for a few moments, every ten or fifteen minutes, with the seating plan and the notebook, thinking and praying and waiting for inspiration to come from his observations.

Three hours later he had his own, minor, epiphany.

It was not a popular decision to re-create the final moments of the dinner party and it took place at the inexact time of five in the afternoon as the guests, or suspects, had only agreed to come on the condition that it did not scupper their plans for the evening. Daphne was being taken to *Madam Butterfly* at Covent Garden, Jennifer and Amanda were due to see Richard Attenborough in *The Mousetrap*, and although the Dowlands had no plans for the evening they were required to cut short their annual expedition to the National Exhibition of Cage Birds at Olympia. Consequently, there was considerable tension in the atmosphere as they sat down in their allotted places and waited for Sidney to conduct them through the events of the previous week.

Nigel was further disconcerted by the idea that he was expected to waste yet another bottle of champagne by deliberately dropping it where he had done so before. Sidney reassured him that he could mime these actions as long as everyone repeated their movements on the night.

'Next thing I know,' Nigel complained, 'you will suggest that I dropped the damn thing deliberately in order to cause a distraction.'

'I have already discounted that,' Sidney replied, rather too punctiliously.

'Are we expected to keep to the conversation as well?' Guy asked.

'You can paraphrase,' said Sidney. 'I would just like to recreate our movements round the table from the giving of the ring.'

'When do we stop?'

'At the moment you were left alone with Miss Kendall and your hosts, Mr Hopkins. The subsequent conversation has no relevance to the disappearance of the ring even though it was certainly of importance to those involved.'

'I'll say,' said Amanda.

'There's no need to bring that up,' Guy snapped.

'I would remind you,' Amanda bristled, 'that we are on "no speaks".'

'Then why are you "speaking" to me now?'

'I am not talking to you. I am "speaking" to Canon Chambers.'

Sidney tried to calm the proceedings. 'Let us begin. We need, of course, a ring. I have brought one in this box from Woolworths. I hope it will suffice. Mr Hopkins, if you would be so good as to give it to Miss Kendall?'

'Very well.'

Guy stood up and walked round. He placed the box in front of her and she opened it. 'I see. Rather better than the one you gave me last week.'

'Oh, for God's sake.'

'Mr Hopkins,' Sidney continued, 'if you would be so good as to return to your seat.'

Amanda handed the ring across the table to Daphne Young. She passed it across to Mary Dowland, who gave it to Sidney. He then placed the ring in front of Juliette.

'I feel quite sick,' she said.

'Now,' said Sidney, 'Mr Thompson, can you please drop the bottle of champagne?'

'I found some rather uninspiring sparkling wine,' said Nigel. 'I am sorry about the waste but I think I might as well repeat the whole blasted thing.'

As he did so his wife gave a shriek and dropped the ring, Johnny Johnson pushed his chair back and brushed the sparkling wine off his trousers with a cry of 'twice in one week'.

'Continue,' Sidney ordered.

Amanda removed Juliette from the room while Daphne fetched a dishcloth and Mary Dowland a dustpan and brush.

After the mess had been cleared up for a second time, the ring from Woolworths remained by Juliette Thompson's place.

'You can hardly expect someone to steal it this time,' said Mark Dowland.

'Please go on,' Sidney insisted. 'Let us repeat our search.'

The guests walked round the room, looking across and under the table.

The maid rang the doorbell. Sidney explained. 'Miss Young, I think you said your goodbye at this point.'

'I certainly did.' Daphne Young opened her bag and emptied its contents on to the dining-room table once more: the same compact, perfume, handkerchief, set of keys, diary, address book and small purse fell out. She scattered her change across the table. 'Here we go round the mulberry bush,' she said.

'Amazing,' said Johnny Johnson. 'That's exactly as you did it before.'

Mary Dowland appeared beside him. 'Then I came up beside you, I think.'

'And Mr Hopkins went through the bag,' Sidney explained. 'Will you do so once more?'

'It's a bit pointless, isn't it?'

'On the contrary,' Sidney said quietly. 'Miss Young, I think you returned to your place and picked up your stole?'

'I did.'

'And then you said your farewells.'

'That is correct. May I go now?'

'Not quite,' Sidney explained. 'We need to continue, if you would not mind waiting. Mr Hopkins must give you your handbag . . .'

'Thank you.'

'And then the Dowlands leave quite shortly. As, of course, do I. So we will just re-enact these movements and then, instead of leaving, we will return to our places.'

'I can't see how that has done any good at all,' said Mark Dowland when the domestic ballet had been completed.

'On the contrary,' said Sidney, 'you have shown me a great deal. And now, I have something unexpected.'

'I don't like surprises,' said Juliette Thompson, returning to her seat. 'They make me afraid.'

'But this is, I think, a pleasant one,' said Sidney. 'You will see that the ring from Woolworths has disappeared.'

'Where is it?' Guy Hopkins exclaimed.

Sidney reached under the table in front of him. 'Instead, I have something else. *Quae amissa salva.* What was lost is safe.' He placed Amanda Kendall's original engagement ring in front of him.

'Where did you get that?' asked Daphne Young.

'Your lodger very kindly retrieved it from The Lanes in Brighton.'

'He is not a "lodger". He is a "paying guest".'

Sidney ignored the distinction. 'In Brighton, there is a second-hand jewellery store, next to some shared accommodation for distressed gentlefolk. Living there is a rather confused gentleman called Hector Young, formerly of the jewellers Braithwaite and Young.'

'You cad.'

Sidney began. 'The ring was reclaimed from your father, Miss Young. How it came into his possession is a matter for conjecture, but my colleague received a rather full explanation.'

'You sent a priest under false pretences knowing that my father was confused?'

'On the contrary, his mission was perfectly straightforward. I sent him under clear instructions to talk to your father and recoup the ring. You often take jewellery down to Brighton, I believe . . .'

'There is nothing wrong with that.'

'Most has been secured on approval so that it can be returned. Some former colleagues also help . . .'

Daphne Young looked down into her lap. 'It is the only thing that keeps him in his right mind. He remembers the treasures he has lost. Sometimes he believes he still has his shop.'

'I am sure he does, Miss Young.'

'He lost everything.'

'How?' Juliette asked.

'He used to rent out things on deposit so that women could make a bit of a splash of an evening and then return the jewellery the next morning. Unfortunately, he . . . he . . .'

Sidney quietly finished her sentence. 'Gambled.'

Daphne was pulling at the handkerchief in her hands. 'He thought he could escape his debts and give his clients a little bit of the proceeds. He went to Epsom and Goodwood and put the biggest bets on the handicaps. He liked to think he could always spot an underrated horse but he was wrong. He didn't mean to lose so he borrowed in order to pay his customers back. He thought it would all come right in the end. Then he started going to the pawnbrokers with some of the stock and without telling his business partner. Now half his mind has gone . . .'

'You were being a dutiful daughter,' said Sidney.

'The jewellery I show him takes him back to the early thirties when I was a little girl and my mother was alive. The shop was a success then. So I've been trying to keep him living there, in the memory of that time, so that he can die with more contentment than he would if he was aware of the world today.'

Mary was unsympathetic. 'So are you trying to tell us that you stole the ring for charitable purposes?'

'I took it without thinking. It was right in front of me.' Daphne looked at Juliette. 'It was there. I couldn't help it.'

'My God,' Nigel exclaimed. 'You stole the ring in the house of one of your best friends. Are you aware of the effect this has had on Juliette?'

'It was her or my father. I made a choice.'

Johnny interrupted. 'How did you do it, Daphne?'

'I am sure Canon Chambers can explain.'

Sidney began. 'It did look as if you were the criminal, Mr Johnson. Miss Young was aware of your father's history and could feel quite confident that you would be blamed; she even tried to do this herself. Then, if that didn't work, there was always Mrs Thompson.'

'But she has never stolen anything,' Mary Dowland cut in.

'No,' Sidney lied. This was not the time for further revelation. 'But she was upset and distracted and it would be a simple matter to make her think she had taken the ring even when she had not.'

Juliette Thompson looked at Sidney. 'So I was right? I never had the ring?'

'It was taken from your place. For the criminal to act in such a way when there were two ready suspects was tempting . . .'

Daphne cut in. 'I am not a criminal. I didn't think of it like that.'

'It must have been when Nigel dropped the champagne,' said Johnny. 'Daphne was picking up bits of broken glass . . .'

'Miss Young, to you.'

'But I would have seen her,' said Mary Dowland. 'I had the dustpan and brush.'

'But,' Sidney explained, 'Miss Young had the dishcloth. It was a simple matter to wipe away the ring at the same time as she mopped the table. If anyone noticed she could easily explain her behaviour as absent-mindedness and put it back. But if no one spotted her . . .'

'But how could she hide the thing?' Johnny Johnson asked. 'She emptied her bag on to the table and opened her purse. There was nothing in it.'

'That was something of a masterstroke. To conceal the ring in an item that had already been searched and then to walk calmly away . . .'

'But how?' Amanda asked.

Sidney began to walk round the table. 'The idea came to me when I was searching the room myself. It was the first time that I have been permitted to be on my own in this house and I was able to think the matter over without distraction. Then I remembered one of my friend Inspector Keating's first questions. "Did you look under the table?" '

'Of course we did,' answered Nigel.

'I don't think you understand. When I say "under the table" I mean something slightly different. Miss Kendall, and Mr Johnson, I would like you to think about your positions at dinner.'

'I was sitting next to the host and Johnny was next to the hostess,' Amanda answered.

'My God,' said Johnny Johnson, 'I think you have got it.'

'You are also sitting, as is Miss Young, at the ridge of the table, where it extends. Of course, this is not noticeable with a tablecloth, but it is common enough. At Miss Young's place there is a slight scratch mark in the ridge where she hid the ring.'

'You mean it was wedged in the ridge underneath the table?' asked Nigel

'Exactly so. And then removed when Miss Young went to fetch her stole. We, of course, were all distracted by the contents of her handbag. The action would have required only the simplest sleight of hand.'

Daphne Young rose from her seat. 'Very good, Canon Chambers. We can all applaud your persistence. If only you had demonstrated the same level of dedication to the priesthood. I presume you have summoned the police.'

'As a matter of fact, I have not. I think it is for Miss Kendall to decide. It is her ring.'

Guy Hopkins cut in. 'I rather think it is mine.'

'You gave it to me,' Amanda Kendall replied.

'But you have turned me down. I think a return is customary.'

One thing Sidney had not expected was the aftermath of his revelation. Daphne Young took advantage of the hiatus and walked to the door. 'I shall leave you all to it. I am expected at the opera. You have my address.'

'Daphne,' Nigel Thompson announced before she left. 'You will never be welcome in this house again.'

His former guest replied without emotion, 'I have no excuse.'

The assembled company listened to her footsteps recede in the hall and the front door open and close. They even heard her sharp whistle for a taxi. 'What an extraordinary woman,' said Mary Dowland. 'She never even apologised.'

'I can't stop thinking about her father,' said Johnny. 'I can't imagine that was the first time. She must have stolen before.'

'I'm not so sure,' said Sidney.

Mark Dowland offered another explanation. 'Perhaps she thought she deserved it more than Amanda. A better cause . . .'

'I've always thought she was a bitch,' said Guy.

'Your thoughts on women are a disgrace,' Amanda replied. It was the first time she had looked at him properly all evening. The ring was still in front of her. She looked at Sidney. 'What shall I do with it now?' she asked.

In 1954, Valentine's Day, which was also Sidney's birthday, fell on a Sunday. He was thirty-three years old. Because he was unable to leave his pastoral duties, his sister Jennifer brought Amanda up to Grantchester to mark the occasion. They came with cards from the rest of the family and a chocolate cake that they had made themselves. The celebration was to consist of a trip along the River Cam and a winter picnic.

It was a crisp but bright winter day and Jennifer and Amanda were sitting in the front of the punt with rugs over their knees and a hamper in front of them. It contained two flasks of milky tea laced with a little brandy; ham and mustard sandwiches; a selection of dainties from Fitzbillies; and the chocolate birthday cake with a candle which they would light at dusk.

Sidney was punting in his clerical cloak and he wore a wide-brimmed hat that made him look like a nineteenth-century eccentric. This was paradise, he thought: to be free of the cares of the world with his adorable sister and her beautiful best friend on his birthday. They would spend an hour or two chatting away and then the girls would return to London and Sidney would take Evensong and allow himself time to contemplate his blessings.

'I have never known anything so unusual as a winter picnic on the river,' said Amanda, 'and I am enjoying it immensely. Where shall we moor?'

'Just a little upstream,' said Sidney. 'Past Byron's Pool. I know a spot.'

He dropped the pole into the water, pushed down, and then as he let the punt move away he began to recite: 'Let us have wine and women, mirth and laughter, Sermons and soda-water the day after.'

'Oh Byron,' said Amanda. 'My favourite poet. "Here's a sigh to those who love me, And a smile to those who hate; And whatever sky's above me, Here's a heart for every fate." '

Sidney smiled. 'I'm so glad that you seem to have recovered from all that sorry business on New Year's Eve.'

'Such a pity we couldn't pin the whole business of the ring on Guy,' Amanda replied. 'I'd enjoy his fury at going to prison.'

'That's not very charitable.'

'We've been generous enough with everyone else.'

'You decided to let Daphne off?' Sidney asked.

'It would have finished her . . .' Jennifer answered. 'And Nigel was keen to avoid a scene.'

'And so a crime has been ignored? That was very forgiving of you.'

'We just have to trust she won't ever do it again.'

Amanda was dubious. 'I don't see how we'll ever know. I don't think any of us will be inviting her again. But I suppose she did me a favour. Not that I'd tell *her* that.'

Sidney manoeuvred the punt round a corner, letting it glide past the frosted willows. 'And you let Guy keep the ring?'

'Oh yes,' she replied. 'He can give it to some other fool deluded by his so-called good looks. I don't want it. It would just be a reminder of the whole ghastly evening. It was very good of your clerical friend to go all the way to Brighton and get it back. Are you taking him on?'

'He should be joining me after Easter.'

'Johnny thinks he might be a pansy,' said Jennifer. 'Do you?'

'I wouldn't dream of enquiring,' Sidney replied as he ducked under a low branch of wych elm.

'Isn't that rather unlike you?' Amanda inquired. 'You have such an inquisitive mind.'

Sidney let the punt glide to the side of the river and moored in readiness for the picnic. 'It is my belief that a private life should remain private. If Leonard Graham has something to tell me I am sure he will do so. I have asked him, in a rather informal way, to shave off his moustache. It makes him look a bit of a spiv and I don't think it suits him. Other than that, I do not intend to pry.'

'Even if your curiosity is piqued?' his sister asked as she unwrapped the picnic.

'I think I pique my curiosity whenever it can be of benefit to others,' Sidney replied. 'Otherwise, I try not to spend too much time on tittle-tattle, however pleasurable it may seem at the time. It never does anyone any good and it makes you feel cheap afterwards.'

'I'm sorry I raised the question,' said Jennifer.

'I don't mind you asking any question you like, my dear sister, just so long as you don't mind my not answering it.'

'But surely *you must wonder*?'

'I try not to think about that kind of thing. It serves no purpose. Discretion is a very underrated virtue, don't you think, Amanda?'

'I suppose it must be. But one can't be serious all the time. Gossip can be quite fun.'

'I am sure it can be, and I can see the temptation; but it's too dangerous for a priest.'

Amanda gave Sidney what he now recognised as one of her quizzical looks. 'I don't think I've ever met someone with such moral certainty,' she replied. 'You make me feel quite the flibbertigibbet.'

'There's nothing wrong with being a flibbertigibbet,' said Sidney. 'In fact, I think the world needs all the flibbertigibbets it can get.'

'Then I am glad to be of assistance,' said Amanda. 'I wonder what the derivation of the word is? "Gibbet" is not very encouraging, is it?'

'I think,' said Sidney, ' "flibber" suggests "flighty"; it's onomatopoeic.'

'And where would you like to fly to?' Amanda asked.

'The moon and back, Miss Kendall, the moon and back.'

Jennifer handed out mugs of tea. 'Are you two flirting?' she asked.

'I think that should remain private,' Amanda giggled. 'I have heard that discretion is a very underrated virtue.'

'I was only asking,' said Jennifer, beginning to find herself quite the gooseberry. 'My brother is something of a dark horse in that department.'

Amanda let her gloved hand skim the surface of the water. 'Well, I always enjoy a day at the races; not that it did Daphne's father any good.'

'I felt rather sorry for her in the end,' said Sidney.

'I love the way you think the best of people. She was quite short with you, wasn't she? When she said,' and here Amanda began to imitate the deep voice of her former friend, ' "if only you had demonstrated the same level of dedication to the priesthood," I thought it was unnecessarily barbed.'

'I don't mind barbs.'

'Really, Sidney. You are almost unnatural. I'm not sure I believe you.'

'He likes to retain an air of mystery about him,' Jennifer explained. 'Although he is yet to realise how effective a ploy that is.'

Amanda remembered what she had been meaning to say. 'Perhaps, one day, you could take me to Newmarket, Sidney. We could have a bit of a flutter.'

Her companion smiled. 'That would be fun. Or, perhaps, we could go to a jazz concert. There's a very good singer coming over from America later in the year, Gloria Dee . . .'

'Oh I don't think so,' said Amanda quickly. 'I draw the line at jazz.'

'Dearie me,' said Jennifer. 'It was all going so well.'

The three friends laughed and Sidney could not remember a time when he had been happier. They lit the candle on his cake, and the two girls sang 'Happy Birthday' in harmony. Then he blew out the candle and wished that he could have more of these moments away from the cares of the world. They remained sitting in the punt, singing and teasing each other for a good half-hour before they found that it was too cold to continue and decided it was time to go home.

There would be a freeze that night and both women were anxious to return to London after Evensong in order to avoid any delay on the railway. Jennifer was starting a new secretarial job in the morning, while Amanda was preparing for the display of a newly cleaned Van Dyck double portrait at the National Gallery. It was, Sidney felt, a familiar Sunday evening experience for those involved in regular employment. The anxiety of Monday morning always seemed to cast a retrospective shadow.

At Cambridge station, Amanda left in search of a cigarette while Jennifer took advantage of a moment alone with her brother.

'I'm glad you two are getting on so well,' she said.

'Oh yes,' Sidney said, almost involuntarily. 'We're thick as thieves these days.'

Jennifer gave her brother a little punch on the shoulder. 'Be careful.'

'I think she's out of my league.'

'Perhaps, my dear Sidney, that is because you are in a league of your own. Happy birthday.'

She let her brother kiss her lightly and then looked out for her friend. The train doors were slamming. The train guard looked at his watch and put his whistle between his lips. Amanda returned. 'We must hurry,' she said, without appearing to do so. 'Although I've told the guard to wait.'

She took Sidney's hand in hers. 'Happy birthday, Sidney. I do hope I can come again. Knowing you is such an adventure.'

'You will always be welcome,' Sidney smiled.

Amanda leant forward to kiss him. As she did so she accidentally brushed her lips against his. 'I think you're wonderful,' she said, looking into his eyes.

'Come *on*,' Jennifer called.

Sidney watched the two women board the London train and waved them goodbye. Then he bicycled back through the dark and icy roads to Grantchester. There were only a few, minor mishaps as he made his dreamy return; a front-wheel skid, a near miss with a cat and a wobble as he waved to a colleague from his college: the usual, unpredictable, moments that made it a relief to arrive home safely.

The next morning Sidney stooped down to pick up a letter that had arrived in the second post. It looked like a birthday card and it had been sent from Germany. The writing was Hildegard's.

Sidney's pleasure at receiving the letter was mixed with guilt about his friendship with Amanda. He passed it from one hand to the other, uncertain whether to open it or not. 'I might just save this for later,' he said to himself. 'I think I've had enough excitement in my life for the time being.'

First, Do No Harm

O NE OF THE clerical undertakings that Sidney least enjoyed was the abstinence of Lent. The rejection of alcohol between Ash Wednesday and Easter Sunday had always been a tradition amongst the clergy of Cambridge but Sidney noticed that it neither improved their spirituality nor their patience. In fact, it made some of them positively murderous.

It had been a Siberian winter. The roads were blocked with drifted snow, rooks fell silent in the deep woods and arctic geese passed over fields where lambs had frozen to the ground. It was a bad time to be old, and Sidney had already spent too much time at the bedsides of elderly men and women who had fallen victim to influenza, hypothermia, pleurisy and pneumonia, a disease that seldom warranted its nickname as the old man's friend. Instead, there was anxiety both in the village and in the town, a sense of unease and even unhappiness in the darkness. It was a world where people seldom looked up, but checked their footing on the road ahead, wary of falling, trusting neither weather nor fate.

What Sidney needed, he thought, was either a single malt or a pint of warm ale – perhaps even both – but he knew that he had to resist.

The strictures of this self-imposed restraint amused Inspector George Keating, who stuck to his regulation two pints of bitter on the regular backgammon night he shared with Sidney, each Thursday, in the RAF bar of The Eagle.

'Still on the tonic water, Sidney? You don't want me to liven it up with some gin? It's cold out.'

'I'm afraid not.'

'Such a shame. Still, if you catch your death I can always slip you a brandy.'

'That won't be necessary. We are encouraged,' Sidney continued dejectedly, as if he had learned the words by heart and no longer believed in them, 'to reject such temptations and observe a time of fasting, prayer and silence.'

Inspector Keating tried to cheer things up. 'You could have just the one. No one would notice. It is only us.'

'But I would know. It would be on my conscience.'

'I wish some of the members of the public had your self-awareness. This town would be a lot quieter if they did.'

'The Anglican Church is supposed to be the conscience of the nation,' Sidney mused. 'We encourage people to believe that a moral life is, in fact, a happier life.'

'People should be good for selfish reasons?'

'Indeed. Shall we begin?'

Sidney laid out the backgammon on the old oak table in the lounge and the two men began to play their favourite game, gambling moderately for a penny a piece. Sidney found this to be one of the consoling moments of his week, a refuge from the cares of the world and the tribulations of office. He took a sip of his tonic water and tried to concentrate on the game. He threw a five and a four and began to move the checkers away from his home board.

Inspector Keating threw in response and was delighted to open with a double six. 'I think it's going to be my night . . .'

Sidney smiled. 'I like it when you have a strong start. It lulls you into a false sense of security.'

'I don't think you need to worry about that. I'm on the top of my game . . .'

Sidney threw a three and a two and tried to think tactically. He moved his pieces and said, quietly, but with a hint of friendly menace, 'Of course I do feel guilty when I keep winning so often . . .'

The inspector did not rise immediately. He threw a four and a one but noticed that he still had the advantage from his early sixes. 'Double?'

'Are you sure?' Sidney asked. 'I wouldn't want another victory on my conscience.'

The inspector smiled. 'I wouldn't worry about that.'

Sidney threw a two and a one and began to realise that he might lose.

'Talking of conscience,' Inspector Keating continued, in a tone of voice that Sidney both recognised and dreaded, 'I think I may be facing what you call "a moral dilemma".' He threw a three and a six, moved one of his checkers nine points.

'Oh really?' Sidney threw once more; a four and a three. 'I have warned you to be careful about such things.'

'The coroner came to see me. Re-double?'

'Of course. I am not afraid. What has happened?'

'It seems a certain lady has asked for her mother to be cremated rather too quickly.'

'A certain lady?'

'It is meant to be confidential.'

'You have my confidence.'

'Isabel Livingstone.'

'I know her, Geordie.'

'I am aware that you do.' The inspector placed the dice back in the cup and threw again: five and a six. He smiled at the resumption of his fortune.

'I saw her only the other week,' Sidney remembered. 'She was with my doctor, Michael Robinson. They are planning to marry. Nice couple, and well suited, I would have thought.' He took a sip of his disappointing tonic water and tried to remember the conversation. 'They told me that they had decided to wait for the ceremony until after her mother had died.'

'Don't you think that is unusual? Most daughters would want their mother at the wedding.'

'They were planning on Easter . . .'

The inspector rattled his dice. 'Well, they can have it now if they like . . .'

'We don't normally conduct marriages in Lent. But I seem to remember that Mrs Livingstone was opposed to the whole idea of matrimony. Her husband had left when Isabel was an infant. After that she had taken a violent dislike of all men.'

'He must have been quite a man to have wrought such havoc.'

'Such a pity, to let resentment fester.'

'Well, it won't be festering any more.'

'And so she has died? I am surprised I have not been informed.'

Inspector Keating was matter-of-fact. 'And so am I. But there may be a reason for that . . .'

Sidney could see that too many of his opponent's pieces were in advantageous positions. He was already anticipating a gammon. 'You hesitate, Inspector . . .'

'I'm sorry . . .'

'You hesitate in a manner that alarms me.'

George Keating threw his dice and began bearing off but his heart was no longer in the game. He spoke without looking at his friend. 'The problem is . . . Sidney . . . that I am not sure that Mrs Livingstone's death was entirely natural . . .'

'I was afraid you were going to say that. You mean?'

'That the lovers might have helped things along? I am afraid I do . . .'

'But it is the winter, and Mrs Livingstone had been in very poor health for a long time,' Sidney observed. 'I would have thought she had a pretty pressing appointment with her Maker.'

'Well, I'm afraid that's not what the coroner seems to think. A friend of Mrs Livingstone came to see him. He asked us to take a look and it's now become a little more complicated.' The inspector threw a one and a six and began to bear off his checkers. 'You remember the Dorothea Waddingham case?'

'The nursing home murderer? You're not suggesting?'

'In the Waddingham case they found three grains of morphine in the first body they examined and then a fatal dose in the second. Sometimes, doctors and nurses get carried away and death comes on a bit too easily.'

Sidney threw again even though he knew it was futile. 'Was Mrs Livingstone wealthy?'

'Moderately . . . but I would have thought the doctor had a good enough income. It can't have been for the money.'

'And why are you telling me this?' Sidney asked.

The inspector leaned back and put an arm over the back of the chair next to him. 'When people come to you to be married, you tend to put the couple through their paces beforehand, don't you?'

'I give them pastoral advice.'

'You tell them what marriage is all about; warn them that it's not all lovey-dovey and that as soon as you have children it's a different kettle of fish altogether . . . .'

Knowing that Inspector Keating had three children under the age of seven, Sidney recognised that he had to be careful of his reply: 'Well, I . . .'

'There's the money worries, and the job worries and you start to grow old. Then you realise that you've married someone with whom you have nothing in common. You have nothing left to say to each other. That's the kind of thing you tell them, isn't it?'

'I wouldn't put it exactly like that . . .'

'But that's the gist?'

'I do like to make it a bit more optimistic, Geordie. How friendship sometimes matters more than passion. The importance of kindness . . .'

'Yes, yes, but you know what I'm getting at.'

Sidney could tell that the inspector was impatient for another drink. 'I think I can guess what you want me to do.'

Keating stood up. 'I'll pay even though it's your round . . .'

'There's no need for that . . .'

'You're not drinking anyway. All I am asking is that you do a bit of digging. Give them a few tough questions when they come and see you. Ask the girl about her mother. Watch the doctor's face. I wouldn't want you marrying a couple of murderers . . .'

'I don't think that's likely . . . they're a very friendly couple . . .'

Inspector Keating ordered his third pint of the evening. 'Well, if they're as nice as you say then we won't have anything to worry about, will we? Another game?'

The winter of 1954 was relentless. Sidney awoke to fierce frosts on his window sills, the days never lightened and rime hung on the trees all day. When Sidney rose the next morning he felt that he had forgotten something. Then the dread returned. 'Ah yes,' he thought, 'Keating. Another distraction. Another death.'

He put on his dressing gown and looked out of the window. In another life, he thought, he might have been a naturalist. He had been reading how it had always been something of a tradition in the church. Gilbert White, the vicar of Selborne, for example, had noticed how, in winter, the rooks in the lane fell from the trees with their wings frozen together. He examined the different techniques with which the squirrel, the field mouse and the nuthatch ate the hazel nuts he had laid out for them, and discovered that the owls in his neighbourhood hooted in the key of B flat. Perhaps, this winter, Sidney thought, he could even emulate Reverend White. So much of life was about noticing things, he thought. It was about *observation*. He would try to be a man upon whom nothing was lost.

It was too dangerous to bicycle to the Livingstone home, he decided. Even walking required caution. He put on his Wellington boots, draped his clerical cloak across his shoulders, and set off through the snow. Hector Kirby, the butcher and churchwarden, with a ready catchphrase and a depressed wife, was clearing a path to his shop; Veronica Hodge, an elderly spiritualist who had once told Sidney that she had been 'mercifully spared the attentions of men', was making her tentative way to the shops, and Gary Bell, the village mechanic, who had somehow managed to avoid National Service, was jump-starting a tractor.

Sidney passed the frozen meadow, where his parents had met before the war, skating at sixpence an evening, and stopped to watch a group of boys in a snowball fight.

As he walked into town he realised that he had never known Cambridge so still. The buildings looked like illustrations to a nineteenth-century fairy tale. The snow had muffled the once audible cries of the world. It was like grace, he decided, or the love of God, coming down silently and unexpectedly in the night.

A slip and a very near fall awoke him from his musing. Perhaps he should daydream less, Sidney thought, as he walked towards a small terraced house in Chedworth Street. Not everything in life could be considered material for a sermon, he told himself, and snow might cover sin just as it could conceal suffering.

He rang the doorbell. As he waited, he remembered Isabel Livingstone as a small, shapely woman with eager brown eyes. Her short hair had begun to grey, perhaps under the pressure of caring for her mother for so long, and she dressed in practical clothes: a white blouse, a green cardigan, a tartan skirt. It was a uniform that never appeared to change and it was hard to tell what age she might be: forty perhaps? Her late-flowering love gave Sidney a quiet hope of his own. After all, if Isabel Livingstone at forty could entrance a doctor might not he have a similar opportunity one day? He remembered the unexpected thrill he had felt when Amanda Kendall had kissed him goodbye at the station and the calm he had felt when he had sat with Hildegard Staunton. How comfortable their silences had been. He really should write to her again, he thought.

Dr Robinson opened the door. He expressed surprise at Sidney's visit. 'I thought we were due to see you at the end of the week?'

'I was passing and thought that I would call in,' Sidney replied, 'since it seems that we now have more than a wedding to discuss.'

'Indeed. Isabel is in the kitchen. I was just leaving . . .'

'I came to offer my condolences; and also to say that the church is, of course, at your disposal should you wish to hold the funeral there.'

'Isabel's mother was not what you might call a churchgoer, Canon Chambers. I am afraid she put herself down for a cremation with the Co-op.'

Isabel Livingstone emerged from the kitchen. She appeared flustered. Sidney apologised for his intrusion.

'I'm so sorry we hadn't got round to telling you, Canon Chambers,' Isabel apologised. 'But there has been such a lot to do. I thought that some day we would be planning a wedding but I suppose I always knew that we would have a funeral service to sort out first.'

'I am doubly sorry,' said Sidney, 'both for your loss and for the unfortunate proximity of events.'

'We did expect it though, didn't we, darling?' The doctor put his arm around Isabel's shoulder and she smiled up at him.

Sidney thought that they looked good together. 'I know you move between birth and sickness as much as I do, Dr Robinson . . .'

Isabel broke free. 'I'll put the kettle on.'

'It makes you appreciate the unexpected pleasures of daily life,' the doctor continued. 'Every time I wake up I try to be thankful that I have spent the night safely, and I try to look at everything as if I am seeing it for the first time; not that I want to philosophise. Come in, sit down . . .'

'I'm sure you've calls to make. Don't let me keep you . . .'

'They can wait. Isabel needs me, I find. And, of course, I need Isabel.'

Sidney tried to make conversation as they moved through to a small sitting room with a two-bar fire. 'It is surprising how often happiness and sadness bump up against each other. It is why I am so opposed to confetti.'

'Confetti?'

'It's upsetting for those who have to attend a funeral when a wedding has taken place earlier in the day. It reminds the principal mourners of what they have lost.'

'I don't think my mother would have minded about that,' Isabel Livingstone interrupted, coming in with the tea tray. 'She was violently opposed to marriage, as you know. Whenever she heard church bells she covered her ears. Weddings just set her off, didn't they, Michael?'

'It's why we didn't discuss our plans with her, Canon Chambers.'

'Sometimes I think Mother kept on living just to spite us,' his fiancée continued. Sidney noticed that she was wearing an emerald ring. 'I had stupidly promised her that I would not marry if she was still alive and so I think she decided to try and outlive me. "Even if I do die first," she said to me, "I'll still be watching." '

'Perhaps you did not need to keep your promise?' Sidney replied.

'Are you, a clergyman, suggesting that I should have broken it?' Isabel asked as she poured from a pot of tea. 'Sugar?'

'No thank you. If it was forced from you, or if it was a bad promise, why, yes of course.'

'Well, in the end, it was not such a long time to wait. We've only known each other properly for seven months,' the doctor continued. 'But you know all this, Canon Chambers. Obviously we are not going to make any public announcement of our engagement until after the cremation.'

'Even though Miss Livingstone is wearing a ring . . .'

'Only in the house. I take it off when I go outdoors. It seems silly because everyone must have guessed by now but when you are supposed to be in mourning it doesn't look right.'

'Supposed?'

'I'm sorry, Canon Chambers; my mother was not a kind woman, either at the end of her days, or even before. I can be grateful for the fact that she gave me life and that she looked after me, but recently, apart from Michael, my life has been misery. It's hard to nurse someone who is so resentful that you are young and she is old.'

Sidney decided to take a risk. 'I know that sometimes, when those close to you die, it can almost be a relief.'

'It was. But you are not allowed to say this.'

'You can say anything to a priest.'

'Or a doctor . . .' Michael observed.

'Not quite anything,' Isabel Livingstone replied.

There was silence.

'Talking of the cremation,' Dr Robinson resumed, 'we were planning to have it next week but now there seems to be some kind of delay. I don't suppose you know anything about that?'

'I did hear,' Sidney replied. 'I think it is a delicate matter.'

'I don't see what is so delicate about it. What have you heard?'

'Oh Michael . . .' Isabel began, but her fiancé cut her off.

'Mrs Livingstone died a perfectly natural death. It was heart failure. I completed the death certificate myself.'

Sidney thought that Dr Robinson was rather too keen to justify himself. 'And you, Miss Livingstone, were you present at the time of death?'

'Of course. I nursed my mother to the end. I gave her sips of water. I mopped her brow. I made sure that she did not become dehydrated as Michael had told me. I did everything my fiancé said.'

'You applied for a cremation immediately?' Sidney asked.

'We were being efficient,' the doctor continued. 'I don't think there is anything unusual in that. It is what Isabel's mother asked for.'

'She had a fear of being buried alive,' Isabel explained. 'She hated worms. She used to say, "Don't let the worms have me." She could be very morbid.'

Dr Robinson was becoming suspicious. 'Why are you asking us this?'

'It seems the coroner is not quite ready to release your mother's body, Miss Livingstone. He may ask for a post-mortem.'

'And why on earth would he do that, Canon Chambers?' Isabel asked in a tone that sounded altogether too innocent.

'I think your fiancé can explain the medical reasons for that request,' Sidney replied.

Dr Michael Robinson rose from his chair and looked out of the window. 'That meddling bastard,' he muttered.

The next day Leonard Graham arrived from London to begin his duties as Sidney's curate. He was looking forward to working both in a parish and in a university town that would allow him to continue his studies into the work of the great Russian writers, most notably Dostoevsky.

Unfortunately, Inspector Keating had sent Sidney off to see the coroner and Leonard's first Grantchester encounter was therefore with the housekeeper. A small, fiercely opinionated woman, five foot three and thirteen stone, Sylvia Maguire told Leonard Graham that he had no need to worry as Canon Chambers was not a practical man and it would be clearer if she explained the way in which the parish, and most notably the vicarage, was run, herself.

She showed Leonard to his room and offered to make him a cup of tea while he began to unpack his suitcase and his boxes of books. After six or seven minutes she called up and told him that everything was ready. Leonard came downstairs, looked at his tea and sponge cake, and prepared for his induction. He already sensed that, rather than talking about the ecclesiastical status of the priesthood or the nature of the holy fool in Russian fiction with Canon Sidney Chambers, he would, instead, be treated to Mrs Maguire's life story. This assumption proved correct.

Mrs Maguire set off on her account of how she was born on 21 January 1901, the day that Queen Victoria had died, and yet, despite this historic date, Sidney never remembered her birthday because he was too busy thinking about criminals. She told him how she had lost three of her brothers in the First World War and how her husband Ronnie had disappeared 'for no good reason' in the second. She explained at length that her sister Gladys, a spiritualist, had been unable to contact Ronnie so he couldn't be dead and she was still waiting for his return; and she reassured Leonard Graham that her husband's departure meant that she was able to 'do' for other people but, even so, and saying that, she regarded both indoor toilets and the bathroom off the ground-floor kitchen of the vicarage as 'unhygienic'. She would be able to offer catering for both the clerics but it would not include too much fish as she was worried about the bones and had never quite recovered from the embarrassment of a choking incident suffered on her honeymoon at Skegness.

Simple meals would be provided, she stated – shepherd's pie, welsh rarebit, toad in the hole, bubble and squeak, steak and kidney pudding – and it was a lot easier now she was coming to the end of her ration book. But washing and ironing would be extra, especially if Leonard wanted his dog collars starched, and she would also be very grateful if he tidied up before she hoovered and emptied his own ashtrays.

Leonard Graham tried to reassure Mrs Maguire when he thought she had finished, 'I am sure that everything will work out beautifully, Mrs Maguire.'

He was then alarmed by her retort. 'Are you indeed? Have you been a curate before?'

'I have not.'

'Then everything will be a surprise to you.'

Leonard was desperate for Sidney's return. 'I am sure I will be able to manage,' he answered. 'My role here will be more spiritual than material.'

'Everyone has to eat, Mr Graham.'

'Indeed they do. I think the playwright Bertolt Brecht even suggested that food must come before morals . . .'

Mrs Maguire did not appear to be listening. 'I don't under-stand why Canon Chambers cannot write his sermons, take his services and visit the sick like any other clergyman,' she complained. 'He has to go poking his nose into other people's business and it's just going to lead to trouble. Before Christmas we had one hell of a time, I don't mind telling you.'

Leonard Graham defended his colleague. 'I don't think he goes out of his way to involve himself in the affairs of other people, Mrs Maguire. They come to him. He is merely responding to their needs.'

'Well, he's too soft and he needs to be careful, you mark my words. Crime always attracts more crime, that's what my Ronnie used to say.'

'I will remind Canon Chambers of his primary duties,' Leonard Graham replied.

'And don't go getting involved yourself,' Mrs Maguire counselled. 'It's bad enough one clergyman trying to be Sherlock Holmes. We don't need the two of you doing it.'

'I will help Canon Chambers whenever I can, Mrs Maguire, but I will not let him distract me,' Leonard Graham answered. 'The church and the parish will be my only concern.'

'Unfortunately,' Mrs Maguire replied, 'that may cause you trouble enough. Grantchester may look like a typical English village, Mr Graham, but I am telling you now that, in reality, it is *a nest of perfidious vipers*.'

'I will do my best to be careful, Mrs Maguire.'

'You will need to do more than that, Mr Graham. Let vigilance be your watchword, that's all I'm saying. I don't waste my words.'

'I can already tell that you don't,' Leonard Graham replied.

The Cambridge coroner had a reputation for efficiency. Never one to linger over idle pleasure, Derek Jarvis was the kind of man who saw every encounter, no matter how pleasurable, as an appointment that had to conform to its allotted time. Tall, slender, and dressed in a single-breasted suit and an old Harrovian tie, he possessed the easy confidence that came with a privileged upbringing. What he lacked in obvious charm he disguised with efficiency.

Sidney had met him once before, after an amateur cricket match in which the coroner had scored a sprightly forty-three runs in a surprise victory against Royston.

'I don't want to appear impolite, Canon Chambers, but I am not sure why this matter involves you at all. It is really between myself and the police.'

Sidney could tell that Derek Jarvis saw his presence as a matter that would take up more time than was necessary. Consequently he needed to be both charming and exact. 'Inspector Keating suggested that I come because Isabel Livingstone and Michael Robinson are my parishioners. They are in mourning and yet, at the same time, they are also about to be married in my church. I am here in confidence, to see how precarious their position might be, and if their wedding might need to be postponed. I am sorry for the trouble my visit may cause . . .'

'It's no trouble, of course. In fact, it's a pleasure to see you, Canon Chambers,' the coroner replied. 'Only it's far more agreeable to meet you on a cricket field than in these less congenial surroundings.'

'Alas, we are still to see the spring,' Sidney replied. 'I look forward to long summer days and lengthening evening shadows; but until then we must set about our daily tasks. I imagine that there must be guidelines in these matters.'

'There certainly are. Mrs Livingstone appears to have died several months sooner than might have been expected. If her death has been hastened, and in suspicious circumstances, then we have to investigate . . .'

'It is the middle of winter, and Mrs Livingstone was a very elderly lady . . .'

'Indeed, Canon Chambers, but, as you will no doubt know, perhaps even better than I do, that we are all God's creatures, young and old alike . . .'

'I am not saying . . .'

'I know you are not. "To every time there is a season." But where a man might propose, it is God who must dispose.'

'I understand.'

'It is a question of *intent*,' Derek Jarvis continued. 'Did the doctor withhold or withdraw treatment? Did he allow Mrs Livingstone to die and, if he did so, was this in the patient's best interests and in accord with her wishes?'

'Mrs Livingstone was very weak. I am sure her daughter would have spoken on her behalf . . .'

'I am afraid that is not the same thing; not the same thing at all . . .'

'Yes, I can see,' Sidney replied hesitantly. 'But if Mrs Livingstone was in great pain . . .'

'Then, of course, morphine may be administered. The exact quantity, however, must be examined.'

'I am sure Dr Robinson knew what he was doing,' Sidney replied.

'I do not doubt. But what was he doing, and what did he *intend to do*? His intentions in this matter are crucial. In addition to preventing pain, as I think you may know, morphine also reduces the depth and frequency of breathing and can therefore shorten a patient's life.'

'A side effect of the reduction of pain . . .'

'Indeed, Canon Chambers. Forgive me if I am stating the obvious, but it is important that the moral principles are clear. I am sure you would agree.'

Sidney admired the coroner's methodical reasoning but worried that he might lack compassion.

Derek Jarvis continued. 'A death that occurs after the administration of morphine is a foreseeable effect, and in these cases, a doctor who gives morphine to a terminally ill patient in order to reduce suffering and foreseeing, though not intending, the earlier death of the patient, has not broken the law.'

'That is good,' Sidney replied quickly, relieved that there might be grounds for hope.

'The quantity of morphine, as I say, has to be assessed and, of course we need to be sure that it was simply morphine that was administered rather than something more serious . . .'

'Such as?'

'Potassium chloride, for example. That is a very different substance altogether. Then it is no longer a matter of foreseeing the death but intending it. Again the matter of *intent* is crucial. It is a form of intervention where death, rather than the relief of pain, is intended . . .'

Sidney tried to keep up. 'It seems, however, that you can only gauge the level of intention by asking the doctor himself.'

'That may be the case but as soon as potassium chloride has been administered, I am afraid that there is only so much a doctor can do to persuade us of his innocence.'

'He may still be acting out of pity for his patient.'

'It would be termed a mercy killing – which, of course, is technically murder,' the coroner replied, as if Sidney had not thought of this. 'And if there is any suspicion that this is indeed the case then a post-mortem will be required.'

'Is that really necessary?'

'I am afraid it is; so much so that I have already ordered one. The results will be due on Wednesday. Consequently I wouldn't do too much about the wedding before then.'

Sidney was disturbed by the coroner's quiet impartiality. At the same time, he could see that anything more he might say could, potentially, jeopardise the future happiness of the couple who planned to marry in his church. 'And after the post-mortem?' he asked.

'I think I have already outlined the possibilities, Canon Chambers. If morphine is found then we may be able to over-look Mrs Livingstone's earlier than expected demise. But in the case of potassium chloride . . .'

'The doctor would then have to stand some kind of trial . . .'

The coroner hesitated. 'And not just the doctor, of course . . .'

'What do you mean?'

'Isabel Livingstone had a duty of care. She was in her mother's house and could have intervened to prevent such actions, if untoward actions there were. She is, potentially, an accessory to the crime and, in consequence, could face the same sentence.'

Derek Jarvis was speaking as if he was already in the witness box. 'The same?'

'In certain circumstances she might get away with manslaughter but in this case, I am afraid they would both, most likely, be charged with murder. And therefore they could both hang.'

'Good heavens,' said Sidney. 'That's terrible. I am sure that what they were doing was in Mrs Livingstone's best interests . . .'

'That may be, Canon Chambers, but it is not the law of the land.'

'Then the law should be changed . . .'

'I will not argue about the ethics but, until such a time as the law is actually changed, if there is any suspicion of foul play, then it is my duty to raise matters with the police.'

'There is nothing to be done?'

'Are you suggesting that I pervert the course of justice?' the coroner asked.

'No, of course not,' Sidney replied.

'I am sorry to have to make myself so clear. The course of any investigation must be allowed to proceed unimpeded. Your best course of action, Canon Chambers,' the coroner suggested, 'is to pray.'

The only event to lighten Sidney's mood, amidst the death and darkness of Lent, was the arrival of his friend Amanda Kendall. At least she would cheer him up, he thought, as he bicycled carefully through the snow and waited for her at the railway station.

It had taken him a good half-hour to get there and the journey had allowed him plenty of time for contemplation. It was so long since he had been anywhere other than Cambridge or London, he thought. He really should broaden his horizons. He remembered Robert Louis Stevenson: 'The great affair is to move.' Yet, since the war, he had hardly travelled at all. Perhaps he could take a holiday in France, he wondered? Or Germany, of course . . .

Hildegard had invited him to stay and he imagined that it would be a considerable comfort to see her again; but Sidney also worried that he had begun to exaggerate the consolation of her company and that absence had, perhaps, made his heart grow too fond.

At least with Amanda he knew where he stood; for despite their affection for each other there was no ambiguity or worry about romantic love or passion. This was a hearty friendship, he told himself, a treat in his life and the dose of liveliness he needed. He only hoped that he could live up to her expectations and that he did not bore her.

'As elegant as expected,' Sidney said, as Amanda stepped off the train. She was wearing a tailored camel coat and carried a chestnut-coloured Gladstone bag.

'I've decided to simplify my wardrobe: lilac in town and brown in the country. It makes life so much easier,' she said.

'This is hardly the country . . .'

'Oh Sidney, Cambridge is not London. You may kiss me.' She stretched out her cheek. 'Where are we lunching?' she asked

'We are going to the Garden House Hotel,' he announced. 'I hope it will do.'

'Then lead on.'

Sidney kept to the outside of the pavement and pushed his bicycle as they walked to the restaurant. As he did so, Amanda told him how extraordinary it was that she had got through the snow at all. She had got talking to a farmer called Harding Redmond who had been complaining on the way up how the turnips in the fields on his farm had rotted, how the ewes had so little milk and the lambs were dying. It was so distressing, she said. His wife bred Labradors and was so worried about a recent litter that she had refused to leave home until she knew that they were safe from the cold.

Sidney asked about the National Gallery and Amanda told him that she was beginning to do the research for a monograph on the paintings of Hans Holbein the Younger. There was, she said, so much more to discover about the cultural life of the court of Henry VIII: the drama, the art and the music, that she felt a whole world was opening up before her. Perhaps they could go to Hampton Court in the summer together?

Sidney told her that would be delightful and replied with parish news, the gossip at Corpus and the arrival of Leonard Graham.

'Has he shaved off his moustache?' Amanda asked.

'Indeed he has. And he is all the better for it.'

'Such a business at the Thompsons,' Amanda continued. 'Poor old Daphne . . .'

'And poor old you.'

'I can never forgive myself for that awful mess with Guy Hopkins.'

'He was a very attractive man.'

'And an absolute brute.'

They arrived at the hotel, handed in their hats and coats and were shown straight to their table.

'To think that it took me so long to notice that Guy was appalling,' Amanda continued. 'I've quite lost my sense of judgement. I was so distracted by a handsome man with prospects that I forgot to think what it might be like to be married to him. Could you tell as soon as you met him?'

'I wouldn't like to say.'

'That means you could . . .'

'Not necessarily, Amanda. I never spoke to him privately or with the two of you alone.'

'But that is what you do before a marriage, isn't it? And that's partly why I've come. I wanted to ask that if it ever happens again, and I do become engaged, that I can come and see you and talk about it?'

'Of course. Do you have someone in mind?'

'Not yet. But there are possibilities.'

'And will I be the first to know?'

'After Jennifer, of course. I can hardly keep things secret from my flatmate.'

'How is she?'

'You mean you want to know about Johnny Johnson? They are just friends, you know.'

'I rather admire Johnny Johnson.'

'And so do I, Sidney. Surely in this day and age we can have friendships with the opposite sex without worrying about what it all means. I am sure you have plenty of female friends . . .'

'Not like you, Amanda.'

'I should hope not. I wouldn't want to be a duplicate.'

'There is no one in the world like you, Amanda, I can promise you that.'

'Oh, I am sure that in the Russian Revolution, or in the French for that matter, I would have been shot with all the other posh girls. But I have to be careful now. I'm worried that when men make an approach they may have ulterior motives.'

'Well, you're quite a catch.'

'Oh, Sidney, you say the sweetest things. But there are times when I just can't be sure of the motives of the men I like.'

'An occupational hazard, I would have thought.'

The waitress arrived with herrings fried in oatmeal but Amanda was in full flow. 'Don't priests undertake to counsel people when they are thinking of getting married? What kind of things do you say to them? And can you sometimes tell that the whole thing is going to be a disaster from the start? I bet you can.'

'That's quite a lot of questions, Amanda.'

'I have more. I want to know everything. How in love do you have to be, for example? Can you tell if it is enough and can you marry if you still have doubts? Does it matter if your parents approve or not? Is it important that your husband has money? Do you have to be of the same social standing? What do you do if there is one aspect of your future husband's personality that you can't stand? Can people change once they are married? All those kinds of things.'

'I don't know,' said Sidney as he started on his herring. 'You cannot anticipate everything. But, at the time, I think you have to be unable to imagine the alternative. I think you have to think that it is impossible to live without someone.'

'But you live without someone.'

'It is different in my case. I live with my faith. What I mean is that it has to be impossible to imagine living without the person you love.'

'But what if you can't find that person? So many people I know seem to settle for second best.'

'Do you know that, Amanda? They may only seem second best to you. And love can be about more than attraction. I sometimes think it is more a question of sanctuary, a case of unassailable friendship.'

'Have you known that?'

'Not quite,' Sidney replied. 'Not yet . . .'

The waitress removed their plates from the table and returned with pork chops and apple sauce. Sidney had not anticipated such close questioning and found Amanda's tone almost confrontational. It was hard to give thoughtful answers to her volley of direct questions.

'Is it lonely being a priest?' Amanda continued.

'Sometimes . . .'

'When is it at its worst?'

'Now, I suppose.'

'You mean at this table?'

'No, of course not, I don't mean that at all,' Sidney blushed, although he did feel out of his depth. 'I think it is when there is a small congregation on a cold February day in the middle of Lent, for example. I feel these waves of depression coming over me. The numbers of the faithful are dwindling, Amanda, and sometimes there is nothing I can do to encourage them. It's like Matthew Arnold's great poem "Dover Beach". I feel the melancholy roar of the withdrawing tide. . . .'

'Then I only hope you have not been diving into any more murky waters,' Amanda replied.

'Sometimes the murky waters come to me. . . .'

Amanda put down her knife and fork. 'I'm so sorry. I have been talking about myself so much that it has taken me a little time to realise. Forgive me. It is clear that something is troubling you.'

Sidney sighed. He wondered whether he should speak openly but he was too preoccupied not to do so. 'I am afraid that it is.'

'Tell me . . .'

'This may not be the place to discuss it.'

'No one is listening.'

'An elderly lady has died.'

'Nothing unusual in that, I would have thought.'

'Indeed not.'

'Then what are you worried about?'

'It is extremely confidential, Amanda. I should not be telling you anything at all.'

'But you are anxious?'

'I am. My doctor has come under suspicion.'

'Whatever for?'

'This is a very delicate matter.'

'I don't know him, do I?'

'No, Amanda, you do not.'

'Then do not tell me his name. Has he been negligent?'

Sidney stopped. He knew that he should not be confiding in Amanda but he could not help himself. 'It's thought that he may have hastened her death.'

'And why would he do that?'

'So that he could marry the daughter without her mother's blessing.'

'Couldn't they just wait?'

'Apparently not. She was a tough old bird.'

Amanda returned to her meal. 'Almost as tough as these pork chops, I imagine. Has your inspector friend got on to the case?'

'He has. We both feel rather uncomfortable.'

'So it is either a medical act of mercy or something altogether more sinister?'

Sidney began to wish he had not raised this subject but it was too late. 'I am not sure the daughter was involved.'

'Well, there is one reason that the mother could have disapproved,' Amanda continued. 'Although I can't see why it makes much difference in this day and age . . .'

'And that is?'

'Oh Sidney, how could you be so dim? She's obviously with child.'

'*Of course*,' Sidney thought to himself. How could he have been so slow?

'If her mother dies before the pregnancy is obvious then they are in the clear; not that they needed to worry that much in the first place. There was nothing else stopping them marrying, I imagine . . .'

'I think Isabel wanted to do the right thing by her mother . . .'

'Isabel? You are on first-name terms with a potential murderer?'

'She is not a murderer, Amanda. She is a woman who has been bullied all her life who has now found late-flowering love.'

'And so her wishes have come true.'

'Love is something to celebrate, Amanda.'

'You never thought of marrying her yourself?'

'Now you are teasing me . . .'

'Is she attractive?'

'She is. But she is not, of course, as attractive as you.'

'Oh Sidney,' Amanda leaned forward and placed her hand on his. 'I can rely on you to say the right thing. You have such perfect manners too. I wish my London admirers would follow suit.'

The waitress returned with a jam roly-poly and Amanda withdrew her hand.

'I think we should be careful what we wish for,' Sidney replied as calmly as he could. 'Sometimes, even when our prayers are answered, there is an ironic twist that we could never have anticipated.'

'Well, let me pay for lunch, Sidney, there's a twist to begin with.'

'I don't think I can let you do that, Amanda.'

'What rot. I think I shall always pay. It will make everything easier . . .'

'Amanda . . .'

'Don't be silly, Sidney. Think of it as a down payment against future marriage guidance. There will probably be rather a lot of it.'

At the beginning of March the snows began to melt and slide off the roofs, taking both shoppers and cyclists by surprise. Hawks hovered over the Meadows, and further out of town, in the fields around Grantchester, the farmers were able to plough and sow at last.

This was the hope of spring. Students unbuttoned their duffel coats and loosened their college scarves, children played football by the river and the first winter hyacinths began to appear in front windows.

Leonard Graham had settled in to one of the upper rooms of the vicarage. Sidney was happy to delegate duties, instruct him in the responsibilities of the ministry and let him preach sermons on the tensions between Kantian and Utilitarian ethics as often as he liked, providing he was kind to Mrs Maguire and was not impatient with those parishioners who had been spared a university education.

'Natural wisdom,' he told Leonard, 'cannot always be found in books.'

'I agree,' his curate replied, 'but to be naturally wise and then to read books gives you even more of an advantage.'

'Over what?' Sidney asked.

'You think I am going to say "other people", don't you, Sidney, but that's not what I mean at all. Reading gives you an advantage over life and time.'

'I am aware of that,' Sidney replied tersely.

'You can travel through history, converse with the dead and live multiple lives . . .'

Sidney thought it sounded exhausting but his curate was unstoppable.

'That is how I spend my free time,' he continued. 'I look to those who have lived before me in order to learn more about how to live now.'

'I wish I had the opportunity to do that,' Sidney replied. 'But, alas, I do not.'

He knew that he was sounding pompous but he was distracted. He was waiting for the results of the coroner's inquest. He still had not quite managed to pin down why Derek Jarvis unsettled him so much. He had thought that it was the black and white nature of his morality and the brisk efficiency with which he operated. But it might also be the fact that he was jealous. Sidney allowed his parishioners so much more time and so much more of a say when they were discussing their problems and their fears than the coroner ever did with his corpses. It was not that he resented this time, but sometimes he wished he could cut his meetings shorter and resolve the issues with which people came with more clarity. Perhaps, Sidney considered, he could even learn something from the coroner's manner?

But no. Like a doctor, a priest had to allow events to run their course.

Sidney hesitated. Was this what Dr Michael Robinson had done? Had he allowed Dorothy Livingstone's life to 'run its course' or had he hastened it towards its end? And if he had done so, were his intentions truly and only honourable and merciful? In short, were his actions those of a Christian?

As both a priest and an Englishman, Sidney liked to give people the benefit of the doubt, but he knew that he would have to find an excuse to see his doctor on his own and ask him a few direct questions.

He decided to make an appointment as a patient even though there was nothing specifically wrong with him. In fact, and in many ways, Sidney had never felt better in his life. He could perhaps go to the doctor's surgery in Trumpington Road with talk of headaches, migraines even, but he did not want to suggest anything that might lead to an investigation or a hospital visit for tests.

'Gout?' he wondered idly. It had done for Milton, Cromwell and Henry VIII but did he really want to be associated with 'the rheumatism of the rich'? Besides, his current abstinence would surely rule that out.

By the time Dr Robinson had asked, 'What can I do for you?' Sidney had still not thought of a convincing complaint.

'I'd like you to take my blood pressure.'

'Any reason?'

'My heart seems to beat at different rates at different times of the day. I am more aware of it than I normally am.'

'Roll up your sleeve. Any pain?'

'No, I don't think so. But sometimes I feel a bit fragile . . .'

'That's normal.' Dr Robinson wrapped a cuff around Sidney's upper left arm.

'Is it?'

'We can all feel a little delicate during difficult times, Canon Chambers.'

'Yes, I suppose it must be very trying for you at the moment.'

Michael Robinson began to inflate the cuff until Sidney's artery was occluded. He then listened with a stethoscope to the brachial artery before slowly releasing the pressure on the cuff.

Sidney did not like to speak during the process but wondered whether people's blood pressure actually rose in a doctor's surgery; if the very act of being there made them tense and their hearts race.

'The coroner hardly helps matters . . .'

'I can imagine . . .'

'Sometimes these things are best left.'

'I suppose he is only doing his job.'

The doctor looked at his watch and then at the dial. 'Well, he won't find anything. I have done nothing wrong.'

'Then you have nothing to fear.'

The doctor unwrapped Sidney's arm. 'Your blood pressure is completely normal, Canon Chambers. Is there anything else?'

'Not really. I do have trouble sleeping sometimes . . .'

'Do you keep regular hours?'

'It's not so much the falling asleep as the waking up in the middle of the night . . .' Sidney replied, thinking how soon he could move the conversation on to sleeping pills, sedatives and painkillers.

'Do you try milky drinks?'

'I do . . .'

'And how long has this been going on?'

'For the past few months.'

'I find exercise also helps. And not eating too late. . . .'

'You don't prescribe sleeping pills?'

'Not if I can help it.'

'You don't approve?'

'Canon Chambers, forgive me for being rude but is there anything that is really the matter?'

'No, I suppose not.'

'I am not sure you came here because you were ill.'

'I did want a quiet word.'

'Anything in particular?'

'It is a delicate matter.'

'I am a doctor, Canon Chambers. There is no such thing as a delicate matter as far as I am concerned. You can raise any subject you like.'

'Miss Livingstone . . .'

'What about her?'

'Is she well?' Sidney realised he had lost his nerve. What on earth was he doing going along with all of this?

'Well, she is sad, and a little nervous, but there is nothing you can't ask her yourself . . .'

Sidney felt rather ashamed.

'You don't suspect her of anything, do you?'

'No, of course not . . .'

The doctor looked out of the window and his confidence seemed to fall away. He looked exhausted. Perhaps he was tired of keeping up his professional demeanour.

'I am sure that you have sat with the dying many times, Canon Chambers. You think that one would get used to it but it is different every time. Sometimes people are ready, and sometimes people hold on, refusing to leave, even though their time has come. They are stubborn and it is uncomfortable but they are indomitable. Isabel's mother was not like that. She wanted to go but death was not ready for her.'

'You know she wanted to go?'

'She told me that she had had enough, that she was looking forward to what she called "the long sleep".'

'And so . . .'

'I relieved the pain.'

'And she was at peace?'

'There's an extraordinary thing I have noticed, Canon Chambers. I hope you won't mind me saying this but in those final moments I don't think faith makes much difference. People are either scared of death or they are not. People divide quite clearly. Even the faithful can be frightened.'

'I know. It is a mystery. But perhaps they are not so much frightened of death as of dying.'

'Yes, they are distinct. Do you ever turn a blind eye, Canon Chambers?'

'When no harm is done.'

'Well, that, of course, is my Hippocratic oath. "First, do no harm." It could work just as well for priests, I suppose.'

'It's a good motto,' said Sidney. 'We have very clear instructions in the Church of England, guidelines as to how life must be lived. But people can't always see what they are, of course. They move in all sorts of directions, like moral dodgems, and the lines are never straight at all.'

'I agree. People don't live neat lives.'

There was a pause before Sidney returned to his questioning. 'But you are convinced that you were acting in Mrs Livingstone's best interests? That you did no harm?'

'I was, even though to tell you so is none of your business.'

'Sometimes I am not sure what my business is, Dr Robinson,' Sidney replied. 'It is everything and nothing, the whole of life, and yet my involvement is not so much on the pages of people's lives but in the margins.'

'You are too modest . . .'

'No, it is true. But this is, of course, the way of Our Lord. Are you a believer?'

'You have asked me that before.'

'That was when you came to see me about your marriage.'

'You will still marry us? Despite what I say?'

'The marriage service asks if there are any *impediments*. It does not require a degree in theology.'

'I was brought up with an intense faith. I know the liturgy. I admire the language and the music. I still hope for revelation. But I am afraid I have seen too much suffering to believe in divine benevolence. The war, you know. I presume you were a pacifist?'

'I am afraid you presume wrongly,' Sidney cut in, a little too aggressively, he thought. 'I fought for what I believed in.'

'Even if it meant killing people?'

'A lesser evil.'

'Ah yes,' the doctor replied, his vulnerability signalled by a furrowed brow that hovered over eyebrows that were darker than his hair. 'A lesser evil. I think we both know about that . . .'

When Sidney returned home he found that Leonard Graham had already left to visit the sick on his Communion round and that, in his absence, Mrs Maguire had decided to pick all his books off the floor of his study yet again, stacking them all over his desk, in order to vacuum the whole house. He had repeatedly asked her not to do this but any request he had made in the past had fallen on deaf ears. He had never seen such a small woman act with such gusto. There was an aggression to her hoovering, a violence that was clearly some kind of displacement activity. He had only seen it once before, after she had been given an unconfirmed report that her husband, who had disappeared in 1944 amidst conflicting rumours of pacifism and bigamy, might actually be living in West London. He guessed that this was not the best time to engage her in any kind of conversation but he was mistaken. Mrs Maguire was all too eager to converse.

She turned off the vacuum cleaner and removed her apron. She had clearly been waiting for this moment and Sidney feared the worst. There were rumours in the village, she told him, and they were bad.

'What do you mean, Mrs Maguire?'

'I will spare you the conversations regarding yourself . . .' she began, as if such a silence was of the utmost difficulty.

Sidney was alarmed. He liked people to think well of him. 'What can you mean?'

'My sister is refusing to see the doctor,' Mrs Maguire announced.

'And why is that?'

Mrs Maguire folded her arms in what Sidney took to be a gesture of defiance. 'She is frightened he's going to kill her.'

Sidney could not believe it. Somebody had been talking out of turn. His own conscience was clear, and he assumed that he could trust Inspector Keating. Could it be the coroner, or perhaps a spurned admirer of Dr Robinson? He would have to visit Derek Jarvis once more.

'That is nonsense.'

'All tittle-tattle, I imagine,' Mrs Maguire continued. 'But you know what they say? There's no smoke without fire . . .' She looked at Sidney as if she had used a phrase he had never heard before.

'I have always found that to be a most unhelpful aphorism,' Sidney answered.

Mrs Maguire took a step forward. 'I don't suppose you know anything about it?'

'I do not,' Sidney replied, unconvincingly. It really was extraordinary the number of lies he had to tell since becoming embroiled in criminal investigation.

'But I think you'll still want to know what they've been saying about *you*?'

'Not particularly, Mrs Maguire.' Sidney tried to sound nonchalant. 'I would rather people told me what they thought directly.'

'Very well. Then I will tell you. They think you're going to marry Miss Kendall.'

'That is most unlikely.'

'That's what I said to Mr Graham.'

'You have discussed the matter with him? What did he reply?'

'That it wasn't for him to comment.'

'Quite right too.'

'But everyone is talking about it,' Mrs Maguire continued. 'You were seen in a restaurant holding hands . . .'

'Only for a brief moment . . .'

'Long enough for the waitress to tell the chef, who told his sister, who is a barmaid at The Green Man. The news will be all round Grantchester by now and tomorrow it will be at every high table.'

'I hardly think that the dining tables of Cambridge colleges are interested in my marital prospects, Mrs Maguire . . .'

'Clever folk love an opportunity to make fun of their rivals, I've noticed.'

'I don't have rivals, Mrs Maguire. I have friends.'

'Call them what you like; but if you hold hands in public there'll be no stopping the gossip.'

Sidney was annoyed. What business was it of anyone else? His relationship with Amanda was private. He hated the idea of anyone talking about them. Now he would have to explain something that he didn't *want* to explain because he liked it all being vague and inexplicable. 'I marry other people to each other. I have no plans to marry myself. Miss Kendall is a *friend*.'

'That's what I said to them,' Mrs Maguire continued before stopping to check. 'So I am right, then?'

Sidney sighed. The quicker this conversation was brought to a conclusion the better. 'Of course you are, Mrs Maguire,' he replied. 'You always are.'

That should do it, he thought.

Unfortunately he was wrong. Encouraged by his response Mrs Maguire put her apron back on and continued, breezily. 'I know you won't mind but I've been telling everyone. She's a fashionable woman from London with expensive tastes. You wouldn't catch the likes of her marrying a clergyman, would you now?'

She turned the hoover back on and resumed her work. After a few vigorous movements back and forth she looked up to see that Sidney had not moved.

'Did I say the wrong thing?' she shouted over the noise of her work.

Sidney said nothing but picked up a stack of books and took them through to the kitchen. On the top of his pile lay *The Confessions of St Augustine*. It was not going to help.

The next morning Grantchester was visited by yet another dose of persistent sleet, warning that winter was still not at an end. 'Where are the songs of spring?' Sidney wondered, forlornly, 'Ay, where are they?' There weren't even any daffodils in bloom. This was a day, Sidney thought, to hunker down; a day for tea and toast and warm fires, for pastime with good company followed by a hearty stew and a good red wine.

Alas, such pleasures were denied to him. It was the thirty-fourth day of Lent. Would it never end?

It would not.

Inspector Keating telephoned. 'You had better come to the station, Sidney.'

'Whatever for? Aren't we seeing each other tonight?'

'This can't wait. Another old person has died . . .'

'Well, it is the time of year. Pneumonia, I suppose.'

Inspector Keating had no time for such musings. 'Yes, I am perfectly aware that it is winter and that these things are likely but it's the same bloody doctor and the second ruddy case. We have to sort this out.'

'It may be a coincidence.'

'Yes, of course, it *may* be a coincidence but if it isn't we can't have an epidemic of old codgers being helped out of this world. That's your job . . .'

'What is the name of the deceased?'

'Anthony Bryant. He was seventy-one. A good age, but people are living longer these days. Modern medicine, apparently . . .'

'Give me half an hour, Inspector. The roads are treacherous for my bicycle.'

'Don't worry about the roads, Sidney, I've sent a car. It will be with you in the next five minutes.'

185

'Your business is as urgent as that?'

'I will brief you at the station. Then the car will take you where you need to go. People are talking and a journalist from the *Evening News* is already sniffing around. We've got to try and stop all this nonsense.'

Sidney sighed. What was he supposed to do? He could hardly find another false pretext to visit the doctor. Perhaps Inspector Keating had other ideas. It was certainly odd for him to send a car. He would have thought that the police had other, more urgent priorities, but then, if the situation was as grim as it sounded, there was nothing more urgent than murder.

He travelled across slushy roads into town with a driver who had clearly been instructed to say nothing. When they pulled up in St Andrews Street Sidney noticed a girl in a duffle coat and a notebook waiting outside the station. She might well have been a student but there was something determined about her. He wondered what she was doing, waiting in the cold, and when Sidney got out of the car, their eyes met and she introduced herself:

'Helena Randall. *Cambridge Evening News.*'

A journalist. Sidney had, of course, been expecting a man. 'I'm pleased to meet you.'

'Are you Tony Bryant's priest, by any chance?'

'Not as far as I am aware,' Sidney hesitated. How had the press discovered news of the death so quickly?

'And are you a patient of Dr Michael Robinson?'

Clearly someone had been talking. Sidney was about to answer when the driver of the police car ushered him away. 'No time for that, Canon Chambers . . .'

'I'm so sorry. Please excuse me.'

'My card,' the girl pressed.

'Yes of course.'

'Come on, Canon Chambers.' Sidney climbed up the stairs into Inspector Keating's office.

His friend was waiting and went straight to the point. 'This is a tricky business. It will take time for the coroner to make his report and, in the meantime, there are a lot of frail, elderly people out there. I am tempted to arrest Dr Robinson and get the whole thing over and done with but we don't have the evidence and I don't want to cause a stir. I have heard that the talk has already started.'

'Indeed,' Sidney replied. 'My housekeeper has been guilty of it herself.'

'Now, Sidney, you may not like this but I want you to go and see the doctor.'

'I have already visited him twice.'

'You didn't tell me.'

'There was nothing to report.'

'Then you need to go and see him again. Make up whatever excuse you like. Plans for the wedding would do it. I want you to win his trust and find out the truth. Is he getting carried away? If he is, I want you to stop him.'

Sidney resented the way that Inspector Keating was speaking to him as if he was an employee, but this didn't seem to be the moment to take him up on it. Instead, he checked that they both thought in the same way. 'And if he is breaking the law then you can arrest him.'

'Of course. But the situation may be more complicated than that. What if he isn't breaking the law but bending it? Going so far but stopping just short?'

'Then he is acting within the law. I would have thought that was perfectly clear.'

'You know what I mean, Sidney. This man may be putting patients' lives at risk. I can feel the tension in the community. Something's not right. People are very worried.'

'I am sure Dr Robinson has their best interests at heart.'

'Are you sure, though, Sidney? That's what I want you to find out. I have a feeling that you also have doubts.'

'How did you know?'

'I am a detective . . .'

'And I am a priest. I tend to give people the benefit of the doubt.'

'Well, I don't. Perhaps that's why we are such a good team. One of my men will take you round to Dr Robinson's surgery. If he's not there I take it he will be in Chedworth Street with Miss Livingstone. I'd like you to talk to him and report back.'

'He'll see through all this, of course. He'll guess that I have come under your instruction.'

'There's nothing to see through. Your visit is perfectly legitimate, unlike the doctor's methods . . .'

'We don't know that, Inspector.'

'But with your help, Sidney, we soon will.'

Sidney decided that the only way to get a straight answer from Dr Robinson was to ask a few direct questions. He arrived at his surgery at midday and was informed by the receptionist that he would have to wait until the doctor had seen the last of his patients. This left Sidney with half an hour to kill, a period of time in which he tried and failed to amuse himself with back numbers of *Punch*. Consequently, when Dr Robinson was ready to see him, Sidney was feeling rather impatient.

'How are your mystery ailments?' the doctor asked. 'Any better?'

Sidney had almost forgotten that this was how the conversation would have to begin. 'I'm sorry. Much better, thank you.'

'Then what can I do for you?'

'I have come about the death of Anthony Bryant.'

'Is he one of your parishioners?'

'I received a telephone call from Inspector Keating.'

'If he was that concerned why didn't he telephone me himself? I can't understand why he's roped you into some completely spurious line of inquiry that is entirely without foundation. I have done nothing wrong.'

'No one is saying that you have.'

'They seem to be implying it. Why can't they just come out and say it?'

'Some members of the family felt that his death came rather more quickly than might have been expected.'

'And are any of them doctors?'

'I don't think so.'

'Old people can't be expected to survive rampant infections, Canon Chambers, and when death comes, as you know full well, it comes at an unpredictable speed. You can't anticipate or measure these things. Nor do I think it at all reasonable for a doctor to come under suspicion every time one of his patients dies. Society has to trust the fact that he knows what is best for his patients.'

'The fact?'

'Yes, Canon Chambers, the fact; otherwise what is the point of a medical training? I make informed decisions about medicine. I have relatively uninformed opinions about theology and the current state of Her Majesty's Police Force. These matters I leave to you and your friend the inspector. I put my trust in you. I do not interfere in your world and I expect you not to interfere in mine.'

'But when people die our worlds collide.'

Dr Robinson leaned back in his chair, let out a long sigh and looked up at the ceiling. Then he spoke once more. 'I don't know if you have seen, Canon Chambers, at first hand, how debilitating a long illness can be; how bleak it is for a patient and how exhausting it is for those who have a duty of care?'

'I have limited experience in this area, I admit; although I do know what it is like when people want nothing more than to die.'

'In the war, I suppose.'

'Yes. It was in the war.'

'So you know how difficult the decision can be? Some pain cannot be eased. Sometimes there is no hope.'

'Yes, and there are times when a decision has to be made very quickly.'

Dr Robinson paused before replying. 'I see you understand the dilemma.'

He was waiting for more. Sidney then found himself telling a story. 'I was in Italy in 1944,' he began. 'It was after the advance on Monte Cassino. We were in the Mignano Gap and had been under heavy mortar fire for three days. We went up the hill, sometimes crawling through the mud, and we faced a machine-gun attack that halved our number. I think I remember the noise more than anything else: the rounds of gunfire, the shouted orders, the cries of the wounded and the dying.

Soldiers, my friends, so many of my friends, were howling for their mothers and their sweethearts. Howling. Then, even when we had pulled some of them to relative safety, their pain became unbearable. My commanding officer gave me a loaded revolver and said simply, 'Do what you have to do.'

'There was a boy of nineteen; red hair and freckles, and he had lost half his face. He would never be able to put his lips together again. There was no hope. His only sensation was unbearable pain. I stopped the pain. And I've never forgotten it. I remember it every day and I pray for him. I ask for God's mercy.'

Dr Robinson sat quietly and thought about Sidney's experience in silence. At last, he spoke. 'I think I can guess why you have been telling me this, Canon Chambers. But I have done nothing wrong. My conscience is clear.'

'I did not intend to tell you. I only came to meet you, and perhaps to advise you to be careful. Sometimes, I think, we are not always aware of how much we have to live with what we have done in the past. We can't predict how these things will affect us.'

'I am always careful, Canon Chambers.'

'I would be very concerned,' Sidney continued sternly, 'if you did anything that might endanger your future, or that of Miss Livingstone, or indeed,' and here he took a wild gamble, 'that of your child.'

'My child? What on earth are you talking about?'

'I think you know perfectly well, Dr Robinson. I would hate to think that somebody so certain of their actions might leave a wife without a husband and a child without a father. Good day to you.'

Sidney was exhausted. He had not undertaken Holy Orders so that he could consort with policemen and threaten doctors. He had been called to be a messenger, watchman and steward of the Lord. He had a bounden duty to exercise care and diligence in bringing those in his charge to the faith and knowledge of God. And he had made a solemn promise at his ordination that there be no place left in him for error in religion or for viciousness in life. Yet, at this particular moment in time, everything was conspiring against him.

One of the problems of being a vicar, Sidney decided, was that you were always available. Just when you had settled down to writing the parish newsletter there would be a knock at the door or a ring of the telephone with news that could be urgent or trivial. It did not seem to matter which. All that mattered was that his attention was immediately required.

The morning after his unsettling visit to the doctor Sidney was at his desk. On it he had placed the figurine of a little girl feeding chickens that Hildegard Staunton had given him: with *Mädchen füttert Hühner* inscribed below. He found it curiously consoling and would sometimes break from his work to think about what she might be doing or imagine what advice she might give him. He took out the letter she had written, thanking him for all that he had done, telling him that he would always be welcome in Germany. He only had to ask, and he could arrive at any time.

'You know that whatever happens in the world,' she had written, 'I will always remember your kindness and be grateful. You know that I am here.'

Sidney put down Hildegard's letter and tried to concentrate. He was trying to work without disturbance before the arrival of

Mrs Maguire with her dusting, her conversation and his lunch. Monday was always shepherd's pie and Sidney was almost looking forward to its simple consoling pleasure when another visitor interrupted him.

It was one of his parishioners, Mrs Agatha Redmond, a farmer's wife, who often helped out with the floral decoration of the church. A smile played across her ruddy cheeks. 'It's a fine morning, Canon Chambers, is it not?' she began. 'Nice to see sunshine after the snow.'

Sidney noticed that Mrs Redmond was holding a black Labrador puppy. Already he began to suspect that something was up. 'Is it about the flower rota?' he asked.

'Oh no. It's nothing of the sort.'

'Then would you like to come in?'

Agatha Redmond hesitated and then looked down at the puppy. 'Isn't he lovely?'

'Yes,' Sidney answered uncertainly. 'I am sure he is. A fine specimen.'

'I'm glad you think so.'

'I do,' Sidney continued as surely as he could. He had never been that keen on dogs. 'Indeed I do.'

'Then I'm so pleased,' Mrs Redmond continued. 'Because Miss Kendall asked me to give him to you. Isn't he gorgeous? He's only eight weeks old.'

'I didn't know you knew Miss Kendall?'

'She met my husband on a train. Then she telephoned.'

'It's very odd that she didn't say anything about it.'

'She wanted it to be a surprise.'

'Well, it's certainly that, Mrs Redmond. Perhaps I am to keep him for her until she comes to collect him?'

'Oh no, Canon Chambers. I don't think you understand. This dog is for you. He's a present.'

For a moment Sidney could not quite take in what was being said to him. 'But why?'

'Miss Kendall thought you were rather down in the dumps. She said that you needed cheering up. There's nothing like a Lab for company, and the black are better for conversation I find.'

Sidney was astounded. He could not understand how Amanda could have done such a thing. Why of all things in the world would he have need of a dog? It was hard enough looking after himself.

'But I've no idea how to . . .'

Mrs Redmond interrupted. 'I've brought a booklet with instructions and there's a basket for him in the car. The important thing is to get him house-trained as soon as possible. When he's older, of course, you can take him on your visits. He'll be very popular.'

'I dare say . . .'

'Shall we set up a space in the kitchen? By the back door, I think. I'll need some newspaper.' Mrs Redmond picked up a copy of the *Church Times*. She was quite unstoppable. 'This will do.'

Sidney gave himself one last chance, 'But I knew nothing about this. I haven't the foggiest idea how to look after a dog.'

'You'll soon get used to him. Try looking at the vicarage from the puppy's point of view. You'll get a whole new perspective on things, Canon Chambers, a dog's eye view of life. I find it so very consoling. After a while, you'll wonder how you ever did without him.'

Mrs Redmond put the Labrador down on the floor and the puppy made a last-ditch bid for freedom. 'Steady now, Archie . . .'

'He's called Archie?'

'You can change the name, of course. But you need to decide soon so he can get used to your commands.'

'I don't think I've given a command since the Army . . .'

'Well, perhaps it's time you resumed, Canon Chambers? There are only five to remember: "come", "sit", "stay", "heel" and "lie down". You need to be clear and consistent. Then you can add words such as "basket". Talking of which I must go and fetch it before I forget. You will keep the vicarage nice and cosy for him, won't you? It's quite cold in this kitchen.'

'It is winter,' Sidney observed, 'and I was not expecting a dog.'

Mrs Redmond failed to detect a tone that hovered between despair and irritation. 'Of course you'll have to keep him in a limited space until he's fully house-trained. He'll need a blanket too. I've brought some food to start you off and I think I have got some old toys as well. They might do when I look in later in the week to see how you are getting on . . .'

Sidney sat down on a kitchen chair as Mrs Redmond busied herself around him and then fetched the dog's basket from her car. 'It will be like having a child . . .' he muttered. 'And without a wife . . .'

Mrs Redmond re-entered the room. 'I am sure you won't have any trouble finding a wife, Canon Chambers . . .'

It now appeared that his visitor had selective hearing. 'People do keep telling me . . .'

'A handsome man like you . . .'

'Do you think so?'

'Of course. Everyone says so. You'd be quite a catch.'

Sidney allowed himself a moment of vanity. He knew that on a good day he had a faint air of Kenneth More about him but he didn't like to dwell on it.

Mrs Redmond put down the dog basket and looked at him. She had sensed his weak spot. 'I am sure Miss Kendall might consider it.'

'I don't think that's likely . . .'

'Oh dear. Never mind.' Mrs Redmond resumed her preparations. 'Still, once you get to know Archie I am sure you can tell *him* your problems instead of Miss Kendall. Then no one else need know . . .'

'I'm not sure my problems are worth discussing.'

'It doesn't matter, Canon Chambers. Archie won't mind. You can tell him anything. Anything at all . . .'

'I suppose I can.'

Mrs Redmond began rubbing her hands together, a nervous gesture that indicated her duty was done. 'I'd better be going now. If you have any problems with him or need any advice just pop round, but I am sure that Archie is going to make a vast improvement to your life.'

'He's certainly going to change it,' Sidney mused. 'I'll see you to the door, Mrs Redmond.'

'Don't you worry about that, Canon Chambers. I'll let myself out.'

Sidney looked down at Archie. He would have to try and pick him up, he decided, but as soon as he made his first attempt the dog proved resistant and gave a small yelp. Indeed, it was a frustrating while before Sidney was able to scoop him up in his arms.

Honestly.

What was he doing?

How could anyone think that such a pet might be suitable?

It was absurd and it quite put him off Amanda. What can he have been thinking when he told her everything? How could she ever have conceived that he might want a dog? What on earth did they have in common? He should leave Grantchester whenever he could, Sidney thought, and find the most remote parish where little happened apart from the need to maintain faith. He thought of Cornwall, West Wales, the Northumbrian border with Scotland: anywhere with a low crime rate and parishioners who were keen to come to church rather than murder each other.

Archie jumped on to his lap. His honey-brown eyes had an expression of helpless trust. This was a creature who was asking to be looked after, whose affection was unconditional, and who would always be pleased to see him. This, surely, would be a more rewarding responsibility, a healing presence amidst the death of the old. Yes, perhaps all might be well after all and Amanda had been right and this would be . . .

Ah.

Perhaps not.

Mrs Maguire was coming through the front door with her shopping bags and Sidney's shepherd's pie.

'It's only me,' she called.

At first Mrs Maguire did not notice the new arrival, walking into the kitchen, putting her things on the table, speaking all the while and telling Sidney that he would have to leave so that she could get on with her work. 'What is the *Church Times* doing on the floor?' she demanded. 'Are you throwing it away? The wastepaper basket is under your desk.'

'It is there for a reason, Mrs Maguire.'

'I can't think what that could be.' She noticed the basket. 'And what, in God's good name, is that?'

'I think I can . . .' At that moment Sidney's new puppy scampered up to Mrs Maguire and gave her right ankle a playful nip.

'Heavens to Betsy!' Mrs Maguire cried out. 'An animal!'

'He is a present from Miss Kendall.'

'What the dickens is going on? How long is he staying?'

'For ever, it seems.'

'What on earth do you mean, Canon Chambers? I hope you don't expect me to clean up after that thing?'

'I certainly don't, Mrs Maguire. At the moment I am not sure what to do. The puppy is an extremely recent arrival.'

'What's he called?'

'Archie. But I think I'm going to change his name. Now you mention it, Dickens sounds rather a good name for a dog.'

Mrs Maguire was unimpressed. 'None of us needs a puppy yapping away. They never stop, you know.'

'I am sure he will grow. I was hoping that he might prove to be something of a companion . . .'

'He'll be nothing but trouble, mark my words. And you, Canon Chambers, have enough trouble in your life already.'

The day did not pass well. Dickens, for that was the name Sidney decided upon, wet the kitchen floor immediately Mrs Maguire had cleaned it, the church roof had sprung a leak under the weight of the melting snow and Sidney forgot his shepherd's pie in the oven. As he ate the burnt remains with his curate, Leonard advised Sidney that he really should see the coroner once more. They needed to know whether Mrs Livingstone's cremation could take place, if her daughter's marriage could proceed and if not, what Inspector Keating was going to do about it.

Sidney found all the demands on his time even more irritating than usual. He knew that he didn't actually *like* Derek Jarvis. But now he decided he was not too keen on Dr Michael Robinson either. Or Mrs Maguire. Or his curate. Or his dog. Or even Amanda. In fact the monastic life suddenly seemed far more appealing than ever before.

Later that afternoon, Sidney rang the bell of the coroner's office and was shown through to a small waiting room. Derek Jarvis was efficiently polite. 'You're taking quite an interest in this case, I see . . .'

'Apparently there is some considerable disquiet in the town. People have stopped going to see Dr Robinson.'

'There are other doctors.'

'We can't hound a man out of town because of an unfounded rumour.'

Derek Jarvis sighed. 'I can assure you, Canon Chambers, that I have been professional throughout this investigation and will continue to be so.'

'I cannot believe that Dr Robinson is a murderer.'

'Well,' Derek Jarvis concluded. 'So far, despite all the anxiety, it appears that he is not.'

'Morphine?'

'A high level but nothing more . . .'

'You sound disappointed.'

'I am not disappointed. I am wary. As I said, a high level of morphine.'

'But within acceptable limits.'

'*Just.*'

'Then you will release Mrs Livingstone's body?'

'I will. However, as I am sure you are aware, other sudden elderly deaths have occurred.'

'Anthony Bryant . . .'

'Indeed.'

Sidney could not let the situation finish like this. He knew that he should act in a more priestly manner. 'I know it is hard to act in good faith with someone you may not like. As a Christian . . .'

'Please, Canon Chambers, do not make such assumptions or jump to conclusions.'

'I was merely suggesting . . .'

'My work is scientific and objective. My personal feelings are kept in abeyance.'

'Very well,' Sidney answered. 'When will you have completed your examination of the second body?'

'All in good time.'

Sidney looked at the coroner and wondered whether there was ever such a thing as 'good time'. It was going to be a long wait.

As he walked back through the streets of Cambridge, Sidney stopped to admire a pipe-smoking snowman that had been given an air-raid warden's helmet. He heard a sudden movement behind him, turned to see who it was, but there was no one there. Perhaps he was being followed? But why would anyone want to do such a thing? He tried to put his suspicions down to the fact that he was cold and anxious, but the feelings of unease grew as he resumed his walk. He was also hungry after the debacle of his lunchtime shepherd's pie. There was nothing for it but to enter Fitzbillies and buy yet another one of their Chelsea buns. He would find a discreet way of eating it on his way home.

Although his purchase was successful, his initial attempt to eat the bun was foiled by the presence of the young female journalist he had seen outside the police station. In the pause in which he tried to remember her name Helena Randall shot out her first question. 'A successful visit to the coroner, Canon Chambers?'

Sidney paused. 'I am not sure what you mean?'

'Are there any positive results?'

Sidney stopped. 'I would like to help you but what I am doing is rather confidential.'

Helena Randall took out her notebook. 'And are there degrees of confidentiality?' she asked.

'I like to think not.'

'And will you be going to see Dr Robinson or his fiancée again?'

Sidney had never met someone so pale and so determined. 'I haven't seen them today.'

'But you have seen them recently? When?'

'In the last few days, but I don't know whether this is anything that might be of interest to your readers. There is no evidence of any wrongdoing.'

'There are coincidences.'

'It is winter, Miss . . .'

'Randall. Helena Randall. I think you are a police spy, Canon Chambers.'

'I have never heard anything so absurd. There may be spies in Cambridge but I can assure you that I am not one of them.'

'So you admit to knowing spies?'

'Of course I don't. Now please; I must be going home.'

'I can walk with you.'

'I'd really rather you didn't.'

'I gave you my card, I believe?'

'You did.'

'Well then. You probably need to know that I, too, am never off duty. I think this has the makings of a story.'

'There's nothing to tell.'

'Not yet, Canon Chambers. But there soon will be. And when the story breaks you will want to tell me your side of it first.'

'I am not sure that I will.' Sidney replied tersely. 'Good day to you, Miss Randall.'

He crossed Granta Place and headed up Eltisley Avenue and glanced up at Hildegard Staunton's old house. He wished she were still there. He could have stopped off on the way home and listened to her play Bach. Now all he had was his bun from Fitzbillies.

He ate it as he walked across the Meadows. It was almost dark. A group of schoolboys were enjoying a snowball fight as people returned from work, bicycling along the high path with books, bags and shopping. Greeting people as they passed, Sidney had a simultaneous sense of belonging and alienation. These were, in the main, decent respectable people, and yet Sidney felt that he had little to do with them. He was detached, separated from their lives and their employment by his calling, by the university and by his dream-like daily musings. Normal

202

life, simultaneously, had both everything and nothing to do with him.

When he returned home his dog scampered up to meet him. It was clear that he expected his master both to give him his full attention and to go straight back out again but the telephone in the hall was already ringing. Sidney had been hoping that he could heat the place up a bit and sit by the fire with some light reading but it was not to be. Who on earth could this be? he wondered as the telephone rang. *What fresh hell is this?*

It was Amanda. 'How is Dickens?' she asked. Already, Sidney thought, her dog mattered more than he did.

'How did you know he was called that?' he replied.

'I telephoned earlier and got Mrs Maguire. She tried to be polite but was really quite ratty. She thought I should come and get him and take him away.'

'Dickens is quite a handful, Amanda.'

'I bought him for that very purpose.'

'Did you indeed . . .'

'He's there to take your mind off all the dreadful things that have been happening. You told me you were lonely.'

'You asked me if I was lonely. That's not quite the same thing.'

'You answered in the affirmative and I have taken steps to address the situation. I thought it was rather thoughtful of me . . .'

'It was Amanda, and I am grateful.'

'How is he?'

'He's perfectly well.'

'You sound grumpy. Are you sure you are looking after him properly? When can I see him?'

'You can come whenever you like.'

'Good. You haven't got the flu or anything like that?'

'No. Why do you ask?'

'Why do I ask?' Amanda was almost shouting. 'Because I don't want you going to see that doctor.'

'What has Mrs Maguire been saying?'

'I am sure you can guess. She thinks that your doctor has been taking the law into his own hands.'

'Nothing has been proved.'

'But by the time it is, it will be too late. You need to be careful, Sidney. In crime stories the murderer is always the doctor. It's why I no longer read Miss Christie. It's always the bloody doctor.'

'But this is not fiction, Amanda. This is real life.'

'I don't want you doing anything silly.'

'There's not much chance of that. All my energy is being taken up with looking after your wretched Labrador.'

'I'm sorry if you think that Dickens is too much for you,' Amanda snapped. 'I meant well. I'm sure I can find another home for him if you'd like. I was just trying to do my best and give you a companion. That's all I was trying to do.'

'I'm sorry, Amanda. It's just that sometimes . . .'

His friend interrupted. 'I'm worried you are so gloomy. Do you think it's because it's Lent? Or something else? Have you taken Dickens out for a walk today?'

'Of course I have,' Sidney replied defensively.

He wondered how much longer this conversation would continue. He had nothing to say and much to think about. Furthermore, he was standing in the cold hall. The windows had frosted completely, and on the inside. It was probably going to snow yet again. When, oh when, Sidney wondered, would it be spring?

Amanda was still talking. 'Are you still there?'

Sidney had switched off. 'Yes, of course.'

'I have to go. Henry is taking me out to dinner.'

'Henry?'

'I've told you about him.'

'Have you?'

'Of course I have. There's nothing you need to worry about.'

'But I do . . .'

'Must dash. Don't go to the doctor whatever you do. Love you.'

Sidney began to remonstrate but Amanda had already put down the receiver. He listened to the relentless sound of the dialling tone. There was nothing that could have matched his mood more exactly.

At last Easter came; the Maundy Thursday washing of feet, the three-hour meditation on Good Friday, the vigil on Saturday evening and then the triumphant alleluia of Easter Sunday. A wave of purple crocuses burst through the grass of the Grantchester Meadows to echo the message of Christian hope.

Sidney was determined that his parishioners should share the joy and redemption of Easter, and took, as the symbol of his sermon, the image of the cloth left in the cave where Jesus had lain. It had been folded rather than thrown away, Sidney told his congregation, a sign, according to the custom of the time, that he would return, to the table, to the meal and to the communion between God and man.

'We are Easter people,' he told the parishioners of Grantchester. 'This is not one day out of three hundred and sixty-five, but the mainspring of our faith. We carry the Easter message each day of our lives, lives in which the pain of the Cross and the suffering of humanity are followed by the uncomprehended magnitude of the Resurrection.'

Sidney spoke with as much passion as he could muster but as he looked down from the pulpit he realised that he was not able to reach every parishioner. The elderly looked benevolent and grateful, but younger widows from the war carried a grief that could not be assuaged. Sidney stressed that God must be one with whom humanity's pain and loneliness can identify, but he could tell that some of his parishioners could only look back at him and say, 'Not this pain. Not this loneliness.'

He wished, once more, that he could be a better priest. He hoped he could bring comfort but there were times when he just had to understand that he could not be all things to all men. Sometimes he had to accept his limitations and take a few hours away from his duties and let life take its course. At least he now had the excuse of walking his Labrador.

This was not always an easy task. Sidney was no disciplinarian when it came to training and Dickens had to be frequently retrieved from hedges, ditches and, on one occasion, the river itself. His presence did, however, make social engagement with other dog owners more agreeable and Sidney had no choice but to leave his desk and get out into the surrounding countryside with a companion who was always loyal and never bored. No matter what Sidney did Dickens was keen to follow.

Sidney only wished that Amanda, the provider of such an unexpected gift to his life, could share some of her caring canine's qualities.

On his return from an enjoyable, if rather breathless walk that Easter afternoon, Sidney was surprised to find the coroner at his front door. He was leaving some wine by the empty milk bottles.

'I'm glad I've caught you,' he exclaimed.

Dickens jumped up against the coroner's knee.

'Playful little fellow you've got there, I see . . .'

'Somewhat too playful,' Sidney apologised. 'Would you like some tea?'

'That would be very kind.'

Sidney opened his front door and Dickens scampered in. 'Do come in. May I take your coat?'

The coroner put down his bottle of wine on the hall table. 'I brought you a small present for Easter, Canon Chambers.'

'That's very kind of you. It's not an egg, I see.'

'It most certainly isn't. It's a Bordeaux. Château-Latour 1937. Rather good, I think you'll find.'

'Oh my,' said Sidney.

'You are aware of the vintage?'

'I'm not sure I am.' Sidney filled his kettle with water and lit the gas ring. 'I'm afraid I'm more of a beer man.'

'You surprise me. I would have thought with all your college feasts you would be quite an oenophilist.'

'I'm really more at home in the pub with my friends. I'm not all that fond of dining at high table.'

'Why ever not?'

Sidney waited for the kettle to boil. 'I think it's because I don't quite belong. A clergyman is always rather an odd one out. Perhaps it goes back to the last century when if a man had several sons then the eldest joined the army, the second ran the estate and the youngest and dimmest went into the church. I fear some of the Fellows still think that this is the case.'

'They do make a great show of finding you intellectually inferior whoever you are. Which is all very well but while they may have brains they certainly don't always have manners.'

'Is that what you find?'

'They are in a world of their own. Sometimes I think they can scarcely talk to each other, never mind their guests.'

Sidney warmed his teapot, added a sprinkle of leaves and then poured in the boiling water. 'It has always surprised me that some Fellows don't actually like their students.'

'I think it's because they want to be students themselves. They are envious of their youth and contemptuous of their intelligence.'

'I wouldn't put it quite as strongly as that.'

'I would, I am afraid. Do you know that line of Kierkegaard's, Canon Chambers? "There are many people who reach their conclusions about life like schoolboys: they cheat their master by copying the answer out of a book without having worked the sum out for themselves." '

'I certainly think that many of them prefer books to people. Do you take milk with your tea?' Sidney asked.

'Of course. But never in first . . .'

Sidney smiled. 'I am not the kind of vicar who would do such a thing.'

'I never suspected that you were; but it's sometimes necessary to say so to avoid disaster.'

Sidney put the teacups on a tray that he had been given to commemorate the Coronation. 'Shall we go through to the sitting room? It's kind of you to bring the wine . . .'

The coroner looked at the bottle as if he was sad to say goodbye to it. 'It's meant as an apology, and as a thank you.'

'I don't think I need either of those. Do sit down.'

'Actually you do, Canon Chambers. I was very brusque with you. I did not like you intruding.'

Sidney poured out the tea. 'You made that very clear.'

'But now I am grateful.'

'I am not sure what I did to deserve this.'

'You averted disaster, something rather more serious than putting milk in your tea first.'

Sidney handed his companion his cup and saucer. 'I don't know what you mean.'

'Dr Robinson and his future wife . . .'

'Oh, I don't think I did anything there.'

'I rather think that you did, Canon Chambers. I know you went to see Dr Robinson. I thought at the time that all of this was none of your business and I'm afraid I may have said so rather too strongly.'

'I am used to people being frank with me, Mr Jarvis. Sugar?'

'No thank you.'

'There's even some of Mrs Maguire's shortbread.'

'I feel you are distracting me.'

'Please. Continue.'

'It's often hard to predict what people might do, don't you find? I can see that Dr Robinson was acting within the boundaries of the law but I could also see that he was in danger of taking that same law into his own hands.'

'The Anthony Bryant inquiry?'

'Again, the quantity of morphine was just within acceptable limits. He was, as we suspected, bending the law rather than breaking it. But sometimes, and I have seen this before, people get into the habit. If Dr Robinson felt that he was performing a useful and compassionate service, and if he imagined that he was acting for a higher moral purpose, then perhaps he believed that he could carry on, take things further and justify what he was doing. I think that by intervening you stopped him doing anything more.'

'I don't know about that.'

'I think I do, Canon Chambers. It could have got out of control.'

'Sidney, please . . .'

'I think not. It doesn't pay for a man to be too familiar with his priest. What you did, Canon Chambers, was to cut off any possibility that he could justify his actions. Your presence reminded him that there were God's laws as well as man's, and that even if he could explain his behaviour with a clear conscience on this earth then he might still be answerable to a stricter ethical power in the afterlife.'

'How do you know this?'

'Inspector Keating told me that Dr Robinson found you rather disconcerting. It was why he sent you. He knew that moral authority would carry more weight than the force of the law. He's cleverer than you think, that man.'

'I do not doubt it.'

'And there were things that you said. They made the doctor pause.'

'I do not think I said very much.'

'It was enough. Of course, I am guessing what passed between you but I know enough to realise that I need to thank you. You did not have to do what you did but you did and I

210

appreciate it. I am sorry not to have been as welcoming as I should have been when you came to see me. I will not make that mistake in future.'

'And I will try not to be disconcerting.'

'To a man with a guilty conscience everything is troubling.'

'I imagine so.'

'And a clear conscience is the only way to live, Canon Chambers, and, of course, a clear head. Now, shall we open the wine? It must be six o'clock and we have an excuse. The Lenten days have passed.'

'I would be delighted,' Sidney replied.

On Easter Thursday the traditional social meeting with Inspector Keating in the RAF bar of The Eagle returned to form.

'It's good to see you back to your old self, Sidney,' his friend began as they settled down to their first pint of the evening. 'Although I wasn't expecting you to come with Dickens. It's a wife you need, not a dog.'

'A dog is all that I was offered, unfortunately.'

'There are women other than Miss Kendall. I thought you were rather partial to that German widow?'

'Too soon, Geordie, and, in a way, too late.'

'People always find excuses. Sometimes it's best just to get on with it.'

'Indeed,' mused Sidney, thinking of Keating's wife and three children.

The inspector took a long draft of beer. 'At least your man seems to have got away with it.'

Sidney gave his friend a stern look. 'He's not "my man", Geordie. And he acted within the boundaries of the law.'

'The coroner's turned a blind eye, if you ask me. He's softer than I thought . . .'

'That he may be,' mused Sidney. 'You still suspect malpractice?'

'I'm not sure.'

'The doctor knew what he was doing.'

'Only too well, it seems.'

'And I think his motives were genuine. It was winter: the season of pneumonia, friend of the aged. A moral decision can sometimes take more courage than we think.'

Inspector Keating did not appear to be listening. He was still brooding over the case and finished his drink at a canter. 'Nonetheless, you have to admit that it's been a difficult business.' He looked into his empty pint glass. 'Sherlock Holmes may have had his two-pipe problem but I'm rather hoping ours are more like two-pint problems . . .'

'Very droll . . .' Sidney replied. 'Another?'

'That would be kind.'

'We will never really know, will we? What goes on in the minds of men.'

'Or women . . .' his friend replied before catching the barman's attention.

The inspector laid out the board of backgammon as Sidney collected the drinks. 'It's a funny thing, the whole business of love, is it not?' He was speaking almost to himself. 'I suppose I take it for granted, I have everything at home, Cathy and the children, and it just felt natural to us but I suppose for other people it's a different story.'

Sidney put the pints down on the table. 'I am sure that most people like to feel their own story is unique.'

'But you, my friend, have a series of different possibilities: books with blank pages about to be filled.'

'I wouldn't put it quite like that.' Sidney could tell that the inspector was trying to turn this into a conversation about Amanda but he wasn't having it. 'I am only relieved that the marriage between Isabel and the doctor can go ahead.'

'When is the great day?'

'A week on Saturday.'

The inspector lit up a cigarette. 'It's a curious thing the way the mind works, Sidney. The doctor probably thought he was acting out of love by bumping off his fiancée's mother.'

'He didn't "bump her off".'

'We both know he did. But he's got away with it by disguising it as compassion.' The inspector threw a double six. 'Do you think the coroner was in on it?'

'I don't think so.'

'I'm still not so sure. It would be an easy thing to sort out amongst themselves. They could have been in it together and the coroner was only drawing attention to the incident as a double bluff. He was getting in first and making sure he was the one doing the investigating rather than any other coroner.'

'That sounds a bit far-fetched.'

'Nothing in crime is ever far-fetched, Sidney. You should know that by now. Anything is possible; and the most unlikely and unbelievable stories are often the truest. I wouldn't mind looking at the wills of the old people who've died. If the doctor's been left anything . . .'

'You can always check, but I think you'll find the coroner is a good man.'

'I've not doubted it in the past, Sidney. You were the one who had reservations.'

'I've rather warmed to him.'

'Have you now?'

'He came to the vicarage with a bottle of wine.'

'Wine? You're easily bought. I thought you were a beer man?'

'It was a Château-Latour 1937. Smooth on the palate and long on the finish.'

'I'll wager he said it was. But wine's a very expensive hobby for a clergyman. I'm not sure you should be developing a taste for something you cannot afford.'

'Corpus does have a very fine cellar . . .'

'It sends out the wrong signals too. You know for a fact that nothing beats a good pub. That's where real people go: not your dons or your rich fancy types. Besides, I thought you didn't like going to your old college?'

'I wouldn't put it as strongly as that.'

'I don't know, man. You seem to have changed character. First you get a dog, and then you develop a taste for wine. God knows what might happen next.'

'I am sure God does know, Inspector. It's just as well we don't.'

'And I'm right glad we don't.'

'Another round?'

'A third pint?' Inspector Keating asked with affectionate surprise. 'Are you sure you can take it, man?'

'Lent is no more,' Sidney reaffirmed. 'You, my good friend, are here. We are talking about wine and crime and love. Sometimes I think there is nothing we cannot say to each other.'

'I suppose that's right.'

'The fire is lit. A dog is by my side. The mood, if I may say so, is jovial. And furthermore,' Sidney continued, 'I am looking forward to some very unsteady bicycling on the way home.'

The following week the air softened and spring came at last. Primroses, violets and coltsfoot bloomed; woodlarks hung suspended in the air all day and sang all night. Lapwings haunted the downs, the stone-curlew returned from the uplands down to the meadows and banks, blackbirds and thrushes laid their eggs.

So late the spring, and yet so welcome. It had come to fruition in perfect time for Isabel's wedding. Sidney was delighted to see the new fashions amongst the female guests: the full skirts, soft shoulders and pinched waists, the figure-hugging dresses and glorious hats with their floral blooms and swirls of organza. The women of Grantchester had cast off their winter darkness and were showing summer colour at last.

Sidney greeted the doctor as he arrived with his best man. 'A happy day,' he said. 'I do hope you enjoy it.'

'I intend to. And I should thank you, of course.'

'I don't think I did anything.'

'You did what you had to do and said what you had to say.'

'That was my duty.'

'It would take a brave man to disagree with you.'

'Alas, Dr Robinson, many do.'

'That's as may be. But you were fair-minded and you said the right things. You made me think differently about the world and its ways. We are both very grateful.'

'I suppose that is a clergyman's duty.'

'Ah, yes. The poet George Crabbe wrote about that, didn't he? The priest as an example to his flock:

Sober, chaste devout and just

One whom his neighbours could believe and trust.

It must be hard to set such an example.'

'It is almost impossible,' Sidney replied.

'Sometimes, it is not the achievement but the intention that matters.' The doctor smiled.

The organist struck up the wedding march and they were off.

Sidney tried to cheer himself up by reminding himself that he enjoyed a good wedding. He was not so keen on the receptions that followed: the nervous bonhomie, the lengthy speeches and the warm white wine, but he had learned to walk through them with a semi-detached benevolence that many people, he was relieved to notice, mistook for holiness.

Isabel Livingstone, soon to be Robinson, was dressed in white taffeta, and Sidney noticed she had chosen an empire line dress rather than the currently fashionable fitted waist and full skirt. She appeared younger than when Sidney had last seen her as if it was only now, at this moment, that she had become herself. The anxiety and grief of the previous months had fallen away, and her walk up the aisle had the air of a triumphal march.

She was followed by two bridesmaids dressed in frocks of buttercup yellow. Both girls were under the age of eight and they walked with a grace and a solemnity of purpose that Sidney hoped might provide an example to the rest of the congregation.

He smiled as he gave the opening welcome but something held him back. He was not going to let the couple off lightly. He spoke slowly, clearly and with authority. He emphasised the fact that marriage had to be entered into reverently, discreetly, advisedly, soberly and in the fear of God. He would explain each of these phrases in his sermon and he would expect everyone to pay attention. This was not just a social event. It was a sombre religious ceremony in which the promises made had eternal consequences.

He would preach, as he often did, on Christ's first miracle, at a wedding feast at Cana of Galilee. The water was changed into wine, as Michael and Isabel would be changed, the two becoming one; but, rather than losing themselves in self-indulgence, the challenge would be to bring out the best in one another. They would have to become different people, better, stronger, more tolerant and more generous.

Even though he told the congregation that the best wedding present they could give the happy couple would be to love, support and be watchful of this marriage, both Michael and Isabel Robinson knew that Canon Sidney Chambers was speaking directly to them. He was telling them to be careful. He was telling them to *watch out*. There was steel, both in his compassion, and in his Christianity. This was not so much a sermon as a moral warning.

God was watching them.

Sidney was watching them.

Six months later Isabel Robinson gave birth to a baby boy.

A Matter of Time

IT WAS THE seventh of May 1954 and Sidney had, at last, perfected the art of boiling an egg. He filled a saucepan with water, lowered a speckled specimen into position and placed it on the stove. As the water began to heat up, Sidney commenced his morning routine. It was vital to complete his shaving at the exact moment the water reached boiling point. Then he would prepare his toast. The time taken to cook, turn and remove the toast from the grill, butter it and then cut it into soldiers, was the exact time needed to boil his egg. If successfully achieved, the toast would still be hot, the butter melted and the egg in perfect condition. It was extraordinary that he was now able to combine the preparation of breakfast with the act of shaving and, every time he did so, Sidney was filled with quiet satisfaction.

On a bright spring morning, as the last of the frost was disappearing from the meadows, Sidney's attention turned to the news on the wireless. Roger Bannister had broken the four-minute mile on the Iffley Road athletics track in Oxford. How odd, Sidney thought, that a man could run a mile in the same length of time that it took to boil an egg. It was also the time needed for an over of cricket, or for that other Sidney, Bechet, to work his way through 'Summertime' on the soprano saxophone. It was extraordinary how much could be achieved in such a short space of time.

He tried to spend a great deal longer walking Dickens as Sidney was, at last, beginning to enjoy the company of his dog. His presence brought new challenges – discipline, training, routine – but also, it had to be said, benefits. Although his desire for attention and reward could be relentless, Sidney found that his Labrador was not only an ice-breaker with new parishioners but also, crucially, a conversation-stopper. In fact Dickens freed Sidney from the time-consuming complaints of the more troublesome members of his congregation. If the dog strained at the leash or made a mad dash after rabbits then his owner would have to break off his conversation and follow Dickens's mazy runs across the Meadows. The dog's sudden bursts of speed or changes of direction were, Sidney decided, like an improvised saxophone solo. You never knew what was going to happen next.

It was, perhaps, not surprising that Sidney should think in these terms for he considered himself to be something of a jazz aficionado. While he loved the concentrated serenity of choral music, and the work of Byrd, Tallis and Purcell in particular, there were times when he wanted something earthier. And so, on his rare evenings at home, he liked nothing better than to listen to the latest hot sounds from America coming from the wireless. It was the opposite of stillness, prayer and penitence, he thought; full of life, mood and swing, whether it was 'It Don't Mean a Thing' by the Ralph Sharon Sextet or the 'Boogie Woogie Stomp' of Albert Ammons. Jazz was unpredictable. It could take risks, change mood, announce a theme, develop, change and recapitulate. It was all times in one time,

Sidney thought, reworking themes from the past, existing in the present, while creating expectations about any future direction it might take. It was a metaphor of life itself, both transient and profound, pursuing its course with intensity and freedom. Everyone, Sidney was sure, felt the vibe differently, although he was careful not to use a word such as 'vibe' when he dined at his College high table.

Jazz was Sidney's treat to himself, and today he was going to share his enjoyment by travelling to London with Inspector Keating to hear the Gloria Dee Quartet in Soho. They were to be Johnny Johnson's guests as a thank you gesture after the business of the missing ring. Sidney had not felt it necessary to admit that the friend he was bringing was a policeman; nor had he told Keating that Johnny's father was none other than the reformed burglar Phil 'the Cat' Johnson. He did not want to over-excite his friend.

Gloria Dee had come over from New York City and was already being tipped as the new Bessie Smith. She had the same dramatic presence, together with a voice that could range from supreme tenderness to gospel power. All the reviewers on the jazz scene had praised both the clarity of her diction and her incomparable phrasing and timing.

Sidney was glad to be so up to the minute in his appreciation of her talents but was nervous whether Geordie would like it. He had him down as a light opera man. He also worried that the inspector would be wary of Soho's seediness.

However, as soon as they arrived in London, Keating seemed unusually cheerful. 'Makes a change from our usual arrangement,' he told Sidney as they left Leicester Square and crossed into Chinatown. 'And it's good to get out of Cambridge. It can feel a bit claustrophobic, don't you think?'

'I worry that you may find the club just as confined.'

'Sometimes you worry too much.'

'And remember, Geordie, we are *off duty*. I am not a clergyman and you are not a detective.'

'We are never off duty, Sidney, you know that.'

'Do you mean to say there's no peace for the wicked?'

They climbed the stairs up to the club and handed their coats to Colin on the door. As they walked in, Sidney began to feel self-conscious. The club was crowded with men in sharp suits and thin ties who sat close to women in tight blouses, full skirts and dancing shoes. They were smoking and drinking, and mellow with the mood. Although Sidney was dressed in civvies – a grey flannel double-breasted suit with two-tone brogues – he still felt like a clergyman. He wondered whether he should have opted for a Homburg hat, or forsaken the tie which, he realised, was an episcopal purple, but it was too late to worry about that now.

Johnny Johnson greeted the two men and, after introductions had been made and the beers had been ordered, they sat down to await the evening's entertainment. A young cocktail waitress with black harlequin glasses approached with a tray of cigarettes. Keating asked for a packet of Players while Sidney declined. As he did so the waitress smiled.

'Stylish suit,' she said.

Sidney was cheered. 'I like your spectacles.'

'Must make a change from all that clobber you have to wear on Sundays.'

'How do you know I'm a priest?'

'My brother pointed you out.'

Sidney guessed. 'Are you Johnny's sister?'

221

'I'm Claudette.'

'An unusual name . . .'

'I think my parents wanted another boy but Claude's a funny name too, isn't it? People call me Claudie, Claudie Johnson. Sure you don't want a cigarette?'

'No, thanks. There are just the four of you then?'

'Three. My Mum died when I was six. I'm Daddy's girl. I'm sure he'll come and say hello.'

Sidney worried that the inspector might recognise Phil 'the Cat', but hoped that a criminal who had done his time should be regarded as an innocent man in the eyes of the law.

He noticed that Claudette was so pale that her eyes appeared very dark. They were like a pair of jet earrings that had fallen in snow. 'I'd best move on,' she continued. 'But you have a good evening, won't you, gentlemen? Put the troubles of the world behind you. And if there *is* any trouble just come and find me.'

'Trouble?' Inspector Keating asked.

'We get some funny types in here.' Claudette leaned in so close that Sidney could smell her chewing gum. 'Some of Dad's old friends. Money in dark corners, that kind of thing. But if you stay by the bar and keep in the light you'll be all right.' Claudette gave him a little wink. 'Stay cool, OK?'

'I'll do my best.'

Inspector Keating looked alarmed. 'I hope there's not going to be any nonsense.'

'I wouldn't worry about that, Geordie.'

He looked across to see Phil 'the Cat' Johnson coming over to greet them. Clearly his daughter had tipped him off. He was a large man with a pockmarked face and a belly like a barrel of beer. He called out to his friends by name as he approached, ordered up drinks and told jokes that he then ruined by laughing through the punch line. 'Have another beer, Sid. I know what you did for our boy.'

'It was nothing, Mr Johnson.'

'You stuck up for him. That's more than nothing. Who's your friend?'

'Geordie Keating,' the inspector replied.

'I'm pleased to meet you, Geordie. You keeping this clergyman out of trouble?'

'I'm doing my best. Sometimes trouble finds him.'

'Well, I'm sure there won't be any of that malarkey tonight. The singer's a corker and the band are great. You both relax and, if there's anything you need, just come and find me, all right? No one messes with me.'

'I can't imagine they do,' Sidney observed.

'They wouldn't dare!'

The room began to fill with more people and more smoke, so much so that Sidney worried whether he would actually be able to see Gloria Dee when she came on stage; but, as soon as she emerged from the darkness, his anxiety melted away.

The first chord sounded on the piano, followed by a walking bass and light drum accompaniment. Sidney did not think he had ever been so exhilarated. Gloria smiled at the audience, shook her body to the rhythm, and began to sing 'All of Me'.

She stood at a microphone, only yards in front of him. Her white satin dress accentuated her dark skin and she wore ribbons in her hair. Her voice was like honey, like molasses, like Guinness, like whisky, like wine. She stretched out the vowels of the lyrics, each one a different piece of elastic, and sang little pieces of scat in between the lines, so that it sounded as if she was singing in a language Sidney had never heard before. She was unpredictable, flirtatious, sensual and sad. She sang 'That Ole Devil Called Love', 'T'Aint Nobody's Business if I Do', 'You're My Thrill', and the daring number: 'Judge, Judge, Lordy Mr Judge, Send Me to th'Electric Chair.'

Inspector Keating leaned over. 'She's quite a girl.'

Sidney thought that this, truly, was heaven. Gloria then sang a song that she said she had composed when the band was on tour in Paris. It was after the explosions at Bikini Atoll in March and she had been thinking about the atomic bomb.

> 'Four minutes
> Just four minutes to Midnight
> Four minutes
> I just want four more minutes with you
> 'If the world ends
> Then the world ends
> But all I need
> Is those four minutes
> With you . . .'

Gloria hummed the next verse and then introduced her band as they took it in turns to play a series of riffs: Jay Jay Lion on piano, Tony Sanders on drums and Milo Masters on bass. Even though he was, he knew, in London, Sidney tried to imagine he was in uptown Harlem, hanging around at the bar with a load of musicians until the last song was sung and the last toot was tooted.

'Hit it, Tiger Tony,' cried Gloria and there then came the moment that always let the side down: the drum solo. Why were jazz fans so partial to this? Sidney wondered. It was like a sneeze, he decided. You could always tell it was coming but you couldn't do anything to stop it.

Tony Sanders did his best but it was still a drum solo. The only bonus was that Gloria Dee wandered out into the audience, singing scat, standing next to Sidney's table, nodding her approval at her drummer's industrial enthusiasm.

Sidney was so excited when he realised that Gloria was close that he dared not look. He only needed to know that she was near. The mingled scent of sweat, gardenia and the heady tuberose of her perfume filled his nostrils. Sidney now knew what the word 'intoxicated' meant. He wanted this moment, with whom he now thought to be one of the greatest jazz singers in the world by his side, to last for ever. This was what it meant to be alive, Sidney decided, in *this* place, at *this* time and listening to *this* music.

Then everything changed.

A girl screamed, her voice piercing the treble line of the music. A man shouted for help. There was a crush for the doors. The house lights came on. The drum solo stopped.

Phil Johnson barged through the crowds to the back of the club. 'What's going on?' he asked.

His daughter, Claudette, was lying motionless on the floor outside the Ladies.

'What happened? Somebody tell me what's going on?'

A frightened girl backed against the wall. 'I just found her.'

'Did you see her fall?'

'I don't know what happened.'

Phil knelt down beside his daughter. 'Fetch Amy,' he shouted. 'Bring some water. She's out cold.' He put his arm under his daughter's head and tried to lift her up. Then he noticed the marks on her neck. 'Bloody hell, what's this? Claudie, wake up; wake up, I say.'

There was no waking her.

She appeared to have been strangled.

Phil Johnson was talking to his daughter. 'Who's done this? What's happened? My little girl, my poor little girl, what have they done to you, Claudie? Get up . . . come on darling . . . get up. Is there a doctor here?' Then he shouted out. 'Is anyone a doctor?'

Keating was already on the case. 'Get me the telephone,' he said. 'Call an ambulance. Then Scotland Yard. No one must leave.'

Most of the customers stood up from the tables and crowded around to see what had happened. The barman and doormen tried to persuade them back to their places while keeping an eye on the exit.

There was nothing for them to go back for: no music, no drink, no conversation. The house lights were on: the late-night atmosphere had evaporated.

'Oh no,' said Sidney, 'Oh no, oh no, oh no.' He looked down at the girl's neck and could already see the bruising. There were fingernail marks under the left angle of the jaw, crescent-shaped abrasions on the skin. He wondered who on earth could have done such a thing. 'Money in dark corners,' Claudie had said to him. What had she meant by that?

A queue formed for the telephone. People could already tell that they were in for a long night. Gloria Dee was poured another drink. 'The poor baby. What'd she got mixed up in? It don't make no sense.'

Sidney wondered whether he would have been more alert if she had not been singing so close to them. Both he and Keating might have seen something, intercepted somebody or been able to avert disaster. But Gloria *had* been standing next to them. And now Claudette was dead. The murder had probably taken less time than it did to smoke one of her cigarettes.

Half an hour later Inspector Williams arrived with men from Scotland Yard. He was a big, burly man who looked like a rugby player. He made straight for the manager.

'I hear there's been trouble, Johnson.'

'It's my daughter. Some bastard's got to her.'

'Keep everyone inside. Cover the exits.'

Keating was by the body.

'Who are you?' Williams asked.

'Inspector George Keating. Cambridge police. I was in the audience at the time.'

'On duty?'

'Incognito.'

'See anything?'

'Nothing conclusive.'

'Everyone still here?'

'There's an exit by the bar that we secured. The fire exit is behind the stage. Apart from that there's a small window in the toilet but no one could get through that. It's just as well there wasn't a fire.'

'They should close this place down. So, as far as you know, the murderer is still in the building?'

'He is.'

'He?'

'Or she.'

'I can count on your assistance?'

'Of course. My friend Canon Sidney Chambers may also be of service.'

'I think this is best left to the professionals, don't you?'

Sidney took a step back as Williams continued. 'I can't imagine a clergyman being good for anything except this poor girl's funeral.'

'You'd be surprised,' Keating intervened.

Williams was keen to press on. 'When do you think the crime took place?'

'We think it must have been during the drum solo. The noise proved a distraction . . .'

'In my experience that's when most people head for the Gents.'

'This audience clearly wanted to stay.'

'Apart from the murderer. There are some familiar enough faces in the crowd. I've spent half my life locking these people up and out they come like cockroaches.'

Gloria Dee walked up and asked. 'Have you found the torpedo?'

'The what?'

'The hit man.'

'We've only just arrived.'

'How long are we gonna have to hang around?'

'All night, madam,' Inspector Williams replied.

'I'm used to late, and I'm real sorry for the girl. Sorrier than I can say. But if you've got questions can you ask us first? We have to play tomorrow.'

'I'm not so sure about that, madam. We may have to close this place down for a few days.'

'Then how am I supposed to live? They don't pay if we don't play.'

Williams had no time for the questions of other people. 'This is a murder investigation. We can start our inquiries with you and let you go home. Clearly you are some kind of performer . . .'

'Let me straighten your wig right off. I'm not "some kind". I'm Gloria Dee.'

'I don't care who you are. I must follow procedure. We have, at the very least, to get the names and addresses of every person here and establish where they were at the time of the murder. I hear that you were in the audience.'

'I was hitting all sixes, scattin' away as the boys were playin'. Everyone was havin' a good time. Then it all went to hell. No matter how many times this kinda thing happens, it still gets to you.'

'You mean this has occurred before?' Sidney asked. He knew that jazz and violence shared a mutual history. He remembered reading about the stabbing of the bandleader James Reese Europe, and of Chano Pozo, the percussionist killed in a bar-room brawl.

'We're jazz people. There's nothin' I aint seen.'

'Then perhaps you can help?' Keating asked.

'I don't know nothin' 'bout nothin'. I'm just sore the baby got herself killed.'

'Can you think why?' Inspector Williams continued.

'Why you askin' me? You're the police.'

'I'm interested in your opinion.'

Gloria sighed. 'If a broad moves in a world of men and darkness she has to watch out. She can't trust no cat. Maybe the baby turned a man down and he didn't take it good, or she saw somethin' she shouldn't have. Perhaps her Daddy was up to somethin'. It's got to be love or money. Those things go together the whole damn time.'

Sidney spoke in the silence. 'I can't understand how something so violent could happen to a girl like her . . .'

'I'm not sayin' it's her fault . . .'

The inspector returned to his questions. 'Whom did you come with tonight?'

'Just the band. Tony on skins, Milo on bass, Jay Jay on piano.'

'Anyone else?'

'There's Liza, Tony's girlfriend. She's around somewhere, and Justin, our driver. He's a dewdropper.'

Williams was not interested in finding out that a dewdropper was a man who stayed up all night. 'Are they still here?'

'I hope so. I need to get back to the hotel.'

'Where are you from?'

'I've been around. New Orleans. New York City.'

'When are you going back?'

'In a few weeks. I hope you're not wantin' me to stay. I have dates at Minton's.'

'Minton's?' Williams asked.

Sidney explained. 'It's a jazz club in New York.'

Gloria Dee smiled. 'You been?'

'Alas, no.'

The singer looked him up and down. 'You plain clothes?'

'No, not at all. I'm a clergyman.'

'A preacher-man? What you doin' here?'

'I'm Canon Sidney Chambers.'

'As in Cannonball Adderley?'

230

'I don't think so.'

'He's a sax player. Eats like a horse. What you drinkin'?'

'I don't think I can. But I'm sure that in your case . . .'

'If I'm havin' to wait I'm sure going to drink.' Gloria turned and walked towards the bar. 'Give me three shots of bourbon straight,' she asked.

Sidney could see Phil Johnson in the distance. He had not moved for a long time. He looked like a man who was stuck in a dream of falling from a high building; someone who knew that he would go on falling for the rest of his life, down towards a ground that was rising to meet him but would never arrive: eternal vertigo.

Already Sidney knew that when, in the future, people asked him about his children or talked about their own, Phil would have to decide how much to tell them or to remain silent; for if he spoke and told them his story no one who had not experienced anything similar would know what to say. It would be impossible for them to compare any grief of their own with his.

He heard Inspector Keating's voice. 'You can go home, you know.'

'Are you staying?'

'I have to, but you don't. I can vouch for you.'

'I think the last train has probably gone.'

'Let's have a look round.'

They parted the black drapes at the back of the stage and found themselves in the clutter of the green room. It was a mess of instrument cases, scattered music stands and empty bottles of booze. A hat stand held a couple of trilbies and a few raincoats, and one of Gloria Dee's red satin dresses fell from a hanger that had been attached to a nail in the wall. The place smelled of sweat, cigarettes and alcohol. Billboards of previous concerts, featuring Jimmy Deuchar, Ronnie Scott and Kenny Baker, were peeling from the walls. Justin, Gloria Dee's driver, was doing a crossword. Liza was pouring herself some rum. 'I'm just having a teensy weenie pick-me-up.' She giggled. 'Now I'm picking up the pick-me-up.'

Sidney could tell that she was intoxicated. 'I need to ask where you were during the concert.'

'Here,' Justin replied.

'All the time?'

Justin set his crossword aside. 'Sometimes we stand in the wings. For the main numbers.'

'You never watch from the front?' Sidney asked.

Liza answered for them both. 'They send for things all the time: water, towels, drink. It's quicker if we're here.'

'And you were backstage during the drum solo?'

'We watched that from the wings. Tony's my boyfriend. The drumming is the best bit.'

'Don't tell Miss Dee that,' Justin added.

'You'll be driving them back to the hotel?' Sidney asked.

'That's what I've been told to do.'

Inspector Keating stepped in. 'So we'll know where to find you if we have any further questions?'

'I live in Earls Court,' Justin replied. 'You can have my address. But, for the moment, I go where Miss Dee goes and I do what Miss Dee says.'

'I hope she pays you well . . .'

Liza sniggered and waited for Justin to answer. 'She pays. It's not always about the money . . .'

Sidney accompanied the inspector back on to the stage, where Phil 'the Cat' was sitting on the piano stool. His body was slumped, as if half the bones in his body had been removed. An abandoned roll-up rested between his fingers.

'Can you think of anyone who would hold anything against your daughter?' the inspector asked. 'Anyone with a grudge?'

'She's a beautiful girl. All I've got. She's never done anything wrong. None of the boys would touch her.'

'Was there anything your daughter could have seen?' Sidney asked.

'You mean a witness to something? It's possible.'

'Was your daughter sweet on anyone?' Sidney asked.

'She's too young for any of that.'

Sidney noticed that Phil referred to his daughter in the present tense.

Inspector Williams continued. 'So you can't think of anyone who would want to do her any harm?'

'No one. I swear to God, Inspector – and in front of this clergyman. Everyone loves my girl. I don't know what to do. I don't know what to say.'

Sidney rested his hand on Phil's shoulder. 'I will pray for her.'

'She was an angel,' Claudette's father replied.

Sidney timed the journey from the stage to the Ladies and diagonally across the room. Even with the crowded tables it would have taken little more than a minute to cross. He tried to think how a murderer could have struck so quickly and powerfully and without being seen. It seemed impossible, and yet it had happened. He watched as two ambulance men took Claudette's body away. There was no beauty or stillness in her death, only absence.

He returned to where he had been sitting and waited as the members of the audience gave their details and statements. Then he put his head in his hands.

Where was God now? he asked himself. Where had He been on the battlefields of Normandy, in the Blitz over London and in the bombed cities of Europe? How could a loving God permit such monumental suffering and what purpose did it serve? And, in contrast with such a widespread human catastrophe, how could God also allow something so small in scale and yet so intimately brutal as the murder of this single girl on this particular night? What could anyone have had against her to provoke such violence? How could there be any reason or justification for her death?

The two friends took the first morning train back to Cambridge. It was already light when they arrived and Sidney had only a few hours before early morning Communion. He would wash and shave and then try to catch some sleep in the afternoon. There was no time to go to bed.

He took Dickens out for his favourite walk across the Meadows but, despite the stillness of the river and the beauty of the light amidst the willows, Sidney's mood could not lift. He was haunted by the murder and what he might have done to prevent it.

He walked across the graveyard filled with trees of yew, holm oak and cherry, and stopped before a broken column: the grave of a twenty-six-year-old man whose life had been cut short in 1843. He passed the memorial for the twenty-five soldiers from Grantchester who had died in the two wars:

They shall grow not old
As we that are left grow old . . .

Inside the church, he began to pray for the soul of Claudie Johnson and for the sorrows of the world. Today, he decided, he would visit the sick of the parish: Beryl Cooper, who had acute arthritis; Harold Streat, the funeral director, whose elderly father was suffering from dementia; Brenda Hardy, the postman's wife, who had breast cancer. He had to stay with each one for as long as possible, providing unhurried comfort, calm and companionship. It was the least he could do, and every time he did so, he realised that the sick and the dying could teach him more than he could ever learn amidst the hurly burly of the everyday. The elderly and the sick had a different view of the world; they were already more than halfway on their journey towards the invisible realm where, it had been promised, all things shall be made known.

That afternoon, Sidney's sister Jennifer telephoned to say that the Johnson family were inconsolable. There was nothing she could do or say that might comfort them. All she could do was offer practical help. Could she therefore ask for her brother's advice regarding Claudette's funeral arrangements? There was going to be a post-mortem, and then a service in a London crematorium but, as not one of the Johnson family was a church-goer, perhaps Sidney could say a few words at the service?

'I'm sure their vicar will be able to do that, Jennifer.'

'They don't have a vicar.'

'Everyone has a vicar. Whether people choose to use him or not is another matter.'

'But they like you, Sidney.'

'Do you know what parish they are in?'

'Somewhere in Brixton, I think. But Johnny has asked for you. They trust you.'

'I'll see what I can do.'

'Johnny's father is so upset that he won't speak.'

'It will take a long time.'

'I can't believe anyone could have done such a thing, Sidney. Claudie was going to be a little sister to me.'

'So it's serious with Johnny?'

'We can't think about ourselves at the moment.'

Sidney tried to imagine what it might be like to lose a sister. It was almost unthinkable. There was so much that he felt that he still had to share with Jennifer that to lose her so suddenly, as Johnny had lost Claudette, without any farewell, would make him regret all the times in his life that he had taken her for granted or been too preoccupied to see her.

He resolved, then and there, and even as Jennifer was speaking, to spend more time with her, to cherish her presence and to be a better brother.

'Do not think you have always to say the right thing,' he began. 'It does not have to be meaningful. It's all right to be silent. All you can do is be alongside them.'

'That's what I am doing.'

'Nothing can be hurried. Grief has to take its time.'

For a moment Sidney worried that his sister was still on the line. Then she spoke. 'There's something else.'

'And what is that?'

'Claudie had a boyfriend.'

'Did her father know?'

'It was a secret. I don't think that anyone knew. She was

always her Daddy's little girl. But the point is that they had broken it off.'

'And so?'

'Sam was in the club with some friends on the night of her death. Now he's terrified of anyone finding out that he was ever her boyfriend.'

'The police have questioned him?'

'Of course.'

'And he gave nothing away?'

'He doesn't think so, but it's not only the police he's worried about. It's the Johnson family. I'm sure they wouldn't do anything but his father does have some nasty friends. They might put two and two together and make five.'

'You mean they might think that he killed her?'

'Exactly. And then take the law into their own hands. They don't trust the police. I know that much. Will you speak to him, Sidney?'

'Me?'

'Who else can he talk to? You are used to sharing confidences and you know how the police work.'

Sidney knew that he should help his sister but he did not want to become personally involved any more than he was already. 'I do have my work to do here.'

'Sam is frightened. Please will you see him? He's willing to come to Grantchester. He'll tell you everything.'

'It's not the type of thing I do, Jenny. I'm not sure anything I say will be of any benefit.'

'But he needs help. That's what you offer, isn't it? And he's a good boy. I know they loved each other but Sam was scared of her family. I think something may have happened that caused it all to end but neither of them would tell me. And now it's too late. Please will you see him, Sidney, as a favour to me?'

'Very well,' Sidney replied. He could hardly refuse his own sister. 'But I can't promise anything.'

'All I ask is that you see him.'

A few days later, a shy-looking boy in a dark suit and a college tie was waiting to speak to Sidney after the Sunday morning Communion service. He made a tentative approach, as if his shoes were too tight for him. 'I'm Sam Morris,' he said.

A wood pigeon flew out of the trees. Sidney steeled himself for another difficult confrontation. 'I've been expecting you, Sam. I normally take my dog for a walk after the service. Perhaps you would like to join us?'

'If it's not any trouble.'

They returned to the vicarage, put Dickens on his lead and set off for the Meadows. On the way Sidney expressed his condolences and established that he had understood the facts his sister had conveyed. He also needed to make clear that anything Sam said was, of course, in confidence, but also that his influence in the current situation was extremely limited. There was only so much he could do; but if Sam wanted someone with whom he could share any anxiety and who would not rush to judge him, then Sidney hoped he could be of assistance.

'Some friends were going to the club and asked if I wanted to come along. They didn't know about Claudette and I wasn't sure she'd be there. She doesn't work every night and I hadn't seen her since Christmas.'

'And did you speak to her at all?'

'I said "Hello" and she looked a bit embarrassed.'

'Did any of your friends notice her discomfort?'

'I don't think so. My friend Max was quite keen on her. But she couldn't stop at any table for long. She had her job to do.'

'And were you hoping to see her alone?'

'She said if I waited until the end then perhaps we could talk but I knew she didn't want us to be seen together. Her father is very protective.'

'I've noticed.'

They had reached the Meadows, and Sidney set Dickens free to explore pastures both new and familiar. 'How long were you together?' he asked.

'About six months. We used to walk by the Thames and hold hands. But then a strange thing happened. I was going home one night and a man started walking alongside me. I thought he wanted to get past so I slowed down but then he slowed down too. I picked up the pace and he did the same. He didn't say anything. He just kept matching my footsteps. Eventually I stopped. I asked what he wanted and he just told me to stay away from Claudie if I knew what was good for me.'

'Could you describe this man?'

'I knew him. He was a friend of her father's. He's called Tommy Jackson. He runs a garage in Tooting.'

'And then he just walked away?'

'He called it a "friendly warning" but I didn't know what to think. I spoke to Claudette and she told me not to worry. Tommy would never do anything. He was probably just having a laugh but it didn't feel like that to me. And then, after that, things never quite felt the same. I was worried every time I saw her.'

'She couldn't put your mind at rest?'

'We came from different backgrounds. I was at university. I couldn't imagine bringing her home to meet my parents. But she was beautiful and she had such life in her. I didn't know what to think or do, but in the end I told her I just couldn't see her any more.'

'What did she say?'

'She thought I was a coward. How did I know, she asked, if she hadn't sent Tommy Jackson herself as a test to see how much I loved her? I told her that if she had done that, it was a mean trick. We argued. Then it was over.'

'And yet you went to the club on the night she died. Why did you do that?'

'I missed her. And I wanted to see if she had found anyone else.'

'Have you?'

'Of course not.'

'So you wanted her back?'

'I wanted to see her. That was as far as I had thought. If we spoke then I hoped to take it from there. I didn't have a proper plan, and it was so crowded I could never get near her. There was no time.'

Sidney realised that Sam Morris was finding it difficult to express himself clearly and decided to ask a few direct questions in order to ascertain exactly what had happened. 'Did you go to the Gents at all?' he asked.

'Of course I did. It was a long night.'

'When?'

'I'm not sure. About half an hour before she was discovered. I went at the same time as my friend Max. There were witnesses if that's what you are worried about.'

'I understand. When you were being questioned did you admit that you knew Claudette?'

'No.'

'You lied?'

'I was frightened.'

'I understand, Sam, but if your relationship does come to light then this will not help your cause.'

'No one will seriously think I was involved, will they?'

'At some stage the police will need to know all the facts. I don't want to alarm you unduly but a secret, whatever the context, is always problematic. If you reveal it, then at least you have control over how it is told and you can explain it in your own terms. If it is discovered, however, then you cannot predict when that will happen or how people might interpret it. It's a matter of timing. If you go to the police, even now, and tell them what happened then you will have control over the information. If you do not . . .'

'I don't think I can do that.'

'If Tommy Jackson knew that you were seeing Claudette then I am afraid that it will come to light. There is no escaping this, Sam.'

'I have done nothing wrong.'

'I know it doesn't sound serious in comparison with murder but, as a matter of fact, you have. You have told a direct lie to the police. They don't take kindly to that sort of thing. Of course you could just carry on and hope that no one finds out.'

'Do you think that's likely?'

'It's possible. But then, once again, if you hope to conceal something, you have no control over the release of information, and so you live in a state of anxiety.'

'Can you help me?'

'I can have a word with Inspector Keating here in Cambridge if you like. He was there on the night and he's a good man. But the information would be far better coming from you directly.'

'I know.'

'Where are you living at the moment?'

'In London University halls.'

'Is it easy to find you?'

'Of course.'

'I need you to tell me if anything unusual happens or if you receive any more warnings. It would be easier if you had told the police at the time of Tommy Jackson's warning.'

'The Johnson family are not very keen on the police, as you can imagine. To go to them would be the worst thing I could have done. Claudette told me that I just had to wait until she was eighteen and then we could do what we liked. It was only going to be another six months but I didn't believe her. I thought there would always be pressure from her father and his friends.'

Sidney was thinking about the events of 7 May. 'I still don't understand why you went to the club that night. You could have sent her a message and arranged to meet elsewhere. You must have known her father and all his friends would be there.'

'I didn't think it through. I was with my friends. I thought it would be all right, and I wanted to see Claudette. But, of course, as soon as I arrived I knew it was a mistake. She asked me what on earth I was doing there.'

'I thought she just said "Hello".'

'No. I bumped into her again a bit later.'

'And when was that?'

'When I was on the way back from the Gents.'

Sidney thought it was incredible that this boy could neither tell his story clearly nor realise the potential trouble that he might be in. 'Did anyone see you talking together?'

'I don't know. I was only looking at Claudette. The barman called her over.'

'So he must have seen you?'

'I suppose so.'

Sidney was momentarily infuriated. There was no *suppose* about it. How could this boy be so hapless?

'I'm sorry, Canon Chambers, I'm scared. I am just a student who wants to become a doctor. I never intended to get mixed up in all this.'

'I can see that.'

Sidney was exasperated. How could Sam Morris be so aware of the trouble that he might be in but remain so ignorant of the implications of his behaviour? What had he been thinking in going to the club that night, seeing Claudette once more and then lying to the police?

As a priest Sidney's first instinct was to listen hard and trust what he had been told, but after they had said their goodbyes and Sam had left, a number of anxieties remained. Had the boy given a clear account of everything that had happened or was he still hiding information? Sidney sensed that Sam was trustworthy and hardly likely to be responsible for Claudette's death, but he had also been extraordinarily naive. He might have charm and intelligence, but he was undoubtedly weak, and he had given up on love too easily. Sidney puzzled over whether he might have done things differently if he had been the same age, and what he could do to help a boy who had got himself into such a mess.

When informed of the conversation with Sam at their regular Thursday night session of backgammon in The Eagle, Inspector Keating responded with a burst of anger Sidney had never seen before. 'Tell that bloody boy to come and see me and make a statement. We can't have him blabbering away to a clergyman even if it's you. There's a procedure to these matters.'

'I only thought it might be helpful.'

'Of course it's not helpful. It's bloody unhelpful. Tommy Jackson was in the jazz club with all his mates. He was sitting at a table by the front of the stage for the entire bloody drum solo. He couldn't have done it.'

'I'm not saying he did.'

'None of them could, as far as I can tell. For all I know this could be a double-bluff – your boy getting his story in early, shifting the blame elsewhere before we get to him; a pre-emptive strike. Does he have an alibi?'

'Not really.'

'What do you mean "not really". Honestly, Sidney . . .'

'And he went to the Gents about half an hour before the murder.'

'So he could have done it?'

'Half an hour before, Geordie.'

'He could have murdered the girl then and moved the body later.'

'But why would he tell me all this?'

'I've said: a double-bluff.'

'He's not that kind of boy.'

'What kind of boy is he, then?'

'I meant that he doesn't seem the murdering type.'

'No one seems the murdering type. That's the whole point, Sidney. If the murdering type made himself known to us then crimes would be solved a hell of a lot quicker.'

The inspector took another sip of his pint. Their game of backgammon had been abandoned. 'Have you got any other ideas? Williams doesn't seem to be getting very far and if I tell him anything about Sam Morris he'll pull him in.'

Sidney wondered whether to offer his friend another drink. This meeting was not going as well as he had hoped. In fact he was troubled by Inspector Keating's aggression. 'I'd rather you didn't.'

'I'll have to. I can't withhold evidence.'

Sidney was alarmed and disappointed. This was surely a breach of trust. 'I told you about Sam in confidence.'

'I know that, and I won't tell Williams right away. But if, in the course of the investigation I am asked, then I cannot tell a lie. I hope you understand that, Sidney.'

'Not entirely.'

'You should have anticipated this. You know me well enough.'

'I am not sure I do.'

'Oh, for goodness' sake. Would you like another drink?'

'I am not sure we have time.'

'I'll get you a swift half.' The inspector signalled to the barman. 'The thing is, that, in future, you should probably think a little bit more about exactly what you want to tell me. Priests and doctors believe in the ethics of confidentiality. I, unfortunately, do not. So I think, at the very least, I will have to suggest your boy is questioned again, if only, perhaps, for his own protection.'

'What do you mean?'

'If he committed the crime then we will have our man. It probably won't take much to get him to confess.'

'But he didn't do it.'

'You say so.' Keating picked up the two half-pints from the bar and then continued. 'However, if the boy is innocent then whoever killed Claudette may be out to get him as well.'

'Unless he is trying to implicate Sam.'

'That is a possibility. But if Sam is in custody then at least he will be safe.'

'You are suggesting he is arrested?'

'I am suggesting he is questioned. In my experience a clandestine relationship is never a secret. There are always people who know. We just need more information: about Sam Morris, Claudette, her father and his associates.'

Sidney still could not understand the need to concentrate on a boy who was surely innocent; unless, of course he had misread him completely. 'If that boy is arrested because of what I have said my sister will be furious.'

'I think there are more important things than your sister's anger. Besides, if he is guilty, and he killed the girl out of jealousy, or because she wouldn't have him back, then the case is closed. Your sister can hardly complain and Williams might even thank you.'

'Sam Morris can't have done it.'

'He can, Sidney. You have to leave your feelings out of this.'

'I don't believe it.'

'Well, if you don't then we need to discover far more than we know already. That's where you can help.' The inspector finished his drink. 'As long as you don't mind acknowledging that we sometimes have to trample over people's feelings. We can't always behave in a Christian way, Sidney. You may find that this conflicts with your principles.'

'I will not let it do so. I will try and bring a moral purpose to any investigation.'

Inspector Keating stood up and put on his coat, signalling that their time together was at an end. 'I don't mind what you bring, Sidney, as long as it leads to a conviction. That's all I care about. I'll let you finish your drink.'

The half-pint the inspector had bought Sidney remained untouched. There was nothing left to say.

The following morning Sidney took an assembly at the local primary school and held a meeting to discuss plans for an elderly people's luncheon club. Although he undertook these tasks with his customary authority and charm, he did not feel that he was giving either of them his full attention. Behind the mask of priestly professionalism was a worried man. He felt that he had betrayed the trust of Sam Morris and that his friend Geordie Keating had ridden roughshod over his careful revelation of the facts.

The feeling of unease now crept into his work as a priest. He had lost confidence in his instinct and he was overwhelmed by the work he had neglected. Sidney had never been very good at differentiating between tasks that were urgent and those which were important, and often those tasks that seemed urgent, but were not important, took precedence over the duties that were important, but not urgent. As a result, the constant, serious business of being a priest was displaced by distraction. He needed time, space and silence in which to reflect on the things that mattered and the things that did not. It also did not help when Mrs Maguire kept interrupting him with news of Dickens's latest misdemeanours.

The two of them were, Sidney decided, mutually exclusive. In the kitchen Mrs Maguire would move Dickens's basket to wash the floor and attempt to mop the dog out of the way. Dickens would then dash round her back and give the ankle of his persecutor a playful nip. If successful, Sidney would then hear his housekeeper cry out: 'Rabies. He's given me rabies, Canon Chambers.'

'Dickens is a puppy, Mrs Maguire.'

'He's a dog. And a ruddy big one too. What are you feeding him?'

'Winalot.'

'I don't know how you can afford it.'

'It's not easy.'

Mrs Maguire gave him one of her looks. 'I should have a word with the butcher's if I were you, Canon Chambers. I am sure Hector can give you some scraps. Especially now meat's off ration.'

'Miss Kendall says he needs more than scraps.'

'Then why can't Miss Kendall pay? After all, she brought him here.'

'Amanda has other concerns.'

'Then lucky her.' Mrs Maguire began to walk up the stairs with a change of linen. 'I notice she hasn't paid a visit for a while.'

Sidney tried to defend his friend. 'She has her work at the National Gallery. She also has quite an active social life.'

His housekeeper was already on to the next task. Even so, Sidney distinctly thought he could hear her mutter, 'A bit too active if you ask me.'

Sidney sat at his desk and tried to get on with his paperwork but found it even harder to concentrate on his clerical duties than he had done before. He could not get excited either by the annual scouts trip to Scarborough or by the plans for the upcoming summer fête, and they had still not found a suitably famous person to open it. He wondered if he could ask Gloria Dee. That would certainly liven things up a bit.

He turned on the wireless and listened to the Light Programme, hoping that there might at least be some jazz to lighten his mood. He managed to find the Charlie Parker Quartet playing 'Moose the Mooche', but it made him feel uneasy. He knew that he was supposed to 'get with' this freer form of jazz and appreciate both its speed and artistry, but he could not find it relaxing. In fact, it made him rather tense. To make matters worse, Mrs Maguire was banging about upstairs, and Dickens was pawing at his shins, keen to get outside. Then the telephone rang.

It was Inspector Keating and he was in no mood for chitchat. 'I've been thinking,' he began. 'When are you next going to London?'

Sidney reached for his pocket diary. 'Tuesday, I think. There is a meeting of the Church Assembly.'

'The what?'

'Think of it as the Annual General Meeting of The Church of England.'

'Never mind that. I've had an idea. Have you got any time?'

'How long do you need?'

'I thought you could look into Phil Johnson's past: old cases, former crimes. We've got the details here, and I'm sending them round to you. They are as long as your arm but some of them are too sketchy. I was hoping you could do some digging around. There's a newspaper library in Colindale. We've got the dates of the trials. You just need to see how they were reported at the time and whether any of the victims said anything; who gave interviews to the press, that kind of thing.'

'You should get that new reporter from the local paper to do it.'

'Helena Randall? I wouldn't trust her as far as I could throw her. No, Sidney, it needs to be someone who is discreet, who can read between the lines and who knows about people. In short, Sidney, it needs to be you. Perhaps you could combine it with seeing Miss Kendall?'

'I'm not so sure about that.'

'Don't be daft. I've given you a perfect excuse. And Gloria Dee is still playing. Take Miss Kendall as your cover story. I'll even pay for the tickets. That lot are worth another look . . .'

'They certainly are.'

'Not for the music, Sidney. Because if Sam Morris didn't do it, as you have suggested, then they, like everyone else, are suspects. We're going to have to go back to the beginning and start all over again.'

'So you want me to look for links?'

'I do.'

'In that case, I'll need a list of the names of everyone who was in the room at the time.'

'I'm sending you that too. But don't let Williams catch you with it.'

'I don't have any intention of seeing him if I can help it.'

'Make sure everything goes through me, Sidney, because if you want to save that boy you had better start making some connections. Williams is seeing him today.'

'They've arrested him?'

'No, they are bringing him in for a few questions. It's routine at the moment but you know how these things can develop. So you should get a move on. Have a sniff around. Look like an ordinary member of the public and see what you can find out. I want your report first thing Wednesday morning. Leads, trails, anyone we should chase up or have followed. You know the kind of thing . . .'

'But Geordie . . .'

'No time to argue. See you Wednesday.'

Sidney sighed. He looked at the notes he had made for his sermon and realised that, although he had made a start, he had so much more to do. He had been called out into the wider world.

It was going to be a long way back to God.

The police records revealed that most of Phil Johnson's crimes had taken place in London: a jeweller's in Hatton Garden, an antique shop in Kensington, a flat in Harley Street, a retired ambassador's house in Mayfair. Johnson would generally access buildings via roofs, upper windows and skylights and sometimes, in the richer neighbourhoods, he even worked in a dinner suit so that he would not arouse suspicion on his departure. His two accomplices were a safe-cracker and a getaway driver, but he often acted alone and he had clearly managed to squirrel away thousands of pounds' worth of goods in the gaps between his prison sentences. He had gone straight either because he had become bored of prison or because he was no longer as agile as he once had been.

What these factual accounts needed was a bit of psychological background, and Sidney recognised that his task was to fill in the gaps with human detail. If Claudie Johnson's death was an act of revenge then Sidney needed to find out more about the victims of these crimes. He wondered how many of them were still alive, what kind of insurance they had taken out – could some of them have been inside jobs, perhaps? – and whether any of them had criminal records themselves. He was going to have to look for inconsistencies, coincidences, potential patterns and unusual details.

He met Amanda for an early lunch on the second floor of the J. Lyons Corner House on the Strand. Sidney had been looking forward to trying the self-service cafeteria, where he would place his tray on a moving conveyor belt and choose the items from the hot cabinets as they moved past, but Amanda instantly dismissed the idea. They were going to have the table d'hôte waitress service and that was that: farmhouse pie with parsnips in a cream sauce followed by either a sponge Neapolitan or a meringue *glace*.

Amanda had been appalled by the murder of Claudette Johnson but intrigued by her father's burglaries. 'Your man was a bit of a Raffles, I imagine. I wonder if he ever met Daphne Young?'

'It's possible. He certainly knew where the rich pickings lay. Some of his crimes were quite close to your parents' house.'

'Belgravia? I can imagine. Lots of antiques round there, and that's just the people.'

'Were any of your parents' friends ever burgled?'

'I should say so. One of them even went mad. A bit like Juliette Thompson, only worse.'

'What do you mean?'

'There was a woman. What was her name? Mrs Templeton, I think. It was after her husband had died. He knew my father, and the burglary took place during his funeral. Can you believe the nerve? Her husband had been an ambassador and so the service was announced in *The Times*. They might as well have added: "We will not be at home for several hours." The thieves just went in and took the lot.'

'*Templeton*, you say, Amanda? That was one of our man's jobs. What happened?'

'As I said, she went mad; she never recovered from the shock of the burglary. They were both gone within the year. Terrible really.' Amanda finished her sponge Neapolitan. 'What are you doing tomorrow?'

'I'm going to Colindale, to the newspaper library, to look through the old crime reports. Then I have to attend a meeting at the Church Assembly.'

'Sounds thrilling . . .'

'After that I'm going to hear Gloria Dee again. Perhaps you'd like to come?'

'Jazz is not really my thing, Sidney. You do realise that Rubinstein is playing Rachmaninov at the Festival Hall?'

'I'm sorry, Amanda.'

'Hang on, though. Wasn't Gloria Dee the singer who was performing when the poor girl was murdered?'

'That's what I've been telling you.'

'I don't suppose any of the band could have done it?'

'They were on stage at the time.'

'The perfect alibi. One of them could have had an accomplice.'

'Will you come?' Sidney asked. He was in no mood for further conjecture. 'It's in Soho, so not far. We can go to the bar and you can meet Gloria.'

'It would be interesting to see what she is like.'

'She is rather fabulous.'

'And she may even be a murderer. Where are you staying tonight?'

'A friend at the Abbey has agreed to put me up.'

'You could have kipped on our sofa.'

'I'm not much of a kipper, I'm afraid, Amanda.'

'No Sidney, you have more soul. Shall I pay the bill?'

'Absolutely not.'

'It's only seven and six. I know the clergy never have any money.'

Amanda had recently discovered that Sidney's annual stipend was £550. There had been an article in *The Times* about clergy salaries and she had asked Sidney if it was true. She was intrigued because her car had cost more than twice his annual income. 'Perhaps the police should start paying you as well?' she asked.

'There's no need for that.'

'Or maybe Miss Dee will sweep you off to America?'

'That is highly unlikely,' Sidney replied.

'But still possible?' Amanda teased. 'You can be such a dreamer. I think it's one of the things I like best about you. Anything can happen.'

'That is not always a good thing, of course.'

'But it does mean that life with you is never dull.'

The next day's visit to the newspaper library took up far more time than Sidney had anticipated. There were reports of some of the original burglaries that Phil the Cat had committed but little information that was not in the police files. Sidney found himself looking for reviews of jazz concerts instead.

He was too excited about the evening trip to Soho to concentrate on much else. He decided to wear his double-breasted suit and this time his Homburg hat, which even attracted the approval of passers-by.

'Hey man, nice lid.'

A thin, blonde woman in a short skirt and a low-cut top was standing in a doorway. 'Need a girl?' she asked.

'Not at the moment,' Sidney replied. 'But thank you for offering.'

He met Amanda at The Moka in Frith Street and then proceeded down a series of dingy alleys where several couples were taking advantage of the darkness to get to know each other better. Sidney knew that Amanda was unused to these surroundings but decided that it was good for her to experience them. When they arrived at the club he ordered her a Martini and found a table to the side of the stage.

'What time do they come on?' Amanda asked.

'Miss Dee likes it late.'

'And how is your investigation?'

'Slow,' Sidney replied.

'The police not much help?'

'They're doing their best but there were so many people in the club. It could have been almost anyone.'

'Do you think it was a *crime passionnel*?'

Sidney felt a presence by his side. 'You talkin' about passion?'

It was Gloria Dee. She was wearing a golden sheath dress. It looked as if honey had been poured over her body and left to set.

Sidney had the look of a schoolboy who had never seen a woman in his life before. 'You remember me?' he asked.

'Sure thing, I remember you, sweetheart. Every time you show up someone gets killed. Who's your baby?'

'This is my friend, Miss Kendall.'

'Pleased to meet you, friend.' Gloria turned back to Sidney. 'You found the cat who killed that girl?'

'I'm afraid not.'

'Better get a wiggle on. Man could've moved miles by now.'

'Or woman of course,' Sidney replied.

'Tell it to Sweeney. I don't think a woman did that. She's more likely to use a stiletto. Stranglin's hard work.'

'I wouldn't know about that.'

'You never killed a chick?' She looked at Sidney's companion. 'I mean the *animal* variety . . .'

'Wouldn't you leave that sort of thing to your husband?' Amanda asked.

'Aint got no husband. You don't keep the carton once you've smoked the cigarette. What you preachin', Sidney?'

'The usual.'

'And what you drinkin'?'

'Whisky.'

'Are you going to fix me one?'

'Whatever you like'.

'I'll take a triple shot and have it on stage.' Gloria signalled to the barman. He had clearly been briefed to keep an eye on her. 'I've got to get myself ready. You're one lucky woman, Miss Kendall. Don't know if I've ever seen an English cat so hip to the jive as your man.'

The lights dimmed, a spotlight moved on to the drums, followed by the bass and then the piano. Sidney realised that Gloria was about to sing one of his favourite songs: 'Careless Love'. He only hoped Amanda would appreciate it.

Almost all of Gloria's songs were about love, disaster and recovery. 'I Aint Got Nobody', 'I'm Wild about That Thing', and 'Gimme a Pigfoot', but they were brightened by one of the most unexpected moments in Sidney's life. Gloria dedicated a song to him.

'When you hear that the preachin' has begin

Bend down low to drive away your sin

When you get religion

You'll want to shout and sing

There'll be a hot time in the old town tonight'

Amanda was not amused. 'How much more of this do we have to up with?' she asked.

'It's a rare treat,' Sidney replied. 'I'm enjoying it.'

Halfway through the song Sidney realised that Gloria was teasing him.

'Please, oh please, oh, do not let me fall,

You're all mine and I love you best of all,

And you must be my man, or I'll have no man at all,

There'll be a hot time in the old town tonight!'

The song came to an end, Gloria smiled, gave a little bow and blew him a kiss.

'That was hardly necessary,' Amanda said.

'She doesn't mean it.'

Gloria Dee thanked the audience for coming. 'Before we take a break, I'd like to introduce the band . . .' she began, and then paused to take a large glass of water and a shot of bourbon.

Sidney whispered to Amanda. 'I need to see what happens in the drum solo; if people leave. It may give me a clue. I think this is the end of the first set.'

'The first set. You mean there's more?'

The band struck up a version of 'Embraceable You' and the introductions were made at the end of each solo. As soon as Tony Sanders's moment on the drums came some of the more experienced punters used his improvisation as an early opportunity to order a sharpener at the bar or get to the toilets.

Sidney realised how easy it would be for a criminal to take advantage of the situation but also how risky. There would only be a very short time, and there was the constant danger of being discovered.

When the first half came to an end a waitress approached the table to ask if they wanted to order food. Amanda said that if they weren't leaving she would like fried chicken with some white wine. As Sidney looked up, a boy and a girl pushed past to go to the bar. He ordered another beer and asked for a steak. When the couple returned he remembered that they were Liza Richardson and Justin the driver. But what were they doing out front? They had told him that they always remained backstage.

'Hello again,' he called out.

'Oh,' said Liza. 'It's you. We were just fetching drinks.'

'I didn't expect to see you amongst the audience.'

'Sometimes we need emergency supplies.'

Sidney looked at the drinks and was surprised to see a key on the tray. He wondered what it could be for. 'This is my friend Amanda . . .' he told them.

Amanda looked at Justin. 'Do I know you?' she asked.

'I don't think so.'

'Was it at the Blakeleys?'

Justin seemed keen to get backstage as the number was about to finish. Perhaps he was scared of his employer. 'I don't know any Blakeleys, I'm afraid.'

'What's your surname?'

'Wild.'

Amanda didn't give up. 'I'm sure we've met. I never forget a face.'

'No, I don't think so,' Justin replied. 'I would definitely have remembered you. But if you'll excuse me I have Miss Dee to attend to.'

After he had gone Amanda was puzzled. 'That was very odd. As soon as he saw me he looked frightened.'

'You do have that effect on some people.'

'No, Sidney, this was different. It was as if he thought I was some kind of ghost . . .'

'Well, I'm sure he'll get over it.'

'And quicker than you'll get over Miss Dee. That singer has quite turned your head.'

'Nonsense.'

'She has.'

'She has not.'

'Then you won't mind if we leave?'

'So soon?'

'It's late, Sidney. I have to be at work at nine in the morning. We can't all live the life of a clergyman.'

'It has its pressures.'

'Only because you create most of them. The next concert we go to will have to be at the Festival Hall. The Düsseldorf Symphony Orchestra are coming next month.'

Sidney sighed. As midnight chimed over Soho he realised that it was going to take a long time to convert Amanda to the wonders of jazz.

The day of Claudette's funeral was one of heat and impending storm. Sidney had been informed that there would be a procession from the Johnson household to the crematorium and was surprised to see not only the mourners waiting outside, but also a brass band and half the jazz community of London. As the white coffin emerged from the house, held by pallbearers who had taken off their hats, the band struck up the old spiritual 'Just a Closer Walk with Thee.'

Three men led from the front with snare drums followed by trombones, saxophone and tuba; then the clarinets, and trumpets, and a bass drummer bringing up the rear.

Sidney's brother Matt came over and spoke directly into Sidney's ear over the volume of the music. 'It's a jazz funeral, New Orleans style. We're all here. Three-line whip.'

'Whose idea was this?' Sidney asked.

'It was mine. We've even persuaded Gloria Dee to sing at the service.'

'That must have taken some doing.'

'I used charm. Apparently it runs in the family.'

Sidney felt suddenly nervous about his ability to say a few appropriate words at the ceremony. He was used to speaking at country funerals and in churches where the congregation were expecting the traditions of the Anglican Communion. A jazz funeral was altogether different.

He wondered what Martha Headley would make of all this. She was the Grantchester blacksmith's wife who sometimes helped out on the organ at funerals but was only confident of her ability to play two tunes, seeing the coffin into the church with Mendelssohn's 'Song without Words', and out with 'Jesu Joy of Man's Desiring'.

Phil Johnson, Johnny and Jennifer led the mourners. Behind them, three women were holding a large floral tribute that spelled out the name CLAUDETTE. As the procession made its way through the south London streets, passers-by took off their hats as a sign of respect to the dead, remembering those they had lost themselves.

Gloria Dee had been waiting in the crematorium. She stood next to a baby grand piano and sang 'Amazing Grace' as the coffin was brought in. She sang unaccompanied, with such poise and intensity that at one point Sidney thought he could hear the timbers in the roof vibrate in response to the force of her voice.

Once the congregation had settled, he read the opening prayer.

'Man that is born of a woman hath but a short time to live and is full of misery. He cometh up, and is cut down like a flower; he fleeth as it were a shadow, and never continueth in one stay.'

Jennifer sat between Johnny and his father, with Matt Chambers just behind her. Sidney found it disorientating to see his brother and sister as members of a different family. A few rows behind them he noticed the rest of Gloria Dee's Quartet: Jay Jay Lion, Milo Masters and Tony Sanders with his girlfriend Liza. Justin the driver sat behind them at the end of a row on his own.

After the prayers, the congregation gave a full rendition of 'Take My Hand, Precious Lord'. It felt a long way from the hymn singing of Grantchester.

Sidney climbed the three steps into the pulpit to give his address. He preached about the sin and darkness of the world and the need for light in that darkness. Claudie Johnson had been one such light.

'Amen,' a man called out.

Sidney told them how Claudette was a girl who carried her goodness into the lives of others; and that this was the task of all us, no matter how weak or strong our faith. We needed to try and leave a better world than the one into which we were born.

This was a moment for reflection, he said; for patience and silence and time. We must be ready not only to offer words of comfort but also to listen to words of grief. Not even the firmest faith was enough to insulate us from the pain of loss, or from the sense that, with the death of someone dear to us, our own life had lost its meaning. Time had to take its course, and in that time we should recognise that where there is sorrow there is holy ground.

Claudette was too soon returned to earth, he continued, but she would live on both as a memory and as an example to all who had known her. There is always a future for our deepest loves.

He ended by quoting Byron's poem 'To Thyrza':

'I know not if I could have borne
To see thy beauties fade;
The night that followed such a morn
Had worn a deeper shade:
Thy day without a cloud hath past,
And thou wert lovely to the last –
Extinguished, not decayed,
As stars that shoot along the sky
Shine brightest as they fall from high.'

There was a silence and then, after the final prayers, Gloria moved to stand by the piano. Jay Jay Lion accompanied her as the coffin disappeared behind the curtains.

She began to sing.

> 'Nobody knows the trouble I've seen
> Nobody knows but Jesus'

Sidney had never heard the song sung so slowly or with such intensity. There was a terrible truth in Gloria's singing that seemed to stretch back over a life. Every phrase was considered; each word could be taken out and understood on its own as well as within the unfolding story of the song. The pauses between the phrases were held longer than Sidney had ever imagined possible. The song defied time and place. It was a blazingly honest performance: a lament for a life and an emphatic statement of readiness for death.

When Gloria had finished, there was silence, shock, applause and then, finally, a loud whistle. The brass band was back and it struck up a boisterous rendition of 'When the Saints Go Marching In'. The sadness was over. The congregation was expected to clap and dance its way out of the building, to thank God for the joy of a life rather than the fact of a death.

Phil did not join in. There was going to be a wake, he told Sidney, in a nearby boozer, and then they were going to have a memorial concert in the club in a few weeks' time. All the jazz musicians in London were coming. 'Just as long as we find the bastard who did this.'

Johnny Johnson shook Sidney's hand and thanked him for the service. His sister kissed him. His brother offered to accompany him to the reception. 'You may feel a bit out of your depth,' he explained.

'I'll do what I can.'

'That was quite a change from the usual Church of England service.'

'Everything about today has been disorientating, Matt. I sometimes feel that I am living in a different world.'

'I don't think that's unusual,' his brother replied. 'Isn't that your job?'

'It's not what I was expecting.'

'You did well. It was a fitting tribute. Everyone loved Claudie.'

'The whole thing is a mystery, Matt. Who do you think could have done such a thing?'

'Jenny told you about Sam?'

'You knew?'

'I saw them together once. I didn't like to say anything. But it all looked pretty innocent. And I can't believe he was capable of violence.'

'Neither can I. But we have to find someone who was.'

'I hope you're not going to get dragged into the whole investigation.'

'I've done a bit of digging around but I haven't really found anything. And I'm worried about Jennifer.'

'You don't think she's in any danger?'

'No, it's not that. I rather like Johnny. I just don't want her to expect too much. I'm not sure how well she knows him.'

'It's early days. You can't expect everything to happen at once. But they're a decent family once you get over the fact of her father's past.'

'He's done his time.'

'Unless, of course . . .' Matt stopped in the street. 'Someone thinks he hasn't.'

'I am afraid we have thought of that.'

'A vendetta?'

'If you think Claudette was not murdered by a lover or because she was a witness to a crime then it's one of the few explanations left.' Sidney replied. 'But it seems such a warped way of thinking.'

'But that is how anyone investigating the crime has to think if they want to find out who did it.'

'I realise that it's necessary to get inside the mind of a murderer. However, it's not something I ever considered doing when I decided to become a priest.'

'You don't have to get involved, you know. The police are dealing with the case.'

'But they don't appear to be making much progress.'

'You think you can make a difference?'

'I have to offer to do what I can, Matt.'

'Even if it's not your job?'

'When I was ordained, I studied the ordinal. It told me what priests are called to do. "They are to resist evil, support the weak, defend the poor, and intercede for all in need." My job is to do the right thing.'

'Even it overturns your life?'

'Even so.'

On the train home Sidney thought over all that had happened. Perhaps his brother was right. There was only so much a priest could do. And he had begun to become embarrassed about his love of jazz. He had to admit that it was a bit of an affectation. He was an English parish priest who had been brought up in North London rather than the hot streets of Harlem. He was never going to be a hipster or a hepcat.

It was also becoming increasingly hard to convince himself that any of the work that he was doing for the police was of any benefit. He had found out about Phil 'the Cat' Johnson's previous crimes, but there was nothing concrete to link any of them to the death of his daughter. When he got back to Grantchester he would have to stop these activities and concentrate on his duties in the parish: chairing a meeting about the church maintenance fund – the winter heating bills had been enormous – discussing the forthcoming music for the choir, as well as organising the teams of volunteers to clean the church and do the flowers. He sometimes thought that being a vicar was a bit like being the managing director of a business in which no one was paid.

He also had to write his next sermon. Although he was tired after his funeral address he was pleased that it had gone well. Perhaps he could use that success to drive his thoughts forward to next Sunday. He would talk about love and time, he decided; human time and God's time; earthly love and divine love; the gulf between the transient and the constant.

The writing would require a great deal of concentration and Sidney was relieved to find a vacant compartment. The freedom from interruption was such an unexpected luxury that he imagined he was travelling in first class. That was what bishops did, he thought to himself, together with successful City types, Amanda Kendall and probably, Gloria Dee. They were not only seeking extra comfort by travelling in such seclusion, they were also desperate for a life without interruption. The main attraction in first class, he realised, was the avoidance of other people.

He began to make notes for his sermon but his thoughts on love and time were interrupted at Finsbury Park when Mike Standing boarded the train. A small, balding man with a prodigious appetite and a heart condition, Mike was the treasurer of Grantchester's parochial church council. No one quite knew what he did for a living but he had a sufficient number of 'business interests' to give him a public confidence with financial matters that he lacked in other forms of social interaction. His wife, Angela, had left him after three years of marriage. No one had quite known why, but Sidney suspected that it was because he did not have as much money as she had first thought.

After an exchange of pleasantries, during which Mike Standing struggled both to regain his breath and find a comfortable position in the otherwise empty carriage, both men settled down into what Sidney hoped would become a companionable silence. Mike Standing took out his copy of *The Times*. Within its pages a party of Italians were climbing Mount Everest, Pakistan were playing Northamptonshire at cricket, and Donald MacGill, the publisher of saucy seaside postcards, had been found guilty of breaching the Obscene Publications Act. It was all rather tame in comparison with Sidney's exploits.

Mike Standing began the crossword while Sidney continued to marshal his ideas. His thoughts, however, kept returning either to jazz or to crime. Furthermore, Mike had begun to mutter. In fact, he could not seem to complete his crossword without providing a running commentary of his progress:

'A blank T blank blank O . . . yes, I see, that must be ANTELOPE . . . but what about three across . . . if that is antelope then this must be RELIQUARY . . . gosh, oh no . . . eight down . . . help . . .'

He turned his attention to his companion. 'You're an educated man, Canon Chambers. Perhaps you could help me with this clue? "No tame Judge for Bacon": two words. The first word has four letters, the second has seven. The first letter of the first word is probably "W".'

Sidney paused for a moment as the train pulled in to Stevenage. Such an unpromising town, he thought. 'Sorry, what were you saying?'

' "No tame Judge for Bacon". Two words.'

Sidney stopped. A chill ran through his body. 'Good heavens,' he said. 'That's it.'

'What's it?'

'I have to get off the train . . .'

'Why? I thought you were going home to Cambridge?'

Sidney gathered his papers and his suitcase. 'I must telephone the police at once and return to London.'

'But you've only just left.'

'Amanda may be in danger. How could I have been so dim? I knew there was something wrong . . .'

'My clue!' Mike Standing called, but Sidney had already alighted and was making his way purposefully towards the stationmaster's office.

He was convinced that the murderer had been working under an assumed name. He telephoned Amanda to test his theory and matched it with a newspaper report from Colindale that he'd made a note of, checking that the dates tallied. Then he telephoned Inspector Keating and persuaded him that an arrest needed to be made. The easiest place to do so, he informed Keating, would be at Phil Johnson's jazz club in Soho that evening.

Inspector Williams was far from impressed that a clergyman had come up with a theory that might threaten the conviction of Sam Morris, but he was sufficiently fair-minded to agree to bring the suspect in for questioning. As a result, the forces of the law gathered together at 9 p.m. Officers in civvies mingled amongst the punters, uniformed police took up positions both at the front and in the back alley, while Keating and Sidney enjoyed a ginger ale at the bar.

Gloria Dee was in the middle of her first half. Sidney had persuaded the men to wait until she had finished as there would be less disruption and the arrest, provided there was no kerfuffle, could be made discreetly in the interval. She ended the session with 'Aint No Grave', accompanied by one of the finest jazz piano accompaniments Sidney had ever heard.

> 'When I hear that trumpet sound
> I'm gonna rise right out of the ground
> Cause there ain't no grave
> Gonna hold my body down'

In the gaps between the verses, Jay Jay Lion let rip on the piano, with Gloria shouting out the odd '*Hey*', as he went into free improvisation. As soon as they had finished, and before the band could get off the stage, four men moved to the green room while two others covered the back stairs. Liza had one hand on a bottle of beer and another on a towel ready for Gloria Dee's exit. Justin Wild was reading a copy of *Melody Maker* and smoking a roll-up. He looked unsurprised at the arrival of the police and made no attempt to escape.

Chief Inspector Williams made the announcement. 'Justin Templeton, I am arresting you for the murder of Claudette Johnson on the seventh of May 1954. You do not have to say anything now, but anything you do say . . .'

'Justin *Templeton*?' Liza asked. 'I thought your name was Wild . . .'

Gloria Dee burst into the room, gathered her towel from Liza and was about to down her beer but stopped when she realised something was going on. 'What the hell are you doin'?'

Inspector Williams explained. 'I am arresting your driver on suspicion of murder.'

'Are you crazy?'

'Never saner.'

Gloria turned to Justin. 'I thought you just met her? What the hell were you playin' at?'

'I wasn't playing,' Justin replied.

'What you talkin' about? You killin' people random style?'

'It wasn't random,' Sidney interrupted.

Gloria Dee turned to confront him. 'Jeepers, it's you. What you doin' now?'

'I have been helping the police.'

'You fingered my driver? How did you figure that one?'

'I looked to the past, what might have been a motive.'

'How far back do you go?'

'Nearly ten years.'

'You mean this has been planned for a decade? Holy moly.'

'I had to look for an underlying reason for the crime.'

Gloria Dee thought for a moment. 'I see. Goin' for the chords rather than the melody.'

'I think that's what Charlie Parker does, doesn't he?' Sidney replied, unsure whether he should expose his scanty knowledge of bebop. 'The improvisation on the chords of "Cherokee"?'

'You're on the trolley, man.'

Chief Inspector Williams interrupted. 'If I could just make this arrest?'

Gloria Dee turned to Justin Wild. 'I never had you down as an ice-man. She was just a baby. Shame on you.'

Justin Wild said nothing. The police led him away.

Sidney held back to apologise to Gloria. 'I am sorry we had to step in. He had been recognised. He could have struck again.'

'You mean he could have killed *me*?'

'No, another woman.'

'That broad you were with?'

'Indeed.'

'You sure attract trouble.'

'I don't mean to, Miss Dee.'

'You may be a preacher-man but I can't see how any girl can be safe with you around. What got you into jazz in the first place?'

'It's a long story.'

Gloria looked at him straight. 'I've got all night.'

'I'm not sure I . . .'

'Why don't you buy me a beer, Sidney?'

'You remember my name?'

'Sure do. Let's ball a little.'

It was nearly eleven o'clock before Sidney was able to extricate himself from the club and he wondered whether he would be able to take the last train home or if he would have to wait for the first in the morning yet again. Mrs Redmond had been prevailed upon to take Dickens in his absence but he couldn't expect her to look after the dog much longer.

However, Sidney also wanted to ascertain that the case that he had presented was watertight. He therefore asked if he could visit Justin Wild in his police cell. Chief Inspector Williams thought it curious that Sidney should want to do this but recognised the work he had done and could see no harm in such a visit from a clergyman while they were waiting for a lawyer.

'What do you want?' Justin Wild asked. 'You can't have come to give me the last rites. I haven't been sentenced.'

'But you will plead guilty?'

'I will, Canon Chambers. I am proud of what I have done.'

'All I want to know is why? Not "how", because I know that: but "why"? I imagine it is a form of revenge.'

'It is. But you know this. The girl's father . . .'

'Robbed your mother.'

'The burglary took place during my father's funeral. It was 1944. Crime doesn't stop, even in wartime. The usual things were stolen: the silver, an antique clock, a few items of value that had been inherited and that no one really liked; but as you will know, Canon Chambers, Johnson was a jewel thief and he took my mother's most prized possessions . . .'

'I understand.'

'No.' The word came out of Justin Wild's mouth like a gunshot. 'You don't "understand". Those jewels may have been valuable, but they were far more than that. They told the story of my mother's life. The police asked if she had insurance or if there were any photographs of the jewellery but of course there were not. Whoever heard of anyone photographing their own jewellery? But do you know what my mother did?'

Justin Wild did not wait for an answer.

'She drew them and she painted them: the sapphire brooch, the pearl necklace, the diamond earrings; everything she had owned. Then, when she had finished, she handed them to the police and started drawing them all over again. She couldn't stop drawing them. After she died I found hundreds of drawings of the same piece of jewellery. The theft made her mad.'

'I'm very sorry,' said Sidney quietly.

'My father had died months before and she was still grieving; not that grief ever stops. They say that love can last beyond the grave but so of course can grief. They had been married for forty-three years.'

'And you were their only child?'

'I was.'

'And you had no one to talk to?'

'I had my mother. Then, because of that man, she was gone.'

'You blame Mr Johnson for your mother's death?'

'I do.'

'Not directly, surely?'

'People don't think enough about the victims, Canon Chambers. At the end of my mother's life her doctor told me that it was possible to go mad with grief. It was a condition. That was the phrase he used. "Mad with grief." The loss of her husband followed by the theft of her jewellery meant that she could not go on. She did not know who she was any more. It may seem a small thing, a luxury even, to have jewellery and then to have it taken away, but it wasn't the objects or their value that mattered.'

'It was what they represented,' said Sidney.

'They were her past. Each ring, every brooch and necklace carried a memory: her mother's wedding ring, the confirmation cross from her father, earrings from her sister. When they disappeared, her memories went with them. By the end she hardly recognised me. As I sat at the end of the bed I thought: I will kill the person that has done this. I will devote my life to finding the man responsible.

'How did you do it?' Sidney asked.

'I started with second-hand jewellery shops and antique dealers. I watched people come and go. I sat in cafés for hours. I read the papers for news of burglaries involving jewellery. I attended court cases. I harassed the police to see if any crimes might be connected to the case involving my mother. And then, in 1949, I found him. Philip Johnson a.k.a. 'the Cat'. He was sent to prison for five years, even though I knew that he would be out in three. It wasn't long enough. My mother could have lived for another twenty years.

'When that thought came to me I realised that I could do much more damage if I *didn't* kill him. I would make him suffer in the way that my mother had suffered. If he died it would all be over too quickly. I wanted his pain to last. So I thought about his family and then, when I saw the way he looked at his daughter, I knew that she was the one who had to die. If I killed her then he would never forget it. It would ruin his life; and he would live with the grief my mother had known.'

'But Claudie was an innocent child . . .'

'She was his daughter. That was all I had to know. It was then just a question of timing.'

'So you found out that he had booked Gloria Dee. You knew the drummer in her band . . .'

'I know plenty of drummers.'

'And you managed to get a job as their driver. That was something that gave you away. You told me that you were not so interested in the money. I thought at first that you might have meant you were receiving something else in return . . .'

'Drugs or favours. I don't think so . . .'

'And neither did I. What she gave you was not money but an opportunity.'

'Exactly.'

'And a club full of criminals, any one of whom might be blamed? How did you do it? It was very risky. You could have been seen at any moment.'

'If you do not care whether you are caught in the end or not, and if you have no fear of retribution, it gives you more courage. You don't have to worry about covering your tracks. We'd already done several nights at the club and so I had established a routine. Miss Dee likes a little junk between sessions and we hid a supply in the store cupboard by the Ladies.'

'You mean drugs?'

'You don't think I'm just a driver, do you? I got hold of the drugs and we kept them in the first aid-kit. Claudette Johnson had the key to the cupboard.'

'Did she know what was in there?'

'She knew not to ask. I don't think there was anything she hadn't seen before. Of course I told Claudette it was all medication on prescription and it had to be kept away from Miss

275

Dee in case she took an accidental overdose. We'd go in the big number before the interval, when everyone was concentrating on the music. After three or four days it became a routine. Claudette knew exactly when to expect me and what to do.'

'And so she was at ease with you.'

'One of a murderer's best weapons is charm. The girl didn't expect anything at all. Why should she? By the time we were used to each other it was easy. All I needed was opportunity and surprise.'

'You strangled her in the store cupboard.'

'It didn't take long; consciousness goes after ten seconds, the brain after three or four minutes.'

'Why didn't you leave her there?'

'Because I wanted to see the look on her father's face when they found her. I wanted to watch his public despair. That's why I went to the funeral. The sadder it became and the more people grieved, the more I enjoyed it. I had to witness that suffering. I needed to know what that man was feeling, even if it was only a fraction of what my mother went through.'

'Phil Johnson did not kill your mother.'

'I believe he did.'

Sidney could see that there was no persuading him.

'How did you discover it was me?' Justin asked. 'I suppose it was Amanda Kendall.'

'You recognised her straight away?'

'We were children, and it was a long time ago, but she's hard to forget. She's cleverer than people think.'

'You also took on an assumed name. That was another, minor mistake.'

'I didn't think anyone would notice.'

Sidney looked at the man opposite. He seemed both deter-mined and careless, unconcerned about anything that might happen next. ' "Revenge is a kind of wild justice." '

'That's Francis Bacon: from *The Essays*.'

'Just- in- wild,' said Sidney. 'Wild justice. Revenge.'

'How did you find out?'

'A combination of luck and memory. But it did seem an unusual name.'

'It's not that unusual. There are plenty of "Justins" about. It will be the death penalty, won't it?'

'Most likely,' said Sidney. 'Unless you plead insanity or show a considerable degree of remorse.'

'I have no remorse. I am glad that I did what I did.'

'Then I'm sorry,' said Sidney.

'On the contrary. I suppose it is I who should apologise. I feel no guilt. If I did it would make it easier for you.'

'There are very few things about my job that are easy,' Sidney replied. 'I'm only sad that someone of your intelligence should have such a distorted sense of justice.'

'I'm sad too. I've been sad for quite a few years now.'

'There is a different way of thinking.'

'A Christian way? I don't think so.'

Sidney stood up. He had thought that he should stay and try to find some repentance in Justin but he knew that it would take longer than a single evening to seek out the remains of his conscience. 'I'm afraid I must go,' he said. 'It's already late.'

'Not too late for a night hawk like you . . .'

'There is my job.'

'I wonder how you find the time.'

'I will pray for you,' said Sidney.

'I don't think your prayers will make much difference, Canon Chambers.' Justin Wild appeared to hesitate. 'But thank you all the same.' He gave a nervous smile.

Sidney gave a little bow. It had become a custom, a signal that the conversation was at an end.

He walked through Fitzrovia to Kings Cross. There was a clear sky of midnight blue with a three-quarter moon. Sidney wanted to enjoy the stillness of the night. For some moments in a life, he thought, perhaps no recovery was possible. A life could be stained, as simply as surely as that, and no amount of peace or prayer could provide lasting comfort. He remembered the words of George Herbert: 'Living well is the best revenge.' That may have been wise advice, but for Justin Wild it had proved impossible. Forgiveness was, Sidney knew, far harder to reconcile than vengeance.

As soon as he returned to Grantchester, he poured himself a large whisky and lay down on his none too comfortable sofa. His Labrador snuggled up beside him. As he did so, Sidney patted him on the back and began to talk to him. Dickens yawned, stretched and laid his head on Sidney's knee. He told him how it had been a testing few weeks and now, surely, he could return to his vocation. He ought to give jazz and crime a rest. It was hard enough doing one job in which he was never off duty; but to combine it with investigations on behalf of Inspector Keating was another matter entirely.

He decided to unwind by reading some poetry and picked out a volume of George Herbert from his bookshelf. He began to read from 'The Temple', a poem in which Father Time pays the narrator a visit.

In the poem, the old man's scythe is dull and his role in human life has changed. Since the coming of Christ, and the promise of eternal life, he is no longer an executioner but a gardener:

> An usher to convey our souls
> Beyond the utmost starres and poles

Sidney remembered how strikingly original the poem was. For George Herbert, the time we spend on earth is not all too brief and transient but too long: because it detains human beings from a life outside time and with God.

Sidney decided to preach on the subject. He would outline the differences between our time and God's time. Human beings live in the threefold present: the memory of the past, the expectation of the future and a perpetual 'now' that passes as soon as it is thought. God, however, is not bound by time. He is outside it. And so our bounded life moves from the world of time to the eternal world of the timeless.

Sidney cast the book of poetry aside and lifted Dickens's head from his lap. He would have to make a note of these thoughts because they would be forgotten by the morning. He moved towards his desk. Almost immediately the telephone rang.

It was two o'clock in the morning. Sidney only hoped that it was not another death.

'It's me . . .'

Amanda.

'Is anything the matter?' Sidney asked.

'Nothing at all. I'm only telephoning to tell you the most ridiculous thing . . .'

'It's nothing serious?'

'Nothing serious whatsoever. I'm sorry it's so late. I did try before but there was no answer. Where were you?'

'It doesn't matter, Amanda . . .'

'I'm only telephoning because we couldn't wait to tell you. Jenny and I have been to the most absurd concert. I can't think why we went but I just wanted to let you know what happened. We've calmed down a bit now but we were spitting with rage.'

'I'm sorry to hear that.'

'The concert turned out to be all that modern plink-plonk music you know I can't stand. We had to have a whole bottle of red wine afterwards . . .'

'The plonk to cope with the plink?'

'Exactly. I'd rather have gone to one of your jazz concerts . . .'

'As bad as that, Amanda?'

'It was atrocious. In the second half a man just sat at the piano and didn't do anything at all. It was most odd. No one knew what to do or say.'

'Nothing? He must have played something?'

'No! That's precisely my point. He didn't play anything. He just sat there.'

'You mean he didn't tickle the ivories at all?'

'Not a tusk. The piece consisted of the audience coughing and muttering and being embarrassed. We were, apparently, the music. The audience. Can you imagine? And to think we paid five bob to get in.'

'Who was it by?'

'Oh I don't know, some American: John Cage, I think he was called. He even had the nerve to give it a title. 'Four minutes, thirty-three seconds.' Can you imagine? It certainly didn't feel like four minutes and thirty-three seconds. It felt like an eternity.

I never knew four minutes could last so long. It was ridiculous. Four minutes! I kept thinking of all the other things I, or anyone else for that matter, could have done in the same time. Can you believe it, Sidney? It was appalling.'

Sidney looked out into the dark night and thought of Gloria Dee's voice, Claudette's simple vulnerability and the terrible murder. He could not begin to explain to Amanda all that had happened or what he thought and felt.

'Are you still there?' she asked. 'You've gone all silent. Is there something the matter, Sidney, or are you trying to pretend you're John Cage? Speak up!'

'I'm still here,' Sidney replied. 'I'm always here, Amanda . . .'

He remembered Gloria Dee's voice in the darkness:

> 'Four minutes
> Just four minutes to Midnight
> Four minutes
> I just want four more minutes with you
> If the world ends
> Then the world ends
> But all I need
> Is those four minutes
> With you . . .'

The Lost Holbein

LOCKET HALL, WITH its grand E-shaped exterior of Ham Hill stone and mullioned windows, had been built at the beginning of the sixteenth century and was one of the finest stately homes in the vicinity of Cambridge. It was the official seat of the Tevershams, a family able to date their lineage back to the Norman Conquest, and an invitation to attend a social function at the Hall was considered an honour, and even a right amongst those socialites whose bible was Debrett's. Accustomed to abbeys and cathedrals, Sidney was not as humbled either by aristocracy or architecture as others might have been, but he still felt apprehensive as Mackay, the butler, opened the door and asked him to climb the grand staircase up to the long gallery, where Lord Teversham was entertaining his guests to midsummer drinks.

Sidney had mixed feelings about the nobility. He enjoyed the spaciousness of their homes and the warmth of their hospitality but he found their sense of entitlement unnerving. 'And if that isn't enough,' he could hear Lord Teversham complaining, 'the government now wants us to open up to the public. This is my *home*, for goodness sake, not a tourist attraction. I might as well give it lock, stock and barrel to the National Trust.'

This was a man who clearly took great pains over his appearance. He was the same height as Sidney, with an angular, matinée-idol jawline and luxuriant silver hair that, despite needing a cut, had been groomed in a manner designed to make bald men tremble. He was dressed in a handmade three-piece suit, with both tie and pocket handkerchief in matching navy blue; while his steel-rimmed pince-nez and silver accessories – cufflinks, fob watch and tie-pin – had all been chosen to set off his coiffure.

He greeted his guest with manners that were so practised that they came without effort. 'Canon Chambers, how very good of you to come; you'll take a dry sherry, I presume . . .'

'That would be most kind,' Sidney answered. There was no point making a fuss.

'Mackay will see to it. I can't remember whether you've met my sister?' He gestured into the middle distance where an elegant lady with similar hair was holding court. 'I think you might have seen her last Christmas at King's after the carols. I must introduce you.'

Sidney knew that the family came to church on high days and holidays, and for social rather than religious reasons. When he was at his most mean-spirited, he sometimes wished that he had the courage to turn such people away.

He looked around the room. There were over a hundred people in attendance but Sidney knew very few of them. He was just about to resort to bland clerical bonhomie with a lady of middle age, who was sporting a pair of unpleasantly practical sandals, when Ben Blackwood introduced himself. 'Lord Teversham sent me over,' he explained.

Ben was an aesthetically pale young man who had studied at Magdalene. He was, he said, an architectural historian, and he was writing the official history of Locket Hall. 'Of course, once they open it to the public it will make the family a fortune,' Ben began. 'Architecturally it's one of the unacknowledged gems of England.' He placed a Black Sobranie into a cigarette holder. 'The art collection alone is worth millions. Have you seen the portrait of Elizabeth I? She sent it as a gift after one of her visits . . .'

Sidney tried to keep up. 'I remember reading that the Royal Progress was very expensive. Hosts had to lay on banquets, masques and hunting expeditions . . .'

'The Queen sometimes stayed for *weeks*! Nearly bankrupted the place. Now the government is trying to do the same thing with its insistence on death duties. It's rather unfair considering the art has already been paid for.'

As Sidney was a guest, his behaviour was restricted by the etiquette of a world in which he only had visiting rights. His only advantage, he thought, was that, as a priest, he could say things that others might not. And so he found himself suggesting that perhaps the loan of a few paintings either to the Fitzwilliam Museum or to the National Gallery might not necessarily be a bad thing.

Lord Teversham overheard him and was unenthusiastic. 'And why would I do that, Canon Chambers?'

'I believe that you can then offset the death duties while retaining ownership . . .'

'But then I have to go to a museum to see paintings that have been in my family for generations . . .'

His sister, Cicely, intervened. 'It's hardly as if you look at them on a daily basis. We could just let them have one or two. I'm sure we wouldn't miss them. And we do have a few pecuniary issues . . .'

Lord Teversham was building towards one of his famous tantrums. 'But they'll want the best ones!'

'If it helps,' Sidney continued, 'I do have a very good friend at the National Gallery.'

Lord Teversham was ill at ease. 'I don't want some chap with a monocle coming down here and eyeing up the family silver.'

'She's not a chap.'

Cicely Teversham interrupted once more. 'I've no doubt Canon Chambers's "friend" would be tactful.'

'I don't like letting go of my possessions,' Lord Teversham muttered. 'Once those people start there'll be no stopping them.'

Ben Blackwood tried to compromise. 'I suppose you could let them have one or two as divertissements – or loan them in lieu of tax. The lesser-known works, obviously . . .'

Cicely Teversham put her hand on her brother's arm. 'What about the lady with the swollen chin? You never cared for her. I am sure you wouldn't miss such a thing . . .'

'I would miss it,' Lord Teversham grumbled. 'This is a collection. That is the point.'

His sister did not agree. 'You don't like the painting, Dominic. You said as much when I sent it away to be restored. You thought it was a waste of money and then complained that she came back even uglier than when she left.'

'Well, you could see more of her. Warts and all.'

'She doesn't have any warts, darling. Don't be ridiculous.'

Sidney tried to calm the situation. 'Perhaps I should not have made the suggestion. I wouldn't want to create discord . . .'

Lord Teversham turned to him. 'Who is this woman of yours, anyway?'

'Miss Amanda Kendall. She is the curator of sixteenth-century paintings. She trained at the Courtauld Institute under Sir Anthony Blunt.'

Lord Teversham was surprised. 'I was at Trinity with him. His father was a vicar. Do you know him?'

'I'm afraid not. But Miss Kendall is a friend of my sister.'

'Why isn't she here?' Cicely Teversham asked. 'You could have brought her along.'

'She is in London.'

Lord Teversham was unimpressed. 'There are trains every hour to Cambridge. It's not difficult.'

Cicely Teversham stepped in to smooth the way. 'Do ask her, Canon Chambers. I am sure the collection will interest her. Only a few people realise what we have here because the insurance is so high. We have to be so careful. The portrait of Queen Elizabeth is known, but there's a Raphael Madonna, and a Titian portrait. Some of our paintings are also without attribution, and so if Miss Kendall has a good eye then perhaps she would like to come and have a look?'

'I am sure she would be glad to do so.'

'I would like to show her our lady in black. The restorer did such a good job.'

'Who is the painting by?'

'We're not too sure,' Lord Teversham explained. 'Netherlandish School, probably. It used to be in the attic. Cicely had it brought down.'

His sister smiled. 'Do bring your friend. Next time you must stay to lunch. It will be intriguing, I'm sure.'

'Intriguing?'

'You speak of her so fondly.'

'Oh, it's not what you think,' Sidney replied hastily.

Cicely Teversham smiled. 'And how do you know what I think, Canon Chambers?'

The painting in question was a sober, almost devotional piece, a full-length portrait of a russet-haired, dark-eyed woman in her early thirties. She wore a black, high-buttoned blouse that covered a long neck, and a headdress edged with pearls. Her hands were half-clasped, but not quite in prayer, and the only lightness of touch lay in the hint of a smile on the lady's wide mouth. Her necklace consisted of a simple medal on a chain. In the background, and to the left, stood a table with a vase half-filled with water containing three carnations and sprigs of rosemary. A painting of Adam and Eve hung on the wall behind the table; a picture within a painting.

Amanda Kendall inspected the panel from every angle, looking at it closely and then stepping back to ascertain its effect. She was dressed elegantly, in a chemise dress by Coco Chanel that made her look decidedly French.

'Do you mind if I take the picture down?' Amanda asked.

Ben Blackwood stepped in. 'Let me help you . . .'

'It's all right. I am perfectly capable . . .' Amanda put on a pair of gloves, lifted the painting away from the wall, and carried it over to the window. She placed it on a side table and then knelt down and looked at it closely, inspecting the edges with a magnifying glass.

She looked at Lord Teversham. 'Could I take it out of its frame?'

He turned to Ben, who nodded in resignation. 'As long as you don't do any damage. It's Tudor wood, you know . . .'

'Indeed . . .' Amanda removed a scalpel from her handbag and prized the panel away from the frame.

Sidney had never seen her at work before.

'The frame is original,' she said before putting the panel back. 'It would be good to get the painting back to the Gallery and take some samples. You've had it restored, I see.'

'Ten years ago.'

Amanda hung the painting back on the wall, and then put her magnifying glass and her scalpel back in her handbag. 'A very unusual piece,' she said.

'Is that all you have to say?' Ben asked.

'By no means. Has this portrait always been in your possession?' she asked.

'Yes, of course,' Lord Teversham replied. 'It's an heirloom. It must have been in the family since the sixteenth century.'

'No, I'm sorry to have to repeat myself. I have to be sure of the provenance. Has this portrait always been in your possession? It has never left the building?'

'Not apart from when it was restored.'

'And who did the restoration?'

'Some chap in Saffron Walden. He was very good value.'

'I imagine that he was. What differences did you notice when the painting was returned?'

Lord Teversham could not understand why Amanda was asking such an obvious question. 'Well, it was cleaner and brighter. You could see everything . . .'

'And he got rid of the woodworm,' Cicely Teversham added. 'I was worried that the panel had a bit of rot and that it would get worse.'

'Well,' said Amanda. 'There's certainly no woodworm now; just a little residue in the frame.'

'The panel is as good as new . . .'

'Tell me, did the panel once have a cartellino?'

Lord Teversham was confused. 'A cartellino?'

'A painted inscription, often giving the name of the person represented.'

'I don't think so.'

'No trace of any over-painting?'

'I wouldn't know about that. Why do you ask?'

Amanda explained. 'The cartellino was a common feature of the Lumley Collection, a group of paintings dispersed in 1785. It is possible the work comes from that collection. Do you have a library?'

'I don't imagine our household accounts go back that far,'

'The provenance is crucial. We do have a copy of the Lumley Inventory at the Gallery.'

'Why are you asking all this?'

'Do you still have the restorer's address?' Amanda asked.

'Yes, I think so.'

Cicely Teversham remembered. 'Frederick Wyatt was his name . . .'

'Although if he recognised the painting I would be surprised if he was still living there.'

'Recognised? Is something wrong?' Sidney asked.

'I'm afraid so,' Amanda replied. She turned to Lord and Lady Teversham. 'I think we all need to sit down with a cup of tea. Or something stronger.'

'Very well; but why are you looking so concerned?'

Amanda was still guarded. 'The frame is the original

sixteenth-century mounting, but the panel itself has been replaced.'

'Replaced?' Ben Blackwood asked. 'Impossible.'

'It's a copy; a very good one, but a copy nonetheless. The paint surface is even; the wood is new. I would need to take a sample to be sure . . .'

'Good heavens . . .'

'Which would not matter so much if this was originally the work of a minor Netherlandish master . . .'

Lord Teversham could not believe her. 'I thought it was . . .'

Amanda continued. 'So did I. But look at the jewellery the lady is wearing. I am pretty sure that it was made either by Cornelius Hayes or John of Antwerp. It is an exact match of a coronation medal in the British Museum.'

'A coronation medal?'

'The carnations in the background are a symbol of betrothal; the portrait of Adam and Eve represents the hope of children in a marriage. The original of this painting can be dated to 1533.'

'Who is she, then?' Cicely Teversham asked.

Ben had guessed. 'You're not saying?'

Amanda paused. 'There is only one of Henry VIII's six wives with no surviving contemporary portrait. If you once had this original painting, and I am only saying "if", then you were the possessors of one of the most valuable pictures in the world: a lost portrait, by Hans Holbein the Younger, of Henry VIII's second wife, Queen Anne Boleyn.'

'A sleeper!' said Ben.

'Exactly,' Amanda replied. 'A work of art that has been misattributed but which turns out to be far more valuable than anyone thinks. I found a Van Dyck in a similar situation only the other day . . .'

Cicely Teversham pressed. 'We had an invaluable Holbein?'

'Possibly . . .'

'And now we've lost it? That painting could have saved our entire estate. How can we get it back?'

'Well, obviously it's not going to be easy,' Amanda replied. 'And we do need to track down your restorer.'

Sidney decided to step in. 'Who else knows you had this painting, Lord Teversham?'

His host was nonplussed. 'Most of the family, of course, and the servants. Mackay always took a dim view of it, but I think that's because it reminded him of the wife who ran off. Then there's Ben, of course, although portraits of pious ladies are quite far from your sphere of interest, aren't they?'

Ben Blackwood looked uneasy. 'Indeed.'

'Some visitors and friends, although most of them prefer horses or dogs.'

'Anyone from the art world?' Amanda asked.

Cicely Teversham spoke up. 'There was also the man from the insurers. He came to value the collection. In fact, he was the person who suggested the painting needed restoring if I remember rightly.'

'It seems peculiar, doesn't it?' Lord Teversham asked. 'If a crime has been committed then it seems rather a bizarre choice – why didn't they take a Titian?'

'That would be harder to sell on,' Amanda replied.

Lord Teversham couldn't quite take in what she had been saying. 'I always thought that this was a perfectly decent but rather insignificant painting. An unknown lady,

Netherlandish School: hardly worth restoring. She's no great beauty, is she?'

Amanda interjected. 'Taste changes, Lord Teversham, but if your original painting is what I think it may have been, then it fills one of the greatest gaps in British art. Holbein was active at the time of the marriage between Henry the Eighth and Anne Boleyn. We know that he designed a table fountain as a New Year's Day gift for the King in 1534, and even, probably, a cradle for the infant Elizabeth I. The theory is that if there was such a portrait it was destroyed or hidden after her execution and Boleyn's name became Bullen or even Butler . . .'

'And why would they do that?' asked Cicely.

'Fear. Anne Boleyn was once the most powerful woman in England. She gave birth to the future Queen Elizabeth, but she could not give the king a son. What I think is interesting is how little she realised the danger she was in. After she gave birth to a girl she thought that she would become pregnant again; and in January 1536 she was. Then, on the twentieth of January she miscarried. In the next few months her enemies rallied, and despite the fact that she had just lost a child, she was accused of multiple infidelity with half a dozen men including her own brother.'

'Seems a bit rum,' Lord Teversham interrupted.

'Half a dozen men, and she had just lost a baby. She was put on trial and condemned to death but as she took the last sacrament she swore upon her soul that had never been unfaithful to her husband. On the nineteenth of May she was beheaded. In less than four months her reputation was ruined. In January she had been the Queen of England. In May she was dead. It is one of the fastest downfalls in English history. Eleven days after her death the king married Jane Seymour. Anne Boleyn's memory was forgotten. Paintings were taken down as quickly as possible, dispersed, disguised and misattributed.'

'Like mine . . .' Lord Teversham cut in.

'We must get it back,' Cicely Teversham exclaimed. 'For the sake of the estate and in the interests of the collection.'

'No,' Amanda cut in. 'We must get it back for the nation.'

After lunch, Amanda returned to London and took the painting back to the National Gallery. There it was examined, photographed and subjected to a series of chemical tests. While she was waiting for the results, Amanda studied the inventory of Mr John Lampton, 'Stewarde of Howseholde to John Lord Lumley', that had been made in 1590. Above an entry for one of the National Gallery's own paintings, 'The Statuary of the Duches of Myllayne, afterwards Duches of Lorreyn, daughter to Christierne King of Denmark, doone by Haunce Holbyn', she had found the following: 'The Statuary of Quene Anne Bulleyne'.

It was a full-length contemporary portrait. There had been no record of where it had gone after the sale of 1785. Amanda's suspicions had been justified.

Lord Teversham had rooted out the address of the picture restorer and, at the beginning of August, shortly after her twenty-seventh birthday, Amanda let Sidney accompany her on a visit to seek him out in the small country town of Saffron Walden.

She drove the cream MG TD which her parents had bought her as a birthday gift, and she wore a scarf and dark glasses against the low autumn sunlight that Sidney thought made her look like Gene Tierney in *Leave her to Heaven*. As they travelled through the lanes of Cambridgeshire, Sidney told her how much he had enjoyed introducing her to Lord Teversham and how proud he was to know her. 'I cannot understand how you recognised that painting so quickly,' he marvelled.

'I do like to think that I am good at my job, Sidney.'

'I have never doubted it.'

'Some do. They think I am merely posh.'

'You are far more than that, Amanda. But do you think we can get the painting back?'

'If the restorer knew what he was doing then he will probably have sold it on. But this is our only lead. I have asked Lord Teversham to check the provenance. It would help if we knew how the family acquired the painting in the first place.'

Sidney tried to catch Amanda's eye but she was concentrating on the road ahead. 'You should have asked Ben,' he said.

Amanda smiled and gave him a glance back. 'I'm not sure about him at all. He's very protective of his position in the house, whatever that might be.'

'First impressions can be misleading,' Sidney replied, 'but perhaps not in this case. He does seem rather effete. Would you like me to look at the map?'

'We're just turning into Chaters Hill. Number one hundred and sixty nine appears to be some kind of souvenir emporium.'

'Are you sure it will be open?' Sidney asked. 'Most of the shops seem to be shut.'

'I thought I saw someone through the window.'

'Then let's go in and ask.'

They parked the car and approached a shop that consisted of toys, trinkets and teddy bears. The owner was a broad-shouldered man with a walrus moustache and twinkling brown eyes. 'What can I do for you both on such a magnificent morning?' he asked.

'We are not sure that we have come to the right place . . .' Sidney began.

The proprietor was unconcerned. 'Ask me anything!'

'I think we must be looking for the previous owner,' Amanda continued. 'Did this building once belong to someone in the arts, a painter or a restorer, perhaps?'

'It did indeed: Freddie Wyatt; the most mild-mannered of men.'

'But he is no longer here?'

'Alas, he is not.'

'He has retired?'

'To Holland, I believe. He went in rather a hurry. He said he couldn't wait to get out of England and just left me with a forwarding address.'

'When was this?'

'A few years ago now. The place was a terrible mess when I bought it. There were bottles of pigment, sugar, tea and alcohol all over the place with no way of knowing what anything was; no labelling, no order. It was chaos. I offered to send on any money received for work that people were late to collect but after three months that would be that. But you have not come to hear about this, I am sure. You have come for a bear, I hope, or a souvenir; something to remember your visit.'

Amanda kept to the subject. 'We were thinking of having a picture restored but it seems we have come to the wrong place.'

'I sell picture postcards, my dear, but not pictures.'

'You knew this Freddie Wyatt?' Sidney asked.

'We used to drink together in The Swan Hotel. Do you know it?'

'Unfortunately, I do not.'

'They do a very fine jugged hare.'

Amanda pressed further. 'And do you know what happened to the work that was left here?'

'The paintings? I put a sign on the door. All work had to be collected and paid for within three months. I gave the rest to the church fête.'

'How many paintings did you give away?'

'About ten, I suppose.'

'Can you remember them?'

The owner tried to think. 'There were some hunting scenes, some seascapes, a few dreary portraits; some of them were even of clergymen.'

'Any ladies?'

'One or two . . .'

Amanda produced a photograph. 'Any that looked like this?'

'She looks rather soulful doesn't she? Is she a widow?'

Sidney tried to help. 'Do you remember seeing it?'

'I can't be sure,' the owner continued. 'Most of the paintings that were collected in time were because a woman came on behalf of someone else to fetch them. She paid for six or seven restorations and framings. I remember because we rounded it all up to five guineas.'

'Do you think this picture could have been amongst them?'

'Possibly.'

'You didn't keep a record?'

'No. I just sent the money on.'

'You cannot remember what the lady was called?'

'I'm afraid not. But she came on behalf of a Mr Phillips.'

'Do you, by any chance, have his address?'

'Alas, I do not. It was all very slapdash, and poor Freddie's bookkeeping was atrocious. Are you sure I can't interest you in a bear or two? We have a couple of very good Stieffs.'

'I don't think so . . .'

Amanda smiled. 'Oh Sidney. Don't be silly. Let me buy you a bear. Then you can take me to lunch.'

'You don't have to.' Sidney wondered about Amanda's gift giving: first a dog and then a teddy bear. He should really get her something himself.

'I know I don't have to. But I want to, Sidney. Let me choose one for you.'

'What an excellent idea,' the proprietor exclaimed. 'I sometimes think that's all you need to be happy: a fine bear and an efficient hot water bottle.'

'If only it were that simple,' said Amanda as she paid the bill.

They remained in Saffron Walden for lunch. Sidney had offered the possibility of a return to Grantchester but Amanda was having none of it. She wanted to have a look round and make a day of it, visiting the ruined castle and the medieval buildings and examining the pargetting on the houses in Bridge Street. 'Also,' she added, 'I don't think I could bear one of Mrs Maguire's toads in the hole.'

Sidney felt that he should stick up for his housekeeper. Not everyone could live in Hampstead. 'Mrs Maguire does her best on very limited means, Amanda.'

It was approaching two o'clock in the afternoon and Sidney was worried that the Swan Hotel might not be serving food. He promised the waitress that they would be happy with anything and, as it was a Friday, both soup and fish would be perfectly adequate. Amanda, however, had other ideas.

'A gin and tonic with ice and lemon together with warm bread rolls while we look at the menu, if you would be so kind . . .' she asked.

The waitress was unimpressed. 'Chef's off in a minute and the gentleman has ordered.'

Amanda looked at the leather-bound menu. 'I don't think he's done so. He has expressed a desire not to be of inconvenience. They are not the same thing. Is everything listed here available?'

'In a manner of speaking . . .'

Sidney tried to alleviate the tension. 'Amanda, please don't cause a scene . . .'

'What would you recommend?' she asked.

The waitress looked at Sidney. 'I would have the soup and the fish, madam.'

'And what kind of soup is it?'

'I'll have to check with Chef . . .'

'Never mind,' said Sidney. 'Let him surprise us.'

'I think it's mushroom . . .'

'I can't abide mushrooms,' said Amanda.

'We do a very good tomato.'

'Tomato will be fine; and then the fish, I suppose. Thank you very much.' Amanda handed the waitress the menu. 'Honestly, Sidney. What a fuss.'

Two bowls of lukewarm tinned tomato soup arrived on the table. A sprig of parsley had been added but a dash of cream only served to lower the temperature further.

'I might as well warm up with another gin,' Amanda said, 'or I could add it to the soup and spice it up. I can't believe we're paying six shillings for this.'

'Let's not worry,' said Sidney. 'I am sure the fish will be tasty. Then we can concentrate on the complexities of the case.'

'There are certainly no complexities about the meal,' Amanda brooded.

There were three other diners left in the restaurant: a silent pair of tourists and a man with a prodigious beard whose response to the inadequacy of the meal resulted in him wearing his food rather than eating it.

'Extraordinary,' Amanda muttered. 'To take so little care . . .'

Sidney took out the photographs of the portrait of Anne Boleyn and looked at them once more. 'We must find this Phillips chap . . .'

'You think he was working in association with the picture restorer?'

'It's a possibility. Or the restorer never knew. It has to be someone who recognised the painting.'

'An inside job? The butler, perhaps. Or one of Lord Teversham's friends?'

Sidney considered the situation. 'I was thinking about the man who came to assess the collection for insurance purposes. The painting was restored shortly afterwards, and he was the person who suggested that it should be done. How much do you think it is worth?'

'I did some research. A Holbein sold for just under £4,000 in 1946. The Anne Boleyn would be worth far more; certainly enough for a nice house in the country.'

Sidney looked at the photograph once more. 'It's a less flattering image than I would have imagined,' he observed.

'It was the beginning of the age of realist portrait painting,' Amanda began. 'Holbein was trying to paint psychologically as well as representationally.'

The fish arrived and looked more promising than the soup. Sidney thought for a moment and then continued. 'Anne Boleyn is, of course, one of the main reasons I am in my present job. Without her there would be no Church of England; no Archbishop Parker at my college, and no Cranmer Prayer Book.'

'But you would probably still be a priest.'

'I'm not so sure about that. But it was probably the moment in history when England first defined itself, don't you think? It's interesting that the picture restorer was called Wyatt. Didn't Thomas Wyatt love Anne Boleyn – his great poem "Whoso list to hunt" and all that?'

'Probably, Sidney.'

'So, in the end, Anne Boleyn may well have inspired both the Prayer Book and the introduction of the sonnet into the English language.'

'Do you think so?'

'Whoso list to hunt, I know where is an hind,

But as for me, hélas, I may no more. . .'

'Sidney, don't get carried away.'

'The vain travail hath wearied me so sore,

I am of them that furthest cometh behind.

Yet may I by no means my wearied mind

Draw from the deer, but as she fleeth afore,

Fainting I follow. . .'

'Stop it. People are giving us odd looks.'

'I was enjoying myself.'

'You mean you were enjoying my discomfort?'

'A bit of teasing shouldn't harm you, Amanda.'

'I don't like being teased. It's embarrassing.' Sidney's companion finished her fish. 'So you think we should find this Phillips man? Perhaps we could ask your friend the inspector to help us?'

'I think you would have to ask him that, Amanda.'

'Me?'

'Yes . . . you . . . . I can't bear to think of the look on his face if I do it.'

'Alternatively, of course, I could telephone Lord Teversham and find out the name of his insurance company. If the man who came was also called Phillips, and he works for a specialist company, then tracking him down should be fairly straightforward.'

'You think you can do that?'

'We have a list of art insurers at work. I am employed by the National Gallery. It's almost my job.'

'But it's probably not the job that you are employed to do.'

'Sidney, that is the clearest case of the pot calling the kettle black that I have ever heard. Let me take you home.'

Wilkie Phillips lived in one of series of ramshackle buildings on the edge of a farm outside Ely. The surrounding land was fenced with barbed wire, the garden had been neglected for years and the house appeared as unloved as it was remote. Yet, on approach, Amanda noticed that the fabric of the building was sound. This was a home where the owner spent most of his time indoors.

A telephone call to Lord Teversham, followed by a visit to the offices of London Assurance, where she had used her considerable charms to good effect, had yielded her the address. She had decided to pursue the investigation on her own, on behalf of the National Gallery, and without troubling either Sidney or his friend Inspector Keating. She would make her visit to Wilkie Phillips as informal as possible, in order to avoid suspicion, and then, if she discovered that the painting was in his possession, or she had any doubts about his trustworthiness, she would summon aid. Until then, Amanda was confident that she was perfectly capable of doing a simple bit of detective work on her own.

On entering the building, she found herself in the hallway of one of the strangest houses she had ever seen. She had been permitted to enter by a small, bearded man who looked like an elderly version of Van Gogh. He apparently worried about neither appearance nor hygiene. The Harris tweed jacket and Fair Isle jumper, which he wore over a Viyella shirt, had clearly never seen a dry cleaner, and his loose-fitting corduroy trousers, in light tan, were held up with string. Although he was in his early sixties he sounded as if his voice had only just broken.

'I don't know what I can do for you,' Wilkie Phillips protested. 'There's nothing of any value here.'

'People have told me that you have a wonderful collection.'

'I don't know who you've been speaking to. I don't have any friends.'

'I am sure you do.'

'Believe me, Miss Kendall. I do not.'

The hallway was filled with paintings of blowzy nudes by Renoir and Degas. Although they were clearly fakes, and not all of them were to scale, the amount of female flesh on display did make Amanda wonder about the owner's state of mind.

'I don't have visitors. When my mother was alive people came all the time but I'm not a great entertainer. Besides, I like to keep the paintings to myself.'

'They're very good.'

'All copies, of course.'

'I can see that. Who did them for you?'

'A friend. Unfortunately he's retired and moved away so the collection is closed. But I find I don't need friends if I've got paintings . . .'

Amanda could see that great trouble had been taken in the hanging, even though the walls were in need of re-plastering. Each painting had its own picture light, and the portraits that hung in the hall were large enough to evoke the sense of a sprawling, but neglected, country house. This was a poor man's Locket Hall; and, like many a stately home, it was too cold and damp for art. However, Amanda did notice an open fire in the distance.

'What is it that you are doing again?' Phillips asked.

'As I explained in the doorway, we are compiling a census of the nation's great paintings so that we know where everything is . . .'

'Then I don't know why you have come here.'

'Yes, I am afraid I must have been misled.'

'Some idle gossip, either in the village or in town perhaps?'

Amanda was not going to give up easily. 'I think you work in insurance?'

'I've been retired for two years. I have a modest pension and I live frugally. I certainly could not afford any original works. Even these copies have cost me a great deal of money.'

'You should come to the National Gallery to see the originals.'

'That is very kind, Miss Kendall, but I like to keep everything close to hand. I do not like to be troubled by the world these days.'

'Then I'm sorry to have bothered you.'

'Not at all. I would offer you tea but I am afraid that I only drink milk. I like it condensed.'

'Oh . . .'

'It's not an affectation . . .'

'I didn't think that it was . . .'

'It's only that life can be so difficult.' Wilkie Phillips wiped his eye. 'I wear the same clothes and I eat the same food every day. Then I don't have to think about those kinds of things. I can just look at my paintings.'

'Is that how you spend your retirement?'

'I spend each day in a different room. There are seven rooms and I have seven days. It's all organised.'

'And where are you today?'

'In the snug.'

'Which is where the fire is?'

'You are observant.'

'May I see?'

'There's nothing there, really. Only a few portraits; they are not very interesting at all.'

'I am sure I will find them fascinating. This is your very own National Gallery, is it not?'

Phillips stepped back. 'I wouldn't go as far as that. But I believe that rooms should have their own themes. Italian Renaissance, Dutch still lives, Venetian views, and a salon of Vermeers. That is my favourite.'

'And what about the snug?'

'My Reformation room: Cranach's Adam and Eve, Quentin Metsys and one or two Holbeins. I've avoided Henry the Eighth because he is too intimidating and, as you have no doubt observed, I prefer pictures of women.'

'Could we go through?'

'You won't be staying long, will you?' Phillips asked. 'Only I haven't finished looking today and I do like to see the paintings in the daylight.'

'No, I won't keep you,' said Amanda. 'I am particularly interested in the Northern Renaissance.'

'You mean the Reformation. Such psychological realism I find . . .'

They entered the room. On the opposite wall was a copy of Holbein's *Lady with a Squirrel* that they had in the National Gallery. She recognised a portrait of Lady Guildford and then there, over the fireplace, was Lord Locket's portrait of Anne Boleyn.

'Oh,' Amanda said, trying to sound as casual as she could. 'I don't think I know that one.'

'Yes,' Wilkie Phillips answered. 'It's rather obscure.'

'It's a copy?'

'They are all copies, as you have noticed.'

'Then where is the original?'

'I can't remember . . .'

'I would have thought you knew where all your paintings came from?'

'They are copies. It does not matter too much . . .'

'But this one seems particularly good. It has a better patina. The sense of age is more convincing. Who is she?'

'No one of any great importance.'

'You don't think so? It seems to have a cartellino.'

'I don't think that means very much.'

'On the contrary. I think it means a very great deal. Could I have a closer look?'

The painting was hung too high but Amanda was convinced that the cartellino read 'Quene Anne Bulleyene'.

Wilkie Phillips shifted on his feet. 'Hadn't you better be getting on now?'

'Yes, of course. Only, it's extraordinary . . .'

'Yes, yes, I suppose it must be very odd to come to a place like this. I'm only sorry you have wasted your journey.'

'No not at all . . .' Amanda hesitated. 'You don't think it might be someone important?' she asked.

'I am not so sure about that. I just saw it and liked it.'

'Yet you can't remember where you first saw it?'

'I suppose that is a bit odd . . .'

'And it's hung in such a prominent position.'

'Well, as I say, I rather like her.'

'Haven't you been curious to do some research?'

'You ask a lot of questions, Miss Kendall.' Wilkie Phillips gave a nervous laugh.

Amanda wanted a closer look at the picture but realised she had outstayed her welcome. She needed time to think. 'Could I possibly use your lavatory?' she asked.

'Must you?'

'I don't *have* to.'

'No, forgive me, I am being unreasonable. I'm . . . I'm not used to guests, you see . . . and I don't like other people looking at that painting. It's a queer thing . . . but please . . . it's along that corridor.'

Wilkie Phillips gestured towards the open doorway with his left arm. 'I'll show you . . .'

Amanda could not resist taking a further step forward to look at the painting. 'I think this is the best work in your collection; the most convincing . . .'

'Do you, indeed? As I said, the lavatory is down this corridor . . .'

Amanda passed Wilkie Phillips in the doorway but was unnerved when he started to follow her.

'It's all right,' she said, trying to get some distance between them.

Her host gave another laugh. 'I don't want you getting lost.'

They turned left just before the kitchen and Amanda found herself in a small windowless corridor off the main building. The lavatory was at the end, with a sink and a small barred window. There was no key in the lock but she closed the door and took time to collect her thoughts.

It was quite simple, she told herself. She would be as polite as possible, leave, and then tell both Sidney and Lord Teversham. One of them would inform Inspector Keating and then the process of investigation would begin. They could requisition the painting, the restorers at the gallery would test her suspicion – for it was still just a theory – and then, if a crime had been committed, the rest would follow.

Amanda washed and dried her hands, adjusted her lipstick and gave her hair a quick brush. She walked down the narrow corridor that led back to the kitchen, already imagining herself on the drive back to London. There was so much to think about that when she first tried to turn the handle on the outer door she thought little of the fact that it was stuck. She tried the handle again. It turned but when she attempted first to push the door away from her and then to pull it towards her she found that it held fast. It appeared that she was locked in.

'For heaven's sake,' she thought.

'Mr Phillips!' she called.

There was no reply.

She banged on the door.

'Mr Phillips!' She looked back towards the lavatory; the only opening to the outside was the small barred window. The corridor was windowless.

She banged again. Then she looked in her handbag. Perhaps she had a pair of tweezers or something that would enable her to pick the lock? She realised that she did not know how to do such a thing and, in any case it was a mistake to panic so soon. Wilkie Phillips was simply a very odd man. He couldn't have locked her in deliberately.

She banged on the door again.

How had she got herself into this and, more to the point, how was she going to get out? 'I'm such an idiot,' she thought.

She returned to the attack, banging on the door and then rapping and calling for a good thirty seconds. Then she stopped.

In the ensuing silence she heard Wilkie Phillips. 'Quite the woodpecker, aren't we? Tap, tap, tap . . .'

His voice was quiet and close and there had been no preceding footsteps. Amanda realised that her host must have been standing on the other side of the door all along. 'Mr Phillips, I seem to be locked in . . .'

'That does seem to be the case.'

'Do you have a key?'

There was a pause in which he appeared to be considering the complexity of the question. 'I do have a key.'

'Then can you please let me out?'

'I am afraid I cannot do that, Miss Kendall.'

'Why not?'

'I saw you looking at that painting.'

'There's nothing wrong with looking at a painting.'

'But you were looking at *that* painting, weren't you?'

'And what if I was?'

'You know what it is, don't you?'

'I'm not sure I do.'

'Would you like to tell me?' Phillips's tone was falsely paren-tal. 'I'm sure you know.'

Amanda sighed. Perhaps she should just get all this out of the way and be done with it all. 'It's Anne Boleyn,' she said.

'Very good.'

'It's from the Lumley Collection. The original was in Locket Hall.'

'It was . . .'

'And it isn't now.'

Wilkie Phillips was still speaking in an insidiously quiet voice. 'Lord Teversham is such a foolish man. As soon as I saw it I knew that I had to have it. And he never even knew.'

'Will you let me out?'

'I am afraid I can't, Miss Kendall.'

'What if I promise not to tell anyone about the painting?'

'I don't believe you . . .'

'The police know I am here.'

'I am not afraid of men in uniform.'

Amanda wished she had brought Sidney. 'I am sure they are on their way even now,' she said.

Wilkie Phillips's reply was both calm and wheedling. 'Well,

we'll just have to wait and see. I'm not sure I'll be letting anyone else come into the building. That would be as much of a mistake as letting you through the door in the first place. In fact, I am rather upset. I was distracted by your beauty.'

'I hardly think so . . .'

'If I could see more of you, of course, I might be a better judge. I could be kinder.'

'Don't be absurd.'

'You are in no position to call me absurd, Miss Kendall . . .'

'What are you going to do?'

Wilkie Phillips still had his mouth close against the door. 'I don't quite know. I haven't made my mind up. Exciting, isn't it?'

The next Thursday evening, on 26 August 1954, Geordie Keating and Sidney Chambers were about to begin their routine game of backgammon in the RAF bar of The Eagle. The inspector was in a good mood: the children were back at school, the football season had begun – his beloved Newcastle United had even won 3-1 at Arsenal – and Scotland Yard had commended him for his help on the Templeton case. He therefore took the opportunity to josh Sidney about his future marriage plans, asking him explicitly about Amanda.

'If you want my opinion you should stop all this shilly-shallying and propose.'

'I don't think anyone would ever see Amanda as a vicar's wife.'

'She could break the mould.'

Sidney threw his dice to begin: a six and a one. 'Besides, I like things the way they are. We are good friends. I don't want to ruin it with romance even if I had the chance. There's a lot to be said for celibacy, you know. More time for God.'

Inspector Keating responded with a four and a three. They were even. 'It's unlike you to be so reticent.'

'I'm being realistic. There is a difference.' Sidney stopped before his next turn. 'Although it's a curious thing, Geordie. I haven't heard from her for a few days. I left a message with my sister and Amanda hasn't replied. That is quite unusual.'

'She's probably found someone else by now.'

'There is always someone else, Geordie. I am quite used to that.'

Keating put down his pint and gave Sidney one of his irritatingly 'concerned' looks. 'It's strange that she hasn't returned your telephone call. Why don't you try her again?'

'I don't want to pester her.' Sidney threw down the dice too aggressively. They bounced off the board and skidded off the table and on to the floor. He could not concentrate at all.

Trapped in the lavatory of a remote farmhouse outside Ely, Amanda was beginning to lose sense of time. As soon as she was sure that Wilkie Phillips had gone to bed, she took the opportunity to wash and brush up. There was no hot water and only a slim bar of Cidal soap. Then she did a few exercises that she had remembered from the Girl Guides: running on the spot, touching her toes and three or four star jumps. She remembered the motto 'Be Prepared' and was furious with herself all over again; a woman who had always prided herself on her intelligence being duped into this!

She found sleep on the cold lino of the lavatory floor nearly impossible. She eventually drifted off and tried to think of the good things in her life but the dawn came all too soon.

Then, what at first she thought to be a strange bird-like sound, turned out to be Wilkie Phillips whispering a high-pitched song through the barred window.

'Oh dear, what can the matter be

Two old ladies stuck in the lavatory

They've been there from Friday to Saturday

Nobody knew they were there.'

'Please let me out.'

Wilkie Phillips's rabbit eyes were visible through the bars. 'I don't think you're in any position to make demands.'

'I'm hungry.'

'I've left you a sandwich.'

'I can't eat it.'

'It's salmon paste. I made it especially for you.'

'I don't want it.'

Wilkie Phillips had a colder tone to his voice. 'I think you'll have to look after yourself if you want to survive.'

'Are you threatening me?

'I might be. And then again, I might not. How unpredictable life is.'

'This is ridiculous. My friend knows I am here. He will bring the police.'

'No sign of him, though, is there?'

'I trust him to come,' Amanda replied.

'Who is "he"?'

'A good man. Far too good for me.'

'You are fortunate that someone loves you. I only had my mother.'

'Why you are doing this? It can't be to make me understand you, Mr Phillips.'

'You can call me Wilkie.'

'Why can't you let me go?'

'Because the painting is mine and I can't let you take it away.'

'I don't have to take it away. I could just leave.'

'But then you will tell your friends and they will come and I will be removed from this lovely home and I will never see such beauty again.'

Amanda saw that she was getting nowhere. She was beginning to understand the nature of his obsession. She decided on another course of action. 'I meant to ask. The Holbein seems an odd choice?'

'Does it indeed? Perhaps so. But it is because the lady in the painting looks unerringly like my mother. As soon as I saw her I knew that I would have to own it. Do you know how old Anne Boleyn was on her coronation?

'Either twenty-six or thirty-two. Her birth date is disputed.'

'You do know your history. I am very impressed. We're going to get along grandly. My mother was in between those ages when I was born, and I think she must have looked very much like this. And now she will always be with me, preserved in the timelessness of art, where death cannot touch her. I can look at her as much as I like: all day if I need too. I don't have many fine qualities but one of them is astonishing patience.'

'But the painting is not of your mother.'

'I can imagine it is her.'

'And why does it have to be the original painting? Everything else here is a copy. You seem perfectly content with them.'

'Because my mother is now the only real thing in a world of fakes, as she was in life. Do you see? It's really rather clever of me.'

'I suppose it is.'

'So do you think I am going to give up the only original artwork I possess? Or perhaps I now have two: you being one yourself. A living sculpture. I am Pygmalion. Together, perhaps, we could have Paphus: a son. Try some of your sandwich . . .'

Amanda was still unsure how to deal with her captor: whether to be defiant or try to befriend him. 'You know my friend will come for me. I have told him about my visit.'

'I am afraid that I don't believe you. You sound too nervous when you tell me. You're not a very good liar, are you, Miss Kendall? Perhaps I should call you Amanda, seeing as we are about to be intimate. Or Mandy. Do you like being called Mandy?'

'No I don't.'

'Milly-Molly-Mandy. You even look a bit like her. Were you pretty as a child? I imagine so. I wonder what you look like without your clothes on. I think I will have to watch when you wash.'

'I won't wash.'

'We all have to keep clean, my dear. There is soap. It's Cidal. My mother used to use it. And a towel. You see how I look after you. I'm a very kind man. I can be even kinder if you are nice to me.'

'I feel faint.'

'Then you should eat something.'

'I do not want to be poisoned.'

'I have left you a banana. You can peel it yourself.'

'You could have interfered with it.'

'It's on the window ledge. I'm glad I put bars across. Another week and you could be such a slip of a girl you'd probably be able to squeeze right through them.'

'Can't you leave me alone?'

'Aren't you enjoying my company?'

'I am not.'

'I thought you liked our little chats?'

'Go . . .' said Amanda. 'Please. Just go.'

'I don't think you should be rude to me. I'm not a very nice person when I'm angry.'

'You're not a very nice person in any circumstances.'

'That's not very generous of you. Have your banana . . .'

'I don't want a bloody banana.'

'When I was a small boy it was my Friday treat. My mother used to take me down to the greengrocer's and let me choose. We would eat them in the car on the way home. I like them when they are a bit sticky.'

'I can't stand bananas. They make me sick.'

'That's a pity. Especially since I brought one as a present.'

Amanda decided to mollify him. 'I'm sorry. I don't want to appear ungrateful.'

'Of course, you should give me something in return. I wonder what that might be. You don't seem to have very much to offer other than yourself. But that would be quite nice. I could look forward to that. In fact, I might save you up as a treat.'

'Please don't.'

'I wonder what you are going to let me do? There are so many choices. I think I'm just going to eat your banana while I decide.'

Sidney had been surprised by Inspector Keating's anxiety about Amanda and found it touching, even though he was not unduly worried himself. She would often disappear for a few days to see friends in the country and their communication had its sporadic moments. After all, their friendship was relatively new and, as he had told Geordie, he did not like to make too many demands. Besides Sidney had concerns and duties of his own, not least Grantchester's upcoming summer fête and the annual scout trip to Scarborough.

He was not even alarmed when his sister first telephoned early on a Tuesday morning to say that Amanda had not been home for several days. Although that was not unusual in itself, Jennifer then explained that the National Gallery had telephoned to ask whether Amanda was ill. Her car was missing, her parents were abroad and a strange address outside Ely had been written down on a notepad together with the name 'Wilkie Phillips'. Did Sidney know anything about any of this and should she be worried?

Her brother pretended that all was well and told Jennifer that Wilkie Phillips was a member of the art world and that Amanda had been keen to talk to him about Holbein. There was nothing to worry about, but if she could just give him the address then he would make some enquiries and set her mind at rest. Jennifer was clearly not convinced by her brother's attempt at a calm response, but obliged.

As soon as he had put down the receiver, Sidney went straight to Cambridge station, where he then took a train to Ely. He took his bicycle with him and, after he had alighted, he headed off across the Fens. A feeling of dread filled his being, a sentiment not helped by the fact that the villages he passed seemed to become more remote by the mile. He asked directions to the private road where Wilkie Phillips lived and turned off down a narrow track. This then widened to reveal the ramshackle dwelling that Amanda had approached three days earlier. Her car was parked outside. The roof of the MG was down but it had been raining and the seats were wet. Now Sidney worried even more.

He approached the front door and rang the bell. There was no reply. He rang again. Then he walked around the house. The main windows were boarded up. There was no sign that anyone lived there. He rang the bell again. Then he banged on the door.

There was silence.

Sidney bicycled back towards Ely but stopped at the first telephone box he saw.

He called Inspector Keating.

'I'm worried about Amanda,' he said.

'Now you tell me. What's wrong?'

'It's not good, Geordie. I think she's been kidnapped.'

Inside the house, Wilkie Phillips was in a cheerful mood. 'I'm sorry you didn't hear the doorbell. I think it might have been your friend. What does he look like?'

'He's quite hard to describe. He's very tall, with a kind face. He stands very straight. He has brown eyes. He wears black.'

'He wouldn't, by any chance, be a clergyman?'

'He is.'

'Oh dear. That will have been him, then. And now he's gone. What a pity I couldn't let him in. We could all have had a little chat. Is he your special friend?'

'Not in the way that I think you mean.'

'Then there's room for me. Perhaps you are, as they say, "unattached", Miss Kendall? Quite a catch, I would have

317

thought. And you know about art. That makes you all the more attractive. We could have a series of discussions about the difference between the naked and the nude.'

'I don't think that would be a good idea at all.'

'Don't you? I could take up life drawing. Or we both could. We could draw each other. That would be fun, wouldn't it?'

'I really don't think so.'

'You do know that you are going to have to be much kinder to me if you want to leave?'

'Mr Phillips, I can see that you have no intention of letting me go.'

'Wilkie, please. I have told you this before. It would be so much easier if you co-operated.'

'And what do you want me to do?'

'Why, take off your clothes of course.'

'And if I do so?'

'I'm only going to look. I don't want to touch.'

Inspector Keating made it clear to his friend that this was the last time he was prepared to go out on a limb and help. It was only because he was fond of Amanda, and recognised that she could, potentially, curb Sidney's more extreme flights of fancy, that he had agreed to step in and provide two cars and six men on what could turn out to be an embarrassingly wild goose chase.

Sidney had already made enquiries in the area, and it was acknowledged that Wilkie Phillips had always been strange, that he had seldom been seen since the death of his mother and that the local vicar had given up trying to pay any pastoral visits since it had been made clear that they would not be welcome.

The local shopkeeper said that Phillips came as little as possible but that, when he did so, he stocked up on condensed milk, salmon paste, bread and bananas. He seemed to eat little else. Whether this made him dangerous, or merely eccentric, was another matter.

Keating asked his men to park out of sight and approach the house across the neighbouring fields. Sidney was to try to make a normal visit once more and, should there be any problems, then the police would be on hand to give immediate assistance. If there were no reply at the door, Keating would issue a warning with a loudhailer. Any further silence would result in them entering the premises and retrieving Amanda by force. He assured Sidney that they would not leave the area without her.

For a short while Amanda had been able to sleep but when she woke she found that her hands and feet had been bound. She wondered if she had been drugged, or if she was still dreaming. Wilkie Phillips was in the lavatory and he was sitting on a stool. He had been watching her.

'I hope you had a nice rest, my dear. I did so enjoy last night. Wasn't I good to leave you alone? I was so tempted to be naughty.'

'What have you done to me?'

'I thought we might play a little game.'

'How did you do this?'

'You were tired, and so sleepy, and I just tampered with the water tank. Only a little, you see, but just enough to send you off. And then I was very careful. You didn't notice me at all. But perhaps all this is a bit tight for you.'

Wilkie Phillips knelt down beside Amanda and began to unbutton her blouse. The speed of his breathing increased. His breath smelled of stale banana and fish paste. As he reached the lower buttons Amanda dipped her head and bit his hand. Phillips leaped back. His hand shook with the pain. She had drawn blood.

His face contorted but his voice remained calm. 'That was a mistake, my dear.'

Amanda noticed a toolbox on the floor by the door. Phillips crossed to it and pulled out some black gaffer tape. He tore off a length and returned. He pulled back her hair and gagged her. He forced her on to her front, lifted up her blouse and undid her bra at the back. He turned her over and pulled the bra away. He leaned forward, over Amanda, but as he did so she twisted her head away to gain momentum and used her forehead to hit him in the face. Phillips's nose began to bleed. He checked the blood. There was a momentary pause. Then Amanda saw his fist coming towards her face.

All was darkness.

The police took up their positions. Sidney approached the front door and rang the bell repeatedly. There was no reply. He walked round the outside of the house, banging on every window and every shutter. It was impossible to see inside until he reached the barred lavatory at the rear of the house. He looked in and saw Amanda half-dressed, bound, gagged and unconscious on the floor. He called out her name. He heard a noise from inside and saw the shadow of a man move across a doorway. He ran back to the front door and waved Keating forward. He shouted out what he had seen.

The officers were summoned. The door was broken down. Two men ran to the back of the house. They found the lavatory unlocked. They knelt down beside Amanda. She was still breathing.

Police officers searched the house. When they came to the snug they found Wilkie Phillips standing before the painting of Anne Boleyn. He was shouting and swearing and blaming his mother for his impotence.

He was also naked.

As he sat by Amanda's bed in Addenbrooke's Hospital, Sidney realised that he had never seen her without make-up. He knew that she would not want him to see her like this, bruised and vulnerable, that she always liked to look at her best; but now that she was sleeping, and unaware of how she looked to the world, he had never felt so fond of her.

He began to pray.

'O Lord, look down from heaven, behold, visit and relieve this Thy servant. Look upon her with the eyes of Thy mercy, give her comfort and sure confidence in Thee, defend her from the danger of the enemy, and keep her in perpetual peace and safety, through Jesus Christ our Lord, Amen.'

He prayed in certain hope of an answer. Prayer was an act of will, Sidney thought; a discipline that had to be learned and practised.

He put his hand on Amanda's.

It was so slender.

He gave it a gentle squeeze and hoped for a response but none came.

He looked down at her pale face.

He spoke aloud. 'The Lord bless thee and keep thee. The Lord make his face to shine upon thee, and be gracious unto thee, and give thee peace, both now and evermore. Amen.'

He kissed her forehead. He kissed her bruised cheek. He laid his hand on hers once more.

Then he stood up and walked towards the door.

He took a last look and left her sleeping.

As he left the building he saw Inspector Keating coming towards him carrying a bunch of Michaelmas daisies.

'Cathy was on a walk with the children and they picked them for Miss Kendall. But you've already taken her some roses, I'll bet.'

'I thought I would wait.'

'Then I will tell her they are from both of us.'

'She's sleeping.'

'I'll just leave them with the nurse.'

'I have to return for Evensong, Geordie. I don't suppose you'd like to join me afterwards?'

'I need to get back to the station.'

'I understand.'

When Keating arrived in the room he found that Amanda was beginning to stir. 'Are those flowers for me?' she asked.

'Of course . . .'

'How long have I been asleep?'

'I do not know.'

'Could I please have some water?'

'I will get some for you,' Inspector Keating replied. 'And I will find a vase for the flowers.'

'Has Sidney been here?' Amanda asked.

'He has just left.'

'I thought I heard his voice. I dreamed that he was holding my hand and praying for me . . .'

'I am sure he was.'

'Do you think so?'

'He prays for us all.'

'Even the man who kidnapped me?'

'Probably.'

'What happened to him?'

Inspector Keating sat down on the end of the bed. 'He is in our custody.'

'Will I have to tell you everything he did?'

'Not now.'

'But eventually?'

'You can tell me everything that you feel able to tell me. Or we can provide a female police officer. It will be in confidence.'

'It could have been so much worse, I suppose.'

'Yes,' Inspector Keating said quietly. 'It could.'

'Should I tell Sidney?'

'If you would like to. He did see you in the house. And he knows that at least . . .'

'I wasn't raped or murdered?'

'Yes.'

'Then perhaps that is enough. Let's not talk about that.'

'You were incredibly brave.'

'And foolish. What has happened to the painting?'

'We have returned it to Lord Teversham.'

'Was he pleased?'

'Very much so. He told me that he is going to invite you to lunch as soon as you are better. I think he is planning a surprise for you; a little thank you. But you do not need to think about that now.'

'And my parents . . .'

'They are on their way.'

'What have you told them?'

'As much as they need to know.'

'I'm so tired.'

'You must rest. Cathy is going to bring in something she's baked. She thinks the food in the hospital may not be up to your usual standards. Sidney has told me that you take a sorry view of the catering facilities on offer in Cambridge.'

'It is because I am spoilt.'

'Or perhaps because you have high standards?'

'Let's just say I am spoilt.'

'Sidney has been worried about you. As have we all.'

'He's such a dear man.'

'He is, and I know he thinks the world of you.'

Amanda turned her bruised face away from the inspector. 'I think it must be hard being a clergyman. You can never do enough for people. But you have a calling and that is what it is. Sidney once told me; "I did not choose. I was chosen." It's quite hard to love a man who will always love God more.'

'Perhaps it's a different love . . .'

'I don't know what it is, Inspector. I try not to think about it.'

'Some things are best left unsaid.'

'What we have is friendship and I do not want to do anything to endanger that. I know that one day he will preside over my wedding and he will be a godfather to my children.'

'One day . . .'

'Yes, Inspector, one day. But not soon. I am not ready.'

'And after that day,' Keating pressed, 'you wouldn't mind if Sidney married someone else?'

'Ah that ... yes ... that is different,' Amanda considered, before turning over to sleep. 'I think I might mind that very much indeed.'

It was three weeks before Amanda felt that she was well enough to revisit Locket Hall. She was weak after her ordeal, and found it difficult to adjust to everyday life, but she told Sidney that she wanted to return both to her work and to her friends as soon as she could. She would not be defeated by events. 'If I have to change my life then that man has won. I will not live in fear.'

Lord Teversham arranged the luncheon party he had promised and made sure that Sidney was in attendance. He was thrilled to see that Amanda had felt able to come back so soon and kissed her on her arrival.

'The vision of loveliness has returned,' he declared, with a triumphant and generous gesture that suggested his guest was appearing on the London stage. 'Aphrodite is in our midst once more.'

'You flatter me, Lord Teversham.'

'I tell only the truth. And you *must* call me Dominic.'

Cicely Teversham hugged her tightly, and Ben Blackwood kissed her for the first time. 'Welcome back.'

'Champagne! I think ...' Lord Teversham called to his butler. 'We can't be having anything as prosaic as sherry on a day like this.' He shook Sidney by the hand. 'I imagine you must be sick of the sight of sherry, eh?'

Sidney smiled. At last people were beginning to get the message. 'It does have its limitations.'

'Then why don't you ever say?'

'I don't want to appear rude.'

Amanda touched him on the shoulder. 'Oh, Sidney, don't be such a saint. Let's get on with the champagne.'

Mackay poured out the glasses while Lord Teversham made a little announcement. 'Miss Kendall, before we go into luncheon we have a surprise for you.'

'I'm not sure I like surprises any more.'

'I think this one will amuse you. Come into the Long Gallery. You too, Canon Chambers. Bring your glasses. Ben will explain.'

They walked out into the Long Gallery and stopped in front of the painting of Anne Boleyn. It looked darker than Amanda had remembered from before. Perhaps it was because the weather had turned for the worse. It was a dull and sombre day and the picture was illuminated only from the windows.

Amanda took a step closer.

'What do you think?' Lord Teversham asked.

Amanda paused. 'Isn't this still the forgery?'

'It is. I knew that you would be able to tell. You are clever.'

'Then where is the original?'

Lord Teversham opened the door beside him that led into a small anteroom. 'Step this way.' He pointed to a large packing case 'It is here.'

'I don't understand.'

Lord Teversham laid a gentle hand on Amanda's shoulder. 'I have been on the telephone to the Director of the National Gallery. He knows what you have done. He reminded me that the painting was priceless. Then he started to tell me about the tax advantages of gifting the painting to the nation. He could take care of it and have it on permanent loan while I am alive, and he could take care of it in such a way that the picture would

never be endangered again. I listened to him very carefully . . .'
Lord Teversham smiled.

'And then?' Amanda asked.

'I thought of you and all that you had gone through. And I thought of what I do. Nothing much happens in Locket Hall, you know? I have my lovely sister, and I have Ben. I shoot, and I have parties, but what have I actually done with my life? Nothing. What will I be remembered for? Nothing. This is one small thing I can do. I am giving the painting to you, Miss Kendall, or rather I am donating it to your employer.'

'Oh . . .' said Amanda. She inadvertently took Sidney's hand and he squeezed it. Then she began to cry. 'That's so kind.'

'It is nothing, my dear.'

'It is everything. I'm sorry. I cry so often these days. I can't help it.'

'There's nothing wrong with crying.'

She let go of Sidney's hand.

He remembered her lying on the hospital bed, and then, her bruised and broken body on the lavatory floor. He had never felt so protective of anyone before.

Amanda gave Lord Teversham a kiss on both cheeks. Then she took Ben's hand. 'Did you have something to do with this?' she asked.

'We all decided it was for the best,' said Cicely, opening her arms.

Amanda collapsed into her embrace.

'There, there,' said Lord Teversham. 'We can't go on like this otherwise we will all start blubbing. We need a good bit of roast beef and Yorkshire pudding and some heady red wine. I have a rather good Mouton Rothschild from '49. Do you know the vintage, Canon Chambers?'

'I can't think of anything more appropriate,' Sidney bluffed.

They walked through to the dining room, where Mackay was waiting. He placed Amanda to Lord Teversham's right and luncheon was served.

The host was keen to hear the full story of the kidnap. 'How frightening it must have been, Miss Kendall. Has Phillips confessed?'

'I believe he has.'

'He sounds a very unnerving man,' Cicely added. 'He must have had a very odd upbringing.'

'Yes,' said Amanda quietly. 'Although, would you mind if we didn't talk about it? I'm still finding it rather hard.'

'Of course.' Lord Teversham turned to Ben. 'It's surprising we didn't notice that the man was mad in the first place. Perhaps it's because we spend so much time with eccentrics in our own family. My uncle thought that pine nuts made you invisible. He used to come down to breakfast naked.'

'I don't think that's the same thing', Cicely said. 'Mr Phillips must have been a different kettle of fish altogether.'

'But that doesn't mean we should take pity on him,' Lord Teversham continued. 'What do you say, Canon Chambers? Even madmen deserve our forgiveness? Surely in some cases people are beyond mercy? There is so much evil in the world.'

'That is true, of course.' Sidney answered.

'You are thinking, I see.'

'It is not the right time to discuss my thoughts.'

'Go on.'

Sidney looked at Amanda who smiled encouragingly. 'He always has something interesting to say.'

'I don't know about that,' her friend began, but he recognised that he should move the subject of the conversation away from Amanda's ordeal. 'People often ask me about the problem of evil,' he began, 'but there is, of course, another way of looking at it.'

'Which is?' Lord Teversham asked.

'The problem of good. If we are all animals why are some of us good, kind, altruistic when we do not have to be? The capacity to behave morally is as interesting as the will to behave badly.'

'Ah, the question of the selfish good,' Ben intervened.

'But that is not always the case.' Sidney replied. 'Some people are selfless. They are good without any expectation of reward. It is almost, or perhaps it really is, natural to them.'

'You do always think the best of people,' Amanda replied. 'If you'd been kept prisoner by someone as vile as that man you might feel a bit differently. Just thinking of him makes me feel sick.'

'Then let's not,' said Lord Teversham.

Sidney explained. 'Amanda's been rather off her food ever since. I just think it's an interesting dilemma that people overlook . . .'

Cicely Teversham began to clear the plates. 'I see you managed the beef all right, Amanda.'

'It was delicious, thank you, and it's so kind of you both to loan the painting. You know that you can come to the National Gallery and see it whenever you like?'

Lord Teversham handed his sister his plate. It was unclear where the butler had gone. 'Perhaps we should crack on with pudding,' he continued. 'I think Cook has organised one of her specials. It's a childhood favourite of mine and now that the tiresome business of rationing is over we have it as much as we like. I hope you will crave my indulgence. I think we've also got a rather agreeable dessert wine to go with it.' He stood up to look for it. 'Let me see if it is here; a rather fruity little Gaillac, I believe.'

Cicely stood up at the same time and moved over to a silver serving dish on the sideboard. She took off the lid. 'Banana fritters!' she announced. 'How wonderful. Can I help you to a couple, Miss Kendall?'

'If you'll excuse me,' Amanda apologised, 'I don't think I'll be having any pudding.'

'Are you sure?' Sidney asked.

'What ever is the matter?' Lord Teversham asked. 'Don't you like bananas?'

Honourable Men

SIDNEY WAS TALKING to himself again. 'Vanity, vanity, all is vanity, saith the Preacher,' he muttered as he walked towards the Arts Theatre for the first rehearsal of a modern-dress production of Shakespeare's *Julius Caesar*.

Why had he agreed to take part, he wondered? At least his was only a small part, that of Artemidorus, 'sophist of Cnidos', who tries to warn Caesar that a group of conspirators are about to kill him. There were two scenes, very few lines and, as Inspector Keating pointed out, 'you can be in the pub by the interval'.

Sidney had convinced himself that his performance was more to do with civic responsibility than with pride. This was, after all, the theme of the play: how to live an honourable life and protect the greater good. To take part in such a drama, he said to himself, was no more than his duty. There was no point in getting into a state or worrying about what people might think. In any case, his ego, he reassured himself, was far smaller than that of Julius Caesar: a man who had, in fact, been assassinated precisely because of vanity.

Derek Jarvis, the coroner, was the director. He had decided to set the play in the 1930s and make much of the similarities between Julius Caesar and Mussolini. The part of Caesar was taken by Lord Teversham with his sister, Cicely Teversham, as Caesar's wife, and Ben Blackwood as Mark Antony.

As soon as he discovered that he was going to be dressed as an Italian blackshirt Sidney forbade both Amanda and Inspector Keating from attending a performance. There was only so much teasing he could take. Why couldn't they have done *South Pacific* instead, he wondered? Then he could have persuaded Amanda to join the chorus and appear in a hula skirt. It would be a lot more entertaining than sharing the stage with a collection of amateur thespians dressed up as fascists.

'I thought you did enough performing in church,' Keating had teased. 'You want to watch it. People will start talking.'

'I think I am on safe ground.'

'This is the way they draw you in, Sidney. Next year you'll be in the panto. I can just see you as Widow Twanky.'

'I will be doing no such thing,' Sidney replied, his sense of humour deserting him. 'This will be my only appearance on the boards.'

Mrs Maguire had been equally sceptical. 'People will think you've got too much time on your hands, Canon Chambers. Either that or you are showing off. No one likes a show-off.'

'I am doing it to feel part of the community,' Sidney replied, 'that is all.'

'You are already part of the community. You should be out walking the dog instead of consorting with people who should know better.'

'But then,' Leonard Graham chipped in unhelpfully, 'if they did *The Two Gentlemen of Verona* Dickens could take a starring role as the dog Crab. There would be no trouble catching him "a pissing" under the Duke's table. He does it often enough.'

'There's no need to be vulgar,' said Mrs Maguire.

'My dear Mrs Maguire, I am quoting from Shakespeare. It's bawdy rather than vulgar.'

'I don't care what it is. It's still rude. But at least it would get that wretched animal out of the house and spare the lino.' Mrs Maguire still refused to call Dickens by his name. Clearly it was going to take her a long time to recover from the latest incident of the laddered stocking.

Mrs Maguire was, however, correct in her analysis of how much time the production would take. Sidney spent hours in rehearsal simply hanging about. He had never realised that most of an actor's life involved waiting around. It made him tense. He remembered the impatience of the prayer – 'Come Lord, quickly come' – and thought that this was a sentiment that could be applied to the all too secular Lord Teversham, who frequently missed his entrances, and who had so much difficulty in remembering his lines that his scenes took far longer than anyone else's. Indeed, Sidney thought, such was the intolerance of the other cast members that he began to wonder if they might even take a modicum of pleasure in seeing their local aristocrat lying in a pool of blood.

There were six weeks of rehearsal before the first night in late October, and much discussion about the inherent themes of the play, such as honour, pride, loyalty and political opportunism. Sidney found it an instructive process, as these were qualities that could also prove useful in understanding the machinations of many a priest in the Church of England.

By the time the first night arrived, he was more than prepared. He strode on to the stage, pressed the letter warning Julius Caesar about the conspirators into Lord Teversham's

333

hands, and infused his lines with as much menace as he could muster.

'Delay not, Caesar,' he hissed. 'Read it instantly.'

Lord Teversham looked at Sidney but then answered by looking straight out to the audience. 'What, is the fellow mad?'

This double-take had not been part of the rehearsal process and was closer to pantomime than politics. The audience laughed and Sidney realised, with horror, that he had been upstaged. He had intended to inspire both anxiety and fear but it now appeared that he was little more than a figure of fun. How could Lord Teversham have done this to him? Was it on purpose or by accident? He left the stage feeling humiliated and watched the rest of the scene from the wings.

Moments later, the conspirators moved in for the kill, kneeling round the aged would-be emperor. Lord Teversham stretched out an Imperial arm, and intoned, impossibly slowly: 'Doth not Brutus bootless kneel?'

Clive Morton, dressed in a black outfit that would have looked more at place in a nightclub than a battlefield, leaped up, grabbed Lord Teversham's neck from behind, and shouted 'Speak hands for me!' before stabbing him in the back.

The other actors rose as one from their kneeling positions to conclude the murderous deed. Simon Hackford pulled back the slouching body by the collar, held the gasping form upright and stabbed Lord Teversham once more in the chest.

His victim gasped. 'Et tu, Brute? Then fall Caesar.'

Lord Teversham clutched his heart, staggered forward to the front of the stage, and fell to his side. As he collapsed the conspirators threw their knives on to the ground. The scattered clatter of metal on the floor was intended to accentuate the drama of the death.

One of the disadvantages of the cast wearing black, rather than the traditional white toga, was the fact that it took far longer for Caesar's blood to show; and, although a stomach sachet had been appropriately punctured, it was only when the conspirators came forward to smear their hands with Caesar's blood that the audience was made aware of the amount of gore involved.

Each actor took off his gloves and knelt before Lord Teversham's prostrate form. A servant arrived to ask that Antony 'may safely come' and Ben Blackwood arrived on stage and took his place by Caesar's corpse.

'O mighty Caesar! Dost thou lie so low?

Are all they conquests, glories, triumphs, spoils,

Shrunk to this little measure?'

His performance had lost the feyness Sidney had noticed in rehearsals and Ben commanded the stage. He took off his gloves and shook hands with the conspirators. The blood on their hands stained his. He knelt over Caesar's body. He was on the verge of tears, choking so much that he could hardly get through his lines:

'Thou art the ruins of the noblest man

That ever lived in the tide of times . . .'

He finished his speech and asked the servant to help him with the body. Then, after he had taken it into the wings and laid it down he hesitated. Lord Teversham had not risen like an actor who had finished his scene but lay motionless. Ben put his head against the heart of his friend and checked the blood once more.

The plebeians took to the stage, picking up the knives the conspirators had thrown down, ready to commit revenge.

Ben Blackwood looked up at Sidney in horror. 'Curtain!' he said urgently. 'Curtain and house lights. For God's sake!'

'Typical,' muttered Inspector Keating after he had been summoned from his home, leaving his wife and three sleeping children behind. 'It could have been any of them.'

'Or all of them, I suppose,' said Sidney. He was already feeling defeated by the events of the evening.

'Steady on. This isn't *Murder on the Orient Express*. Only one blade did the damage.'

'But who carried it? That is what we need to know. And where is it now?'

'If it is in this building my men will find it. No one who took part in the play will be allowed to leave . . .'

Sidney realised that the design of the play was going to hamper the investigation since its fascist theme had necessitated each of the assassins wearing black shirts, black boots, and, crucially, black leather gloves. There were no fingerprints from the murder itself, and all the plebeians had handled the knives in the ensuing tumult. The actors playing Marcus Brutus, Cassius, Decius Brutus, Metellus, Cinna, Casca, Ligarius and Trebonius were all suspects.

The stage area was sealed off and the investigation began. Inspector Keating called Sidney aside. 'I'm assuming that I will have your help on this case?'

'As a member of the cast I am of course a witness. And, I suppose, a suspect.'

'Now you are being plain daft.'

'I would hope to be one of the first to be ruled out of your investigation.'

'You can take that as read. Where do we start?'

'With the director: Derek Jarvis. He should know what everyone was supposed to be doing and who was meant to stab Lord Teversham and where. He's quite thorough about that kind of thing.'

'I can't imagine that the coroner is best pleased to have his night of theatrical triumph ruined by his professional duty. As soon as we know the angle of the crucial blow we will have to do a re-enactment.'

'Tonight?'

'Tomorrow. Once we have heard everyone's statements. It's going to be a long evening. You must be getting used to these by now.'

'They are,' Sidney agreed, 'becoming alarmingly familiar.'

Police were stationed at the public entrance and the stage door. The cast was asked to wait in the auditorium while the stage and backstage areas were searched for the murder weapon. The coroner made a preliminary examination of Lord Teversham and organised his removal to the mortuary. His distraught sister had been in the audience and accompanied the body. Ben was alone in the bar. Frank Blackwood gave him a stiff drink and wrapped him in a blanket. He sat in the corner, shivering, without saying a word, unable to leave until the police had taken his statement, a hipflask of brandy beside him.

Inspector Keating commandeered the theatre manager's office and went through the list of official suspects on a blackboard.

Marcus Brutus: Simon Hackford, auctioneer and art dealer

Cassius: Frank Blackwood, engineer

Decius Brutus: Hector Kirby, butcher

Metellus: Stan Headley, blacksmith

Cinna: Michel Morel, *le patron*, Le Bistro Bleu Blanc Rouge, Mill Road

Casca: Clive Morton, solicitor

Ligarius: Tom Rogerson, stationmaster, British Rail

Trebonius: Mike Standing, businessman

Inspector Keating briefed his men. 'According to the coroner's preliminary examination Lord Teversham was stabbed between the chest and the stomach with a single blow which twisted first to the left and then to the right. He suggests a short blade, three or four inches in length. It must have been sharp as the wound was clean and deep. To disguise a stage dagger and conceal its sharpness would take skill. All the knives used in the production were put back on the prop table after the murder. There are no missing stage weapons and they are all blunt, retractable and safe. The real weapon has disappeared. We need to find it.'

PC Roger Wilson asked a question. 'An additional knife?'

'Possibly disguised as a stage weapon.'

Wilson continued. 'We are assuming, then, that the murderer would be some kind of expert . . .'

'It seems likely but . . .'

'Which means the butcher, the chef and the blacksmith?'

'They would be obvious suspects. At the same time we must establish a motive. Why would Hector Kirby, for example, a butcher, want to kill Lord Teversham? Why would a French chef? It doesn't make sense. We need to ask each man where he struck his blow, find out any inconsistencies and proceed from there . . .'

'Can we rule any of them out?' Sidney asked. 'We know that the actors playing Ligarius and Trebonius did not stab Caesar at all and were nowhere near his body. Furthermore, Clive Morton, who played Casca, stabbed Lord Teversham in the back.'

'Very well, but he still had a weapon, Sidney.'

'I do think that after we have taken their statements we can probably discount Mike Standing and Tom Rogerson.'

Inspector Keating took out his blackboard duster and rubbed the names away. 'Very well. That would still leave six main suspects, all of whom were known to the victim. Clive Morton was his lawyer, Simon Hackford dealt with his art, Stan Headley sorted out his horses, Hector Kirby provided his meat, Le Bistro Bleu Blanc Rouge was his favourite restaurant, and Frank Blackwood was father to his personal assistant. They all knew the victim, and any one of them could have had a grievance. We have to find out what that was, and who had the nerve to risk committing such a public crime.'

The interviewing strategy was agreed, tasks were allotted and the actors were asked for their statements. Those who had not been on stage at the time of the murder were questioned first and allowed to leave. Actors playing the conspirators were given a more thorough investigation.

The police began with Derek Jarvis. He was attempting to remain calm. 'If I'd known they were going to start murdering each other I would have put them all in togas,' he complained. 'There would be so much more evidence. I should have thought about it in advance, I suppose, but you can hardly expect something like this to happen.'

'Was there any tension between members of the cast in rehearsal?' Inspector Keating asked.

'There's always tension. Lord Teversham certainly made a meal of everything and he never listened to what anyone else was saying. It's a pity I cast him but I thought he had the right gravitas.'

'Did you witness the death?'

'Of course. I was watching from the front. It was as if I had directed the whole thing.'

'And you saw nothing unusual?'

'No. It unfolded like a nightmare:

"Between the acting of a dreadful thing

And the first motion, all the interim is

Like a phantasma, or a hideous dream . . ."

Who would have thought the play should be so apt? You could almost think I had chosen it deliberately.'

'I'm sure it's not your fault.'

'I provided an opportunity. It will be on my conscience.'

'Then let us help ease it by finding the person responsible. I am going to need all your help on this, Jarvis.'

'We're going to need each other,' the coroner replied, looking at Sidney. 'And we'll have to be at the top of our game because I think whoever did this must have been planning it for weeks.'

Keating leaned forward, with both hands resting on the table. 'You mean he could have joined the cast specifically in order to murder Lord Teversham?'

'It is a possibility.'

Sidney thought this through. 'Someone who has never appeared in amateur theatricals before?'

Keating snapped. 'I don't think he means you.'

The coroner left to make preparations for the post-mortem and the investigators turned their attention to Clive Morton, the local solicitor, who had played Casca. He had changed into his usual blazer and flannelled trousers. 'I don't know why you need to ask me any questions,' he began. 'I stabbed him in the back. Lord Teversham fell forwards and the others did the rest. I can hardly be a suspect.'

'We are not saying that you are,' Keating replied. 'But perhaps you saw something else?'

'It's hard to think. We are all shocked. It must have happened so fast. We were at it hammer and tongs. Derek Jarvis told us that in order to get into the mood we should remember the war and imagine that Lord Teversham was a Nazi who had killed our children. That certainly did the trick.'

'Did you get carried away?'

'I admit that I stabbed him a couple more times for effect. I wanted to be seen to be doing something.'

'And did you notice anything else? A real blade, blood, anyone acting suspiciously?'

'We were all acting suspiciously, Inspector, if you can call it acting. That was the point.'

'And can you think of anyone who might want to kill Lord Teversham?'

'No one at all.'

'You were his lawyer?'

'I was.'

'And you have heard or seen nothing untoward; either on stage or off?'

'I am afraid I have not. I suppose, when the time comes, you will probably want to have a look at the will.'

'The time *has* come, Mr Morton.'

'Then I will bring it to you first thing tomorrow morning, which is almost upon us. Do you think I could go?'

'Provided you come to the station in the morning.'

'I am at your service.'

Inspector Keating summoned Michel Morel, the French chef, a thin, vain man who was wearing a black polo-necked jumper under his suit. 'In France this does not happen,' he began. 'We are careful in our passions. When people are angry they drink some wine and they find another woman. We do not kill each other like this. It is not good. Have you discovered the correct knife?'

'All the stage weapons have been returned. They are blunt.'

The chef was unsurprised. 'Of course. They would be of no use in a murder.'

'Could any of them have been modified or replaced?'

'Why do you ask?'

'Because you deal with knives every day. Have any of yours gone missing recently?'

'I do not think so.'

'Have you trained anyone in the use of knives?' Inspector Keating asked.

'No one who was in the play. I have a sous-chef, Gavin, but he is Scottish and he hates the theatre. He was cooking that night. We had many customers. But, of course, we always need more. It is one reason why I was taking part. I have to persuade more people to come and eat at my restaurant.'

'What did you think of the stage knives you were given?'

'They were toys. They were short and no good. We painted them black.'

'You did not see the flash of a blade under the lights?'

'I thought it was a reflection or a mirror.'

'So you might have seen something?'

'In the middle of it all I saw a glint, I think. Is that the word?'

'In the middle of the assassination? You are sure? Not at the beginning or the end?'

'No. It was before my turn. Not after.'

'And who was holding the knife?'

'I cannot tell. It was quick – like the back of a fish in a river. You see it and it is gone.'

'But it was not at the very beginning?'

'No. I do not think so. Not the first or the second person.'

'You are sure?'

'It was very fast. But I think so.'

'You could not have imagined it?'

'I always tell the truth. I am a man of honour.'

The inspector turned to Sidney. If what Michel Morel was saying were correct, then that would rule out Clive Morton.

'How well did you know Lord Teversham?' Sidney asked.

'He was one of my best customers.'

'How often did he come and who did who did he come with?'

'They were business meetings. First with Mr Hackford but not recently not so much; they argue, I think.'

'You saw them do this?'

'Of course.'

'What were they arguing about?'

'They talk about paintings and money. It was last year. Then Lord Teversham comes with a different man.'

'Ben Blackwood?'

'*Bien sûr*. Now they include me more. Lord Teversham is happier. They talk to me about art. We have a little joke. I say the French are always best; David, not Gainsborough, Poussin not Constable, Rodin not Henry Moore. They were amused that I know so much. But most of the time, you must remember, I am in the kitchen. I say hello and goodbye. I do not have the time to listen. Mr Blackwood came once with your beautiful friend, Canon Chambers.'

'My friend? You mean Miss Kendall?'

Inspector Keating interrupted. 'Where did you stab Lord Teversham?'

'I was to the left. I stab him in the guts. I ask if I can do this. More passionate.'

'I don't think this murder is about passion.'

'You do not think so?'

'These were all men.'

'You do not think men can have passions with each other?'

'It's not considered decent in this country.'

'Sometimes passion is deeper than we think, Inspector. People have feelings. Even in the police, I am sure . . .'

Inspector Keating was in no mood for insinuation and cut short the interrogation. 'That will be all, thank you very much. We are not here to discuss the feelings of my officers.'

Once Michel Morel had left, Keating rose from his chair and started to pace around the room. 'I think that chef saw more than he was letting on . . .'

'Oh, I don't know,' said Sidney. 'I rather liked him.'

'We'll have to sound him out again. Perhaps you could go to his restaurant.'

'He must wonder why he ever came to England.'

'He's never going to make any money,' Keating continued. 'I looked at the menu in the window. Who is going to eat snails? Or artichoke? As soon as you've peeled the leaves off there's nothing left. We don't like waste in this country, and I don't like him wasting my time.'

'He was teasing you, Inspector, but I can't believe he is a murderer. Who have we got next?'

'Frank Blackwood.'

'Ben's father?'

'Not the most restful of people to be interviewing in the middle of the night. We had better call him in. Offer him some tea while you're at it.'

Such thoughtfulness was not appreciated. 'I'm sick of bloody tea,' Frank Blackwood began. Sidney had always thought that he had been miscast. He was too bulky to have the lean and hungry look the part of Cassius demanded. In fact, thought Sidney, his son might have been better. 'I've had nothing but bloody tea all night,' Frank complained. 'What do I have to do to get a decent drink round here?'

'I saw you giving your son some brandy,' Sidney observed.

'He's taken my hipflask and drunk the lot, most likely. I needed it for a bit of Dutch courage, not that the Dutch make any brandy as far as I am aware.'

'You were nervous?' Sidney asked.

'Of course. I've never acted in a play before.'

'Then why did you agree to take part?'

'Ben was in it and I thought it might be a lark. I quite fancied meeting an actress. Although I didn't realise how few women were in it. They should have done a musical.'

'That's what I thought,' said Keating. 'Or a panto.'

'The woman playing Calpurnia's all right. I've had a few chats with her, even if she is more crackers than biscuit. What do you want to know?'

Inspector Keating began. 'Can you tell me how you killed Lord Teversham?'

'I didn't. Or is that a trick question?'

'At the moment we are trying to establish who stabbed Lord Teversham when, where and in what order. Could you remind us of your movements leading up to the murder?'

'I was on stage. Lord Teversham was on my left . . .'

'And you stabbed him with your right hand?' Keating asked. 'Whereabouts?'

'In the chest. That's where I was told to do it. I was to go second so the old man fell forward before Hector did the stomach so the blood came out. Then the others followed.'

Sidney joined in once more. He wished he had more of a photographic memory. 'And what did you do with your knife afterwards?'

'I threw it on the floor. We all did.'

'And then you stood back?' Keating asked.

'That was the idea. It's terrible that it took us so long to notice that something was wrong but that's what happens when you all wear black. Someone might have been able to save him.'

'You weren't shocked when you realised what had happened?'

'Of course I was shocked. It's murder.'

'And you saw nothing suspicious?'

'Nothing. No one can believe what's happened. You don't expect this kind of thing, do you?'

Inspector Keating began writing down a few notes but Frank Blackwood had had enough. 'Do you think I can go now?' he asked. 'I've got a seven o'clock start and I need to be at the factory for the men. You can always find me at the works.'

Sidney stood up to open the door and stretch his legs. He wondered how much longer they were going to take. There were just a few people left to interview. The situation had been so confused and it was difficult to think it through when everyone was so tired. He needed to sleep, wake refreshed and then make some notes, recalling everything he had seen during rehearsals. He closed his eyes and tried to remember the movements of everyone on stage during the performance.

'Last one for now, I think,' Inspector Keating announced. 'Simon Hackford of Willows Farm. Art dealer, auctioneer and former business associate. I hope you're not falling asleep, Sidney?'

'Not at all. I was thinking.'

'I hope productively?'

Sidney was not sure that he was. His thoughts had roamed from the question of dignity and status in the play – 'Set honour in one eye and death i'the other' – to the idea of reputation in general. Could there be a clue here?

The presiding ethic of the aristocracy was to be noble; and yet, perhaps Lord Teversham, in some aspect of his life, had lacked nobility and fallen short? But where? Could it be in his financial dealings, in his personal relationships, or in the management of his estate? Where might such a gentle man have behaved dishonourably? Sidney would have to talk to those who had been closest to him.

Simon Hackford, Lord Teversham's former business associate, had been waiting for three hours and was in no mood for a close examination. 'This is ridiculous,' he began. 'How can I possibly have committed this crime?'

Inspector Keating looked to Sidney to calm the situation. 'You were playing the part of Brutus. The last man to strike,' he said, 'and therefore the most important. Can you remember how much stage blood there was on his costume before you struck the blow?'

'It was all over the place . . .'

'So you did not need to puncture the sachet?'

'I did not.'

'And where did you strike him?'

'In the heart. I had to pull Dominic's head back from his slumped and stabbed position with my right hand. Then he was to look me in the eye and say: "Et tu, Brute?" I stabbed him on the nearside left, the same side as his heart, so the audience could see us both. After I had done this he was to say "Then fall, Caesar"; but by the time I lifted him up he was already limp and half-dead and I couldn't keep him upright.'

'You think he was already wounded?'

'I do now: although I didn't think so at the time. I thought he was just over-acting. The director told him that he should be as passive as Jesus and that this would be a Christ-like moment. I was supposed to hold him by the hair at the back of his head and let him stand centre-stage with the conspirators in a semicircle around him. It was a version of the Last Supper, I suppose, and Caesar was then meant to open his arms, as if he had the stigmata, and fall forward, only turning on to his side at the last minute. But as soon as I let go of his body he just crumpled.'

'Why did it take people so long to realise what had happened?'

'Because we thought that Dominic was having his great moment. It didn't occur to any of us that he was paying for the performance with his life.'

Inspector Keating allowed a moment's silence. 'Of course, it could still have been you that administered the fatal blow. You were playing the part of Brutus, the noblest Roman of them all.'

'Yes, it could have been me, I suppose. But it was not. I loved that man. I would never have harmed him; no matter what happened between us. He was my friend.'

'What do you mean, "What happened between us"?'

'We used to work together; as I am sure you know.'

'What was the state of your relationship on the day of the murder?'

'We have always been perfectly civil to one another. There was no animosity, if that is what you are implying. We both acknowledged that some things have to come to an end.'

'And you didn't mind about that?'

'There is no point dwelling on what might have been. My passion is for silver and for antiques, rather than paintings, and I set up a new business after I stopped working for Lord Teversham. Dominic even lent me some money.'

'May I ask how much?'

'A thousand pounds.'

'Rather a lot.'

'I was paying it back. I think he felt guilty that our working relationship had come to an end.'

'And why did it?'

'There was nothing specific. If anything, the feeling was mutual. I had always wanted to start something on my own and

I had neglected my wife. I'm sure you know how it is, Inspector. When a man works too much his wife often complains.'

Sidney looked to his friend for a reply, but he said nothing. Instead, he nodded, encouraging Simon Hackford to continue.

'Now I have my antique shop and I work with my wife all the time. That is why I would like to go home. I start to feel ill when we are apart. It's almost a physical sensation. Have you ever felt like that, Inspector?'

Keating answered at last. 'To be honest, most of the time I'm quite glad to get away from home; but I can see what you might mean. There's no need to detain you any longer, Mr Hackford.'

It was three in the morning and Sidney was exhausted. If he had been a monk he would be getting up for the first prayers of the day. Instead he was at a crime scene, having a cup of tea with a police inspector who was becoming increasingly exasperated.

'You would have thought it would be a simple matter, wouldn't you, Sidney? One of the stage knives is tampered with, or replaced. It goes missing. We find it and then we discover who did the deed. But, in fact, we have no suspect, no finger-prints and, so far, no knife.'

'I was wondering,' Sidney said at last, 'if the choice of murder scene might be deliberate?'

'More than opportunist?'

'What I mean is that there might be clues in the play itself. Caesar is killed for different reasons: partly because he is vain, and partly because of mob desire. But Brutus kills him out of civic duty: "a piece of work that will make sick men whole." It could perhaps boil down to a question of honour, social obliga-tion or revenge.'

The inspector gave one of his familiar sighs. 'I'm all for revenge as a motive, Sidney, but you mean someone might also be doing it for the good of society?'

'It's a thought. The German poet Schiller, for example, referred to the theatre as a moral institution.'

'With respect, I do feel you may be barking up the wrong tree, Sidney. This was cold-blooded murder. It wasn't an act of social justice.'

Sidney hated the phrase 'with respect'. It always meant the opposite. 'I don't think we can discount anything.'

'Of course not.'

'I think the idea of honour and reputation is important.'

'It often is.'

'People are terrified of losing face.'

'Men like Simon Hackford?'

'Indeed.'

Inspector Keating would not be committed. 'Nice man; a bit weak, I would have thought.'

'Too weak to do the deed?'

'No. It doesn't take much to stab a man, especially in those circumstances.'

'He would be your chief suspect?'

Keating thought for a moment. 'I wouldn't like to say. But I wouldn't mind you finding out a little more about his relationship with Lord Teversham. It doesn't sound right. Perhaps you could go to Locket Hall and give them the once over?'

'Very well.'

'You hesitate, Sidney.'

'I do; but that is nothing to do with Locket Hall. A further thought troubles me . . .'

'Which is?'

'Was the person holding the dagger aware that he was doing the deed?'

'What do you mean?'

'We have to be sure,' Sidney began, 'that the person who administered the blow knew that the dagger had been switched. If he did not know, then he could have killed Lord Teversham by accident, leaving the real murderer with the perfect alibi. In fact, I might even be surprised if the murderer was one of the assassins. I would suggest it could equally well have been someone who switched the daggers and left the scene of the crime, knowing that the fatal blow would be administered in his, or even her, absence.'

'That's the kind of thing I'm supposed to come up with. It means the murderer could be anybody.'

'Not if we find a motive. We need to look into the character of Lord Teversham.'

'I agree. But there are six suspects and a reconstruction to get through first. By all means make a start on your theory. Any background you can get on Simon Hackford, then tell me in the pub on Thursday. Any foreground information or immediate suspicions, then come to me immediately . . .'

Sidney bicycled home, lights flaring, across the fields and against a harvest moon. He met no one. Everyone in the city appeared to be asleep. He wondered how many of them had said any prayers.

'Forasmuch as all mortal men be subject to many sudden perils, diseases, and sicknesses, and ever uncertain what time they shall depart out of this life . . .'

He bicycled quickly because he was worried about having

left Dickens for so long but, on opening the kitchen door, he was reassured to find him asleep in his basket and a note on the table: 'Have walked dog. No mishaps. Leonard.'

That was a relief. He really would have to try and be more responsible about his dog in future. Sidney made himself a pot of tea and wondered why he had stayed and taken part in the investigation. There was no need, really. Inspector Keating had said as much.

So why had he done it? Was it vanity, he wondered, the idea that they could not manage to conduct a police inquiry without him? It was absurd to think like this, but he now had to admit that he was never far from the sin of pride. He tried to convince himself that his motives were born out of a desire to understand what had happened, to stand alongside people in their difficulty and also to be, in Bunyan's words, 'valiant for truth'. But it was going to take a long time both to justify his involvement and to find out the truth behind this particular murder.

The next morning, unsurprisingly, Sidney overslept, missing the eight o'clock Communion service. Over a late breakfast, Leonard Graham told him that he had been informed what had happened, that he hadn't wanted to wake his boss and that there was little point in having a curate if he couldn't be relied upon to take a service on his own.

There had been four people in the congregation: Agatha Redmond, the Labrador breeder; Isabel Robinson, the doctor's wife; Gervase Bell, the local historian; and Frances Kirby, the wife of the butcher who had played Decius Brutus, a woman who made sixty toffees for her husband every week and could be relied upon to spread news of the murder, together with her personal opinion as to the most likely culprit, by lunchtime.

'We must try to discourage any unnecessary rumours,' Sidney urged Leonard after finishing his boiled egg. 'The last thing we want is people jumping to conclusions.'

'I am afraid,' his curate replied, 'it is too late for that.'

'And what are they saying?'

'They think it was Simon Hackford.'

'That is ridiculous.'

'He did play Brutus . . .'

'But he is the most mild-mannered of men. And it is most likely that the fatal blow was administered before Simon Hackford got anywhere near Lord Teversham. 'Why are they saying these things?'

Leonard Graham gave his vicar a steady look. 'I think you can guess.'

'Simon Hackford is a married man.'

'But Lord Teversham was not.'

'There is no proof of any indecent involvement on anyone's part.'

'Of course there isn't, Sidney. If there was any evidence for that then both men would be in prison.'

'I do think that is harsh.'

'Do you?'

'Some homosexuals receive longer sentences than burglars. It's absurd. But surely this is all gossip?'

'People are saying that there is no smoke without fire.'

'That is one of Mrs Maguire's favourite phrases. I have told her to stop saying that but she never listens. I can't abide the way in which our country is losing its sense of discretion. Even

354

if there was something between Simon Hackford and Lord Teversham, the fact of the matter is that it is none of anyone else's business. People should have a right to privacy.'

'I didn't know you felt so strongly.'

'We must think the best of people, Leonard, or we are lost. I think I'll have to preach along those lines on Sunday.'

'That would be a brave thing to do.'

'It isn't brave at all,' Sidney replied. 'It is necessary.'

'Matthew chapter 7 would be an obvious text,' Leonard advised. ' "Judge not that ye be not judged." There is also the Book of Proverbs: "The words of a talebearer are as wounds . . ." '

'That's a better idea . . .

' "And they go down into the innermost parts of the belly." Do you think it's a bit too apt? Lord Teversham was stabbed, after all.'

'I'd like to give it to them straight: shake them up a bit.'

'I think they are already quite shaken, Sidney.'

The telephone rang. It was Amanda. Sidney asked how she was feeling and if she was all right.

'Never mind me,' she began. 'I hear Lord Teversham has been murdered.'

'I'm afraid it's true.'

'Ben telephoned. He could hardly speak. This is a disaster.'

'I know. It was, it seems, the perfect murder.'

'How can a murder ever be "perfect"?'

'There were multiple weapons and everyone in the cast was wearing gloves. It could have been any of them.'

'But who would want to kill Lord Teversham? You could hardly hope to meet a kinder man. It's so cruel.'

'It's hard to find a genuine motive, I must admit.'

'Ben has asked me to come and stay. He said that it would be a comfort. Then I can see you at the same time. Are you all right?'

'I think the correct word would be "preoccupied".'

'I was thinking of the five o'clock train. Would you like to come to Locket Hall for drinks? I just need to see you, Sidney. For both of our sakes.'

Sidney thought how good it would be to see Amanda once more, but worried about exposing her to the darker side of life once again. He tidied his desk, took Dickens for what was now becoming yet another brief walk across the Meadows and returned to his neglected paperwork. As soon as he did so, Mrs Maguire seized the opportunity to remind him about the peeling wallpaper in the bathroom.

'I do have more important things to think about than wallpaper,' Sidney snapped.

'If you weren't so involved in all that crime then you would have plenty of time.'

'I am aware of that.'

Mrs Maguire continued to grumble. 'They should never have put a bathroom and toilet next to the kitchen. That sort of thing belongs outside.'

'It is 1954, Mrs Maguire. Times change.'

'Some things never change,' the housekeeper replied, ominously. 'Just like people.'

Sidney was not going to rise to the challenge of yet another gnomic remark. He pretended that he was writing a sermon.

'You're busy, then?'

'I'm always busy, Mrs Maguire.'

'Then I suppose I'll have to let you get on. I've left you a steak and kidney pudding,' she added. 'I hope you don't burn it.'

'Very good, Mrs Maguire.'

When she had finally left him alone, Sidney picked up his pen and wrote out the list of principal suspects.

Simon Hackford: he and Lord Teversham had been former business partners; there had clearly been a row of some sort, and there were rumours of intimacy. But he seemed an unlikely murderer.

Clive Morton: Sidney would need to check the will. There could be a financial motive.

Michel Morel: unlikely, Sidney thought, but he did have considerable expertise in knives.

Frank Blackwood: it was hard to know what he was doing in the production in the first place. It was out of character, Sidney thought ruefully. But if he had joined the cast for the explicit purpose of murdering Lord Teversham, then what was his motive?

Ben Blackwood: despite not being a conspirator, Sidney had to admit that, however unlikely, it was not impossible. Perhaps he stood to inherit the art collection? He could have had a concealed weapon when he was crouched over the body and committed the crime while pretending to weep. But his behaviour on the night in question, and his grief after the death, were surely genuine? If Sidney were to pursue this line he would have to be careful.

Later that day he put down his pen, fetched his hat and coat and set off on the half-hour bicycle ride to Locket Hall. After he had ridden through Trumpington and carried on for a few miles he realised that, rather than burning Mrs Maguire's steak and kidney pudding, he had completely forgotten about it. No wonder he felt hungry. But it was too late to go back. Perhaps Leonard Graham would help himself and finish it off? Sidney certainly hoped so, because if Mrs Maguire discovered that it had not been touched when she returned the next morning with her welsh rarebit, then there would be hell to pay.

But how was he supposed to remember everything? Sidney thought to himself. The things he had to keep in his head . . .

On arrival at Locket Hall, Forbes Mackay took his hat and coat and offered him 'a wee sharpener' to steady himself 'in these coal-black times'. He warned his guest that the mood upstairs was more sombre than he had ever known.

The butler gestured to the staircase and Sidney climbed it to find Ben and Amanda sitting together on the sofa.

'Forgive me for borrowing your friend but I've been in a funk,' Ben began. 'Cicely has taken to her bed, the staff have been stunned into silence and I don't know how what to do. I keep thinking of Dominic and wandering about the house. I forget why I have come into a room. I'm unable to listen to anything people are saying or make any reply. Nothing has any point any more.'

'You need to rest,' said Sidney. 'And sleep.'

'I try, but then, just before I fall asleep I remember what has happened and all I can think about is that appalling crime.'

'The police have been to see you?'

'They wanted a lot of personal information. I suppose it is understandable. Is Mackay getting you a drink?'

'He is . . .'

Amanda turned to Sidney and asked, 'Why do such terrible things have to happen? Surely it shakes your faith?'

'Not in God. It shakes my faith in people.'

'Have the police finished with their interviews?' Ben asked.

'They will probably have to go round again. Do you know who benefits from the will?'

'Most people get something. I think Clive Morton has handed it over.'

'Yourself?'

'I have been bequeathed some of the lesser paintings. A Palmer landscape that I always admired, a charming Landseer and a beautiful set of Bewick engravings. It was incredibly thoughtful of Dominic but I'd rather he was still alive. The works don't mean anything without him.'

'Anyone else?'

'Cicely inherits the whole collection but there are a few other bequests: Simon Hackford, for example. I think Dominic changed the will recently to cut his inheritance down. At one point he was going to give Simon a Turner. That would have raised a few eyebrows.'

'I think they were already raised. Did Simon Hackford and Lord Teversham work together?'

'I thought you knew that?'

Sidney smiled. 'I don't always admit to what I know, Ben.'

'They were the greatest of friends. They went to auctions together. In fact, Simon is responsible for many of the items in the collection. He would spot the painting, Lord Teversham would buy it and then they would either keep it or sell it on. Simon's really an expert on silver, but he knows his eighteenth century, although he did manage to miss out on an unattributed Gainsborough . . .'

'He failed to spot what you might call a "sleeper"?'

'Very good, Canon Chambers, you're catching up on the lingo.'

'Why did Simon Hackford stop working here?'

'Dominic told me that he began to doubt his abilities. He didn't feel that he could quite trust him any more and then, after I came along, they saw rather less of each other. I don't think there was any great falling out: just a drifting apart. Sometimes friendships fade away, don't they?'

'You're a bit young to know that.'

'I saw it at university, Canon Chambers. People develop sudden likings for each other and then, when they get to know each other better, that knowledge isn't as exciting as the initial promise . . .'

Amanda sighed. 'It happens in London all the time. It's so hard to know whether people are genuine or not. Don't you agree, Sidney?'

'I have to give people the benefit of the doubt, of course.'

'But not when you are investigating a murder, surely?'

'No,' Sidney agreed. His thoughts were becoming alarmingly familiar. 'Then, it seems, I can't think like a priest at all.'

The next day Sidney and Amanda met for an early lunch at Bleu Blanc Rouge. Sidney had not been inside the restaurant before and was unsurprised to discover that it lived up to its name. With its white walls, red gingham tablecloths and blue napkins, everything about it suggested the tricolour. Enlarged photographs and framed copies of old newspapers celebrating the 1945 liberation of Paris covered the walls and the menu offered unremittingly French fare: pâté, onion tart, omelettes and *potage parmentier, boeuf bourguignon, coq au vin*, rabbit and turbot.

'Would you like a glass of champagne?' Michel Morel asked as he took their coats.

'It's a bit early, isn't it?' Sidney asked, wondering how his host could afford to make such an extravagant gesture.

The chef ignored him. 'Where I was trained the *cuisinier* began each day with champagne. He is the greatest chef in France, Fernand Point.'

'I think I've heard of him,' Sidney replied. 'Some friends of mine went to his restaurant after the war. La Pyramide . . .'

'Exactly so. He shares a bottle with the barber who shaves him each morning.'

Amanda smiled. 'He must be drunk before he starts work.'

'Not at all. He is always *de bonne humeur. Gardez le sourire, mes amis!* he says. Sometimes I think all the meals he has ever eaten are still in his stomach. I will bring you the menus.'

Once they had sat down at their table Amanda told Sidney that she was nervous. 'I hope we don't put people off . . .'

'Why would we do that?'

'People will think we are discussing the murder.'

'The whole of Cambridge is discussing the murder.'

Amanda took a sip of champagne and then put her glass down. She was not in the mood for it. 'I'm worried about Ben, Sidney.'

'I'm sure.'

'Yesterday he told me something that's rather haunted me.'

'What is it?'

'He was almost talking to himself. I think that he had almost forgotten I was in the room. He was speaking out of grief, as it were, and then he suddenly said something that struck me as incredibly moving.'

'What was it?'

' "Dom gave me the love my father never did." '

'Did he explain what he meant?'

'Not entirely. But he had rather a brutal upbringing. His mother died when he was away at school and he was not allowed to come home for the funeral. He was bullied for being small and effete and he lost himself in his work. He was the first member of his family to get into Oxford but his father resented him for reading history and wanted him to study engineering and join the family firm. When Ben refused, his father kicked him out and cut him off. Ben's very frightened of him.'

'Then why were they both in the play? It does seem very odd.'

'Perhaps you should go and see Frank Blackwood?'

'I do have a few questions.'

Amanda continued. 'Fortunately, Ben made some friends at Oxford and one of them arranged the job with Lord Teversham. Then, just when he was happy and had prospects, this happens.'

'How well do you think he knew Lord Teversham?'

'Is that a leading question, Sidney?'

'Only if you take it to be one.'

'I don't think there was anything funny going on, if that's what you are getting at.'

'But perhaps other people did? The love that dare not speak its name . . .'

Amanda leaned forward. 'Do you mean someone like Simon Hackford?'

'I'm not sure.'

'You're suggesting that Ben might have been considered some kind of replacement for Simon Hackford in Lord Teversham's affections?'

'It is possible.'

'You think Simon Hackford and Lord Teversham were more than friends?' Amanda asked.

The waiter came to take their order but they asked him to wait. Sidney continued. 'You know how deeply such a secret has to be kept.'

'In the art world, half the people I meet are pansies. People pretend that they are not, their true friends understand that they are and everyone knows not to ask too many questions.'

'Not everyone, of course. And in a small town, or with a reputation to keep up, you can imagine how frightened they might be of exposure.'

Amanda put down her menu. 'But why would either of them betray the other? I don't think blackmail works with homosexuals. If you are an adulterer and you go to the police and complain that you have been threatened then you can put them on to the blackmailer without any fear that you will be punished yourself. All you have to worry about is a scandal. But if you are homosexual and you complain that you are being blackmailed then the police can start with your arrest and you can be put in prison whether they deal with the blackmailer or not.'

'So you don't think Simon Hackford was doing any such thing?'

'If he was, then he would be the one that was killed. I suppose he might have felt murderous after being replaced by Ben. He had a good thing going with Dominic, financially at the very least . . .'

'He says he is happier now, with his wife.'

'A lavender marriage, perhaps,' Amanda replied. 'He must have found the sight of Ben unbearable. But do you think that's sufficient motive for murder? It seems a bit desperate.'

'Perhaps that's often what murder is,' Sidney replied. 'People are desperate.'

Bleu Blanc Rouge was situated in the same street as the Blackwood works, and after Amanda had taken a train back to London Sidney decided to pay Ben's father a visit.

'Dom gave me the love my father never did.'

The factory was classified as light rather than heavy industry, making wireless components, valves and transistors. Serious young men in open-necked shirts and sleeveless jumpers stood at workbenches in a large, open-plan space, stripping wire, applying solder or clamping boards in vices. A phalanx of economically groomed women with Amami-waved hair typed out invoices, arranged deliveries and answered the telephone. The layout, the lighting and the method of work all subscribed to the idea that every part of the building, both human and manufactured, was a key component in an overall machine for modernity.

'We run a tight ship here,' Frank Blackwood began, 'with no time for layabouts. If this new, modern Britain is going to have to compete with Europe and the rest of the world then it needs every engineer it can get. We're on the go from seven-thirty in the morning until four-thirty in the afternoon with half an hour for lunch. I'm moving away from wireless to television parts. You have to keep up with demand.'

'That would be a wise decision, I would have thought,' Sidney replied. 'Everyone wants a television these days.'

'Have you got one then, Canon Chambers?'

'Alas, on my stipend . . .'

'They're expensive but the price will come down.'

'They also seem rather cumbersome. Do you think they will get smaller?'

'I imagine so. But there are a lot of parts, the cathode rays, the tubing, the switching.'

'Can I see inside one?' Sidney asked. 'I've always wanted to know how they work.'

'Of course.'

'The on–off switch is spring loaded, I see.'

'We have a lot of sprung mechanisms in here. I started by making bagatelle machines. We nearly moved into pinball but the Americans have got the market covered so we changed direction and went for technology. But I am sure you haven't come to talk to me about this, Canon Chambers. Are you any nearer finding the murderer?'

'We have some ideas, but it is too soon to say.'

'People who were close to Lord Teversham, for example?'

'We are not suspecting your son.'

'That is a relief,' Frank Blackwood replied. 'Although I was never keen on Ben working there.'

'Why not?

'I didn't like him being cooped up and out of the way. I can't believe that it is a proper job either. He doesn't seem to have any prospects. What kind of a business is looking at paintings or writing a book about a place no one can visit? He should be working for me or down in London. God knows what he will do now.'

'What do you think will happen?'

'They might give him some kind of pay-off. Simon Hackford's likely to take over. He and Lord Teversham have been friends for years. You should go and talk to him. There was something fishy going on there, but I suspect you know about that.'

'I have seen nothing to make me think that Simon Hackford is anything other than a decent man.'

'You're being too Christian.'

'I have no choice.'

'I don't mean to be rude, Canon Chambers, but you only have to look at that man to know that there's something not quite right.'

Sidney cut the suggestion short. 'I am seeing him later today.'

'Then he is a suspect?'

'Everyone is a suspect, Mr Blackwood. Even you, and even me.'

'I don't think that's likely.'

'The police do say that it's often the unlikeliest people . . .'

'But you are a priest.'

'And you run a tight ship,' Sidney replied. He smiled with as much ambiguity as he could muster. 'I am not a murderer, Mr. Blackwood, but sometimes priests can be more devious than people think.'

'Is that so, Canon Chambers?'

'I wouldn't like anyone to take me for granted.'

Simon Hackford's antique shop was situated in Trumpington Street, almost opposite the Fitzwilliam Museum, with four clear windows in which were displayed a tasteful collection of eighteenth-century paintings and traditional English furniture. Whenever Sidney decided to bicycle home via

Sheep's Green and across the Fen Causeway, he liked to slow down, glance into its windows and imagine what he could have afforded had he chosen a different profession. The Elizabethan walnut chest would look handsome in his hallway, he decided, and he had always fancied a pair of Queen Anne candlesticks.

'Is there anything you are looking for specifically?' Simon Hackford asked. 'We have some Apostle spoons that came in a few days ago. As you probably know, Canon Chambers, there are only four sets in the country.'

This was one of the areas in the field of antiques where Sidney had a smidgeon of knowledge. He was keen to impress. 'Is the bowl marked with a leopard head?'

'Indeed.'

'And are the rest of the marks stamped across the back of the handle?'

'They are.'

Sidney nodded as thoughtfully as he could. 'And is each apostle recognisable, with his own halo?'

'The nimbi are intact.'

'Can I see them?'

'I am sure you have not come simply to look at my silver, Canon Chambers.'

'Indeed not, although now that you are about to show me these spoons . . .'

Simon Hackford had seen right through him. 'Your visit is about Lord Teversham, I presume?'

'I am afraid so.'

The antique dealer walked back to the counter and produced a small green case. He put it down on an oak dining table. 'A terrible thing,' he said, before returning to fetch a pair of white gloves. 'We were such friends.'

'Although perhaps less so, recently,' Sidney said.

'Why do you say that?'

'At the theatre you told us that you did not like to spend time apart from your wife. Is that because you once did so?'

'I don't think that is any business of yours.'

'I hope you don't mind me asking.'

Simon Hackford turned and his tone changed. In fact, he became positively hostile. 'I do mind you asking, as a matter of fact. We had rather a rough time of it lately and Marion doesn't like me to talk about it.'

'I'm sorry.'

'I can understand why you might be interested. Lord Teversham and I were friends and business partners. I had no reason to dislike him. Our arrangement simply came to an end when Ben Blackwood arrived.'

'I presume you do not like him.'

'No one likes to be replaced, Canon Chambers. You do not think that anyone can do the job as well as you or that arrangements might change. Fortunately, I have a good eye and other clients. I do not need the support of anyone other than my wife.'

'I am glad to hear it.'

'You can talk to her if you like . . .'

'I may need to do that. But in the meantime, please show me the spoons.'

Simon Hackford put on his white gloves. His hands had a slight shake to them. Sidney wondered if he was a secret drinker.

'I think they may need a bit of a polish.' Simon Hackford undid the gold metal clasp and opened the box. Then he stopped. 'Oh my God.' He stepped back in horror. 'How did that get there?'

All the spoons had been removed. Instead, resting on a crumpled piece of white satin, lay a short bloodied dagger.

'That's our man,' said Inspector Keating.

'I think he is innocent,' Sidney replied.

Inspector Keating sighed. 'You never trust a simple solution, do you, Sidney? I suppose you think the weapon was planted deliberately in order to implicate Simon Hackford?'

'I do.'

'The man is a former business partner of Lord Teversham. God knows how close they were. He ceases to be a business partner. He stops being a friend. His own business has its difficulties. He plays the part of a murderer in the play. He is the last man to stab Lord Teversham. It could hardly be more obvious.'

'Too obvious, Inspector.'

'I'm sorry that you think that. But until you can come up with something better Simon Hackford is under arrest.'

Sidney knew that he was probably the only man in Cambridge who could help the accused. 'I believe that you are innocent,' he told Simon Hackford. 'But I must have more information if I am to find out who did it. I need to know the names of all the key-holders and everyone who has come into your shop since the arrival of the Apostle spoons.'

Simon Hackford was so distressed that he found it difficult to speak. 'Some of them were strangers; customers. But my wife knows most of the regulars who have been in to see us. Is there a way in which you can ask them questions without making it clear what has happened?'

'We can be discreet,' said Sidney. 'It is a matter of making connections. It would be helpful if you could have some idea about who might have committed the murder other than you.'

'I need to be sure that what I say will go no further.'

'You have my assurance.'

Simon Hackford stopped for a moment. He looked more frightened of what he was about to say than any confession of murder. 'I am not sure if I can trust you. You are in cahoots with the police.'

'I am, but my first duty is as a priest. It outweighs all other concerns.'

'What if I were to tell you that I was guilty of something else?'

'I would urge you to be discreet if what I think you may be about to tell me is correct.'

'Then you have guessed what it might be?'

Sidney paused. 'I imagine that you had a close relationship with Lord Teversham?'

'That is correct.'

'Then that is all you need to tell me. You will let me read between the lines?'

'I will.'

'However, you had a falling out?'

'We did.'

'When Ben Blackwood arrived?'

'I am not saying they are as intimate as we were, or that Blackwood is a murderer. But I do not think he is entirely innocent. He wheedled his way into Dominic's affection and he's probably after the paintings. But if I say all that . . .'

'Then he could retaliate . . .'

'Exactly. You know what it is like.'

'I don't know what it is like but I can imagine it.'

'Even though the law may change, we cannot talk about such things for fear of exposure. This makes us vulnerable.'

'You think the murderer may have been Ben Blackwood or perhaps even another, equally intimate, friend of Lord Teversham?'

'It is not impossible.'

'But who?'

'That, Canon Chambers, is what you need to discover.'

Sidney felt out of his depth and he decided to ask his curate for advice. There was a world of secrecy, suggestion and innuendo around this case that he could not fathom. He suspected that Leonard had opinions on the matter even if he did not voice them explicitly.

The time came when the two men were sitting at the kitchen table and eating a frugal lunch of sardines on toast. Sidney had conveyed the news of Simon Hackford's arrest and suggested that he considered this to be a mistake. He also noted that the mutterings about homosexuality in general had increased of late, both in Cambridge and within the pages of *The Times*, and he wondered if his curate had an opinion on the matter.

'The Archbishop of Canterbury has, of course, made the position of the Church on this subject perfectly clear,' Leonard explained carefully. 'He has publicly stated that homosexual indulgence is a shameful vice and a grievous sin from which deliverance is to be sought by every means . . .'

'Do you think this applies as much to consenting adults over the age of twenty-one, and acting in private, as it does to what the archbishop might call "other deviants"?' Sidney asked.

'The archbishop makes no distinction. Every act is equally sinful.'

'And do you think it applies just as much to gestures of affection, holding hands, kissing and so forth, as it does to what Lord Samuel recently referred to in the House of Lords as "the vices of Sodom and Gomorrah of the cities of the plain"?'

Leonard began to start on the washing up. 'Again, the archbishop makes no distinction.'

Sidney picked up a tea towel and continued. 'Yet many of those who are homosexually inclined have begun to suggest that their inclinations are a misfortune, or even a fortune that they cannot control and which, with a clear conscience they can indulge . . .'

'The archbishop has directed us to think that they are mistaken and that they should see their doctors.'

'Do you agree with the archbishop, Leonard?'

Leonard placed a dish on the rack to dry. 'It is not my place to make any public pronouncement contrary to my archbishop.'

'And what should be done with such people?'

'There are, a recent report in *The Times* newspaper informs us, "physical measures to diminish the sexual impulse". The main difficulty, however – and it is, to those in the medical profession, apparently a "baffling" one – is the frequent unwillingness of the offender to face his problem and co-operate in seeking a solution.'

'The offender feels that his behaviour is not a crime but a natural condition?'

'That is what has been suggested, Sidney. Whereas His Grace firmly believes that such behaviour is a shameful vice that must be punished, ultimately by imprisonment, for the protection and well-being of society as a whole.'

'And do you think His Grace believes that locking such people up for eighteen hours out of twenty-four, in solitary confinement, where a perpetrator of such vice may meditate on his past and contemplate his future, is likely to result in the reform of his character?'

'His Grace has not vouchsafed to comment on the matter.'

Sidney began to dry the water glasses. 'I also wonder whether one might possibly consider that personal feelings, expressed in private, should be a matter for legislation? It could, perhaps, be argued that the more of an individual's private life you bring within the criminal law, the less you leave to be lived on the basis of free moral choice.'

'You ask a valid question, Sidney, but it is one that I do not feel qualified to answer. I would, however, draw your attention to the fact that of the Ten Commandments, only three are embodied in criminal law: theft, perjury and, of course, murder.'

'And it is on murder, rather than any attendant moral deviance, that you feel we should concentrate our thoughts at present?'

'Exactly so, Sidney. I do not think an investigation into any man's private life can be as important as that.'

'Then we are agreed,' Sidney concluded, uncertain quite whether he had discovered anything other than his curate's relentless ability to answer every question with a straight bat.

However, before Sidney could continue with his investigation into the death of Lord Teversham, and while he was preparing to write the introduction to his parish magazine, Amanda telephoned and insisted that he come to London as soon as possible. She had something to tell him and it was, apparently, urgent.

Sidney knew that he did not have the time, and that her urgencies existed in a strangely privileged parallel universe, but his affection for Amanda had reached a level where it had become impossible to refuse her requests, and so they met for cocktails at the Savoy. This was the hotel, Sidney remembered grimly, where Oscar Wilde had once stayed with his friend Lord Alfred Douglas.

Outside, a man was pacing up and down with a placard declaring 'THE WAGES OF SIN IS DEATH'.

'There's no need to rub it in,' Amanda remarked as they passed him.

She took off her coat to reveal a black cocktail dress with a low neckline and a string of pearls that made her look like Ava Gardner. Sidney felt positively seedy in her company and wished either that he had the kind of income that would allow him to dress as Frank Sinatra or that they had arranged to meet in the more comfortably raffish surroundings of Soho.

He looked nonchalantly at a comely blonde singer with The Savoy Hotel Orpheans singing 'I'm a Fool to Want You' but loitered too long. Amanda pulled him away to a reserved corner and insisted they drink champagne cocktails. There was something she wanted to say, she told Sidney. She needed cheering up.

'My father thinks that I am being too independent,' Amanda began.

'I thought you liked being independent?'

'He also thinks, extraordinarily, Sidney, that you are not a good influence upon me. He said that I should stop seeing you. I refused point-blank of course. I told him that what he was saying was rot and that what's been going on could have happened to anyone but it was hard to argue when he pointed out that, as a result of our friendship, I have been part of two criminal investigations, kidnapped and assaulted; all within the space of a single year.'

'I agree that it does not look good.'

'That is what he said.'

'And what does he want you to do?'

'Marry, of course.'

'I see.' Sidney knew that he had to be careful. 'Do you have someone in mind?' he asked.

'There are always people around, but there is no one specific. It would be so much easier if I could marry you but we've agreed that I can't possibly marry a clergyman.'

'We have?'

'You know that I would be absolutely hopeless as a clergy wife and I don't want to ruin what we already have. You understand that. Don't you?'

'I do, Amanda. The only problem is that if you marry someone else things might change. Your husband might not like us seeing each other.'

'I can sort that out. I am certainly not prepared to "obey" if that's what you mean. And, by the way, if I ever do marry I obviously want you to take the service.'

'Of course. Although I might find it rather difficult.'

'You mean you would be jealous?'

'I am afraid so.'

Amanda thought for a moment. 'And how do you think I will feel when you marry yourself?'

'I don't think that's likely.'

'I am not so sure about that. For all I know I could be in Germany next Christmas, sitting in the front row of a cold Lutheran church while you tie the knot with Mrs Staunton.'

'How do you know about that?'

'From Jennifer, then from Inspector Keating, and even from Leonard Graham. They all think something's up. You never talk about her at all and that, my dear friend, is a bit of a give-away. I've also heard about the prominence of a piece of porcelain on your desk. I presume you correspond?'

'We do.'

'And do you have any plans to see her again?'

'I don't think she will return to Grantchester.'

'But you might go to Germany?'

'I would like to see her; that is true.'

'Well, there you are then. I don't know why you are worried about the possibility of my marrying when you might be doing so yourself.'

'That is a very distant possibility.'

'Then you admit it is a possibility?'

'I still don't think it's *likely*. It's certainly not as probable as you marrying one of your suitors. Who does your father have in mind?'

'Eddie Harcourt.'

'And who is he?'

'An old Etonian. His father owns half of Somerset, and they have a large home in the centre of Bath. I think it may even be in the Royal Crescent. So the family have money and Eddie's a decent enough sort but he's awfully dull. I don't think I could last more than ten minutes with him before running off with the nearest blacksmith.'

'Do they have blacksmiths in Bath?'

'I imagine so.'

'And did you tell your father this?'

'I did, as a matter of fact, and do you know, he was quite cross with me? "After all I've done for you," he said, before going on and on for so long that I had to stop listening. The gist was that he didn't want me to be a disappointment like my brother.'

'He doesn't approve of David?'

'He's furious with him. As you may remember, David ran off with a divorcee and now Daddy thinks he's lost control of us both. He still believes that I should have married Guy Hopkins. He said that we were in danger of ruining his reputation; and that if neither of his children did what he said then he would cut us out of his will and then either emigrate or kill us. Obviously he was exaggerating and it was quite a ramble because it was the three gins that were doing the talking but it's quite upsetting when your father threatens to kill you, don't you think?'

Amanda stopped talking. 'Are you listening, Sidney?'

'Sorry, I . . .'

'Why have you got that strange look on your face? I've seen you drifting off like this before. You're meant to hang on my every word.'

'I do, Amanda. I do. It's just that I was thinking.'

'What about? What could possibly be more important than what I am saying to you now?'

'Murder,' said Sidney.

'But how? I was talking about Eddie Harcourt, my brother, the divorcee and my father's drinking. What has any of that got to do with events in Cambridge?'

'I must get back there as soon as possible, Amanda.'

'Now?'

'Come with me, if you like.'

'I am supposed to be having dinner with Eddie.'

'Tonight?'

'Yes, tonight. What shall I do?'

'Turn him down, Amanda.'

'Very well. If he asks for my hand in marriage, I will. And if Daddy kicks up a fuss I'll tell him that I did it on your advice.'

'No, don't say that,' Sidney answered distractedly.

'It's the truth, isn't it?'

'Yes, but you don't need to tell him that.'

Sidney was already thinking about the Teversham murder. He knew that he had not been listening properly to his friend. 'It has to be your decision, Amanda. But you can tell your father that you are not prepared to marry without love. That is, I am afraid, the minimum requirement.'

'Can you grow to love someone?'

'There has to be something there in the first place, I would have thought.'

'As we have, you mean?'

'Yes, Amanda,' Sidney sighed once more. 'As we have.'

Before taking the train home, Sidney telephoned Inspector Keating and alerted him to his suspicions. He was informed that due to the unexpected nature of the revelation the suspect was hardly going to anticipate that they were on to him. Any further interview could wait until the next day. It therefore wasn't until well after nine o'clock the following morning that the two men walked in to a small engineering works off Mill Road and asked for a few words, in private, with Frank Blackwood. Two uniformed officers waited outside.

Ben's father was unwelcoming. 'I've already told you everything I know. What more do you require?'

'We wanted to ask if you had ever acted in any amateur drama before the current production of *Julius Caesar*?' Sidney asked.

'What's that got to do with it?'

'It doesn't seem your type of thing.'

'We've been through all this. I had taken a shine to the woman playing Calpurnia. I told you before. Not that it's done me much good.'

Inspector Keating chipped in. 'Did it make any difference that your son was taking part? I would have thought that it might have put you off.'

'I didn't mind.'

'And you also didn't mind that your son failed to follow in your footsteps?'

'I've already told Canon Chambers that I did. But what can you do if your son swans off to Oxford? He was always a mummy's boy. He would have been better off doing an apprenticeship and a bit of National Service.'

'And what did you think about him working for Lord Teversham?' Inspector Keating continued.

'I wasn't keen on the idea. But what's all this got to do with him? You don't think he killed the old bugger, do you?'

'No, we don't.'

'I can't imagine Ben killing as much as a fly.'

'That may, of course, be a good thing,' Sidney observed.

'Wouldn't have done us much good in the war, though, would it?'

'Fortunately he didn't have to fight.'

'I don't suppose you did, Padre.'

Inspector Keating was, on his friend's behalf, getting tired of this assumption. 'As a matter of fact, Canon Chambers did fight. He won the Military Cross. Can I ask you where you were standing on the night of the murder?'

'We've been through all this.'

'How well did you know Lord Teversham?' Keating asked.

'Not well at all. He's an aristocrat so we didn't have anything in common.'

'Your son worked for him.'

Frank Blackwood was annoyed to be interrupted. 'How much do you want me to go on?'

'As long as you like. We'd like to know what you thought of Lord Teversham.'

'Well, he wasn't really one of the lads, was he? You were in the play, Canon Chambers. You saw what he was like. He's not what you'd call one for the ladies.'

'You suspect his inclinations lay elsewhere?'

'I don't suspect. I *know*. What do you think he was doing with my son?'

'Employing him.'

'It was more than that. They went swimming together.'

'Swimming is not illegal.'

'They shouldn't have behaved the way they did.'

'They were friends.'

'They were more than that.'

'And what evidence do you have?'

'I saw the way they looked at each other.'

Sidney tried to interject. 'I don't know what they did or did not do together. It is none of my business. I think adults should be given their privacy.'

'Do you indeed? It shouldn't be allowed. The things they do.'

'Why do we need to know what people do in private, Mr Blackwood?

'It's a sin, whether it's in public or in private. You know it is. And the police turn a blind eye.'

Sidney answered calmly and sternly. 'Sin is a very emotional word.'

'Spare me the Church of England line.'

Keating said nothing but his friend would not be distracted. 'Sin involves choice. Sin is when you make the wrong choice.'

'Which is what my son did.'

'What if he had no choice?'

'Of course he had a choice. Or rather that man did. He corrupted him.'

'But what if he could not help being, in your words, "corrupted"? What if he was born with feelings for men rather than women?'

Inspector Keating interrupted at last. 'Oh Sidney, don't start on this . . .'

Frank Blackwood pushed his chair back. 'You mean you're saying he was born like that? If you go on like that I'm going to punch you in the face.' He turned to Inspector Keating. 'What's this man doing here anyway?'

'He is helping in the investigation. He is my friend.'

'Not you as well, Keating? I thought you were married.'

'I am . . .'

'Although that doesn't stop some people. You just have to lift up the carpet to see the vermin underneath. Why doesn't anyone do anything about it? It's against the law.'

'And what do you think we should do?' Sidney asked.

'Get rid of them.'

'Is that what you think?' Inspector Keating asked.

Frank Blackwood continued. 'People like you don't have the guts to do anything about it. Do you know what it's like to have your own son living like that?' he asked. 'You can't stop thinking about it. I know the way the men in the factory talk about it. Some of them pity me, others think it's funny; the boss's son unable to work with heavy machinery because he's too busy looking at another man's etchings.'

'And because you thought your son was one of them you decided to take the law into your own hands?' Sidney asked.

'I'm not saying that.'

'I think you just have,' Inspector Keating replied. 'I am suggesting that you killed a man because you thought he had feelings for your son.'

'And what if I did?'

'That is murder,' said Inspector Keating.

'No, it is not. It is justice.'

Sidney interrupted. 'Lord Teversham and your son had done nothing wrong.'

'You think there's nothing wrong with sodomy? Have you read your Bible recently?'

Inspector Keating interrupted. 'Frank Blackwood, I am arresting you for the murder of Lord Teversham. You have the right to remain silent but anything you do say may now be used in evidence against you.'

Sidney left the room to fetch the officers who were waiting outside. Frank Blackwood complained as he left, 'People should be grateful, not threatening to bang me up . . .'

Keating persisted. 'Do you want to make a statement?'

'I'll decide what I want to say in my own good time. In the meantime I've had enough of this pantomime. I'm off to do some work.'

Keating persisted. 'I don't think you understood what I said.'

Frank Blackwood was at the door. 'I am the one in the right. I did what no one else was able to do.'

'What you have done is against the law.'

'What they were doing was illegal.'

'We don't know that, Mr Blackwood. All we do know is that you had a choice. You chose murder. It was the wrong choice.'

Everyone thought it best if it was Sidney who told Ben Blackwood about his father's guilt. Inspector Keating had volunteered to send a couple of police officers but he made the offer half-heartedly. He knew that his friend would offer to take the responsibility and, indeed, Sidney was accustomed to being the bearer of bad news. During the war, and shortly afterwards, he had often had to ring a doorbell with news of a death. Sometimes a mother would faint; a father would punch the wall; a sister would stare out of the window. The presence of a priest confirmed the worst, and nothing Sidney could say could ever bring people comfort. All he could do, once the news had been given, was to sit with the bereaved in silence and let grief take its insidious course.

And yet, at Locket Hall, it was different. After Sidney had told Ben what had happened, his host looked stoic. It was almost as if he had been expecting the information.

'My father has always tried to ruin my life,' he said. 'And now he has succeeded. He should have murdered me. I was the disappointment, not Dom.'

'He could not kill his own son.'

'But Lord Teversham had done nothing wrong.'

'He had taken a son away from his father.'

'I had gone a long time ago. I would never have worked in his factory. You can't want the best for your child, educate him away from the family and then expect him to come back as the same person. We lived in different worlds.'

'Perhaps your father was not ready for your world.'

'How did he do it?' Ben asked.

'He had a spring-loaded knife strapped to the inside of his arm.' Sidney mimed the actions. 'He shook his arm down and the knife projected forward in line with the palm of his hand. He raised his hand high, as in a fascist salute, and the blade retracted with the upward movement. The invention suited the gestures made during the play. It was ingenious.'

'Dad the inventor. How did you find out?'

'I saw the spring-loaded mechanisms at the factory. I realised how it could be done, but I could not prove anything.'

'The blade at Simon Hackford's?'

'Planted. We're not sure how your father did that. We could only ascertain his guilt by extracting a confession.'

'You provoked my father's anger?'

'He wanted to be proud of you. It was a matter of honour.'

'And I was not honourable?'

'It became a question of shame.' Sidney quoted from *Richard II*, 'Mine honour is my life, both grow in one. Take honour from me, and my life is done.'

'I like art, Canon Chambers. I like beauty. Is that so very bad?'

'Of course not. It was your friendship that your father thought was wrong.'

'And do you?'

'Think it wrong? I am a great believer in privacy. It is none of my business.'

'What people don't understand,' said Ben, 'is that you can be intimate with someone, whether it is a man or a woman, without being physical. In fact, to be physical sometimes ruins the whole relationship.'

'Are you sure you want to tell me this?'

Ben continued. 'You can hug someone, and kiss someone, and go for walks or a picnic or go swimming but this is not something that is governed by passion. It is ruled by friendship.'

'I understand.'

'Passion is such a strong emotion that it dominates everything. It's like a strong spice in a meal, or a dominant red in a painting. Your senses are drawn to it at the expense of everything else. Dominic and I were not physical friends, so to speak. But I did love him. We can't help loving the people we do, can we? But that love doesn't have to be physical. You can be equally intimate. It doesn't matter. Do you understand what I mean, Canon Chambers?'

Sidney was thinking over what Ben was saying. Out of the window he could see a pair of swans flying low over the river and into the distance. He wondered where they were going.

Amanda had agreed to come down on 5 November for Grantchester's annual fireworks party. A vast bonfire had been built on the Meadows and a display had been planned for 6.30 p.m. Potatoes wrapped in foil had been placed at the base of the fire and refreshments were on offer in the pavilion. Most members of the village were in attendance and Sidney hoped that the same number might come to his carol concert in a month's time. Dickens, who was scared of the noise, was hiding under Sidney's bed.

'It was good of you to come, Amanda, especially on a weekday.'

'I'm always keen to see you, Sidney, and, I know you've all had a terrible time. Poor Ben; and poor you . . .'

'I just want the year to end.'

'It's been so eventful. But at least we've got to know each other. That is one consolation, don't you think?' Amanda asked. 'We can tell each other anything, I hope.'

'That is true.'

'It doesn't matter whether it's God, crime or my new fur coat, does it?'

'Of course it doesn't, Amanda. Sometimes I wished we could talk about the trivial a little more. By the way, where did you get that coat? Did Eddie Harcourt give it to you?'

'He did not.'

'Then . . .'

'I turned him down, by the way.'

'Good. I'm pleased.'

'Daddy's not, although he's already lined up someone else.'

'Hence the fur coat.'

'Indeed. But there's no need for you to worry about any of that. As soon as I meet anyone serious you will have power of veto and I can't imagine you approving of any of them.'

'There's bound to be someone in the end.'

'Probably; but we don't have to think about that now, do we? Is there any beer?'

'I think there's a whole barrel from The Green Man,' Sidney replied, wondering how limitless Amanda's supply of suitors might be.

'Do you imagine they'll give me a whole pint?' she asked. 'It's not very ladylike.'

'I'll get one for you. They'll probably give it to you on the house. You're becoming rather well known round here.'

'Well, I do hope people are talking. I like to create a bit of interest.'

The first of the fireworks exploded in the sky. The two friends took their pints out of the pavilion to watch the night rainbows of crimson, silver and gold.

'What a sight!' Amanda cried. 'And what a sound! There's enough noise to cover all manner of murders, I would have thought.'

Sidney smiled. 'Don't.'

'What do you mean?'

'You are beginning to sound like me.'

She put her arm through his and the warm light of the bonfire lit up her face. 'Is that a good thing or a bad thing?'

'A very bad thing, I would have thought,' Sidney replied. 'Especially if you want to keep up with your friends.'

Amanda gave his arm a tug of reassurance. 'You remember when I came to lunch last winter? It was when we thought the doctor might be polishing people off . . .'

'It was the first time we were alone together.'

'You said something to me then that I have never forgotten. Can you remember what it was?'

Sidney thought for a moment. Children raced in front of them, waving sparklers, shouting with delight. A Catherine wheel fizzed chaotically on the side of an oak tree. Rockets exploded in the sky.

'You were advising me about marriage. You said that love was "an unassailable friendship". Now, we're not married, of course, but do you think we've got that now? With each other?'

'Unassailable friendship?'

Amanda gave a little tug at his arm. 'What do you think?'

'I certainly hope so.'

'So do I,' said Amanda, kissing him lightly on the cheek.

The following Thursday Sidney was sitting with Geordie Keating in their accustomed positions at The Eagle. Their first pints of bitter were half-empty and a game of backgammon was well under way. The Inspector was convinced that he was on the cusp of victory while Sidney was mulling over the implications of the recent crime.

'So complicated, the whole business of reputation, isn't it?' he mused. 'So intangible, and so hard to know if you are maintaining it well.'

'Isn't it just a matter of keeping a clear conscience?' the inspector asked.

'I'm not sure that it is. I think it is worth thinking about the way in which other people see you. A man's reputation can be more fragile than he thinks.'

'You just have to be true to yourself, don't you?' the inspector asked. He threw a three and a one. 'That's what I try to do, even though sometimes, inevitably, the black dog comes; and I don't mean your Labrador.'

'Everyone has his moments of depression, Geordie . . .'

The inspector looked down at the board. 'It's your turn.'

'I am sorry.' Sidney threw his dice. 'Oh good. A double six.'

Keating continued. 'And then, when it does come, I sometimes think that everything I do – whether it is in the Force, at home, for the wife, for the children, or out in the streets – anything and everything – is a waste of time. Nothing I do, in the grand scheme of things, can ever make much of a difference.'

'I can assure you, Geordie, that everything makes a difference. The world would be a poorer place without you.'

Keating threw a two and a four. 'I don't know, Sidney. You solve one crime and then, as soon as you've done that, a hundred others spring up to take its place. The process is never-ending.'

'We have to keep faith.'

'I think that's rather easier for you to say than me.'

'I don't mean religious faith. I mean faith in our own abilities. We have to do the best we can with the talents we have, Geordie. The future is too unpredictable for anxiety.'

'And yet the anxieties come.'

'Let us concentrate on the game, Geordie.' Sidney threw a five and a three. 'I can see that you need cheering up.'

'I'm hardly going to cheer up if you keep winning all the time.'

Sidney leaned forward over the board. 'Do you want me to lose deliberately? I am sure you would find that rather insulting.'

Keating smiled. 'I don't mind, Sidney, there are worse things in life.'

'Indeed there are. And we must remember that there is much to look forward to: Christmas, for example, and your birthday too. A double celebration.'

'I don't know about that. I like the hullabaloo and the excitement of the children but Cathy always gets tense when her
mother comes to stay. She feels judged all the time.'

'Judge not that ye be not judged.'

'Well, Sidney, perhaps you could come round and tell my
mother-in-law that? You would be welcome at any time.'

'That's very kind of you.'

'But what are your plans, Sidney? Will you be seeing
Amanda?'

'I think so. Although she gets very booked up at this time of
year.'

'I would imagine you had first call.'

'Not necessarily. She leads a pretty active social life. I am
sure she will marry soon.'

Inspector Keating pretended, without success, to return to
the game. 'I have told you what I think about that.'

'We are friends; nothing more.'

'That's a good enough reason, isn't it?'

'I don't think so. I have thought about it, as you know only
too well; but I don't think it could possibly work. Her world is
too different; and, of course, in many ways, I am married to
my job.'

'But you can't be a bachelor for ever, Sidney. It's too lonely.'

'Perhaps that is the price of the priesthood?'

'Nonsense, man. There are plenty of married clergy. You see
them all over the place.'

Sidney was beginning to feel uncomfortable. He didn't like
talking about himself and realised that he found it far easier to
ask questions than answer them. 'I am aware of that.'

'So what are you going to do?'

Reluctantly, Sidney realised that it was time for a little confession. 'Well, Geordie, to tell you the truth, I thought that, after Christmas, I might have a little holiday.'

'But where on earth would you go to at this time of year?'

'I was thinking of Germany.'

'I see.' Inspector Keating gave Sidney one of his steady looks. 'You've kept very quiet about that. You're going to see Hildegard Staunton?'

'I hope so.'

'Does Amanda know of your plans?'

'Not at the moment, no.'

'And are you going to tell her?'

'I am sure she won't mind.'

'I, however, am sure she *will* mind.' Inspector Keating finished his pint. 'Well, well, well. Your secret is safe with me.'

'It is not a secret, Geordie.'

'I think it should be. Still waters run deep, eh?'

'I haven't been to Germany for quite a while.'

'I don't think you are going for the landscape or the beer. Admit it, man.'

'I don't really want to talk about it, Geordie. I may have got completely the wrong idea. But there is something about Hildegard. I don't know how to express it: but when I was with her, I felt at home.'

'I will expect a full report.'

'I am not sure I can promise you that, Geordie. We must have some secrets from each other, surely?'

'I've told you before, Sidney. We can have no secrets, and we are never off duty.'

The publican threw another log on to the hearth and the fire blazed up once more, giving a comforting glow to the faces of the two drinkers. The two men resumed their backgammon and played in companionable silence until Sidney threw a four and a three to gain yet another unlikely victory.

'I don't know how you do it,' his friend complained.

'Think of it as part of the game we call life,' Sidney replied.

'It's not much of a game if you keep winning all the time.' Geordie Keating leaned back in his chair and accepted defeat. 'Sometimes, Sidney, I really do think that you must have God on your side.'

'I certainly hope so,' his clerical companion replied. 'Another round, Inspector?'